Publisher's Note:

Thank you for purchasing this book. It began as an idea, was shaped by the creativity of its talented author, and was subsequently molded into the book you have before you by a team of editors and designers.

Like all EDGE books, this book is the result of the creative talents of a dedicated team of individuals who all believe that books (whether in print or pixels) have the magical ability to take you on an adventure to new and wondrous places powered by the author's imagination.

As EDGE's publisher, I hope that you enjoy this book. It is a part of our ongoing quest to discover talented authors and to make their creative writing available to you.

We also hope that you will share your discovery and enjoyment of this novel on social media through Facebook, Twitter, Goodreads, Pinterest, etc., and by posting your opinions and/or reviews on Amazon and other review sites and blogs. By doing so, others will be able to share your discovery and passion for this book.

Brian Hades, publisher

The Sic Transit Terra Universe:

Novellas:
Lydia's Royal Ace
Candles
Novels:
The Genius Asylum (Book 1)
The Otherness Factor (Book 2)
The Relativity Bomb (Book 3)
The Genome Rally (Book 4)
The Cockroach Crusade (Book 5)
The Identity Shift (Book 6)

SIC TRANSIT TERRA 6

THE IDENTITY SHIFT

ARLENE F. MARKS

EDGE SCIENCE FICTION AND FANTASY PUBLISHING
An Imprint of HADES PUBLICATIONS, INC.
CALGARY

The Identity Shift
Sic Transit Terra Book 6

EDGE SCIENCE FICTION AND FANTASY PUBLISHING
An Imprint of HADES PUBLICATIONS, INC.
P.O. Box 1714, Calgary, Alberta, T2P 2L7, Canada

The EDGE Team:
Producer: Brian Hades
Acquisitions: Michelle Heumann
Cover Design: Brian Hades
Cover Art: Lynn Perkins
Book Design: Mark Steele

ISBN: 978-1-77053-205-2

EDGE Science Fiction and Fantasy Publishing and Hades Publications, Inc. acknowledges the ongoing support of the Alberta Foundation for the Arts and the Canada Council for the Arts for our publishing programme.

Library and Archives Canada Cataloguing in Publication
CIP Data on file with the National Library of Canada
ISBN: 978-1-77053-205-2
(e-Book ISBN: 978-1-77053-204-5)

FIRST EDITION
(20200524)
Printed in USA
www.edgewebsite.com

Those who cannot remember the past are condemned
to repeat it.

(George Santayana, *Reason in Common Sense*)

Memory … is an internal rumor; and when to this hearsay
within the mind we add the falsified echoes that reach us
from others, we have but a shifting and unseizable basis
to build upon. The picture we frame of the past changes
continually and grows every day less similar to the original
experience which it purports to describe.

(George Santayana, *Reason in Science*)

Chapter One

On Daisy Hub

There was an old Earth saying: "The road to hell is paved with good intentions." Out in Sector Five, the road from a planet called Helena to a star nicknamed Purgatory was still paved with space debris four Earth years after the end of the Corvou war. It had taken nearly three of those years for all the frozen bodies (and body parts) to be recovered from the various battle sites and returned to their respective home worlds for identification and respectful disposal.

Except for the Corvou corpses, of course. Coravon was still enveloped in a pocket of space, sealed shut by the Kularian brotherhood's heavy ship. Since the ship was gone and the brotherhood weren't responding to attempts to contact them, there was no alternative but to bundle the Corvou dead together and send them straight into Purgatory.

It was, Drew Townsend thought, an apt and fitting way to treat the insectoid race that had unleashed such a devastating conflict on the galaxy. Frustrating though it might be to know that the remaining Corvou were now safely beyond the reach of a war crimes tribunal, it was also a tremendous relief to have them out of the picture while the allied races who'd defeated them were grieving, regrouping, and rebuilding their space fleets.

It recalled another old Earth saying: "Out of sight, out of mind."

But the Corvou would never be completely out of mind for Townsend, the *Hak'kor* of House Daisy Hub.

Earth space had been the sole theater of this war, and Humanity had been the only race to suffer civilian casualties. The cost in Human lives had been staggering. Entire colonies had been wiped out when moons and planets had been incinerated by the invaders' superweapon. Space installations had been blown apart. Millions had died.

Eleven of them had been members of Townsend's crew. They'd left the safety of the *Marco Polo* and returned to the station, knowing full well that they could be killed defending it. Each of them had been a willing volunteer, but that didn't make it any easier to accept that they were gone. Not when Townsend knew in his soul that the reason he'd even given them the choice had been his knee-jerk compulsion to avenge his own parents' deaths on Schweitzer Hub.

He'd gone *hartoon*, and people he'd cared about had paid the price.

As soon as the Hub's losses had been tallied, the conviction that he was responsible for them had burrowed inside him, aggravating his already troublesome peptic ulcer. Diet and medication had eventually brought the ulcer under control, but only just. It would continue to be a problem, he was told, until he'd confronted and dealt with the deep-seated emotional issue that was eating at him, the one he refused to discuss.

That would be Olivia. Unfortunately — or maybe not — the chances of brother and sister ever being face-to-face again were laughably slim.

No matter. Drew had long ago resigned himself to carrying around a lot of pain and anger. By now, they were like a favorite pair of shoes, broken in through constant wearing until they felt like part of who he was. The guilt, however — that was new and stiff. Four years of therapy had managed to bend it a little and knock the sharp edges off it. By keeping himself busy and his mind otherwise occupied, he could almost forget that it was there. But he seriously doubted whether anything could rid him of it entirely.

Warmaster Vixor ban Jorisam had once told him that there was no justice in a war, only victory or defeat. The Nandrian hadn't elaborated at the time, but after some reflection, Drew thought he understood.

Every life cut short in battle was a senseless death, until the fighting was over. Then the survivors could decide what to do next. Seeking vengeance meant bringing further violence and even more losses. (That was probably why the Nandrians considered *hartoon* to be a form of insanity.) The reasoned response, the one that honored both the lives and the deaths of the fallen, was to create a legacy that would rise from the rubble and keep their memory alive.

It made perfect sense. It was why every Nandrian House had a wall of heroes. And forty-one other *Hak'kors* were probably inscribing names on their walls right now, to commemorate the courage of every last warrior who had died in Earth space.

However, in Townsend's case, there was a hitch: unlike the alien allies who had entered the conflict willingly in a noble cause, the crew of Daisy Hub had been, purely and simply, fighting their way out of a corner. The Humans on the station had been motivated less by courage or altruism than by sheer dogged desperation, and they knew it.

Gavin Holchuk had run away from his past, onto a doomed Nandrian warship. Devanan Singh had put himself and five others in harm's way out of grief over the death of his daughter. The other nine casualties on the Hub had simply been in the wrong place at the wrong time. None of those deaths had been heroic, and none of the survivors were hypocrites. A wall of heroes would have been a false and empty gesture of recognition. So would a medal, awarded by the same government that had earlier exiled them all the way to the margins of Earth space and then turned its back on them.

Nonetheless, nagged a voice inside Drew's mind, *there ought to be a legacy.*

"Be glad that you're alive, Chief."

Townsend glanced up and found Ruby McNeil standing in front of his desk, gazing at him with unaccustomed sympathy. She was the fourth person to say that to him today.

"Are my feelings that obvious?" he inquired.

"No more than anyone else's right now," she told him, dropping onto a chair. "It would be nice if what ails us could be cured by a good night's sleep, but it can't. On the bright side, at least the Daisy Hub crew and Zulu detachment are all back together again. They're even letting us keep Yoko and Akiko." She paused and narrowed her gaze. "That's your doing, isn't it?"

"Mine and the Doc's. It's amazing what you can get with a series of logical arguments and a faked panic attack."

Ruby flashed him a wicked grin. "You ran a con on Earth Medical Services? And the Doc went along with it?"

He dipped his head in confirmation. "She went with the flow, and we got exactly what we were after. Med Services agreed that we needed therapy animals aboard the Hub, and that it made more sense from a psychological standpoint to simply give us back the two rats we'd already had. Now the status is returned to quo, and Yoko's and Akiko's secrets are still safe. It's good to know I haven't lost my touch."

"So, what now, Chief?"

"That depends," he told her. "Has everyone had a chance to settle in?"

"Well, it's only been a few days. Some of them are still trying to wrap their heads around the fact that the Zoo is now based aboard the station," she reported. "And some of the Rangers are apparently wrestling with the idea of Space Installation Security topping up the detachment with female constables. Five of them, to replace the men Rodrigues lost in the battle. And Chief, you're going to love this — one of them is Madeline Holchuk."

Somehow, he wasn't surprised. Madeline was not only Gavin's daughter, she was also a natural warrior. She'd fought her way to Daisy Hub to find him, only to lose him again when the Corvou attacked. Under those circumstances, Drew wouldn't have wanted to return to his previous life on Earth either.

"Is everyone aboard who should be?"

"By my count, yes. Odysseus is on the new Mitradean home world in Sector Two, with the rest of his people. Its exact location is being kept secret for security reasons, but he has promised to visit us from time to time."

"Karlov?"

"As soon as the Directorate found out he was alive, they recalled him to Stragon to be debriefed. No one's heard a word from him since then."

That wasn't right. The Stragori Directorate had sent Max Karlov to the Hub originally to ensure that Yoko didn't fall into the hands of the radical faction. With polarization continuing unabated on Stragon, and Daisy Hub now situated just one Gate and three days away from that world, it was the worst possible time for the Directorate to be withdrawing their protection.

If they thought the Rangers had been put aboard the Hub to take over that duty, they were mistaken. However, something told Townsend that the Directorate didn't usually make that kind of error.

"If Max isn't coming back, then we have to assume that someone else will be taking his place," Drew decided. "Reserve quarters for whoever it turns out to be."

He raised a hand to pause the conversation, then opened the top drawer of his desk and uncovered the control pad concealed inside it. There was a brief buzzing sound as the privacy shield activated around his brand new office space. "All right," he continued, "I want you to set up an all-crew meeting in the caf, to begin in one standard hour." He'd lowered his voice, even though it wasn't necessary. They were surrounded by a wall of white noise, and any surveillance hardware that might be inside its perimeter was jammed.

Ruby leaned in and lowered her voice as well. "Are we including the Rangers?"

"No. This is a family conference, and Zulu's an unknown quantity right now. I'll brief Captain Rodrigues privately later on and let him decide how deeply he wants his detachment involved in our next mission."

She reared back as though to avoid a blow. "Our *next* mission, Chief?" she echoed uncertainly. "I thought we had just the one, for Earth Intelligence."

"We do, and it's ongoing. But you don't really think the threat to Humanity ended with the Corvou war, do you?" He paused, then explained, "When I was a field investigator in New Chicago, my captain wouldn't let us close a criminal investigation until we'd neutralized all the parties involved — the tools, the henches, and in particular, the one giving the orders. The Corvou were tools. Now that they're out of the way, we can go after bigger game."

"You're not talking about trying to solve the Corvou queen's murder, are you? I mean, they're still—" She gasped her next breath, abruptly understanding. "The Great Council?" she whispered. "That's pretty ambitious, Chief. We're still finding our footing again after the war, and they'll be coming into it fresh."

"And that's exactly what I want them thinking too. Call the meeting, Ruby. We've got a lot of work ahead of us."

«»

Before the Corvou war, an all-crew meeting would have completely filled the caf. Today, as Townsend's gaze swept the room, it snagged on all the empty spaces and vacant chairs that spoke of the Hub's losses. Cargo Inspectors Teri Mintz, Robert O'Malley, and Lu Xensiu sat together at a table for four, reserving a spot for their leader, Gavin Holchuk, as usual — except the Chief Cargo Inspector was gone. Other details had done the same for their missing members. There was no idle chatter, and no one was smiling.

It felt to Townsend as though these pointed reminders of death had somehow rarified the air in the room, forcing him to inhale more deeply before he could speak.

"Well, here we finally are, rock-throwing distance away from Stragon, aboard our new and improved Hub. Either Earth's government was feeling guilty as hell about the way they'd treated us in the past, or the High Council realized what might happen if they gave House Daisy Hub any reason to complain to our Nandrian allies. Either way, this station has nearly everything we asked for."

Deliberately making eye contact with the crew member who had requested each one, Drew enumerated the items they'd put on the wish list. "A Mark Six shuttle for Ruby to fly and Soaring Hawk to tinker with. A separate landing deck for the Rangers' three shuttles. Upgrades to all our technology, including the Doc's lab, Jensen's kitchen, and the solar energy capture system. A factory-installed on-board security package. Additional space for food production. Vastly increased data storage capacity, together with state of the art VR programming for our SPA room. AdComm is now permalinked to Zulu's communications console, extending and broadening our sensing capabilities. Hull integrity is back up to one hundred percent. Our spare parts locker is full once more. And they've replaced our death trap escape pods with ones that are more spacious, better outfitted, and actually maneuverable.

"They've also kept us just within the border of Earth space, and they've reclassified the Hub, from 'deep space experiment' to 'deep space way station'. That not only changes our legal status and obligations, it also alters the relationship between Daisy Hub and Zulu. In short, we're not detainees anymore, and they're not our wardens. We're just another hub that happens to have a Ranger detachment on board. We're going to have to do some things for ourselves that they used to do for us, because they're going to be out on patrol, helping to take care of whatever other installations survived the war in this sector of Earth space.

"The memo informing me of this reclassification came from the Space Installation Authority. That doesn't mean it was their decision. At the moment, I can't tell you where the idea originated, or whether its advantages outweigh its disadvantages. I guess we'll just have to wait and see how things shake out. One thing that I can tell you with certainty, however, is that no matter what Earth chooses to do with us, we remain, and always will be, the Shields of House Daisy Hub."

"What about the Nandrian victory parties?" hollered Security Chief Orvy Hagman from the back of the room. "Are we still going to be hosting those?"

Townsend exchanged a look with Ruby. "Like I said, we'll have to wait and see. Now that we've formally allied ourselves with Trokerk, we probably won't be able to claim neutrality anymore. In any case, the Nandrian fleets took a heavy hit during the war, so it's doubtful whether any of the Houses are ready to resume *tekl'hananni* just yet."

Engineer Spiro Gouryas rose from his chair to ask, "Since we're no longer in isolation, will Earth be sending us new crew members to round out our manifest, the way Space Installation Security did with the Rangers?"

Townsend pressed his lips together. It hadn't been Earth's government that had originally assembled the Hub's crew. It had been Earth Intelligence, using the Earth Relocation Authority as a blind. But none of his people were ready to know that yet. Meanwhile, the Relocation Authority was reduced to tabulating numbers and updating the population database as census reports came in from distant hubs and colonies. Could the EIS find an alternative way to send more operatives to Daisy Hub? Drew wouldn't know that until they began arriving.

Fortunately, Ruby noticed his hesitation and got to her feet to answer the question. "Eventually, they'll have to, Spiro. However, until the census is complete and the various branches and levels of Earth's government all get their acts together, it's highly doubtful whether any new postings will be opening up in Earth space. Bottom line is, there may be a reshuffling of titles and responsibilities to ensure that every detail is covered, but I'd say that for the next couple of years at least, we can expect to be on our own out here."

And that was apparently how they liked it. Townsend saw heads bobbing in approval as Ruby sat down again.

"All of this is our reward for saving Earth's ass at the battle of Daisy Hub," he continued, opening his arms in an encompassing gesture. "Wow. They think we saved Humanity. That would be quite a feat, if we'd done it without needing the assistance of forty-two alien fleets. Forty-two," he repeated, and paused to let the number sink in. "So many lives have been lost. Too many of them belonged to people that we cared about. If you're like me, you've probably been wondering: What can we do in the names of our fallen friends and crewmates and family members, that we can actually claim as our own achievement and — just for good measure — that will top what Earth thinks we've already done?"

The room began percolating with murmurs.

"It may sound like an impossible order, but I've had four years to think about this," Drew said, raising his voice to cut through the chatter. "There is something more important than saving Humanity — saving Humanity's future. Our greatest enemy has not been defeated. It's still out there, and it's not the Corvou, or the Thryggians, or any other individual race.

"After our disastrous first contact with the Corvou, Agnosk, the Chief Officer of the *Nannssi*, told me that the Great Council had ordered all its member worlds and their protectorates not to warn us about that particular race. They wanted us to be ignorant, most likely to ensure that we would offend the Corvou deity and provoke a declaration of war. According to Agnosk, there is also reason to suspect that the Great Council might have been behind the event that launched the swarm into the galaxy in the first place. I'm talking about the suspicious and untimely death of the Corvou queen."

"Wait a damn minute!" said Hagman, leaping to his feet. "You're telling us that the Great Council has it in for us? *That's* the enemy we need to bring down now?"

"That's exactly what I'm telling you, Mr. Hagman. And if they're so determined to annihilate Humanity that they would murder a queen and trigger a war in order to do it, then it's safe to assume that they will try again. And again. And again, unless ... we ... stop them."

"Why us?" demanded a female voice. "We've done our part. Why can't we just sit the next battle out?"

"Excellent question!" Drew declared before anyone could shout her down. "Here's the answer: Because it's not force of arms that will defeat this enemy. It's something else, something they won't be expecting. Something that Humans have been practicing on one another for centuries." He permitted his lips to curve upward and saw several answering grins in the audience. "Something that, quite frankly, has become sort of our specialty here on Daisy Hub. Guile and deception."

The grins were contagious. They were sprouting up all over the room.

Ruby's was especially impish. "We're going to run a con on them, Chief?"

"We are. It won't be a rapid victory," Townsend warned. "The setup alone could take years. But it's the only way to defeat an enemy that powerful without bloodshed. And I think you'll all agree that there's been more than enough of that already."

"What about Earth's government?" said Jason Smith. "And what about Zulu? Are we going to read them into this operation?"

"Earth's government, maybe, once we're further along," Drew replied. "They've already got as much on their plate as they can handle for now. In any case, it's easier to ask for forgiveness than it is to obtain permission. In fact, if I can show them that we have a reasonable chance of success, they might even agree to participate. The Rangers will be briefed separately, once Captain Rodrigues has had a chance to assess and orientate his five new constables.

"First things first, though. We can't let on to anyone what we're doing, not even Zulu yet. I put a privacy shield in place around the caf before we began this meeting. It's one of the new security features on the Hub, and I suspect we'll be using it regularly. Thanks to the war, there are now settlements of Terran refugees living on alien-controlled worlds, and if word gets out that we're plotting against the Great Council, we'll be putting potentially millions of Human lives at risk. That's why we need to tread lightly and take things one small step at a time."

"And what's the first baby step, boss?" called O'Malley.

As if he didn't already know.

Composing his features, Townsend called back, "A good con artist always researches the mark. Our first order of business will be to gather and verify as much intel as we can about the Great Council and its dealings with member worlds, from every available source. Any crew members with connections to off-Earth databases — or talkative aliens — are instructed to report to me as soon as possible. I'll be meeting with each of you individually over the next interval or so, beginning with O'Malley, in my office, in half a standard hour. If there are no further questions...?"

Heads turned to and fro, but no one spoke up.

"Then we're done here."

———— ⟨⟩ ————

Daisy Hub's diameter had increased a little, and most of its interior had been reconfigured to contain all the tech upgrades, not to mention an entire Ranger detachment. It was still only about a kilometer in length — a runt compared to the other hubs that had survived the war. Still, in keeping with its new role as a deep space way station, it had been outfitted with a docking ring and fixed airlock-to-portal passageways that replicated the daisy petal shape at the north end of the original Hub. (Judging by the scorched and scored condition of the ring's exterior, it had probably been salvaged from another, destroyed installation. If so, Drew decided, he didn't want to know which one.)

The most impressive InfoComm and security technology could be found on AdComm. The control center of the Hub on C Deck had been subdivided. To the left as Townsend stepped out of one of the tube cars were three consoles with viewscreens suspended above them. The largest belonged to Ruby's main work station. The other two were for communications and ops, both security and tactical. Unlike the first Daisy Hub, this one was equipped with defensive armament. Officially, the weapons and ordnance were under the control of the Rangers. Whether Rodrigues would agree to train Townsend's crew to use them as well remained to be negotiated. Drew suspected it would depend on how much his "merry band of lunatics" had been changed by their experiences during the war.

To his right were the offices. The largest was the station manager's work space. It contained his desk and chair, along with seating for several guests and a medium-sized table for holding meetings. The desk was a technology unto itself, equipped with everything that someone on Earth apparently thought a station manager might need. Fortunately, that someone had also provided documentation outlining all its features. Townsend had been able to bring himself up to speed in less than an hour.

The other two "offices" were glorified cubicles, unfurnished at the moment. All three backed up against a bulkhead and were enclosed and separated from one another by clear plastiplex panes. Each of their occupants thus had an unobstructed view of the rest of the deck. And vice versa. The privacy shields were auditory only.

Sitting behind his desk, Drew felt as though he was inside a fish bowl. He couldn't even rebuild his wall of filing cabinets. They'd been scrapped and replaced with a memory bloc the size of his fist.

Be careful what you put on a wish list, he thought wryly.

At least the data in O'Malley's stash hadn't been lost. In the intervals leading up to the Corvou invasion, the ratkeeper had had the presence of mind to back up the Hub's entire system onto a pair of portable memory cores. He'd then packed them into anti-mag carrying cases and taken them with him aboard the *Marco Polo*. (Yoko and Akiko hadn't been his only reason for remaining aboard the *Hak'kor*'s ship during the battle.)

Exactly thirty-two standard minutes after the conclusion of the meeting in the caf, a tube car door slid open and Robert O'Malley strode onto AdComm. It was evidently his first time on C Deck. He paused for a look around, uttering a low whistle when he saw all the shiny new toys in the room. Then he headed to the office where Townsend was waiting for him.

The last four years had aged everyone on the Daisy Hub crew two or three times over, including O'Malley. The ratkeeper had finally left his thirties behind. He still had the face of someone half his age, but his demeanor was definitely changed. The old O'Malley would have been the portrait of youthful overconfidence. He would have spun a guest chair around and straddled it as though mounting a moto, grinning toothily as he asked, "What can I do for you, boss?"

The man who now sat down on the other side of Drew's desk was a more sedate and thoughtful version of that previous self. He'd even shed his unruly mop of dark brown hair in favor of a shorter, more conservative style.

"Well," O'Malley remarked, "we did ask for upgrades."

"And we got them, in spades." Drew opened his desk drawer and activated the privacy shield. Then he asked,

"Have you begun populating the new servers from the memory core?"

"Yes, but it's going to take a while before the process is complete. As well as all the files I took from the *Marco Polo*'s intranet, we have Earth's entire database, both civilian and military, from 2250 to the day you gave the order to pack up and move to the *Hak'kor*'s ship. Then there's approximately one third of the Galactic Central Archives. That by itself is a huge amount of information. And I'll have to enter all the new stuff that's come in from the census over the past four years. I estimate it will be a dozen days, at least, before our system is back up to date. After that, I'll resume data mining."

"As soon as Earth's pre-war database has uploaded, I want you to make backup copies, plural. Make sure they're protected. Then bury them in separate locations and give me the decryption key. You can update the original as the census reports come in, but I want a pre-war snap of the Human population. We may need to show an interplanetary tribunal how Humanity was affected by being deprived of vital intel."

"Not a problem."

"When the rest of the data has uploaded, I want you to do the same thing for it as well," Townsend continued, explaining, "Apparently, I made a powerful enemy back on Earth when I dressed down General Bascomb in front of a Fleet admiral and vice-admiral and got him recalled by the High Council. For the past four years, he hasn't been able to touch me. Now that's changed. This man has a far longer reach than someone in his position ought to command. I'm guessing he pulls strings using blackmail. So, I want everything that happened aboard the station prior to the final battle to be documented and secured, in case I need to prove that he's lying."

"See, that makes no sense to me. He knows that we're a House allied with the Nandrians, and that you're its *Hak'kor*. Anyone attacking you would be starting a war with *them*."

"I don't think he cares about that," Townsend said grimly. "I did some checking before we came out here. Vice-Admiral Nelligan wasn't the only person who warned me about him. He's apparently a vindictive bastard, the kind who would blow up a ship full of passengers in order to take revenge on just one of them. At some point, he's going to make a move, on me or on the Hub. When he does, I want to be able to put him down quickly. We can't let his personal vendetta distract us from the greater mission."

O'Malley leaned back in his chair, a new level of respect in his eyes. "You're serious, then. You're really going after the Great Council."

"Absolutely. However long it takes. But even if I weren't, the first and unwavering mission of Earth Intelligence is to uncover and preserve the truth. You of all people ought to know that."

"You're right." Rearranging his arms and legs, he met Drew's steady gaze with one of his own. "How long have you known?"

"You were my prime suspect in the murder of Karim Khaloub. I figured out early on that he'd been terminated so that I could replace him as station manager. That meant there had to be another agent on board, taking orders from someone higher up than me. I wasn't sure it was you, though, until you found all those relatives of crew members, including at least one that the EIS had placed deep undercover years earlier. You'd pulled off some impressive hacking feats in the past, but there was no way you could have found Walt Garfield, let alone gotten a message to him, without some help from his handler."

"You could have exposed me as a mole four years ago and put me out of your misery," he pointed out mildly. "Why didn't you?"

"You'd proven that you were a brilliant hacker. I figured the risk of having you around was outweighed by how useful your talent could be to us, going forward. And we were on the same side."

O'Malley hesitated. "And are we still on the same side?"

Turn him or terminate him. They both knew what the options were.

"I would say that's up to you. We're about to embark on something completely unsanctioned and without the knowledge of anyone on Earth. I didn't mind that you were reporting over my head earlier, but now I need to control the narrative. I want you to report only what I tell you to report, when I tell you to report it, without letting anyone at the EIS find out that your cover has been blown. Do that, and I'll exercise my right as *Hak'kor* to give you amnesty for Khaloub's murder. Otherwise..."

There was no need to elaborate. O'Malley was smart enough to complete the thought on his own. "Now that I've seen how you operate, I've got no problem with that."

"Good. And there's something else I want you to do. Go back undercover as the cocky, blabbermouth kid that everyone else still thinks you are, and don't breathe a word about the EIS. Once the upload is completed, I'll be putting you together with Lydia and Walt on a research detail. Neither one of them is a fan of Earth Intelligence right now, so it's in your best interests to keep them from finding out about it. When the time is right, I'm going to reinvent Daisy Hub as the Earth Intelligence Service. Then we can all stop pretending. But I'll decide when it's time, and I'll be the one to make the announcement. Is that understood?"

O'Malley's expression cleared. In an instant, the kid was back, giving him a broad, confident grin. "Crystal clear, boss."

When the meeting was over, they left Townsend's office together. O'Malley went to check on the progress of the upload, and Drew crossed the deck to join Ruby at her console. "Find out where the *Marco Polo* is right now," he instructed her. "Give my best regards to Captain Takamura and ask when he'll be available to come and tour our new facilities."

"On it, Chief."

Chapter Two

On The Island On Stragon

The knife in Isabela Bakshi's hand was elegantly curved and exquisitely sharp. It was of Stragori design, with a quantum blade that vibrated at a molecular level, turning the act of slicing and dicing from a physical assault into a technological achievement. As she stood in the school's kitchen, contemplating what she could do with such a knife — the justice she could administer, the pain she could end — a faint, mirthless smile stole across her lips.

"Mrs. Bakshi? Are you ready?"

With a sigh, Isabela dropped the knife back into its tray compartment and nudged the cutlery drawer closed. No, she wasn't ready. But she had promised to take the children out that afternoon to gather samples for a botany lesson. They were probably standing at the classroom door with their jackets on, eagerly waiting for her to lead them out into the wild. At least, she *hoped* that was what her teaching assistant, Joanne, was talking about.

"I'm ready," Isabela replied, consciously relaxing her shoulders and pinning a pleasant expression on her face. "I've put the snacks and drinks into the cooler."

Joanne knelt and placed her thumb on the insulated metal container's control button. When the light beside it flashed green, she asked, "And what's our destination?"

Their destination? At the moment it felt to her as though the Terran colony on Stragon was headed straight to oblivion. She would never say such a thing aloud, of course, not when children were present. And as far as Isabela was concerned, her teaching assistant could be counted in that category, being only sixteen years old.

Back on Earth, Joanne had rated above average on the emotional intuitiveness scale. She looked up now, her eyes brimming with empathy, and said, "Mrs. Bakshi, if you'd rather postpone this excursion, I think everyone will understand. Your husband's funeral was just three weeks ago, and Doctor Quinian told you that you could take as much time off as you need."

"What I need is to stay busy and be with my students," Isabela replied firmly. "And what *they* need is to experience nature, not just read about it on a computer screen. Program the cooler to meet us in that clearing I pointed out to you on the satellite image the other day."

"Yes, ma'am." The girl's fingers darted rapidly in the air, entering the coordinates on a keypad only she could see. For Joanne, and for a disturbingly large and still growing number of Humans on their island, this was normal behavior. They were optimized, their brains connected directly to the Stragori intellinet.

Beginning with the first arrivals on Stragon some five years earlier, the refugees from Earth had been continually bombarded by messages from Stragori government agencies — and by advertisements from Stragori businesses — touting the benefits of cybernetic implantation. According to these authorities, connectivity was the key to success and happiness in the modern-day world.

Joanne's parents had given her the procedure as a birthday gift as soon as she reached the minimum legal age to undergo it. And now their only living child was walking around with alien technology grafted onto her neural network, and with an eighty to ninety percent chance that removing the implants would kill her. Had anyone bothered to calculate the odds that this technology could be hacked? That commands could be downloaded as well as uploaded, and that information could also travel both ways? It made Isabela shudder just to think about it.

"Done," Joanne declared, straightening up. "All the children are dressed appropriately, I've packed the protective gloves and the first aid kit, and the baskets were nested together in the store room, right where you said they would be."

Isabela mustered a smile. "Then let's go for our walk."

It was a beautiful spring day outside, crisp and clear. The overcast skies of winter had finally dissipated, the haze of summer was months away, and the sun hung in a vibrant blue sky, igniting growth and energizing the senses. It energized the children as well. As soon as the door to the outside was opened, a couple dozen six-to-ten-year-olds spilled through it onto the manufactured turf of the schoolyard, laughing and chattering and chasing one another in circles.

Isabela and Joanne stood together on the paved walkway, keeping watch while the youngsters blew off some steam. Their field trip today was to the Wilderness Zone of the island, half an hour away on foot, where the navigation satellite had detected a blossoming of wildflowers in an area overlooking the shore. The students would be collecting samples to draw, classify, and catalog, as part of a multidisciplinary study. They would also be comparing their findings with the plant life native to Earth.

Dr. Quinian would probably not be pleased about that last part. Isabela didn't care. They'd butted heads quite vigorously on this subject more than once. It was no secret that the Directorate was aiming to assimilate the Terran colony as rapidly as possible into Stragori society. Keeping fresh the memory of the world they'd left behind was, in Quinian's words, "counter-productive". Too bad. In another thirty years, perhaps, Stragon might feel enough like home for the current generation of refugees to let go of Earth. But not today. And certainly not while Isabela Bakshi had any say in the matter.

Today, she and her students would be visiting a part of the island that always reminded her of The Flats back in Americas. It was a glorious expanse of natural flora: uncurated forest, unmanicured grasses, and untamed growth of a thousand different varieties of flowering and non-flowering vegetation. And — what was most important — other than being visible to the navigation satellites in high orbit around the planet, it was free from the technology that seemed to loom over and pervade every aspect of Stragori life.

For homesick Terrans, the Wilderness Zone was a sanctuary, in many ways a balm for the spirit. It had been her and Vikram's salvation when her brother Carlos had succumbed to illness shortly after their arrival on Stragon. Now Vikram was dead as well, and despite the depth of the void his loss had left in her life — or perhaps because of it — Isabela had purposely avoided going back to the Zone.

She'd known she would have to return there eventually, to pick the ingredients for her special recipes. There had been no demand for them since just before the funeral, most likely out of respect for her grief. But she was the only Earth Intelligence chemist embedded on Stragon, and life (and amnesia, and paralysis, and occasionally unconsciousness) had to go on. Soon the orders would resume coming in from the other three EIS cells. Today was as good a time as any to return to normalcy.

Besides, today she would have the care of twenty-five children to keep her occupied and, hopefully, prevent her from sinking into sadness about things she could not change.

Isabela's school was one of the smallest in the district, a Junior Advanced Education facility with a teaching staff of two — herself and Joanne. It was also, by happy coincidence, the school nearest the tall fence that marked the boundary between the residential areas and the Wilderness Zone.

About a kilometer away, at the end of a long, straight gravel path, sat the first gate. As the students passed through it, they each pressed a thumb to the glowing green square mounted halfway up the gatepost. Everything was monitored on this island, especially movement in and out of fenced areas. The sensor atop the post conducted a head count. The thumbprint matched each head with an owner. The data was probably time-stamped and stored on a server somewhere. Whether and how it was being used was anyone's guess.

Isabela had given up wondering about it. Alone or with Vikram, she sometimes "forgot" to record her identity. So far, no one had sent her urgent reminders or come pounding at her door, but that didn't mean no one ever would. So, when accompanied by students, she played strictly by the rules.

The second gate, another thirty or so meters farther along, was the entrance to the Wilderness Zone. Once again, each member of the group was thumbprinted for tracking purposes. Isabela called a halt just inside the barrier so that she and Joanne could conduct a "bare skin check", making sure the bottoms of the children's pant legs were securely fastened around their ankles and covered by their socks and the tops of their boots. The cooler hovered nearby for a bit, getting its bearings. Then it scooted off to its programmed coordinates to wait for them.

Joanne led the way into the woods, guided by her invisible map. Eventually the trees thinned out, prompting some of the older children to race ahead. Less than a minute later, the entire group had emerged from the forest to line up, goggle-eyed, on the borders of a dense, richly colored carpet of vegetation.

There were more than a dozen different kinds of wildflowers growing here. Fiery orange and red flamebirds hung suspended from long, bowed stalks as though flying in formation. Dark blue nightlilies and hot pink passion flowers made a striking, velvety mosaic on the ground. Bright yellow and purple delphins with curlicued ribbon-like petals clung in pairs to tall stems that swayed in the cool breeze off the water. White whispers and pale blue chin-a-wags bunched together, looking and sounding like old women gossiping. And the fragrance! All these blossoms seemed to be competing to fill the air with their heady perfumes.

Images taken from orbit could only hint at the voluptuousness of this place. That was why her students had to experience it for themselves. How else could they appreciate it with all their senses? And how besides bringing them here could Isabela have safely reimmersed herself in the peace and deceptive beauty of the Wilderness Zone?

For a long moment, no one moved. At last, Joanne waded into the field, brandishing a pair of gloves in one hand and a basket in the other, and turned to face the class. "All right, kids, you know what the assignment is. Make sure you're wearing gloves before you handle these alien plants. If you don't, some of them may burn your skin, and others can make you terribly sick. Finding out which ones are safe to touch will be part of the lesson later on.

"You'll work in pairs. When you've collected your samples, put them into the nearest basket. I'll be placing these at intervals around the field. When the baskets are filled, we'll take everything back to the facility for study. Remember, we want some of every kind of flower you see growing here, so each of you will need to pick at least six different ones."

The students waited for her to regain the margin of the field and distribute the gloves. Then, their hands protected, they partnered up, spread out among the wildflowers, and set to work with focused intensity.

Watching from the sidelines, Joanne fretted to Isabela, "Oh, dear! I should have specified that we only need stems and blossoms. Some of them are yanking out roots as well. I'd better make an announcement—"

"Don't bother. Their gloves will keep the children safe. I'll trim the root bulbs off before we start back home."

Joanne relaxed and resumed monitoring the class. Meanwhile, Isabela swallowed a sigh. The roots of the plants on the island acted as natural filters and therefore contained the highest concentration of toxins from the soil. Cutting them off and leaving them behind felt like a waste of perfectly good poison. But this was a school field trip. What else could she do?

After a pause, Joanne remarked, "I think I know why you like the Wilderness Zone so much."

"Because it is so bright and beautiful?"

"Because it's the only part of the island that isn't fenced in and spied upon. My parents worry about me, so I'm constantly getting pinged. But someone without implants could sneak through that gate behind us and disappear off the grid. As long as you stayed out of sight of the satellite eyes, you could literally lose yourself here."

Isabela gave her a narrow look. "Are you having second thoughts about being optimized, Joanne?"

The girl started guiltily. "Me? No, of course not! I was just thinking out loud."

"Mrs. Bakshi! Mrs. Bakshi!"

Isabela turned and saw three of her students racing toward her, in tears.

"What's happened?" she demanded. "Is someone injured?"

"An ugly old man came out of the woods and ordered us to get off his property," blubbered Carmen, the oldest.

"He says this is his garden and we're not allowed to pick the flowers," added her sister, Ione. And the youngest girl, Stephanie, concluded with, "He went back into the trees, over there." She pointed with a chubby forefinger. "He says if we're not gone when he comes back, he's going to kill us all and eat us for dinner."

"Oh, really?" said Isabela coolly. "Joanne, take the children to the clearing and give them their snacks. Keep them all calm and together until I return."

"Where are you going?"

"I am going to find this 'ugly old man' and set him straight about a few things. And do not worry, *chica*," she added, heading off Joanne's expression of concern. "It's my experience that bullies only threaten those who are smaller and weaker than they are, and I am neither."

With that, Isabela set off across the field, determined to give Moe a piece of her mind.

She knew exactly where he would be.

———— «» ————

"There was no need to frighten the children," she scolded him.

Seated on a tree stump, he tilted his overlarge, vaguely reptilian head with its randomly distributed tufts of blond hair and looked up at her. He didn't have the lips for it, but the rest of him was pouting.

"Isn't that what monsters are supposed to do?" he growled back.

Isabela felt her temper flare and barely managed to control it. "When have I ever called you a monster?" she demanded.

"Your students did. Bright little creatures. They knew what I was the moment they laid eyes on me. They were expecting me to scare them off, so I did. Besides, I've been stuck here in the woods, with no visitors for weeks on end. I've read and reread all the books you gave me, at least three times each. Since I can't use technology if I want to stay off the Directorate's screens, how else is a monster supposed to amuse himself?"

"Stop describing yourself that way, Moe! It insults everyone who cares about you."

He stared at her for a moment. "And speaking of... Where is your little man?"

Sudden tears burning her eyes, she had to clear her throat twice before replying. "Vikram was killed four weeks ago. He was knocked down while trying to break up a fight. He hit his head and died instantly. I tried to press charges, but the tribune threw them out. She said an aging dwarf should have known better than to insert himself into such a dangerous situation. So, my husband's death has been ruled an accident, and the men who caused it have paid their fines for brawling on the street and have put him out of their minds," she concluded, with effort filtering the emotion out of her voice.

"I'm sorry he's gone," Moe murmured. "He was my friend. And I know he meant a lot to you."

"Yes, and he still does."

Isabela gazed over Moe's shoulder at the shelter where he had been living for the past four years. From the outside, it looked like a carelessly stacked woodpile. Vikram had purposely engineered it that way. Isabela's breath caught in her throat as a guerilla memory squeezed her heart. Vikram had made Moe a hiding place. For just a moment, she wanted nothing more than to curl up inside it, away from everyone and everything on this unfriendly world.

Moe had been watching her. He tilted his head the other way. "Have you been able to locate my twin brother?"

Yanked back to the present, she told him, "Not yet. I'm sorry it is taking so long. A friend of mine with connections has been making inquiries. With luck, I should have some news for you soon. And I apologize for not visiting you more often. Even before Vikram's— before the funeral, my ... *supe-*

riors were beginning to question the amount of time I spent out here. And the things I was seen carrying back and forth."

A grin split his face, like a seam slowly coming apart. "Monster isn't the only word you hate, is it? It chafes you having to take orders and account for your whereabouts all the time. Back on Earth, *you* were the one in charge."

"My brother was. Carlos enjoyed being the boss of Veggieville. I was the one who occasionally pulled his strings from behind the curtain."

"Is that what you're doing now? Secretly pulling strings?"

Recomposing herself, she replied, "To help you, yes. And to help my students. We both know that field is not your personal garden. So, you are going to leave the children alone while they pick flowers. And I will bring you new books to read when I come back in a couple of days. Agreed?"

"Add in some more pain pills and we have a deal."

Frowning, she reached into her pocket for the bottle she'd been carrying with her. There weren't many doses left. The stress of the past few weeks had given her a series of grinding headaches.

She handed him the medication. "Is it getting worse?"

He showed her something that she guessed was his version of a brave face. "Nothing I can't handle, with one or two of these," he said, giving the bottle a little shake.

"I'll bring you more next time."

Now pensive, Isabela headed toward the clearing where the students were waiting. Helping Moe had been an easy decision to make. Equally easy had been the choice to become a teacher. She'd taken to the giving professions naturally, having been taught from an early age to put the welfare of others ahead of her own. But now that she'd been so cruelly robbed of the ones she cared about the most, that would have to change.

As she had told Juno Vargas back in Veggieville so many years earlier, power worked differently for women than it did for men. A man's power was born of entitlement and built on conquest. Winners gained power; losers lost it. A woman's power grew from the calculated unpredictability of her choices, fueled by icy rage. Rage was something Isabela had in abundance right now. She could feel it burning colder inside her with each passing day.

A power game was being acted out on this world. Once she'd learned the rules and identified the players, she would find a way to flip the board over. And then, Vikram would receive the justice that he'd been denied, and she would have the closure she needed before returning to Earth.

———— «» ————

Carefully cradling the pitcher of wildflowers in the crook of her arm, Isabela returned to her apartment at the end of the school day and found a technician kneeling at her door.

"What are you doing?" she demanded.

He glanced up, then returned to his work. "I'm reprogramming the lock. It's standard procedure when there's a change of occupancy."

She drew herself erect and informed him frostily, "There is no change of occupancy. I have been living here for more than four years, and I am not moving."

"You may not be moving out, ma'am, but someone else is moving in. I'm sorry for your loss, but it's the rules. Grace period is over, space is at a premium, and double occupancy is required."

Isabela swallowed the next razor-sharp words to land on her tongue. It wasn't fair to abuse this man over a decision that had obviously been made higher up. So, she composed herself and asked, enunciating each syllable crisply, "Do I at least get to choose who my new roommate will be?"

He pulled out his compupad and called up a file. "It says here that you already did."

"What? When?"

"When you first arrived here and filled out the residence form. She was your third choice, after Vikram Bakshi and Carlos Calvera. Anna Sturtevant. Does that ring a bell?"

A second later, the memory clicked in. Anna Sturtevant was Angeli's birth name. She had apparently resurrected it when adding herself to the passenger manifest of the evacuation ship bound for Stragon.

Clearly, she'd also taken the liberty of adding herself to the Bakshis' residence forms. Not that Isabela would object.

The two women had been well-acquainted back on Earth. They'd reported to the same handler at Earth Intelligence and had been sent here on the same mission, Isabela as chemist and Angeli as operation coordinator.

Now that Carlos and Vikram were gone, Angeli was the only Terran on Stragon who knew why Isabela was really there. For the sake of the mission, that secret had to be kept. So, if Isabela had to have a roommate, she reasoned, Anna Sturtevant was the best possible choice.

"And when can I expect Ms. Sturtevant?" she asked.

The technician had been eyeing what she carried in her arms. Now he shifted position, as though preparing to duck. (*Madre! Throw one vase at one delivery person and you are branded for life*, she thought irritably.) Slipping the compupad back into his pocket, he replied, "Her belongings have already been transferred inside, so she knows about the move. My guess is, she'll be coming here directly when her work shift ends."

Two hours later, Isabela heard the apartment door chime and slide open. Leaning from the kitchen into the living room, she watched as a familiar figure strolled in and dropped onto the beige and barely-green sofa.

Angeli was wearing her hair differently. It was darker and much shorter — a flattering style, Isabela thought. And she was dressing like a businesswoman now instead of like an agricultural worker, and wearing lip rouge, and painting the lids of her pale blue eyes to bring out their color.

"I like your new look, *chica*," she called out.

Gesturing for silence, Angeli reached into her pocket and pulled out something that resembled a gem-studded brooch. Then she noticed the blinking green light set into the lid of the small metal box on the side table. "Is this what I think it is, Bela?"

"If you mean is it a signal jamming device, then yes."

Angeli slipped the brooch back out of sight. "I should have realized you'd have one of your own."

"Carlos detected the microphones in our apartment right after we arrived. He requested a change of quarters for us but was turned down. So, he and Vikram built that to ensure privacy at appropriate moments. You found covert technology in your place as well?"

"Four remote ears. They're easy enough to block when necessary. At first, I thought the Stragori had pegged us as spies. But then I sent the other agents out to do some door-to-door work, pretending to be safety officials on a random inspection tour. They sampled residences in each district on the island, and found listening devices in just about every room they entered."

"Could they tell whether the microphones were live?"

"According to the reports, they appeared to be, but I was never able to determine what, if anything, was happening at the other end of the feed. The problem is, if we simply kill or remove them, we could be blowing our cover. These mics are well-hidden, and concealed surveillance is something ordinary folk wouldn't even think to check for."

"So, it is business as usual. We remain careful while continuing to do our jobs," Isabela summed up.

"As for my outward appearance," Angeli reminded her, "don't get too attached to it, Bela. It's just my way of getting into character." Glancing around the room, she made a face and added, "Pale neutral colors? Your house in Veggieville was full of energy, all bright gold and shades of blue and orange. But this place... just looking at it makes me want to yawn."

Isabela returned to the kitchen counter, where she had been slicing vegetables with a quantum-bladed knife nearly identical to the one at school.

As the first Terrans to arrive here had been dismayed to learn, the soil on the island was not just alien, it was also dangerously toxic to Humans. Plants might grow here, but very few were safe to handle, and none of them were safe to eat. Therefore, all the produce at the island markets was imported from the mainland.

The Stragori versions of carrots and celery were nutrient-rich but much too bitter to be eaten raw, and too tough-skinned to be cut with an ordinary kitchen tool. A little like herself right now, she mused darkly.

"To paraphrase someone I know," she said, raising her voice to be heard in the next room, "it is just a temporary accommodation. The apartment was already furnished and decorated this way when we moved in. Changing it to suit our own tastes would have required an investment of time and effort, which neither of us felt like making after Carlos passed away. Fortunately, a bland environment is easy to remedy. Whenever I find it difficult to bear, I bring home something colorful to liven it up. Like those flowers on the coffee table."

Angeli came to stand in the doorway. "I'm afraid that may not be enough. If you intend to complete your mission, then you're going to have to demonstrate a much stronger commitment to this place, Bela, and soon," she warned. "Once the Stragori fleet is at full strength again, they'll be ready to ferry revenants back to Earth. There's a lot of civil unrest on the mainland, and considerable resentment building toward those of us who resist assimilation. If it continues, the Directorate may not be able to guarantee the safety of neutral aliens anywhere on the planet. Humans who still identify themselves as Terrans will probably be sent home."

Home? It was a concept without meaning for Isabela, now that Vikram was dead and the Veggieville that she and Carlos had shaped and overseen together no longer existed. But the three of them had been entrusted with a vital role, backing up the efforts of all the other EIS agents on this world. Those operations were still ongoing. And what about Moe? And the students in her care? And Joanne? She couldn't just abandon them. She wouldn't!

Isabela paused to steady her hands and her voice. "Do not worry, *chica*. In spite of all that's happened, there is more for me here than there is on Earth right now. I plan to stay where I am needed, for as long as I am needed."

"I guess we'll be going to a store on the mainland, then, to pick out new furniture. I know someone who can give us a deal, since I'm related to Dennis Forrand." Jerking herself erect, Angeli spun and looked around. "Where's my stuff, Bela?" she demanded.

"It was cluttering up my living room, so I borrowed some anti-gravs and moved it into Vikram's work space. You can sleep on the sofa tonight. Tomorrow, you can help me turn his office into a bedroom." She swept the last of the vegetables off the cutting board and into the cooker, sealed the lid shut, and selected "Stew" and "Meatless" from the programming menu. Then, picking up a bottle with one hand and two stemmed glasses with the other, Isabela stepped past her new roommate, rounded the end of the sofa, and sat down, inviting her with a glance to do the same.

"Did you look inside any of the containers?" Angeli inquired.

"No, of course not. I respected your privacy."

Isabela set the bottle and wine glasses down gently on the long packing container that a previous occupant had repurposed as a coffee table. Angeli had moved the jamming device, she noted. It now sat in front of them, next to the vase of frilly orange damselflowers that Isabela had picked during the field trip earlier that day.

Damselflower was one of the few naturally growing plants whose stems and blossoms could be safely handled without gloves. However, it had properties similar to those of the *digitalis purpurea* of Earth. A powder made from its parts could be slipped in small amounts into a target's food or drink to induce a whole range of noxious effects, including temporary arrhythmia. (Why this should be one of her most popular recipes, she preferred not to speculate.)

Only half joking, Isabela added, "And I knew what you had been up to lately and wanted to have deniability if someone came to arrest you."

She charged the first glass, then moved the mouth of the bottle to the second one and froze as a sudden thought occurred to her. "*Am* I going to need deniability?" When Angeli didn't reply immediately, she rephrased the question. "Are there stolen goods in those containers?"

"Not exactly. They're datawafers containing encrypted files that I copied during my various stints in the Data Management office."

"They're restricted?"

The other woman shrugged. "Like I said, they're copies, made during a download requested by a user with valid and appropriate authorization. The originals are still on the servers, so no one is going to miss them. However, in the unlikely event that someone decides to initiate a forensic analysis, trust me, the trail won't be leading anywhere near you or me."

"And you are certain that no one suspects you've been doing this?" Isabela persisted.

"Please, give me some credit! Anna Sturtevant has embraced her new life on Stragon and has been training diligently for promotion from her entry level job as a data clerk in the Directorate's office. I've also been taking extra courses at the Technikum to improve myself and my computer skills, whatever they're offering that doesn't require optimization.

"The big hats on the Directorate's staff must have a very low opinion of Terran intelligence. Maybe it's because of my accent when I speak Stragori. Or maybe I'm just really good at acting dumb. Anyway, I've figured out how to co-opt a data request without leaving anything traceable behind. I've been careful, Bela. By the time anyone is able to figure out what I've done, I'll have gone off the grid. You'll have total deniability, and your cover will remain solid, I promise."

It was nice to hear that things were going as planned for *some*body, at least. Isabela poured the second glass of wine and lifted it off the table. "I am pleased to see you again, *chica*. It has been a long time since you last slept under my roof."

Angeli picked up the other wine glass. "When we tested Juno Vargas. That was in 2374, so it's been ... about thirty-two Earth years. Wow. That *is* a long time." She took a sip, then let out a sigh. "The experts are all telling me I'm in the prime of my life right now, but it doesn't feel like it. Some days, I'd swear I must be a hundred years old. I was sorry to hear about Vikram, by the way. I didn't know him that well, but I know you cared deeply for him. And this is going to sound cold, but there's a silver lining to his passing. Now that you and I are sharing the apartment, we'll be able to confer privately face to face, instead of having to arrange dead drops or accidental meetings in public places."

She was right. It did sound cold. Savagely redirecting her thoughts, Isabela said, "Speaking of that, I saw Moe earlier today. His pain is worsening. I don't think he has much time left. Please, tell me I can give him some news."

"Well, I was able to call in a favor or two from contacts with access to restricted data, and the good news is that he does have a twin."

"But there is bad news?"

"He's on Nandor, in the custody of House Trokerk."

Isabela nearly dropped her glass. "In custody? He's a criminal?"

"No, but— How much do you know about Nandrian rituals?"

She shrugged. "I've heard a great deal about them, but I know very little for a fact."

"Well, in the course of my inquiries, I was given some interesting information about one in particular. About fifty-five years ago, Stragon entered into a formal alliance with House Trokerk of Nandor. The ritual that sealed the alliance was supposed to be a blending of gene pools. Between two Nandrian Houses, it would have been a simple matter of cross-fertilizing eggs. For an interspecies alliance, that was not possible. So, the Stragori scientists figured out how to splice the genomes of the two races together, creating *Homo saurius*. In their laboratory, they made two hybrid infants, one to give to the Nandrians and one to keep for themselves, as living symbols of the alliance between them."

Isabela paused thoughtfully. "Moe is a living symbol and his twin is on Nandor. This is becoming extremely complicated."

"Yes, it is, even more than you think. What does Moe remember about growing up here?"

"He hasn't told me everything, I am quite certain. However, he says he was well-treated. His guardians gave him everything he needed, including a formal education. In all ways, he was raised as if he were the only child of a high-ranking Stragori family. Until he learned about his twin and expressed a desire to find him. That was when things changed.

"Bars went up on the windows, and a lock was installed on the outside of his bedroom door. He lived in confinement for most of his life after that, provided with every creature comfort but constantly feeling incomplete somehow. When the Directorate ordered the relocation of everyone on the island to make room for Terran refugees, he saw an opportunity to escape to the Wilderness Zone, and he took it."

"Does he remember having any contact with Stragori children his own age?"

"Not that he has mentioned to me. Why?"

"Because the folder where the lab records and the alliance ritual information are stored also contains an incident report with an order from the Directorate appended to it. I wasn't allowed to copy anything, but the report and the order were very kindly decrypted for me to read. Moe wasn't locked up just because he found out about his twin. He's a chimera, Bela, part Stragori and part Nandrian, and Nandrians have a lethally venomous bite. Moe's guardians were ordered to take safety precautions because he apparently became excited one day and bit a Stragori child who'd been brought to the house to play with him. The child was rushed to a Med Services center but was pronounced dead on arrival. After that, Moe was allowed no more young visitors, only adults. And anyone who might come into contact with him had to wear specially reinforced clothing."

Stunned, Isabela sank backward against the sofa. "Was he told the other child was dead?"

"No. He was deemed to be incapable of understanding what he'd done. Truthfully, if he'd been just an ordinary chimera, he probably would have been destroyed after something like that. But he was special — a living symbol of Stragon's connection with the Nandrians — so they had to protect him. The bereaved parents of that little boy were handsomely compensated for their loss and were sworn to secrecy. It probably ate them alive, knowing that his killer could not be punished."

The irony of her situation was not lost on Isabela. Still, she countered, "Of course he was punished. How could he not be? His caregivers must have looked at him differently afterward, must have whispered things they thought he could not hear. Why else would this child have become convinced that he was a monster?"

Angeli let out an exasperated breath. "Perhaps because, by most definitions, he *is* one."

Isabela's vision clouded with tears. "Moe is an intelligent, articulate being who has accepted the fact that he is dying. Two months ago, he entrusted us with his final request. Now Vikram is gone, and I am the only friend he has in the world. Moe is counting on me, Angeli. So I am begging you. Please! Tell me there is a way to put Moe and his twin in the same room together."

Angeli set her wine glass down and stared at it as though daring it to move. Her lips pursed, then deked side to side a few times. "It may be doable," she admitted at last. "I made a friend a couple of years ago. He's been working closely with the Directorate and has a history with Daisy Hub, which, according to his sources, is also allied with House Trokerk."

"*Is* allied? I thought the station was destroyed during the war."

"It was badly damaged, but it's been rebuilt. This isn't going to be easy. But if we can get Moe off the island and all the way to Daisy Hub without anyone finding out about it, we just might be able to grant his wish. And if we do, Bela, you are going to owe me *so large*…!"

Chapter Three

"What's this I'm hearing from your students about a monster in the woods?"

Dr. Reston Quinian was barely five and a half feet tall, a slender man with the deep, resonant voice of someone much more physically imposing. Most days he wore a disapproving frown, but today he was looking especially displeased. Isabela knew the reason for that even before he spoke to her. She braced herself, knowing from experience that once he'd asked a question, he wouldn't let up until he'd received a full and satisfactory answer.

Quinian had been waiting by her classroom door when she'd arrived at school that morning. Glancing inside to assure herself that Joanne had everything under control, Isabela composed her features and gestured to him to take one of the seats in the hallway.

He chose to remain on his feet. She sighed inwardly and did the same.

"There is no monster in the woods," she told him, "just an old man who prefers to live like a hermit. He can be irritable when his solitude is disturbed, but I assure you that he is harmless."

Quinian scowled at her. "Harmless? He threatened to make a meal of your entire class."

"It was an empty threat. In any case, I have given him a stern lecture about the consequences of frightening children. He will not be doing it again," she promised him.

"I gather you'd met him before." Quinian's eyes now reminded her of a hawk's, bright and piercing. Searching for prey.

"Yes, when my—" Her voice fogged up, forcing her to clear her throat. "My husband and I were picnicking one day.

He tried to scare us off, but instead of leaving, we invited him to share our lunch. Since then, I have visited the Zone to check on him periodically. Sometimes I bring him things to make his life a little easier."

"Did he say he was Stragori?"

Mentally crossing her fingers, Isabela replied, "Actually, he has never told me what he is. He might be Stragori, I suppose. Perhaps someone who did not want to leave his home when the Directorate ordered the island to be evacuated."

But Quinian was shaking his head. "We keep careful records. Every resident was accounted for, both leaving the island and arriving on the mainland. And traffic across the strait is strictly controlled, so he couldn't have landed and then stolen back. Your hermit must be a Terran."

"If you say so."

"Did he tell you his name?"

"No. We gave him a nickname, but I guess that does not help."

"Well, whoever he is, it sounds as though he's having problems fitting into society and is in need of professional counseling. You should have reported his presence the first time you and your husband encountered him. Now that we're aware of him, someone will have to come and collect him for psychological evaluation."

"I understand. When do you suppose that will happen?"

The soberness of his expression was belied by a twitching at the corners of his mouth. "I'm not sure. How long did you say he's been out there?"

She widened her eyes and gave a little shrug. "I have no idea. We met him only a couple of years ago."

"And he's healthy, not in imminent danger of expiring?"

These were strange questions, she thought. And Quinian was settling for evasive, even untruthful answers. That wasn't like him at all. Her skin prickling a warning, she replied, "Apparently."

"Then it's not an emergency. I'll be on the island for the next three days, conducting curriculum assessments. As long as your hermit keeps out of sight and doesn't bother anyone else while I'm here, I'll wait to submit the report until I return to the office. It will take several days after that to generate and process the removal request. The rescue team should be arriving to pick him up in, I would estimate, a week to a week and a half from now."

Carefully rearranging her expression, Isabela thanked him and walked into her classroom.

These children had a busy day ahead of them: seven different tasks out of twelve. The menu included a follow-up to the previous day's botany study, a docuvid and quiz on the physics of flight, a flutterball game in the exercise room, and some quiet reading time. It was a far cry from the basic literacy and numeracy skills Isabela had taught in whole class sessions back in Veggieville. Here, students were expected to work independently, performing the assignments in whatever order and at whatever speed best suited their mood, temperament, and personal learning style of the day. Each completed task was then checked off on the teacher's master list.

After four years, Stragori was the language most commonly spoken on the island (with Standard coming in a close second), and most of the Terran students and teachers had acclimatized to Stragori educational methodologies. With all of her young charges caught up and learning at the appropriate levels, Isabela had settled into the role of facilitator. She assembled the menu, organized the materials, and oversaw the children's practice as they honed their skills.

On a normal day, she would be at her computer, monitoring and formatively assessing each child's work in progress. However, this was not a normal day. Her disturbing conversation with Dr. Quinian had set Isabela's thoughts racing and put every instinct she possessed on high alert.

A Stragori week was eight days long. If Quinian had been truthful with her, about delaying his report, about the time it would take to go through channels, about any of it at all, then they had at least that long to get Moe safely out of reach of the authorities. If not, he might already be out of time.

The question was: Could Quinian be trusted?

The answer came back at once: They couldn't risk it.

Signaling to Joanne that she needed a five-minute break, Isabela hurried to the school's hygiene room. There, she locked herself inside a stall and tapped out a quick message to Angeli in Anglo, using the DNA-keyed encrypting device and commpad each EIS agent had been issued on departure from Earth: *Quinian knows about Moe.*

Fortunately, Isabela thought to flush the waste disposal unit and sanitize her hands before coming out again. Dr. Quinian had been waiting for her in the hall. "Mrs. Bakshi, I want to go over your records for the past three months," he said sternly. "In light of the incident in the Wilderness Zone yesterday, we need to discuss certain irregularities in the curriculum you've chosen to present to your students."

Several choice responses occurred to her and were swallowed before they could reach her tongue. He had most likely already informed the Directorate and just needed to keep her busy while they lined up their "rescue mission". If she refused to engage in a debate about her educational practices, did she really want to find out what else he might drag her into?

Selecting her most charming smile to display, Isabela replied, "Of course, Dr. Quinian. I'm sure Joanne can manage on her own for a while."

———— «» ————

There were fifty districts on the island, each roughly the size of an urban district back on Earth, and each able to house about half a million people. Every district was surrounded by something resembling a greenbelt and enclosed by a tall physical barrier with multiple openings. Noticed but never discussed were the markings at each opening that indicated the former presence of a locking gate, and the thumbprinting and constant monitoring that bore disturbing similarities to a detention center security system back on Earth. This suggested that the Directorate might have emptied a gulag in order to accommodate the nearly 27 million Terran refugees. If that were true, it explained a lot, but it also raised some questions that Isabela felt uncomfortable even contemplating.

As she left the school building late that afternoon, she averted her eyes, purposely ignoring the securecam perched atop its pole in the corner of the yard, as well as the ones that sat at intervals along every street on her way home.

It had been mild and sunny all day, but by now both the sun and the temperature were falling. Fortunately, she had thought to bring a jacket with her that morning. Isabela stuffed her hands into its pockets and kept up a brisk walking pace. Five blocks of low- and medium-rise apartment buildings lay between the school and her quarters. Occasionally, an awareness of movement at the corner of her eye made her glance to her right, where her lengthening shadow lay like spilled ink across the pavement. The sight of it hastened her steps even more.

To her surprise, Isabela found Angeli waiting for her outside the main door of the quadplex that contained their apartment.

"I got your message," Angeli called, strolling over to meet her. "And I like your idea. We do deserve a meal out. So let's go to the food kiosk near the park and have dinner *al fresco* to celebrate the coming of spring."

"Isn't it a little chilly for that?"

Angeli leaned toward her and murmured, "It's part of the plan, Bela. Just trust me and go with it. And stop looking so tired and worried. I'm pretty sure we're being watched."

"I cannot help it," she whispered back. "Dr. Quinian had my teaching records under a microscope all day. I had to justify every assessment I have made for the past two years. Now I know why he travels around so much. A moving target is harder to kill."

Angeli let out a snort of laughter, then fell silent.

Several moments later, she leaned in again and explained softly, "You were right to mistrust Quinian. I was able to check his comm records. He did place a call this morning, but it wasn't to the Directorate. It was to a woman who's been flagged by Security as a radical. The content was encrypted, but I think we both know what he was telling her. Smile, Bela, as if I just made a joke."

Of course. Isabela tilted her head and forced her lips to curve upward.

Angeli continued: "You don't see as much of this on the island as the rest of us do on the mainland, but the fringe radicals are becoming more and more active. And dangerous. The public isn't supposed to know about this, but Security has intercepted and foiled at least two attempts to set off explosions in government buildings.

"Quinian hasn't openly declared for either side — he knows that having radical leanings would cost him his job — but if he is a radical, then he and his friends pose a serious threat. The radical faction hates everything the Directorate stands for, and Moe would be a perfect target for all that rage. In fact, it's possible the Directorate arranged for him to escape into the woods in the first place, simply to keep him out of enemy hands."

Isabela was confused. "But aren't we trying to keep him out of the Directorate's hands?"

"In a way. Remember the friend I was telling you about? He agrees that we have no time to lose. He's going to sneak ashore by boat and move Moe to safety tonight."

Isabela nearly tripped over her feet. *Tonight?* This was too sudden. Moe wouldn't be prepared. *She* wasn't prepared.

If Angeli noticed her reaction, she gave no sign. "But my friend needs our help," she continued.

"What kind of help?"

"To begin with, Moe's location, marked on a map of the island."

"I do not have a map."

"Not a problem. I do. Second, he'll need a way to make Moe understand that he's being rescued, not captured. Since you're the only person he trusts right now, something that proves you're on board with this operation would go a long way to ensuring it runs smoothly. Maybe there's a code phrase you use, or a detail that only the two of you know?"

"No," Isabela decided. "What will convince Moe is something better. Bound, hard copy books from Earth, printed in Anglo. I promised to bring him some. They will have to be titles Moe has not read yet."

Angeli gave her a look. "Moe reads Anglo?"

"For three years now. And since I am the one who taught him, and I am also the one providing the books, no one else would know which titles he has read."

"All right," Angeli said thoughtfully. "I guess we'll be bringing my friend back to the apartment."

At this time of year, the food kiosk was open twenty hours out of twenty-five, offering a limited range of processed meals and a broad array of snacks and beverages. The foodstuffs were Stragori, but almost every item listed on the large printed menu came with a name or description that Terrans would recognize.

"What can I give you ladies?" asked the perky young woman behind the counter.

"Are we really doing this?" Isabela wondered aloud. "Having dinner here, I mean."

"Yes, we are," Angeli informed her. Addressing the server, she said, "I'll have the ground meat sandwich with spicy *heggen* sauce and fried *dannoli* on top, and a citrus soda. Go on," she urged Isabela, thumbprinting the debit screen. "It's my treat."

Thinking longingly of the vegetable stew sitting in the refrigeration cabinet in the apartment, Isabela thrust her hands more deeply into her jacket pockets and searched the menu for something remotely appetizing. "Cheese fingers with puréed fruit dip. And plain soda." *And some antacid for my friend, because she's probably going to need it*, she added privately.

Carrying their trays, the two women made their way to a vacant bench across the street. As they sat down, Isabela repressed a shiver. It was only partly from the nip in the air. If they were being watched, as Angeli had said, distancing themselves from the crowd around the kiosk didn't strike her as being a very intelligent idea.

"Relax, Bela. Enjoy your meal," the other woman murmured. "We're about to put on a show."

As though on cue, a man appeared before them, carrying a tray of his own. He was tall and well-built, with rugged features and a shock of light blond hair. Isabela caught a *click* of recognition in his bright blue eyes when they alighted on Angeli's face.

"Excuse me, ladies. Would you mind if I join you?"

Angeli glanced up. She looked pleasantly surprised to see him. "Vin Trager? What are you doing all the way out here?"

He grinned and eased himself onto the bench. "I've just been notified that the date of my departure has been moved up. I'm leaving for my new assignment first thing tomorrow morning, and I didn't want to go without saying goodbye to my favorite Terran." He popped a fried stick of something into his mouth and made a face. "Is this supposed to be Earth cuisine?"

"It's the Stragori version of it," Angeli told him.

"Well, it's definitely not the farewell meal that I had anticipated having with you, but I guess it will have to do."

Giving her a reassuring pat on the arm, Angeli said, "Isabela Bakshi, meet Vin Trager. We worked together on the mainland for a while." To Trager, she added, "Do I want to know how you knew I would be here?"

He shrugged. "I'm former military. We have connections."

She raised knowing eyebrows. "Uh-huh. So, are you all packed for the voyage?"

"No. It was short notice. I've got some work ahead of me."

"Then you're probably scrambling to find containers."

For just an instant, his gaze narrowed. Then Isabela saw that *click* of recognition again, and he said, "In fact, I am. You wouldn't happen to have a couple sitting around, would you?"

"You're in luck. I just moved in with Isabela and can spare you a few."

"And Anna comes through again!" he declared heartily. "Thank you, I would appreciate it. Would it be too much trouble if I picked them up right after dinner? Much as I enjoy your company, I'd rather not have to make another trip from the mainland tonight if I can avoid it."

"No trouble at all. We live not far from here, and these containers are the kind that break down flat," she told him. "We'll bundle them so you can carry them onto the ferry with you."

"Sure, that works."

Isabela was remembering yet again why she generally avoided buying "fast food" at the kiosks. Apparently, she wasn't the only one. Leaving the rubbery cheese fingers and watery fruit dip on her tray, she sipped her soda and watched as Vin Trager stuck another fry into his mouth and forced himself to swallow it. Angeli, on the other hand, had polished off most of her sandwich without blinking twice. Clearly, the younger woman's digestive tract was made of sterner stuff than her own.

A few minutes later, they emptied their trays into the organic waste receptacle and began walking back toward the quadplex. Vin and Angeli strolled arm in arm, occasionally bending their heads together in what appeared to be intimate conversation. Meanwhile, Isabela was becoming increasingly uncomfortable. She knew this meeting had been contrived as part of a plan and they were all playing roles for the securecams. Nonetheless, her part — extra body tagging along on a friend's date — felt depressingly close to reality right now.

Then she overheard Angeli murmur, "You're picking up paper-and-ink books, brought all the way from Earth. Bela's the only person in the galaxy who would have spent her mass allowance that way, so they'll prove she sent you. And when we get to the apartment, be careful what you say. We're most likely under audio surveillance."

He nodded, apparently unsurprised to hear this. Then Angeli whispered something into his ear and they both laughed as if at a dirty joke.

Inside the apartment, Angeli pointed out the location of each of the listening devices. Then she loudly offered to make their guest some tea, and he accepted. The signal jammer remained off this time. After all, as Angeli had said earlier, they were putting on a show.

Two cups of *jekhailla* blend and an hour of inconsequential chatter later, Vin Trager left, carrying copies of *Don Quixote* and *A Christmas Carol* inside his jacket, a map marked with an X in his pocket, and a bundle of five telescoping packing containers under his arm. With luck, whoever might have been eavesdropping on them had heard nothing to arouse suspicion.

The stress of the day had been draining. Isabela's muscles were begging her to sit down. However, a nameless urgency kept her on her feet. She was certain that something important had slipped her mind, something meaningful and necessary that still remained to be done.

Visibly concerned, Angeli watched her pace back and forth for several moments, then said, "Bela, you look exhausted. You ate hardly anything for dinner. Let me warm up some stew for you."

Not trusting herself to speak, Isabela gave her head an emphatic shake. Then she went into the bedroom to tidy the pile of books she had brought from Earth — the treasures that had used up most of her mass allowance. As the first title caught her eye, a sob escaped her lips.

It was the only book she'd decided never to let Moe read: Mary Shelley's *Frankenstein*. Like the creature in the novel, her friend was about to disappear into the night, without hearing a single soul tell him how much he would be missed.

She hadn't had a chance to say goodbye to Vikram either. Just all at once, a piece of her had been torn away. And now it was happening again.

Isabela lay down on her bed and wept.

Chapter Four

On Daisy Hub

Townsend and Captain Paul Rodrigues were sitting together in the caf, sipping from mugs of Chef Jensen's famous sludge and munching on samples of Nora Duvall's latest baking experiment.

With the station's change of classification had come freer access to a variety of non-perishable Earth-grown foodstuffs. Inspired by the ready availability of such things as nuts, dried fruit, whole grain flour, and honey, Jensen and his *sous chef*, Nora, had immediately begun trying out new recipes. Today, she had left a platter of date and oatmeal squares on the snack counter. Drew and Rodrigues had each taken two. Everything Nora made was tasty, both men agreed, but it was difficult not to compare her offerings with Karlov's spiced shortbreads (which she had not yet managed to duplicate).

"How are your five new constables settling in, Paul?"

"About as well as can be expected, given that they're women, outnumbered two to one by the men in the detachment. I'm just glad there will be female civilians in the vicinity. Being part of a community should ease the transition considerably for them. How are your people handling things?"

Drew gave him a wide-eyed look. "Things?"

"You know what I mean. The whole detachment won't be on patrol all the time, and on- and off-duty personnel are going to have free run of the station. I'm sure your crew can't be happy about the prospect of Security being constantly present in what used to be their private territory."

Mentally crossing his fingers, Townsend replied, "I've laid it out for them. There will be adjustments to make, and perhaps a little friction at first, but I think we'll be all right. What about Madeline Holchuk? How is she doing?"

Rodrigues hesitated, visibly trying to choose his words, then apparently giving up. "To be blunt, she's a firecracker, Townsend, and a rabble-rouser, just like her father," he declared. "Did you know that she's the reason there are now five female constables in my detachment?"

"She pulled strings? How is that even possible?"

"When she'd completed her training on Mars, she marched into the base commandant's office and demanded to be posted to Zulu. He pointed out that it was an all-male detachment, and he wasn't about to put a lone woman in a situation like that, especially not on the borders of Earth space. She promptly went out and rounded up four more female constables awaiting assignment, and all five of them marched into the base commandant's office demanding to be posted to Zulu.

"He was taken aback, but only for a moment. Then he decided to teach them a lesson by giving them what they'd asked for. Fortunately, he sent me a heads up so I wouldn't fall off my chair when they reported for duty. I've been ordered not to give them any special treatment. Still..." He paused. "I want your honest opinion, Townsend. You knew Gavin Holchuk. Would you say he was a warrior?"

"Truthfully, I would not, not really. The Nandrians thought he was, and at the end he was trying to be one — felt he had something to prove, I guess — but he was just a sociology post-grad student with a dead wife and a missing daughter when he arrived on the station. Lots of grief. Plenty of anger. No training, outside of Lu's martial arts classes. Why do you ask?"

"I've been scanning the service records of the new arrivals, and Madeline's contained an addendum to the intake report from the recruitment office on Mars. She knew all the right things to say to the psych officer to get herself approved for the training program, but he noted that Madeline had severed herself completely from her adoptive family on Earth. She told him quite adamantly that it didn't matter what the database said — her biological father's death during the war had made her an orphan."

"That's understandable. In order to reclaim her true identity, she killed off the one that had been foisted on her when she was a baby. As far as Madeline is concerned, Irene Bauer was a lie. She never existed."

"Well, lie or not, Irene Bauer was Regional Security-trained, tough as nails and hard to stop. Madeline Holchuk has the skills and the mindset of a warrior. Normally, that would be an advantage in our line of work. But her father jumped aboard a Nandrian battleship and got himself a hero's death and a posthumous medal for bravery. According to the psych officer, if she's identifying with him, then she might also feel the need to live up to his example.

"I don't need any berserkers in my detachment, Townsend. I like things quiet. So, I've ordered my sergeants to keep an eye on her. In the meanwhile, it's clear that she has some issues to work out. If there's anyone in your crew who could befriend her, maybe provide a sounding board and some additional guidance, I'd appreciate it."

"I'll see what I can do."

"Thanks. The other four women seem to have their heads on straight for now. I'll let you know if any red flags pop up. And there's one more thing. I've learned who gave the order to reclassify the Hub. A confidential source told me that it was a new appointee to the Space Installation Authority's executive committee, a fellow named Darren Bascomb."

Townsend felt a sudden chill. "Bascomb. Any relation to General George Bascomb?"

"His son. Apparently, he's got two more, and he's begun insinuating them into the power structure on Earth. The EIS is opening files on all of them.

"Townsend, you need to be careful. The only reason Bascomb's first attack on you failed was that Daisy Hub was considered to be an experiment, and protecting it was Zulu's sole assignment. We were able to bring the entire detachment to bear on any perceived threat to the station. By changing your status and making us responsible for patrolling the entire sector, the SIA has also made you much more vulnerable to outside interference. I suspect this is what Bascomb wanted — to strip away most of your defenses so he could try again."

Drew had already figured this out. "Earth Intelligence needs to be careful too, Paul. If they move against him and his family, he's liable to accelerate his timetable and come after us before we've prepared for him."

Rodrigues leaned back and narrowed his gaze. "I had a hunch that you were working on something. Do you want to tell me what it is?"

"I can't read you in just yet. I have a contingency plan, but it hinges on Daisy Hub's servers being restored and back online. O'Malley estimates they'll be ready in about one interval. In the meanwhile—"

Drew's wristcomm chose that moment to buzz.

"Chief, I think you'll want to come up to AdComm," said Ruby's voice.

Deliberately ignoring Rodrigues's inquisitive stare, he replied, "I'm on my way."

"And I'll be waiting for you here. This discussion isn't over, Townsend," the Ranger captain called after him.

As Drew stepped off the tube car on C Deck, Ruby swiveled her chair and informed him, "We've got inbound traffic. A Stragori ship just popped through the Gate, ETA in approximately sixteen hours."

The image that had resolved itself on the screen above her console was nothing at all like the primitive display that they'd been accustomed to seeing on Daisy Hub's old monitors. The new medium- and long-range sensors had registered the approaching vessel's configuration and identification code and had pulled the most relevant data they could find out of the tactical computer's memory. What Drew and Ruby were looking at now was a shuttle profile that combined the fluid lines of an Eggenali Night Cloud with the heft of an Earth-made Mark VI.

The computer was identifying this ship as a diplomatic transport, and a warning was crawling across the bottom of the screen, repeating continuously: *Diplomatic immunity. Do not scan.*

It felt as though the words were crawling across Townsend's flesh as well, raising goosebumps as he came to stand beside Ruby's chair. "All right," he told her. "We can't scan, but we can initiate contact."

As the final word left his lips, a green light began flashing on the console.

"Looks like he's saving us the trouble, Chief," Ruby observed. "It's audio only. Do you want to respond, or shall I?"

"Put us on speakers," he decided.

She nodded and found the right button to push, and the pilot's hail filled the air around them.

"Daisy Hub Control, this is the Stragori shuttle *Shortbread*, requesting clearance to dock and tie down on your landing deck."

Drew and Ruby exchanged startled looks. "*Shortbread?*" they exclaimed in unison.

"Karlov, is that you?" Townsend demanded.

A deep chuckle gave him his answer.

"Mr. Townsend, it's good to hear your voice again as well."

Beside him, Ruby was shaking her head in disbelief.

"And do I want to know what you're doing piloting a diplomatic vessel?" Drew asked.

"It's not stolen, if that's your concern," came the response, accompanied by further laughter. "I'm here to take up my new post as liaison officer between House Stragon and House Daisy Hub. Once the *Shortbread* is safely aboard your station, I'm going to need a private audience with the *Hak'kor*, and I do mean private."

"There have been some changes around here, Mr. Karlov. The most private place I can think of would be inside your ship."

"That would be quite acceptable, *Hak'kor*. And you should be informed that there have been changes at my end as well. Karlov was the name your friend on Earth gave me. From now on I'll be answering to my birth name: Vinson Trager."

That gave Townsend pause. "I see. Tell me, then, Mr. Trager, are both your eyes the same color now?"

They heard a gusty exhalation, followed by his reply: "Yes, but not for the reason you may think. I'll explain everything to you when we meet in person."

Ruby's expression had hardened. Townsend gave her the throat-cutting signal to mute the audio feed.

"What are your thoughts on this?" he asked her.

She pursed and unpursed her lips. "If he's connected back up to the intellinet, I think it's going to be damned difficult for us to keep anything secret from the Stragori government," she said. "On the other hand, they did fight and die to protect millions of Human refugees during the war. If he has legitimate diplomatic status, I don't see how we can refuse to let him dock."

She was right. "Okay," he told her, "assign him a tie-down space and confirm that I'll meet him on the landing deck once his vessel is in place. I'll listen to what he has to say. Or rather, what the Directorate has to say. I suspect that's more to the point."

When Drew returned to the caf, he found Rodrigues still sitting at their table with half a mug of cold java in front of him and a pensive cast to his features.

"My sergeant on watch tells me that a Stragori diplomatic vessel has entered our sector, on distant approach to Daisy Hub. Any idea as to what that's about?" he inquired stiffly as Townsend resumed his seat. Chef Jensen had seen the station manager enter. Moments later he bustled over, bringing them a fresh pot of steaming brew.

"Nothing definite yet, but I have a theory."

"Uh-huh. Care to share it with the class?"

"As a matter of fact, I would, Paul," said Drew, pausing to refill his mug and freshen Rodrigues's, "but you'll have to promise me that nothing I tell you will end up in any of your reports, to anyone, anywhere."

The Ranger captain muttered something in an old Earth language that sounded lyrical but was probably a malediction. "You're doing it again, aren't you?"

Townsend stared a question at him.

"Don't give me that look. You're thinking about mounting a rogue operation, I can tell. Listen to me. Figuratively speaking, you and I got away with murder before, because of what Daisy Hub was and where it was located. We were off in the shadows and there was next to no oversight. Now we're in the mainstream, practically center stage. We'll have everyone and their uncle breathing down our necks, making sure the mavericks and dissidents on Daisy Hub don't step out of line.

"The SIA and SIS will be monitoring the hell out of us, springing surprise inspections and putting our reports under a magnifying glass. And the icing on this cake is that Bascomb and his boys will be keeping us in their crosshairs as well, praying for one of us to make a false move. Pre-war Daisy Hub may have been a gulag, Townsend, but it wasn't a prison. This station is going to feel like a prison."

"You're right, Paul. But you're wrong. The Bascombs are a threat, but they're hardly the icing on the cake. There is now a possibility that the Stragori Directorate might be looking over our shoulders."

Rodrigues's jaw dropped. "You're telling me that there's a Stragori agent aboard that ship?"

"I'm saying it's possible."

"Well, the good news is, he's not here yet. As station manager, you can refuse to let him dock."

"Can't. It's Karlov. Before the war, he was a Stragori agent aboard the Hub. I turned him, but the Directorate knew about it, so he more or less became our liaison. After the war, he was recalled to Stragon. Now he's coming back, with official diplomatic status and a new name, and quite possibly a fresh set of implants linking him to the Stragori version of the InfoComm network. We won't know about that last one for sure until I've met with him face to face."

"The one-eyed man," Rodrigues mused. "He was the one I was told to warn you about, wasn't he? He was looking for a rat, as I recall. Yoko?" Townsend bobbed his head in confirmation. "And you said you turned him?"

"He didn't have implants then. If he does now, we've got a problem. It won't be enough to turn the agent. We'll have to turn his handlers, and maybe the whole damn Directorate as well. And *that* will be the icing on our cake."

——— «◊» ———

One of the features of the new and improved landing deck was that it was now equipped with an airlock and an antigrav platform, both specially designed to wrangle small craft in a gridded space. No longer was it necessary to empty the deck of living personnel each time a ship was cleared to enter the station. Once the air had cycled back in and the inner doors opened, the platform would bring the vessel onto the landing deck, delivering it to the next available tie-down position. For outgoing traffic, that process reversed itself.

By now, every pilot on the Hub's crew had tested this technology, some more than once, to make sure it was working perfectly. That was their story, at any rate.

Trager's shuttle occupied less deck space than Drew had expected. As he stepped aboard the *Shortbread*, he also noted some amenities that wouldn't normally be found inside a ship this small — like a cabin decked out as a fully furnished living area. Complete with artwork mounted at eye level on the bulkheads, it put the station manager's quarters on the station to shame.

"Do all Stragori diplomatic vessels have such well-appointed interiors, Mr. Trager?"

"A great deal of thought went into deciding what to put in here," the other man told him. "And that's why I needed to speak with you privately, *Hak'kor*."

"I'm the wrong person to be asking for decorating advice."

He smiled thinly. "This isn't about the paintings, or the color of the upholstery. It's about the survival of Stragon itself. My *Hak'kor* wishes to beg a favor from the *Hak'kor* of House Daisy Hub."

A favor? This was a new wrinkle in Townsend's decidedly untidy life. "Go on," he said.

"There's no longer much doubt in anyone's mind regarding who would win a civil war on Stragon, Mr. Townsend. Many of our losses during the Corvou war were moderates, and with each day that passes, the radical faction becomes stronger. But the Directorate's main concern is not for their own safety. They worry that if there is a planetary war, the servers containing all the historical records of Stragon may be damaged or destroyed during the fighting. They also don't want their collective knowledge to be lost. So, they've downloaded everything from the intellinet's database onto memory blocs and backed up their own personal server as well."

He turned and pressed his hand against the bulkhead. A panel slid aside, revealing a hidden alcove. Inside it, Townsend saw what appeared to be a row of three metal suitcases.

"The Directorate would be most appreciative if you would agree to safeguard these until the danger of a war is over," said Trager.

"Memory blocs," Townsend repeated, his thoughts and his pulse beginning to race. With effort keeping his voice conversational, he added, "Containing historical information about Earth as well?"

"Containing copies of every document in the Stragori Archives. You wish to read them." It wasn't a question. Drew bobbed his head in confirmation. "The files are encrypted," Trager told him, "but I have the key. And I'll share it with you on one condition: that you also grant sanctuary and a favor to my passenger."

Common sense pulled Drew up short. Naturally, there would be a condition, and it was probably something hazardous, or even illegal. In fact, it would have to be, to justify the awarding of such a valuable prize. "That will depend on the identity of your passenger," he said stiffly.

"Of course. He's over there."

Drew's gaze followed Trager's pointing finger to a corner of the cabin, where what appeared to be a carelessly dropped blanket was now stirring. Warily, Townsend stepped closer. As he bent to get a better look, the huddled figure stared back at him, then slowly straightened up, snugging the blanket around its shoulders. Reflexively, Drew leaned away.

This creature was alien. Standing at about shoulder height to the station manager, it had a greenish cast to its complexion and random tufts of yellow hair sprouting from its scalp. Its facial features reminded him of one of the reptilian races, except around the eyes, which were bright green and definitely Human. They were also filled with pain and pleading silently for help.

"You remember what I told you years ago about the *ssalssit essendi* between Stragon and Trokerk?" said Trager. "About the twin infants?" His gaze riveted on the creature's face, Townsend nodded in reply. "Well, this is one of them. Meet Moe."

Drew glanced at Trager, then did a double take. "Moe?" he repeated.

Improbably, the creature's nonexistent lips parted in a smile. Then it spoke, in a voice that sounded incongruously deep and cultured. "It's short for 'homo', as in *homo saurius*. Not terribly original as names go, but it's what they kept calling me, and it stuck. Now I'm used to it. And you are…?"

Equally improbably, Townsend found himself returning the smile. "Station Manager Drew Townsend. They keep calling me *Hak'kor*, but you can call me Townsend if you wish." Addressing Trager, he demanded, "Does the Directorate know about this?"

"That he's here, you mean? Yes, but that's all they know. They have no idea about the rest of it — where he wants to go next and what he wants to do there."

"And that's the favor he needs from me?"

"That and some pain relief. We ran out of analgesic half a day ago. He's dying, *Hak'kor*. This favor is his final wish." He paused. "Help him and I'll unlock the memory blocs for you. The entire recorded history of Stragon, including its dealings with other worlds. You can even copy the files relating to Earth onto your own servers. But we'll need to hurry. Moe does not have long to live."

Townsend had run enough cons to be able to smell one in progress, and this situation was setting off an entire chorus of mental alarms. The bait was far too attractive, and the deadline disturbingly close. On the other hand, this was Karlov. Since being outed as a spy and then turned, the Stragori had earned the trust of everyone on the station by proving to be an extremely reliable source of intel.

Moe let out a soft moan, drawing their attention. "I'm sorry. I just need to…" As the alien crumpled slowly to the deck, Drew made his decision. It was a gamble, but what wasn't these days?

"Mr. Trager, we have a deal." He buzzed AdComm. "Lydia, please alert the Doc that she has an alien patient on the landing deck, and that he's in extreme pain."

"Right away, Drew."

Returning his gaze to the Stragori once more, Townsend adopted a *Hak'ko*resque posture and said, "I have many questions."

Trager bowed formally from his shoulders. "Ask them."

"If the Directorate knows Moe is here, then why go to the trouble of smuggling him off-world in a diplomatic craft?"

"To prevent the radical faction from finding him. He's the living symbol of our alliance with the Nandrians. The radicals would love to turn that — and him — to their own political advantage. However, he went off the grid several years ago, assisted by the First Shield, and nobody knew where he was. The Directorate felt it would be best if that status remained quo."

"So they made you a diplomat in order to send him here for safekeeping?"

Trager flashed him a grin. "Along with three cases of memory blocs. They probably got the idea from your friend on Earth. He made me your bodyguard in order to send Akiko here, full of encrypted information. And you have to admit, we're both very good at our jobs, Townsend. Even in the middle of a war, Daisy Hub emerged as one of the safest places to be."

Drew's jaw clenched. He could list the names of eleven people who might dispute that claim. But there were more important issues to debate. So, shoving the thought to the back of his mind, he leveled a narrow gaze at the Stragori and demanded, "Are you optimized again?"

"No. The Directorate didn't want anyone on Stragon tracking me prior to this mission. They kept me offline and let me grow a replacement eye. The artificial one I got on Earth was quaint, but it made people uncomfortable."

"You have no implants whatsoever?"

"None," he replied. "As your doctor can easily verify."

"And your diplomatic status as liaison is strictly between House Stragon and House Daisy Hub? Earth is not involved?"

"Exactly, and for the good of all of us, it would be best if the reconstituted Terran government remained ignorant of everything we've just discussed."

At that moment, Doctor Ktumba arrived, propelling an anti-grav gurney ahead of her. With their assistance, she moved Moe off the ship and onto the gurney, where she rapidly checked his vital signs.

Scowling, she glanced up at Townsend and shook her head. Then she left, pushing her patient in the direction of the tube car doors.

———— 《》 ————

How long did Nandrians live?

It was a good question. Townsend had been mulling it over for a while. As he sat at his desk on AdComm, sipping from the last of his daily java allowance, he realized once again just how integral Gavin Holchuk had been to the operation of the station. Holchuk had been the man with all the answers about the fearsome warrior race. He'd spent more than twenty Earth years studying their culture. He'd rhymed off information about them reflexively.

Holchuk would have known off the top of his head what the average lifespan of a noncombatant Nandrian was, and whether Moe's imminent death was probably from natural causes. Unfortunately, Holchuk was dead. Townsend could only hope that he'd recorded his notes somewhere on the Daisy Hub intranet, and that they would turn up once the servers were restored. Otherwise...

"Congratulations, boss man. You've just passed your tekl'han-anni." said Holchuk's remembered voice inside his head.

Great. He'd passed his final exam before any real learning had taken place.

His deskcomm buzzed. It was Lydia. "Drew, you're wanted in Med Services," she told him.

Townsend turned and saw her watching him through the transparent wall of his office. He waved to let her know he'd heard her, then swallowed the last mouthful of his java and headed for the tube car door.

Trager was already at Moe's podside in the Trauma unit when Drew arrived. As in every other part of the station, the contrast between the old Daisy Hub and this new, upgraded version was dramatic. Med Services was now equipped with an impressive array of cutting edge diagnostic and monitoring equipment. Instead of beds, Townsend saw a double row of enclosed transparent biopods, each with a control console mounted beside it and readout screens at its head and foot.

Moe lay inside the one farthest from the door. He was covered from the waist down by a thermal sheet, naked above it. His eyes were closed, his limbs and features relaxed. He looked pale, Drew thought. Almost too pale.

His midsection somersaulting, he turned to Trager and blurted, "He's not—!"

The other man shook his head in reply.

A moment later, the Doc joined them. "His biochemistry was degrading, so I've put him into stasis while I figure out what's causing his condition."

"And what is his condition, Doctor?" said Trager. "Besides the fact that he's now dying more slowly."

She gave him a sour look. "Judging by what I've seen so far, he appears to be suffering from some form of autoimmune disease. And until I have a more complete medical history for him, that's as much of a guess as I'm prepared to hazard. What I need from you right now is information, Mr. Trager. You're the one who brought him aboard the station. How well do you know this patient?"

"I know that he's a Nandrian-Stragori hybrid, fifty-five years old, but that's about all. I met him for the first time five days ago, and for obvious reasons he was very quiet during the voyage."

"A Nandrian-Stragori hybrid?" she echoed, her eyes widening. "Like the *in vitro* infants you told us about earlier?"

"Not *like* the infants, Doctor. Moe *was* one of the infants," Trager confirmed.

"Was he able to tell you anything before you put him under?" Townsend asked her.

"Not much," she replied. "Certainly not enough for a full diagnosis. But at least now I understand why his DNA looks like gumbo. Tell me, Mr. Trager, what is the average lifespan of a Stragori?"

He frowned. "About two hundred and fifty years. Why?"

"Do you know what's wrong with him, Doc?" Drew cut in.

"I have a theory. I'll need to perform some additional tests to confirm it. Until then, I'd rather not say anything. I'll do my best to help him, Mr. Townsend," she promised. "But right now, it appears as though there's a war going on inside his body. It may be between the Nandrian and Stragori elements of his DNA, or it may be something else. Keep digging for information about him meanwhile. Whatever you're able to find. It could well put me closer to a diagnosis and possibly even a cure. And now I want the two of you out of here. I have work to do."

—— «» ——

Three days later, she called them both back to Med Services and made her report.

"You're absolutely certain of this?" Townsend demanded.

Standing across Moe's biopod from him and Trager, the Doc straightened her shoulders and replied, "I wouldn't be sharing my results with you if I weren't. My theory was correct. The tests have borne it out. Moe's condition is eminently survivable. We've all gone through it and are here to tell the tale. But his case is complicated by the fact that he is a Nandrian-Stragori hybrid."

"And you're saying that you can cure him?" said Trager.

"Cure him? No. I can treat him," she corrected him primly. "Moe has already consented to the extraction procedure. He'll have to have it done every seven or eight standard years for the rest of his life. And you can tell your fancy geneticists on Stragon that this is what happens when you forcibly splice the genomes of incompatible races, one viviparous and the other oviparous, without taking into account what happens at puberty. The sudden rush of Stragori hormones most likely triggered a response from the Nandrian genes that regulate egg production. Moe can make an egg, at great cost to the Stragori parts of his body, but he has no way to expel it. So, it's been sitting inside him like a tumor, causing him pain and making him believe he was dying."

Trager's face acquired a speculative expression. "Will his egg be viable, do you think?"

"I have no idea," she replied. "Why? Are you thinking of having someone fertilize it, just in case this situation isn't unconscionable enough already? And who should that be? A Nandrian? A Stragori?"

"What about another hybrid identical to himself?" the Stragori suggested evenly. Turning to Townsend, he added, "Moe's dying wish was to be in the same room as his twin brother. If we took that one step further...?"

"Until I've removed the mass from this patient's belly, the only steps you'll be taking will be straight out the door," the Doc scolded them. "Now leave, both of you, and let me get to work!" And with both her hands, she mimed sweeping them out of the room.

"Think about it, Townsend," Trager urged him once they were standing in the corridor. "Instead of simply begging a favor from the *Hak'kor* of Trokerk on behalf of someone else's symbol of alliance, you could be *exchanging* favors with him, saving your request from *ssalssit essendi* for something that will benefit your own people."

It made a lot of sense, especially considering the scope and nature of Daisy Hub's next mission. If everything went south, being able to call in a marker from the most feared warriors in the galaxy could save them all from a very messy end.

Chapter Five

On Earth

Juno Vargas was sitting on one of the benches in the square fronting the District Administration building, soaking up the unexpected spring warmth that some kind soul had programmed into the weather dome over New Chicago. It felt like a gift, today especially. The people who flowed steadily back and forth around her were like worker bees, single-mindedly going about their business. They barely noticed her at all, and that was a gift as well.

Tomorrow, everyone on the planet would know who she was and what she had done. The scandal would be splashed across the tabs, its details part of every InfoComm unit's news feed.

Today, however, she was just another stranger sitting in the square, wearing a gentle smile on her face and watching the world go by. Juno closed her eyes and focused on absorbing the moment — the staccato tapping of footsteps, the occasional sibilant rush of a passing vehicle, the faint fragrance given off by the flowers blooming in their wooden tubs. Tomorrow, this memory would be a treasured possession.

All at once, a familiar female voice piped up close to her left ear, "Shouldn't you be packing up your office?"

Juno's eyes blinked open. She reached into her pocket and activated the jamming device that she carried with her constantly now. Maintaining a neutral expression, she turned toward the source of the voice. "Good afternoon,

Supreme Adjudicator Ellenshaw. Shouldn't you be in the High Council chambers, voting on whether to have me arrested?" she returned.

Ellenshaw's hair and eyes were blue today, the same shade as her blouse. Dark-skinned and imposing, she rounded the planter at the end of the bench and sat down beside Juno, letting out her breath in a sigh. "I'm sure Patricia Chen is looking forward to that, but there can't be a vote until she has a quorum, and she won't have a quorum until the last two High Councilors are officially sworn in. Rhys Amis and Arbo Lugaparathan actually did you a favor, running away off-world and getting themselves killed during the war. And all the Regional Councilors and District Councilors who bribed their way onto the evacuation ships, jumping the queue and leaving Earth in political chaos...? You owe them a debt, Juno. They bought you an extra four years in office, and pretty much a free hand to continue doing whatever you and Dennis had cooked up between you."

"The Reformation. It was his plan. I just—" Executed it, she'd been about to say, then changed her mind. In her current circumstances, it would have been an unfortunate choice of words. "How long do you think I have left?"

"The swearing-in ceremony is scheduled for tomorrow morning, and the motion will most likely be made right afterward. I can argue against it and stall the vote for a few hours, but there's nothing I can do to change the outcome, I'm afraid. You extorted the High Council and bent it to your own political will by making the Councilors believe that their families had been kidnapped. I know it was just a con job and that you did it for the greater good, but in the eyes of the law, it fits the definition of treason."

Now that the word had been spoken aloud, it seemed to settle like a heavy weight onto Juno's shoulders. "They mustn't put everything back the way it was, Lynette," she said. "You can't let them."

Leaning in confidentially, the other woman assured her, "Don't worry. They already know they won't be able to. You released the genie from the bottle when you expanded the New Chicago District Council to include representatives from the 'Industrial Wilderness'. That was — what? Two years ago? By now, every governing council in every political union on the planet is aware of what you've accomplished here. And, as I believe someone once said, nothing is more powerful than an idea whose time has come."

Whoever had said that was right. There might not be much left of the Earth Intelligence Service at this point, but Juno was still its Chief Intelligence Officer. She had contacts in several critical locations, keeping her apprised of developments worldwide. According to their reports, the idea of democratizing the District Councils was steadily catching on.

In Americas, Vancouverville and Lakeshore Ontario had already adopted the expanded model; and Atlantica and Havana were in the process of screening candidates from the surrounding Industrial Zones so that they could follow suit. Under pressure from the masses, three urban districts in Greater Europe, two in Pacifica, and another two in Indo-Asia were exploring the feasibility of switching over as well.

"Because of the way Earth's government is structured," Ellenshaw continued, "you've created a path to political power for any citizen with the will and the abilities to take it. If this continues, the Regional and High Councils will cease to function as an elite private club. That's what has their members in such an uproar." Her expression grew somber. "You've figuratively torn down their fence and peed in their sandbox. Now they're determined to make you pay, and there's nothing I can do to stop them. I wish there were. I don't know whether Dennis foresaw this happening, or what he had in mind for you, Juno. All I can say is, I'm sorry."

"Don't apologize," Juno said mildly. "I'm the one who chose to cross the line, and as you said, if not for the war, I would probably have been arrested years ago. Did Forrand ever tell you how I became his protégée? I was sixteen years old and Eligible, and determined to take back control of my life from the Relocation Authority. So, I sneaked into his office and got him to agree to teach me how to be as powerful as he was."

"And he taught you well. You've changed the world."

"Yes. But the exercise of that kind of power exacts a price. He warned me. The greater the power, the higher the personal cost. He talked about losing my privacy, and about sacrificing relationships. The rest of it he let me find out on my own. It's ironic, really. All I wanted was to rule my own life, but by the time I was able to, I didn't have much of a life left."

Ellenshaw's eyes filled with sympathy. "Sadly, it doesn't surprise me to hear you say that."

"And here's a further irony for you, Lynette: Tomorrow morning, Richard Bascomb will be the new Chief Adjudicator for New Chicago, and I'm the one who made that possible. He joined the Council last year, representing the Agricultural Zone." She uttered a syllable of laughter. "Well, he may be my enemy, but at least I know he won't be overturning my changes to the composition of the District Council."

Ellenshaw was shaking her head. "Richard isn't your enemy, Juno. His father is. In fact, George Bascomb is the reason his son ended up working in the Industrial Wilderness in the first place. I don't know about the other two boys, but as much as George hated Dennis, that's how much Richard hates the general."

Now, *that* was interesting. Juno widened her eyes and inquired, "Really? How do you know?"

"George and Dennis and I grew up together, so I've known the family for a long time. Darren and Hugh have inherited their father's mean streak, but Richard takes after his late mother. He's a decent, honest man. Trust me when I tell you that if he's your successor, you'll be leaving the District Council in good hands."

"And you're certain he can't be influenced by his father?"

"Positive. General Bascomb only pulls strings at the highest level."

Juno arched her eyebrows. "Patricia Chen?"

"He's been pressuring her to arrest you for some time. It appears he wants you in a cell even more desperately than she does." A pause, then, "It's because of your connection to Dennis Forrand, you know. Up until the age of about seventeen, Dennis and George were best friends, practically inseparable. Then, overnight, that changed. I have no idea why. I only know that of all the enemies Dennis managed to acquire over the years — and there were many — George was always his most tenacious and vindictive adversary.

"When Dennis died, the hatred should have died as well, but it didn't. George simply transferred it from the mentor to the protégée. I know how much Dennis trusted you, Juno. He made you the guardian of his legacy, knowing that you would do everything in your power to protect it."

"Unfortunately, it appears my power is about to end. Last time I checked, the penalty for treason was death."

"Very true. However," she went on in a low, intense voice, "last time *I* checked, death was not necessarily a permanent condition in Dennis Forrand's world. You're too smart not to have planned for this. Let me know if there's anything I can do to help."

Juno considered for a moment. "There is one thing. Be a friend to Richard Bascomb, the way you've been for me. I have a feeling he's going to need someone higher up watching his back from now on."

"Of course I will. You know, there's a Regional Council meeting tonight. Until you're replaced as District Chief Adjudicator, you're still a member. Will we see you there?"

This time she only pretended to think about it. "I'm a member in disgrace, about to be arrested," she said. "I think it would be better for all concerned if I just went home instead."

"Then this is goodbye?"

Ellenshaw's eyes were shining. Fortunately, she didn't lean in for a hug, and Juno was able to resist the urge to reach out to her. They'd been associated politically for many years, sometimes as allies, sometimes as opponents; but at this point, with charges of treason hanging over Juno's head, it was vitally important for Ellenshaw's career that they not be perceived as friends.

"I'm afraid so, Lynette. Take care of yourself."

The Supreme Adjudicator hardened her expression. Then she got to her feet and walked rapidly away.

———— ⟨⟩ ————

Juno had known for some time that her house was being watched. She swept each room regularly for surveillance technology but could do nothing about the eyes trained on the exterior of the building. According to Novak, their owners reported to several individuals, including George Bascomb. That fact was going to prove quite useful in the days to come.

Juno made a final circuit of the house, ensuring that she wouldn't be leaving anything important behind. The vote wouldn't be taken until late tomorrow morning. The arrest warrant wouldn't be issued and therefore couldn't be legally executed until sometime in the afternoon. Not that a technicality like that would stop anyone on the High Council — or General Bascomb — from giving the order to swoop in and take her into custody tonight.

It was a quarter to midnight. She glanced at her suitcase, packed and sitting in the foyer. She was ready.

Five minutes later, she heard the crunching of tires outside as a vehicle pulled up in front of her verandah. Juno peered through the clear pane beside the door. The car bore Security markings. Two uniformed officers stepped out and stood for a moment, staring back at her. One of them touched the weapon at his side, as though warning her not to resist. Then they marched up to her front door, in tandem, and one of them pounded on it several times.

No words were spoken. In the glow cast by the porch light, she could clearly see that the officers' jackets were dark blue and bore the insignia of Planetary Security. Of course they did, she thought as she swung the door wide for them.

"Madame Chief Adjudicator?" said the first man stiffly. "You know why we're here?"

"Unfortunately, I do," she replied, stepping back to let them enter, then shutting the door behind them. Once she knew they couldn't be overheard by the watchers outside, she added, "That color suits you, by the way."

"Thanks," said Novak. "I always figured these uniforms would come in handy again." He gestured toward the suitcase. "That's it?"

"You told me to pack light. I'm taking only what belongs to Olivia Townsend. As for the rest ... it should remain in the Forrand family. I'll leave it to the advocates to handle the details."

"You've filed a will?"

"Weeks ago, and a hard copy letter in an envelope marked, 'If anything should happen to me'."

"Then we're all set," he declared. "Is Madame Vargas ready to die?"

She made a face. "It's going to hurt, isn't it?"

"Not at all." The other officer stepped forward now, and she recognized him as Doctor Nayo Naguchi, still going under the name Randall Chin. "Not here, anyway. But they will need to find some fresh blood at the secondary crime scene in order to draw their erroneous conclusion. Relax, my dear. I'll be extracting it from your arm." He was grinning from ear to ear, clearly enjoying this little adventure in the field.

"Kill the outside lights, Olivia," Novak ordered. "Then pretend I just knocked you unconscious."

Minutes later, two shadowy forms emerged from the house. Observers would later report that one of them had appeared to be carrying the limp body of a third person, which he had then placed across the back seat of the vehicle. The other one had been carrying something that might have been a suitcase, which he had apparently deposited in the trunk. It had been too dark to be certain of details, but one verifiable fact on which they would all agree was that the vehicle in question had come from the transportation pool of Planetary Security — the High Council's special force, commanded by General George Bascomb.

"Wait a minute. Where are you taking me?" Olivia demanded from the back seat as they sped through the streets of New Chicago. "The Zone is the other way."

"There's been a change of plans," Novak replied gruffly. "We get one chance to do this right, so stay down and stay quiet."

She swallowed hard. The plan had been hers, but the op was Novak's. Now he was in charge and she had no say in the matter, because Juno Vargas was dead. A corpse couldn't dictate where it would be disposed of.

Her stomach writhing uneasily, she lay down across the seat. They were on the urbanway, apparently headed for the greenbelt. To keep her mind occupied, she focused on counting the overhead lights that slipped across the window above her feet.

After thirty-seven, there was only blackness.

"You can sit up now, my dear," said Naguchi, adding unnecessarily, "We've just reached The Flats."

Olivia pushed herself erect and peered outside. Behind her, the lights of New Chicago shrank to a galaxy of distant stars, then finally winked out, smothered by the pitch darkness that lay over the landscape like a blanket. Up ahead, the car's headlamps revealed a narrow, rutted path, like the one that had taken her to Veggieville so many years earlier. Now, as then, she was riding helplessly at what felt like breakneck speed, deep into the wilderness.

Mustering as much indignation as felt safe under the circumstances, she asked, "Would one of you care to read me into this change of plans?"

"Nope," Novak returned tightly. "We've got this, Olivia. We know what we're doing."

Really? She was beginning to have some doubts about that. With each passing second, the trail grew bumpier and the bouncing and swaying of the vehicle more pronounced. Novak was forced to slow down. All conversation ceased. At last, Olivia noticed a light, off to their left. It was moving back and forth, describing an arc in the air. Abruptly, Novak steered off-road toward it, driving the vehicle straight into a thicket of wildgrass tall enough to grope the windows. Then, just as abruptly, he braked and turned off the engine.

"We're here," he announced, and got out of the car.

The dome light came on in the cabin. As Olivia blinked against the sudden brightness, Naguchi turned in his seat. "And now, Ms. Townsend, if you wouldn't mind lying down again, I'll be needing about half a liter of your blood."

She did as he asked, feeling strangely more comfortable with the notion of having a needle stuck into her arm than she'd been with the way Novak had been driving.

"He seems angry," she remarked.

"He received some disturbing information earlier today."

Naguchi didn't elaborate, and she decided not to pursue the matter.

He'd been right — the needle didn't hurt much. However, as she discovered when he gave her a hand getting out of the vehicle, the blood loss had left her a little unsteady on her feet.

With Novak supporting her on one side and Naguchi carrying her suitcase on the other, she managed to wade through the wanton growth of vegetation without passing out or turning an ankle. The swinging light had moved as well, leading them forward like a will o' the wisp, into the woods and along a footpath to a clearing where three motos stood waiting. One of them sported a sidecar. The person who had been holding the light raised it to illuminate his face, and she recognized Zane 'Man Mountain' DeWitt, Novak's second in command.

"Status?" Novak asked him.

"The pilot's waiting. He's ready to take off as soon as she's aboard," DeWitt reported. Then, without warning, he scooped Olivia into his arms and lowered her gently into the sidecar while Naguchi fastened her suitcase behind the rider's seat.

"Where are you sending me, Barry?" she demanded, with effort keeping her voice steady.

"As we discussed, your final destination will be Stragon. Here — you're going to need this to get through the checkpoints," he added, handing her a biowafer. "Your transportation is already arranged and paid for. Zane will drive you to an old airstrip, where you'll board a privately-owned shuttle. It will take you to Transfer Point Charlie. From there, I've arranged for an independent ship owner to pick you up and carry you the rest of the way, with a stopover at Daisy Hub."

"Daisy Hub? But we were supposed to—!"

"No arguments, lady!" he cut her off sternly. "We spent a lot of time formulating our exit plan, and I spent even more time setting it up. Now the next step is yours. Everything you need will be aboard that shuttle." Softening his tone, he continued, "You also asked me to help you put Olivia back together, and that's what I'm doing. The final pieces are waiting for you on Daisy Hub. Reunite with your brother. Look him in the eyes and tell him what you've been wanting to say all these years but couldn't. Then go conclude the op on Stragon, as we agreed."

"And what about you?"

"I'll be tying up the loose ends here on Earth."

"After that, will you be joining me?"

"I don't know how long the clean-up is going to take. And when I'm done—" He paused for a breath. "No promises, Olivia, but I'll try."

"Then I may never see you again. Barry, I—"

"It's Tommy," he corrected her, his gaze so intense that she could practically feel its heat on her face. "Tommy Novotny. Go now. And when you get to Daisy Hub, give Snooper my best regards."

He stepped back to let DeWitt mount the moto. A moment after that, Olivia was on her way.

Several days later, a vehicle from the Planetary Security transportation pool was discovered, abandoned in tall grass in The Flats. The back seat was soaked with blood. DNA testing proved that it had come from Juno Vargas's body. A medical expert confirmed that the quantity of blood lost would have been fatal. A scarf that Vargas had been seen wearing was subsequently found on the shore of a nearby pond. Dredging the pond turned up a suitcase containing more of her possessions, including some clothing and her biowafer. Of the body itself, however, there was no sign at all.

Chapter Six

On The Island On Stragon

"Son of a bitch!" Angeli's voice carried all the way from her bedroom to the kitchen of the apartment, where Isabela stood patiently stirring a bubbling mixture of root extracts. Reduced to half its original volume, this liquid would be a quick and effective paralytic agent, similar to the Earth drug curare.

Four years earlier, she might have wondered about the intentions of the operative who had placed the order. She might even have worried about them. Now, Isabela didn't want to know. Her part of the EIS mission was simple and repetitive, and she was just as glad to keep it that way. The product needed to be at the dead drop by a certain day and time. She made sure it got there. After that, it was out of her hands. Until the next order came in, she would focus on her students. Their futures, at least, merited conscious concern.

Isabela had stopped wondering about Angeli as well.

The other woman had taken leave from her mainland posting two weeks earlier and sequestered herself in the bedroom with her cache of encrypted documents, emerging only to eat and use the hygiene room. Every few days there would be an outburst of profanity, followed by a sharing of some revelation that had jumped off her screen.

Apparently, she'd just unearthed another one. Isabela hoped the revealed information would have some bearing on their mission. The way Angeli had explained it to her, this was turning out to be a hit-and-miss proposition, with many more misses than hits.

Progress had been slow during the past four years. To begin with, none of the EIS agents on Stragon could risk being optimized, and that immediately put them at a disadvantage. They were having to gather useful intel the old-fashioned way, by infiltrating organizations and cultivating relationships, a time-consuming process that produced only a trickle of data because — surprise, surprise — people who refused to connect to the intellinet tended to engender distrust in others. Hence, the reliance on Isabela's expertise.

Angeli's approach was more technological. Planted inside the bureaucracy, she had access to a wide variety of public documents, and plenty of opportunity to cull them for practical intel. However, the Directorate's dedicated servers were her real target, and their security protocols were formidable. Novak had impressed on her the importance of the operation coordinator keeping her hands clean. In order not to get caught and blow potentially a dozen covers, therefore, Angeli had had to settle for stealing a copy of every restricted document retrieved by someone with the proper authorization, while it was being downloaded. Every half-year for the past four years, she'd taken her mandated three weeks of leave and gone into seclusion with a batch of co-opted files. She'd spent that entire time decrypting and analyzing them, all the while keeping her fingers crossed that something significant would pop out.

So far, no luck. Travel requests and budget meeting memos raised more questions than they answered and moved the EIS operatives no closer to heading off a Stragori civil war.

Isabela slid the pot of serum over to the counter to cool and set about preparing an evening meal for two.

"*Son* of a *bitch*!"

Without warning, Angeli stormed out into the living room and proceeded to pace back and forth, blowing out gusty breaths. Her hands were curled into fists. She looked as though she wanted to break something with them.

Isabela eyed her warily through the kitchen doorway. "What is wrong, *chica*?"

The other woman halted and spun to face her. "I think we may have a serious problem, Bela. I've just broken the encryption on a folder someone was downloading from the main server. It contains documents mentioning two of our agents by name."

"Are the agents compromised?"

"Not anymore, but I'm afraid others may be. Tell me, when Carlos died, what did they tell you was the cause?"

What did they *tell* her?

With a sudden lump in her throat, Isabela stepped into the living room and eased herself down onto the royal blue sofa. "What did you find?" she asked hoarsely.

"Answer my question first. What were you told?"

"It happened after one of our visits to the Wilderness Zone. Carlos had been bitten by an insect. We went straight to a Medical Services center, where a doctor identified the insect and gave my brother an injection. It was supposed to mitigate the effects of the bite and protect him from a pathogen that is sometimes carried by that particular beetle. It did neither. Carlos was dead within a week.

"When I demanded to know what had gone wrong, the doctors told me that he might have had an allergic reaction to one of the ingredients of the vaccine. They said it happens once every four hundred injections or so. They also suggested that his immune system might have been compromised by exposure to something else he'd encountered in the Wilderness Zone, and that would have impaired his ability to deal with the weakened strain of pathogen used to formulate the vaccine."

"And what about Vikram? I know you had suspicions, because you did your best to bring the case before a tribunal."

Another whole set of unpleasant memories arose now, pushing the others into the background of Isabela's thoughts. "They said it was his own fault for putting himself in harm's way unnecessarily." She raised widening eyes to meet Angeli's steady gaze. "I was right, wasn't I? It was not an accident at all."

"I can't say that for sure, Bela. All I know is that we have two deceased agents and far too many unanswered questions. And sifting through a bunch of bureaucratic nonsense is getting me nowhere. I can't believe all this garbage is considered important enough to be restricted. It's time to take some risks." Angeli leaned forward, her body tensed as though preparing to pounce. "Tell me, what was Vikram working on just before he died?"

"Besides adding flourishes to Moe's cabin in the Wilderness Zone, you mean?" Isabela paused to think. "Vikram had just submitted a proposal to get funding for a hydroponic greenhouse for our district, like the ones we had in Veggieville. He wanted to grow Terran vegetables in the park. As part of the proposal, he'd completed a study to see whether some of the soil on various parts of the island might be chemically treated to convert it into a growth medium."

"Did he show you his proposal before it was submitted? Did he keep a copy of it?"

"Of course, and yes. We're both scientists. It's standard procedure. Why do you ask?"

"In my experience, when someone is targeted for termination, it's for one of four reasons: what they are, what they've witnessed, what they know, or what they've been investigating. If I'm right about this, the proposal he submitted has already been destroyed. I need you to give me the copy he held back. And pray that my hunch is correct, and that no other EIS agents on Stragon are compromised and walking around with targets on their backs."

A sour taste invaded the back of Isabela's throat. She swallowed hard to clear it. "What did you find in that folder, Angeli?" she demanded in her most teacherly voice. "Tell me."

Reluctantly, the other woman replied, "Two documents. One of them is a confidential memo instructing the Data Management Office to suppress the results of your brother's last two blood tests, in order to avoid 'public distress'. And the second contains the findings of a confidential inquiry into Vikram's death. The conclusion they reached was the same as what you were told: lack of probative evidence, ruling of death by misadventure."

Isabela's eyes sprang wide. "Someone secretly ordered an inquiry? And is there another name on that report besides my husband's?"

"No, but even if there were, it wouldn't mean anything without corroborating documentation."

"There must be one on the memo, then," she persisted. "If this is a cover-up, we need to expose it and hold to account whoever is behind it."

Angeli brought her up short with a hand gesture.

"Wait a second, Bela! You want justice for your husband. I get that. And I'll help you, as long as investigating his death does not jeopardize our primary mission here."

"You said it was time to take risks," Isabela reproached her.

"Yes, to learn whether any other agents are compromised! In any case, without further information, we have no way of knowing where following this trail may lead us. It could take us nowhere at all. Or it could bring us up against an individual, a corporation, or even the Directorate itself. As the operation coordinator, I'm ordering you not to do anything rash, regardless of your personal feelings. Is that understood?"

Isabela let out an exasperated syllable. "If you didn't want me doing anything about their deaths, then why did you even bring the subject up?"

Angeli gave her a thin smile. "Because I agree with you that finding these two documents alone together in the same encrypted folder is highly suspicious and ought to be investigated. But we need more intel before deciding how best to go about it. Intel is my department, not yours. I'll keep digging. And if it turns out that someone can be held responsible for the deaths of your brother and your husband, then we'll find a way to make them pay. I promise. Do we have a deal?"

Justice for Carlos and Vikram, at last? It sounded almost too good to be true. But if anyone could wrest the truth from the grip of an alien bureaucracy, Isabela decided, it would be the woman sitting across from her.

"Deal."

Chapter Seven

On Earth

George Bascomb walked through the front door of his home in Millbrook Enclave and reset the alarm. He'd spent the entire day in meetings, some on the record and others not, and all of them frustrating. Two weeks had passed since the recovery of the vehicle, two and a half since Juno Vargas had gone missing. He was convinced that her murder had been staged in order to get everyone on the High Council pointing fingers at one another. Unfortunately, the strategy was succeeding. The harder he worked to convince people that they were being conned, the more suspicious they became that he was the one who had disappeared her. He'd had to back down and use his influence just to avoid being arrested.

"Hello, General. You look like a man who could use a drink at the end of a long and tiring day."

Startled, he whirled and found a stranger ensconced in Bascomb's favorite easy chair, holding a goblet of wine. The bottle sat on the table beside him, label facing forward. It wasn't a name he recognized. Oddly, it didn't seem out of character for this man to have brought his own wine. He looked to be in his late forties or early fifties. Lean and sharp-featured, well-dressed and impeccably groomed, he had such a casually civilized air about him that one could almost forget he was an intruder. And there was something else about him, something indefinable that set Bascomb's teeth on edge.

"Care to join me?" Producing a second goblet, the stranger charged it and offered it to him. "It's European, from a small vineyard just east of España. I like this red especially. I think you'll agree that it's very full-bodied. Please!"

Against his better judgment, Bascomb took the glass and sat down. If this was a home invasion, it was the most bizarre one he could have imagined. "Do I know you?"

"Not yet."

"How did you get past my security system?"

"I designed that system. It makes sense that I would know how to circumvent it."

In fact, it was the only thing that was making sense right now. Bascomb waited for his visitor to drink from his own goblet, then took a tentative sip himself. The wine really was delicious. The thought must have shown on his face, for the man said, "I told you. European vintners make the best *bordeaux*." Then, with a hard gleam in his eyes, he added, "So much for the pleasantries, General. Now, let's talk business."

Bascomb stiffened in his chair. "Listen, if you think you can intimidate me—"

The man let out a syllable of laughter. "Intimidate you? While you're enjoying my wine? Don't be ridiculous."

"If you're here, then you must want something from me. What is it?"

"You're going to give me some information."

His arrogance was stunning.

"Oh, really! Just like that!" said Bascomb.

"Pretty much. But as an act of good faith, I'll tell you something first."

This was growing curiouser and curiouser. Bascomb drained his glass and set it down. "All right. Tell me something I don't already know."

"My mother was Gloria Novotny."

The name struck Bascomb with almost physical force. She was dead and gone, a plague casualty on some obscure backwash of a planet. All his sources had assured him that he would never have to think about her again. And yet ... there she was, in the shape of this man's chin and around his eyes and nose.

"You must be Tomasz," Bascomb said quietly. The other man dipped his head in confirmation. "You were supposed to go off-world with your parents. What happened?"

"I got into some mischief when I was thirteen years old and lost my Eligibility, just before they were posted to a colony on the edge of Earth space. A bunch of us from the enclave got left behind that day. We stuck together. Formed a gang. We helped one another to survive on the streets, since no one else seemed to give a damn what happened to us."

"From the look of you, I'd say you've done very well for yourself, in spite of that rocky beginning."

"See, I knew you would say that. And I'm guessing that you were really glad when Gloria accepted your bribe and got on with her life. It must have been a huge relief for you when the Novotnys were relocated and you could finally put a career-ending mistake behind you.

"That's all it was to you, wasn't it? A mistake. Not a rape — a misunderstanding. The payment to her credit account was supposed to make the problem go away. But it didn't, because she found out later that she was pregnant, with me. When she told you, you probably tried to force her to abort the pregnancy, but she refused. Good thing for me she knew what to expect from you by then. She'd evidently made damn sure you couldn't harm either one of us without even worse consequences to yourself."

Bascomb drew himself up in his chair. "I gather you've discovered her 'insurance policy'," he said stiffly.

Novotny's reply was a smile. "You're a piece of work, General, I'll give you that," he continued. "But so am I. I can understand why you didn't want me to be born. I was an inconvenient reminder of what you'd done to her. When I went off the grid, I'll bet it lifted quite a weight from your mind."

"It did. But now you're back, no doubt with a price tag attached to your silence."

"Yes, I'm back." He paused. "In order to facilitate the census program and rebuild the population database, they've decided to make DNA testing freely available to anyone who requests it. Did you know that?"

Bascomb swallowed hard. "I heard about it. Is that how you learned that we're related?"

"Related?" the other man echoed. "Hell, no! We're *family*." He chuckled. "You can relax, General. You're not the only one with friends in high places. My test results are being kept off the record. Your dirty secret is safe, for the moment. That's part of *my* 'insurance policy'. And now it's your turn to provide information."

Of course it was. Bascomb's back and shoulders tensed in anticipation.

"I've heard nothing but rumors and suppositions so far, and I want to know the truth," said Novotny. "What made you blow up your close friendship with Dennis Forrand?"

For several heartbeats, Bascomb was at a loss for words. Given the tenor of the conversation so far, he had been expecting to hear a demand for something entirely different. He was the Commander in Chief of Planetary Security, after all, with access to all sorts of military secrets. Novotny had designed Bascomb's home security system. A criminal with that kind of expertise should have been asking for classified intelligence — contingency plans or High Council Security passwords — not interviewing him about his personal past.

"Forrand? Why the hell would you be interested in him?"

"Never mind my reasons. Just answer the question."

"I can't tell you."

"You're wrong. In fact, you're the only one who *can* tell me. What did he do at the age of seventeen that was so terrible that you would still be warring against him even after his death?"

Bascomb's heart was racing, and a cold sweat was tattooing his forehead. This was the scenario he'd been dreading. He'd always known that there would be a reckoning. He'd even drawn up a plan to circumvent it by gradually divesting himself of the secrets he'd been protecting for most of his life. Unfortunately, he hadn't figured on Tomasz Novotny barging into his living room with a bottle of truly excellent *bordeaux*.

"It wasn't what he did. It was what he was. What he told me he was. Trust me, you don't want to know this truth.

It's twisted my entire life out of shape. It's not something I would wish on anyone, let alone—"

The rest of the sentence stuck in his throat. Tomasz Novotny was a stranger, he reminded himself. At best, he was a new acquaintance, with no desire to become anything more. And after this evening, he would be just another name on Bascomb's long list of enemies to be dealt with.

Novotny put his glass down on the table and pulled something small and colorful out of his pocket. "This is a jamming device. I activated it the moment you walked through the door. Nothing we've said so far has been recorded, and nothing you tell me now will be on the record either. And just so you know, I'm already privy to some truths that would make your teeth fall out of your head if I shared them with you. I'm pretty sure I can handle one more."

"All right, then," said Bascomb grimly, settling back in his chair. "You want the truth? Here it is. When we were seventeen, Dennis and I were returning from a party together. We'd had some drinks and were a little toxed. Dennis suggested that we seal our brotherly friendship by exchanging secrets, each of us entrusting the other with some knowledge about himself that could never be revealed for as long as we both lived. When he told me his secret, I thought he was joking. To prove that he was serious, he took me to his house and woke up his father..."

"...who confirmed that he was telling the truth?"

"And who threatened to personally eviscerate me and destroy the lives of everyone I cared about if I ever revealed it. It had to do with where the Forrand family had come from."

"Let me guess," said Novotny. "Stragon?"

Bascomb was floored. "Yes! But how could you—?"

"In light of recent events that I'm aware of, it was the most logical conclusion to draw. Not such a terrible secret anymore, is it? And the one you shared with him?"

"It came out later, when I applied to become an advocate. My acceptance into the program was rescinded as a result."

"You thought he'd broken faith with you and revealed your secret. You couldn't retaliate, though, because his father was still alive."

"Forrand Senior died in 2375," Bascomb went on bitterly. "By then Dennis was a Supreme Adjudicator. I couldn't touch him."

"I can understand how all that would have poisoned your friendship with Dennis Forrand while he was alive, but it doesn't explain why you're making war on his legacy."

"His legacy? That's what they're calling it? It's a damned cheat! A con job! Dennis Forrand and I were closer than brothers. We were evenly matched in strength, and intelligence, and ambition. We should have been equally successful in life as well, but we weren't."

"Because his father used his influence to create short cuts and opportunities for Dennis as he climbed the political ladder? He wouldn't have been the first parent to pull strings on behalf of a son or daughter," Novotny pointed out. "From what I've seen, that's pretty much a standard practice among the elite."

Bascomb shook his head. "Dennis didn't need anyone's help. He would have made it to the Supreme Adjudicator's chair on his own. Either way, I wouldn't have begrudged him his success, if his father hadn't also used his influence to make sure I failed. Everything Dennis touched turned to gold, and everything I touched—? Well, I knew who was responsible for that, but I couldn't stop him. I tried, but I couldn't do a thing to either of them."

"So, you kept score and outlasted them. You waited until Dennis Forrand died, then started taking your revenge on everyone and everything he'd cared about, just as his father had threatened to do to you."

Letting out a sigh, Novotny brought the bottle over and refreshed Bascomb's wine glass. Then he returned to the easy chair and pointed out, "You're right about being twisted out of shape, but I'm not convinced the Forrands are to blame for it, General. Did it ever occur to you that you might simply have had a run of bad luck? Or that you kept trying to succeed at things you weren't cut out for? After all, you did eventually find a way to rise to the top. Quite rapidly, I've heard."

Bascomb downed his wine in three long swallows. Then he stared at the empty glass for a moment. "Yes, I did, and it wasn't easy. But I'd learned to play hard ball by then, thanks to the almighty Gilles Forrand. I made some enemies. Then I took care of them." *Like I'll take care of you*, he added mentally.

If Novotny was at all affected by the implied threat, he gave no sign. "Tell me about my half-brothers."

"Ha! They're *my* legacy. They'll carry on the battle after I'm gone, bringing down everything Gilles Forrand ever touched, and burying all of Dennis's so-called 'good works' in pieces. The Bascombs won't rest until the entire Forrand family is driven off the planet, back to Stragon where they belong. And now I think you'd better leave."

Bascomb tried to get up from his chair but had to fall back. His legs were refusing to follow orders — they wouldn't accept his weight. His head seemed a lot heavier than usual. His vision was blurring. Too late, he realized his mistake.

"You've poisoned me!" he tried to rail, but his lips and tongue weren't working properly. As he struggled to speak, the words stretched out, distorting like images in a warped mirror.

Novotny came to stand over him. "Kill you before you can be found guilty of the murder of Juno Vargas? I wouldn't think of it ... Dad. For now, I've only drugged you. It's a special cocktail created by a chemist at Forrand Pharmaceuticals. When you wake up, you'll have no memory of my visit here today. The past hour will be a blank. But I'll remember every scrap of the information you so generously shared with me. Thank you for that."

One by one, Bascomb's senses deserted him, until he was only dimly aware of movement nearby. Then the room blinked out of existence.

——— «» ———

His mind churning, Novak took the scenic route back to EIS Operations Headquarters in the Zone. It was only partly to ensure that his moto was not being followed. This had been a week of staggering revelations for him. He needed time and space in which to fit all the pieces together and make sense of them.

George Bascomb was Tommy Novotny's biological father. Learning that he was the offspring of Dennis Forrand's nemesis had been bad enough. What had been even more disturbing, however, was the realization that Forrand had to have known it all along.

Forrand had always kept a close watch on his family and friends, and an even closer watch on his enemies. George and Dennis had been irreconcilable for years when Gloria Novotny came into Bascomb's life. That meant Forrand must have known everything about their relationship, about the sexual assault, about the pregnancy, and about Tommy's birth. Hell, Gloria might even have been on Forrand's payroll from the beginning — a honey trap, paid to seduce Bascomb so that Forrand could ruin him afterward.

At what point, Novak couldn't help wondering, did Forrand decide to use Bascomb's "mistake" against him? Was this the "insurance policy" that protected Gloria from Bascomb's wrath when she told him she was having the baby? Did Forrand foresee an opportunity to hurt Bascomb by turning his own blood against him? Was that the real reason Forrand had approached the Warrior Kings to help him build the EIS?

Turn him or terminate him. As the EIS mantra spooled through Novak's brain, he could taste bile rising at the back of his throat. Yes, Dennis Forrand had known all along who Tommy Novotny was, and had coldly and callously used him. In fact, he had used everyone in his life, pulling strings from as far away as Stragon to make sure they did his bidding.

As Novak had discovered while freeing Olivia Townsend from Forrand's surveillance teams, the Supreme Adjudicator had assembled an extensive network of agents loyal only to him, both inside and outside of Earth Intelligence. Many of them had originally worked for his father. The rest he had recruited and trained himself. It had taken Novak years to identify and neutralize the ones assigned to watch Juno Vargas, and he was certain there were more, waiting and watching and reporting to Forrand on encrypted channels.

He probably thought he was safe, back home on Stragon. Good. Let him keep thinking that.

At Ops HQ, Novak rode his moto down to the second parking level, then took the lift to the top floor and charged into Nayo Naguchi's lab.

The scientist had evidently been expecting him. He barely glanced up from his computer screen as Novak came to a quivering halt beside him. "Well?" Naguchi said evenly. "How did your family reunion go? Did you get answers to your questions?"

"Everything that I've suspected about Bascomb is true. Unfortunately, it's not only the general that we'll be fighting. He's weaponized his sons against anything associated with Gilles and Dennis Forrand."

"Does that include Forrand Pharmaceuticals? I'm asking because the governing council of Earth Medical Services has just instructed my department head not to place any further orders with this particular supplier. When I reached out to our inside contacts for information, I discovered that the company is downsizing. Three of our chemists there have been let go, and the other two are expecting to be laid off any day. And once they're gone, the supply chain Forrand set up for Earth Intelligence will collapse."

Novak had to consciously relax his jaw. "We're being cut off?"

"Intentional or not, that will be the final result. It would appear that your decision to fold the EIS on Earth is fortuitously timed."

"That vindictive bastard! I don't know how he's doing it, but—" Novak pulled up a stool and slid onto it. "Bascomb is bent on destroying both legacies, Dennis's and his father's. The irony here is that the only thing Forrand about Forrand Pharmaceuticals is its name. Gilles Forrand's grandfather turned it over to a board of directors shortly before he died, because no one else in the family was interested in taking over the running of it. I'd have to look up the details, but I'm certain that Gilles and his heirs were just shareholders. Gael Dedrick was Dennis's last legitimate heir, so he ended up owning about ten percent of the company, which he sold off just before the war, to help pay for his ship. Oh, jeez!" Novak moaned, struck by a sudden thought. "The board of directors. Pull up their names, Nayo."

A moment later, Novak's suspicion was confirmed. Two new members had recently been voted in. One of them was Hugh Bascomb, the general's oldest son.

"Damn! He must be the reason they're downsizing."

"I gather you're thinking termination," said Naguchi. It wasn't a question. After a beat, he continued, "If I may speak candidly…? Perhaps purging Earth Intelligence of Forrand's private agents wasn't the wisest course of action to take."

Naguchi was right. The EIS on Earth had been pared down to a skeleton crew consisting of the SecuriTech staff and about half a dozen agents in the field. The bulk of the organization was currently located on Daisy Hub, and Novak could think of no way to bring any of Townsend's people back to Earth without jeopardizing everyone's cover.

"Perhaps not. In any case, we have to work with what we've got, Nayo."

"What we have on Earth may not be enough," the scientist pointed out.

"For an open confrontation, maybe. But once I've framed him for Juno's murder—"

"Then you'll still have to deal with his sons. You're fighting a hydra, Barry. Cut off its head and the neck stump grows three more. I think we need to ask ourselves, 'What would Dennis Forrand do?' Or perhaps we should simply ask Dennis Forrand."

This was such wishful thinking that Novak had to smile. "First we would have to find him on Stragon. You know I can't spare any agents for that kind of off-world search. I only have a handful, and they're too thinly spread as it is."

"On Earth," Naguchi repeated patiently. "However, just because I spend most of my time in this laboratory, that doesn't mean I'm unaware of what everyone else in the organization is about. There were some familiar names on the passenger manifest of the last refugee transport bound for Stragon. I'm thinking that you and Juno Vargas were most likely planting agents inside the colony, either separately or in concert. If it were my operation, their first assignment would have been to establish a secure means of communication with EIS Headquarters on Earth."

Now Novak had to chuckle. "I should know by now not to underestimate you."

"Yes, you should. So. Confirm or deny: Are you in contact with a cadre of EIS agents on Stragon?"

"Yes, but for critical messages only. They're working undercover and have gone silent rather than risk detection by either of the warring factions. Meanwhile, General Bascomb is most likely plotting to destroy Daisy Hub, and our resources on Earth are dwindling." He thought for a moment. "It will take everything we've got and then some to bring him down."

"Which warrants my asking: Do you intend to wait until it's a dire emergency before calling for help?"

Novak scowled. "No, of course not. Not a *dire* emergency, anyway."

"How comforting," Naguchi remarked drily. "Well, be careful, Barry, because you're only going to get one clear shot. Bascomb possesses enough clout to quash anything short of an iron-clad case against him, and the fact that you're his son is not going to protect you from his wrath should you fail."

Novak was well aware of that. Even if he were an advocate — or knew one he could trust — it would be reason enough to go outside the legal system for the means to eliminate this threat to Earth Intelligence. That was where his loyalties lay now. Not to Dennis Forrand. Certainly not to the Forrand or Bascomb families. Not even to the Warrior Kings, come to that. As Olivia had pointed out earlier, he and his crew had outgrown them. Of course, that didn't mean they couldn't be useful.

The general wanted a war? All right. He would get one. He had no idea of the havoc Tomasz Novotny could send his way.

Chapter Eight

On Daisy Hub

The pain was back. Not as bad as before, but definitely there. A slow-burning fire between the lower halves of his ribcage, toasting his heart like a marshmallow.

Drew had just spent half an hour on Deck C-1, where the data mining detail had set up their office. True to his word, Trager had handed over the decryption key, along with a translation matrix offering both transliterated Standard and direct-to-Anglo versions (among others) of each document. The search of the Stragori memory blocs was underway.

It was already yielding results — results that had landed in his gut like a smoldering ember as they confirmed Townsend's worst suspicions.

Earth was being gradually annexed by the Stragori. His inner cop hated to admit it, but maybe that xenophobic fringe group, Earth For Terrans, had had the right idea all along.

Drew had known since before the Corvou war about Adam Vargas and the Reorganization. The aliens had arrived on Earth at its weakest moment, a period of chaos following a pandemic, and had implemented a plan they'd brought from Stragon — a social and political system modeled on their own. According to the documents in one of the memory blocs, Earth's space colonization program had come from Stragon as well, complete with the coordinates of about thirty already-terraformed moons or planets for Terran explorers to "discover".

Karlov (now Trager) had kept insisting that the Directorate had only the best interests of Humanity at heart.

Townsend had always been a little skeptical about that. Now, he couldn't help wondering how deeply the alien influence might have permeated Terran society over a period of more than two hundred years. Had the Stragori infiltrators tweaked Earth's educational system to resemble their own? Had they imperceptibly, decade by decade, aligned Human health care practices with the ones on Stragon? How about the design of fashions? The construction of home furnishings? The way a table should be set? Was any aspect of life on Earth still completely Human?

His stomach knew the answer to that.

Townsend left the tube car, crossed AdComm, and lowered himself onto the chair behind his desk. The Doc had given him a bottle of antacid tablets to keep in his desk drawer for moments like this. He shook a couple of the pills into his hand, then popped them into his mouth.

"Rough day, Chief?" Ruby had come to stand in the doorway of his office.

He motioned her inside, then activated the privacy shield.

"The data detail has been busy."

Her eyebrows went up. "And...?"

"They think they've figured out why half of Stragon wants the Directorate reined in and the other half wants them gone. Which doesn't really bear on either of our missions, but it did get me thinking."

"Not about good things, I gather. Well, maybe this will cheer you up. We've got inbound traffic. It's the *Liberty*, captained by our friend Gael Dedrick, and he says he's bringing you a special passenger."

"Did he say who it was?"

"No, but he guarantees that you will be surprised. His ETA is ten hours, give or take."

Drew frowned. He wasn't fond of surprises these days. Too often, all they did was exacerbate his stomach pains. But maybe this time would be different. "All right. Assign him a ring station and notify me when he docks."

Nine and a half hours later, rested and showered and hoping for the best, Townsend was waiting in front of Portal 4 to meet this mysterious passenger. His jaw nearly grazed the deck when she stepped through the opening.

Over the years, he had seen still images and videos of Juno Vargas at various stages of her career. Even as an intern, studying to be an advocate, she had always shown the world a polished public figure, impeccably dressed and groomed and bestowing a practiced smile on the vidcams. But that woman was nowhere to be found in the person now standing in front of him. Her clothing was rumpled. Her hair was almost as short as his own, an unruly thatch beginning to gray. And her face was scrubbed of makeup, her complexion pale and blotchy, with weariness etched into every feature.

She halted just inside the portal and looked him up and down as well. "Drew?"

He stiffened, remaining where he was. "Juno?"

"Olivia," she corrected him. "I'm Olivia Townsend again. Juno Vargas is dead."

"I see," was all he could bring himself to reply.

The silence stretched out between them. It had considerable mass.

"This is a lot harder than I thought it would be," she said at last, in the voice laced with frustration that he remembered from his childhood. The picture now completed, the reality of this moment struck him with almost physical force.

He waited until he could trust his own voice before responding, "I know. Thirty-two years is a long time between hellos."

"And for that I apologize. It wasn't my choice, believe me."

She *apologized*? Townsend felt his gorge rise. Diplomats apologized. Politicians apologized. Siblings said, 'I'm sorry,' and asked for forgiveness. Clearly, that wasn't what they were to each other anymore.

He hardened his expression. "If you're here to make excuses—"

"No excuses," she told him, raising her chin. "I know how hard your life was at first. Forrand wouldn't let me interfere, but I persuaded him to let me keep track of you. He put us both through some difficult tests. He was planning to hand his legacy over to us, and he needed to make sure we'd be up to the job."

"And were we?"

"You were, and still are, little brother. But I'm afraid I may have been a disappointment to him."

"Don't call me 'little brother', Olivia. You gave up that right when I was twelve."

Her head snapped back as though he'd slapped her. Then, dropping her gaze to the deck around his feet, she said softly, "I guess I did."

With effort, he kept his hands relaxed. "How long will you be staying on Daisy Hub?"

"Not long," she told him. A note of resignation had crept into her voice. "I'm on my way to Stragon. Some of us are trying to head off their civil war."

"Well, I wish you good luck with that. Enjoy the rest of your voyage."

As he turned away, she called out, "Wait! There's a reason I stopped here, Drew. But I need to speak with you privately about it."

He halted with his back to her. Urgently, she continued, "It's really important that we talk. If you won't let me onto the station, then meet with me aboard the *Liberty*. Right after that, I'll leave. Please!"

Townsend took a moment to listen to his gut. Then he buzzed AdComm. "Control, are you seeing this?"

"I've been monitoring, sir," said Jason Smith's measured voice.

"Then you know where I'll be for the next half hour."

For a blue collar vessel, the *Liberty* was surprisingly comfortable inside. Not as well-appointed as the *Shortbread*, of course, but certainly homey enough to serve as living quarters for a medium-sized family or a tightly-knit group of friends. Townsend joined Olivia at a dining table large enough to seat eight on dark green, high-backed, falsahyde chairs. Dedrick was nowhere in sight, but that didn't mean he wasn't listening. Drew knew they were cousins. Did Dedrick? Did Olivia? Did it even matter?

"What's this important reason that you wanted to discuss?"

"It's about the EIS. The Corvou war hit us hard, Drew. We've lost most of our operatives, and our enemies are gaining ground every day. In short, the organization is falling apart back on Earth. So, we've decided it's time to move our headquarters to an off-world base. As per your original assignment, that's Daisy Hub."

He scowled. "Then you won't be proceeding on to Stragon?"

"Actually, I will. But they won't."

His gaze followed her pointing finger to a pair of suitcases placed next to a bulkhead in a corner of the cabin. A sudden wave of *déjà vu* made him glad he was sitting down.

"Is that what I think it is?"

"Backup copies of all the intel on the EIS servers," she confirmed. "When Forrand stepped down in 2385, he made me Chief of Intelligence. As I said before, you're better equipped to handle that job now than I am. So, I'm turning it over to you. Each of those cases contains a portable memory core. To decrypt the data, you'll need this." She reached into a pocket and extracted a datawafer. "These are the VICTOR codes. It's an acronym: verification, identification, communication, travel, ops in progress, and retrieval of data." As she slid the wafer across the table toward him, he searched her expression for any sign of emotion and found none. Her years in politics had either taught her how to conceal them or made her incapable of feeling them.

As he considered the second possibility, it occurred to him that Olivia might have been damaged even worse by Forrand's manipulations than Drew himself had been. The thought sent a guerilla ripple of sympathy through him.

Quashing the impulse to pick the wafer up just to get it out of sight, he asked gruffly, "What about Novak? Is he on side with this?"

"Yes. Originally, Dennis Forrand ran the whole show himself. Then he divided the leadership, making Novak Chief of Operations and me Chief of Intelligence. All that did was create conflict at the top of the reporting structure. So we decided, for the sake of the organization's future, that we needed to revert to Forrand's original model and have one person in charge. Someone who was familiar and new at the same time. We agreed it should be you. There's no one better qualified, Drew. You've got the experience and the training, and heaven knows you've got the smarts for the job.

"When I left, Novak was beginning to tie up loose ends on Earth. I have no idea how long it will take him, but he says he's going to join me on Stragon when he's done. I imagine he'll be stopping here to update you first and hand over any remaining codes."

Townsend was having trouble drawing a full breath. "You're really making me the head of the entire organization?"

"Everyone in it will eventually be reporting to you, so, yes."

"Eventually?"

"Until Ops is wrapped up, all the active field agents will remain under Novak's command. We're letting you step into your new role one foot at a time, beginning with Intelligence. There's a lot of data on those memory cores. It will take you a while to familiarize yourself with it."

"Who else is aware of this change of command?"

"Outside of the EIS, no one even knows for certain that we exist. Inside the organization? A handful of trusted aides who are assisting with the shut-down on Earth. For security reasons, Novak, you, and I are the only ones who know that the EIS will be continuing to operate from Daisy Hub. I've instructed my data sources on-world to go quiet until they're reactivated using the established verification codes. At that point, they'll be *your* data sources and you can change the codes to whatever you want."

"And your off-world contacts?"

"Sadly, that information network got blown up in the war. Literally. Some of my people may have survived, but none of them have gotten in touch with me. That leaves just my sources on Daisy Hub. We do have operations in progress on Stragon, but those agents are reporting to Novak, not me. As far as they're concerned, everything will be business as usual until their assignments are completed. After that, they'll be turned over to you, to be left in place, recalled to Daisy Hub, or sent elsewhere."

"What about the agents you'd planted on the station before I arrived? Do they know why you've come here?"

She shook her head. "They've been purposely kept out of the loop. The worse things got on Earth, the less we wanted them to know." She paused. "Rodrigues will keep reporting to Novak for the time being. O'Malley and Singh were reporting to me. Singh's gone. I'll leave it up to you to read O'Malley in, whenever and however you decide it's appropriate."

"And Ruby McNeil?"

Olivia gave him a blank look.

All at once Townsend's mental alarms were shrilling. Ruby was the first operative Dennis Forrand had planted on Daisy Hub, back in 2368. If she was using an EIS encryption device, then she had to be reporting to someone. Forrand had been her original handler, but Forrand was dead. So who, Drew wondered, was her handler now?

"She's your second in command," Olivia pointed out, breaking into his thoughts. "If she's good at it and you trust her, then you can give her that responsibility in the organization as well. If not, I'm sure you'll know what to do."

Yes, he did know.

Turn her or terminate her. It was the EIS mantra.

It looked as though he and 'Mom' would have to have a long, heart-to-heart talk as soon as he returned to the station.

Olivia leaned across the table, earnest gray eyes fixed on his face. "You've spent thirty-two years hating me," she said in a suddenly husky voice. "I get that. Maybe I even deserved it. But I want you to know something. I twisted Forrand's arm to let me keep track of you because I needed to make sure you were all right. I may not have been in your life, Drew, but you've always been in my thoughts. I know how it must have felt to you. You thought you'd been abandoned. But the truth is that I've never stopped caring about you, and I never stopped watching your back. When I found out what Forrand was planning for you, I made sure O'Malley and Singh would be here when you arrived. Their reports to me kept me updated about your health and your state of mind, not just your activities.

"Now you're the one who'll be running things, and I'm the one leaving on a mission. I won't have the resources to check up on you, so I want you to be extra careful while I'm gone. Don't get me wrong — there's no one I trust with this responsibility more than I do you, and I know you'll do a stellar job. Still, there will be risks, and you may be tempted to stick your neck out. Promise me that you won't try to be a hero."

Funnily enough, it was the one thing that he *could* promise her.

He scooped up the datawafer and slipped it into his pocket. "You've got my word."

When he returned to his office, he found Lydia waiting for him. She was sitting on one of the guest chairs, her expression pinched with concern. For him? Of course it was. For just a moment, he considered getting back on the tube car, maybe going to the caf for a glass of milk surrogate to douse the embers sitting in his belly.

Lydia had an uncanny knack for showing up just as he was ready to put his fist through a bulkhead and forcing him to talk about his feelings. She'd first done it when he was grieving the loss of his friend Bruni Patel. She'd done it several more times since then. Each time, she'd offered herself as a sounding board, and the emotional release had lightened his mood.

This time, he didn't deserve to feel better. He'd just unloaded thirty-two years of resentment onto someone who'd tried to reach out to him. Then he'd sent her away. Her final words to him had been, "I never stopped caring about you." His final words to her had been, "Goodbye, Olivia."

"Goodbye" wasn't going to work with Lydia, he could tell just by looking at her. Neither would hiding in the caf. Swallowing a salt-flavored sigh, Drew walked past her and sat down behind his desk.

"Jason showed me the vidclip before he wiped it from the system," she told him. "I thought you might want to talk."

"There's nothing to say."

She leaned forward, her blue eyes brimming with sadness. "Then don't say — *do!*" she urged. "Call them back, Drew. It's not too late to mend your relationship."

"There's nothing to mend. I'm not sure there ever was a relationship."

"She's your sister. You must have loved her once."

"No. When she left, I was twelve, a selfish, arrogant brat. I didn't love — I needed. I wanted. She'd promised to protect me. And on the one day when I needed protection the most, the day that would have made all the difference in my life, she wasn't there. The first person to show me any kindness after that was Bruni Patel, six years later. Bruni was persistent. He broke through my walls and taught me about friendship. About trust. Eventually, we had a relationship, he and I. But Olivia? She died that day, thirty-two years ago, before I even knew what love was."

Lydia reached out and touched his hand, and it was all he could do to keep from pulling it away.

"Maybe you didn't know, but it sounded to me on the video as though she did. Regardless, I'm here for you if you change your mind," she said. Then she stood up and headed for the tube car. His spine rigid, he watched the door close behind her. He counted to ten before getting up from his chair.

Townsend went to his quarters and sat on the edge of his bed, waiting for the release of tears. They never came. In his stomach, the embers continued to burn.

Chapter Nine

On Earth

Loudon Beecher was twenty-seven years old and compactly built, with dark brown skin and enough attitude to fill an arena. Watching him swagger through the door of the sixth-floor meeting room at EIS Ops, Novak couldn't shake the feeling that history was about to repeat itself. Thirty-two years earlier, a nineteen-year-old Rex Regum had sauntered confidently into Dennis Forrand's office, invited by the Supreme Adjudicator to receive an offer he couldn't possibly refuse. A clean slate. A fresh beginning. An opportunity to make a difference, maybe even to change the world.

Forrand must have been certain he would accept it. He'd obviously been tracking young Tommy Novotny and had known what sort of bait to dangle. And he had had the wherewithal to make good on every one of his promises.

Novak had no such advantages. He'd picked Beecher to succeed him as leader on the streets because the other new members — born Ineligible, unlike the original crew — had shown they were willing to follow him. To his credit, Beecher had upheld his predecessor's code of honor, ruling his gang of petty criminals with a firm hand. Now it was time for a change of direction. Novak had no idea what it would take to persuade this new crop of Kings to turn spy, let alone whether he would be able to afford it. Still, he had to try.

Beecher paused inside the doorway and glanced around. "Nice castle," he remarked. "You've been hiding up here the whole time?"

"Not exactly hiding, but yeah, this is where the original Warrior Kings have been living," Novak replied. "How's our former residence holding up?"

Beecher dropped onto a chair and gave him a broad grin. "Oh, you'd love what we've done with the place. Running water, curtains... We even scored some appliances last year. The girlfriends and boyfriends have moved in ... it's like an effin' hotel now. But you didn't call me here to talk about that, did you?"

Novak gathered his thoughts for a moment, then dived in. "No, I didn't. I have a proposition for you. But first, I need to know something. Are you happy with the loyalty of everyone in the gang?"

"I trust them with my life every damn day. But if you're asking whether *you* can trust them...? That would depend on whether they can trust *you*."

Of course, it did. Some things never changed, even after thirty-two years.

"They will if you vouch for me," Novak supplied impatiently, "which you'll do if I make you a sweet enough offer. I've traveled this road before, Loudon."

Beecher leaned back in his chair and spread his arms expansively. "So make us an offer, O Mighty One."

"I need snoops. Insiders to gather information at specific locations and outsiders to follow targets and report their activities. I can arrange for training for any Kings who are interested, but you'll have to guarantee their loyalty before they start. Worth a nibble?"

"Maybe. I can discuss it with the gang and get back to you. And if we decide to take you up on your offer, what benefit do we get in exchange for providing this service?"

"Besides the training and preparation, each snoop will get a clean identity to use while carrying out an assignment, complete with a dedicated credit account. My going rate for valid intel is twenty credits on verification and another thirty if it enables a successful operation."

"That sounds an awful lot like spying, Mister Novak."

"I know. Think of it as skills enhancement to reduce the risk for all the other stuff you do."

"Actually, I prefer to think of it as try-outs for doing all the interesting stuff *you* do."

Novak feigned surprise. "You know about that?"

"Your HQ is in the middle of my turf. So, *hell* yeah, I know about it. And some of us want in." Beecher's chin was elevated, fairly broadcasting a challenge.

Novak nodded thoughtfully. "That's something I'd have to discuss with my crew and get back to you about, but if they agree, you'll have a deal."

As Beecher strutted out the door, Novak permitted himself a moment of satisfaction. They would have to be vigorously trained, of course, and that would take time. However, ten or a dozen new recruits would make Tommy Novotny's job immensely easier.

《》

The Warrior Kings' old hideout wasn't the only place that now resembled a hotel. Nestor Quan had been in custody and behaving himself like a model prisoner since before the Corvou war. His room — it could hardly be called a cell anymore, since he'd been pretty much entering and leaving it as he pleased — was now supplied with more amenities than some people's homes. He'd been a wealth of information about Stragon, making it feasible for the EIS to initiate covert operations there. As his reward, a tracking device implanted in his wrist had removed the need for him to be guarded around the clock, and he'd been given free access to the roof.

That was where Novak found him later that day. 'The ninja' was lying bare-chested on a blanket, his eyes closed, absorbing some afternoon light. He'd evidently been making good use of the workout equipment in the Kings' exercise room. Novak announced his presence by purposely casting a shadow over the Stragori's lean, muscled torso.

Quan let out a long-suffering sigh. "Somehow I knew you would come looking for me, Mister Novak. You've uncovered some new information, I gather, and it has raised questions in your mind. But are they the right ones?"

Novak strolled over to the railing and turned to face him. "You know, if you weren't so damned useful to us, that attitude alone would probably have gotten you terminated years ago."

A smile trickled across Quan's face.

"Did you know when you came to me to propose an alliance with the radicals that the EIS was the brainchild of a Stragori?" Novak demanded.

"That's not the right question, but I'll answer it anyway. Yes, I did." He opened his eyes and sat up. "I was also aware that he was continuing to monitor its activities from Stragon. Are you now wondering which faction he supports, and whether, by collaborating with me, you are betraying him? Because if I were you, that is something I would be concerned about. On both our worlds, the Forrand family members are extremely influential."

That was putting it mildly. Looking back, Novak realized that he hadn't been in full control of his life from the first day he'd met Dennis Forrand. Neither had Bascomb after attracting Gilles Forrand's notice. Unbidden, the thought popped into his head: Like father, like son. Savagely rejecting even the idea of kinship with the general, Novak snapped out a response. "Quite frankly, Quan, I don't care which faction the Forrands support, or whether Dennis Forrand agrees with them. He's not running this organization anymore. I am."

"Your honesty is refreshing, Mr. Novak. And your courage. It bodes well for our eventual partnership."

"You're still holding out hope for that?"

"Always. As long as my intel proves to be reliable, you treat me as a guest — albeit one who cannot leave. Compare that with the abuse that was heaped on me when I first came into your custody. You cannot deny that my situation has been steadily improving. Therefore, why wouldn't I hope?" Letting out a relaxing breath, he leaned back on his elbows. "Now, unless there is something else you want from me...?"

"There is," Novak decided. "Years ago you said you wanted Humanity to know the truth about the Directorate's plans for us, and you also said you were bringing it to me specifically because you knew I would have the means and the will to act upon it."

"Yes. None of that has changed."

"But you also knew about the Forrands' involvement with Earth Intelligence. Weren't you concerned that they would find out what you were doing?"

"No. Once my fellow radicals were certain that I was safely in your hands, they counterfeited a death notice from Earth's government and transmitted it to the Directorate, enabling me to remain here undisturbed for as long as necessary. I'm sure you are familiar with the strategy."

Novak stared down at him. "As long as necessary to do what, Quan?"

The ninja brows rose in a parody of innocence. "Why, to answer your questions, of course. What other reason could there possibly be?"

Now Novak's gut was churning. He crouched down, putting his face closer to the other man's eye level. "Then answer me this one. I want to know everything you know about the Forrand family. I want to know what part they've played in the Directorate's plans for Earth."

Quan leaned forward and folded his legs into the lotus position. "Now you're asking the right question," he declared. "You may as well make yourself comfortable, because this won't be a short answer." He waited for Novak to settle down facing him, then continued, "Gervais Forrand was part of the team led by Adam Vargas that was dispatched to this world to restore order following the pandemic of 2172. When that assignment was completed, the team received further instructions from the Directorate. They were ordered to remain on Earth, mate with Humans, and create as many hybrid offspring as possible. Vargas's team was the first wave of migrants. Essentially, it was the wedge that enabled the Directorate, over a long period of time, to relocate many more Stragori to your world, all with the same orders — to blend into the Human population, and then to be fruitful and multiply."

Novak felt a sudden chill. "And take over Earth?"

"Actually, it was part of a much grander scheme — the Directorate's long-range plan to modify the Human genome through interbreeding, making you more like us and facilitating your eventual assimilation into the Stragori race."

Assimilation. Novak's brain fumbled that word, dropping it hard and cold into the pit of his stomach. Assimilation was a form of genocide. It was the death of identity of an entire people. And it was completely at odds with what Quan had earlier stated regarding the Directorate's plans for Humanity.

Novak had to clear his throat before he could speak again. "That's not what you told me before, Quan. You said the Directorate was dedicated to the preservation of the Human race. And before that, you told me they had chosen not to reunite with Humanity."

"Both statements were truthful, Mr. Novak. What I said was that they had decided not to openly acknowledge our shared history and reunite with our distant cousins of Earth. You may recall that I also told you I supported their goals but not their methods. The Directorate's plan has always been to bring the Terran and Stragori halves of Humanity back together. However, the way in which they've elected to do it is by covertly merging our genomes. This is not reunification. It's absorption. The Directorate claims that Humanity will benefit from this, that we're 'upgrading' the Human genome by combining it with our own. They may be acting with the best of intentions, but as far as the radical faction is concerned, that does not make it right."

"So this is the Directorate's plan that you were talking about, the one that you intend to throw a wrench into?"

"It's one of them. Obviously, we cannot 'unhybridize' the hybrids. But the Directorate has been meddling with your planet in other ways as well. With your help, the radical faction can make Terrans aware of what has been happening, and together, we and they can put a stop to it."

"By overthrowing the Directorate," Novak supplied. "That's why you came to me."

"Quite so. However, the truths your people now need to learn can't come from the Stragori on your world. All that does is add fuel to an existing xenophobia. We don't want to be the targets of violence on Earth. We want that violence to be harnessed and directed against the government on Stragon."

"I still don't see how—" In an instant, Novak's words dried up as he finally understood what Quan had been talking about. "You sneaky bastard! It's not the Terrans on Earth you want me to recruit to your cause. It's the ones on Stragon."

"All twenty-seven million of them, yes," Quan replied.

"That makes no sense. You were my prisoner before the Corvou came to Earth space. How could you have known that there would be a Terran colony on Stragon?"

"Not every poison takes effect immediately, Mr. Novak. The Stragori have agents in interesting places. We knew the Corvou queen's fate was sealed long before the swarm was launched, and the Directorate's response to Earth's cry for help was quite predictable. As is the Human response to learning that one has been deeply betrayed. Once you have exposed the Directorate's plans, the colonists will react just as you did, with outrage. They'll join with us gladly in armed rebellion."

"Once *I* have exposed their plans?"

"Through the network of Terran spies that I've helped you to plant on my world."

Of course. Novak should have known there would be strings attached to the Stragori's assistance with that. He shook his head, not sure whether to be angry or to laugh out loud.

"One thing I still don't understand, Quan. You've been locked up here for seven years. You could have told me all this at any time. Why wait until now?"

"I had to be certain that you would give serious consideration to what I said." The dark eyes were glittering. "My presence on this roof clearly indicates that I have earned a degree of your trust. And now that you have seen the light, Mr. Novak — as I once predicted you would — I want you to think about how you're feeling right now.

"Willingly or not, the Humans of Earth are being drawn into a Stragori civil conflict. So my question to you is this: Now that you have heard the truth, can we count on the support of the Earth Intelligence Service? It's a small thing I'm asking, Mr. Novak," he added. "All you have to do is pass factual information along to your operatives and instruct them to disseminate it to the other Terrans on Stragon."

"It may be a small thing to you, but it's not why I sent them there. Their mission is to find a way to prevent a bloody war, not help you stir one up. Therefore, I'm afraid I must turn down your request for assistance."

"That's a shame. I was hoping not to have to do this. However, since you are adamant... You should be advised that my people on Stragon have been aware for some time of the agents that you've slipped in among the refugees. By now they will have identified a number of them — perhaps even all of them — and will be keeping them under surveillance until their intentions can be determined."

A chill stabbed through Novak's core. He got to his feet again, took a step forward, and loomed over the Stragori.

"Are you threatening me, Quan?" he said with quiet menace.

"You? How can I? I'm your captive. Your operatives, on the other hand? Virtually from the moment they set foot on Stragori soil, their fate has been in our hands. And now I am placing it in yours.

"In light of this new information, you may wish to reconsider your position regarding the impending civil war. When you arrive at the correct decision, I'll tell you how to notify the radicals on Stragon. And then your agents will be considered turned, and ours will stand down. If open conflict breaks out before then, of course, we'll have no choice but to eliminate the alien influence in our midst. In either case, the responsibility for what happens to your people will fall squarely on your own shoulders."

Turn them or terminate them.

Novak's hands were itching to form fists. Meanwhile, his thoughts were a blur. Olivia Townsend was on her way to Stragon. Angeli had been there since just before the war. Would the Forrands protect their own? Would Olivia even think to approach them?

Quan had been watching Novak expectantly. "If you need time to think about it, you know where to find me," he said. "But don't wait too long, Mr. Novak. Hostilities could break out any day now." With maddening unconcern, 'the ninja' lay down again and closed his eyes.

Novak stood there for a moment, imagining what it would feel like to put his boot on the other man's throat and shift his full weight onto it. Then he had a better idea.

Tommy Novotny headed for the door to the lift. He'd played by the rules long enough. Now it was time to put Barry Novak away and mete out some street justice.

Chapter Ten

Daisy Hub

"You wanted to talk to me, Chief?"

Townsend tore his gaze away from his computer screen and saw Ruby leaning against the jamb of his office door with her head tilted and her arms crossed.

"Yes. I have a question for you."

"And I have many answers," she replied, straightening up and bowing, Nandrian-like, from the shoulders. "Ask your question. Maybe we'll find a match."

He beckoned her inside the office and waved her onto a chair. Then he activated the privacy shield.

"You told me that Forrand had gotten you posted out here when the station first went online. That was several years before the EIS was established, so I'm assuming he also gave you a secure way to communicate with him. Once the technology existed, you were issued an agent-specific decryption device, just like the rest of us. When Forrand stepped down from running the EIS, you must have been assigned a different handler as well. I want to know who that is."

Her brows drew together in puzzlement. "He stepped down? That's news to me."

"Well, it's hard to manage an outfit this size when you're a corpse." She chuckled as though he'd just made a joke. Instantly, Townsend's brain began to itch. "Listen, I've identified all the agents aboard the Hub now, and I know who each of them has been reporting to. Except for you.

You're the only one I can't place in the organization. You're my second in command, Ruby, and with all the changes that have been happening lately, and the scope of the mission we're about to embark on, I can't have unanswered questions about any member of my crew. So tell me: Who is your current handler?"

She gave him a shrug and a benign, infuriating smile. "You said it yourself, Chief. I've been reporting directly to Dennis Forrand."

"This whole time? Come on, Ruby, that's imp—" He halted as a sudden realization seemed to suck the air from the room.

Convincing people that their loved ones were dead was Forrand's favorite manipulation technique. In fact, he had practically made it an EIS trademark. Faking his own death would have been a simple matter for someone with Forrand's resources. It would also have given him the perfect cover while he continued to monitor those he'd placed in positions of responsibility — for example, the station managers of Daisy Hub.

"Damn!" Falling backward against his chair, Drew tried the words out to see whether his brain would accept them without imploding. "Dennis Forrand is alive."

"Yes. He's using a different name now," Ruby said breezily, "but he's alive and well and living on Stragon."

Of course he was. And Olivia had apparently lifted a page from Forrand's playbook, killing off her Juno Vargas identity before leaving Earth for that same alien world. According to her, Tommy Novotny would soon be following suit, shedding Barry Novak like an old skin. More than once, Drew had longed to be able to do exactly that. For just a second, he felt a pinch of envy.

"So, for the past nineteen Earth years, you've been sending confidential information about Daisy Hub to someone on Stragon?"

"Yes." She frowned. "It doesn't sound very good when you put it that way. But Daisy Hub was Dennis's pet project. I'm certain he wouldn't do anything to jeopardize the station or anyone on it."

"Even if we set off in a direction he didn't approve of? Like mounting an attack on the Great Council?"

Her lips drew into a hyphen. With evident reluctance, she conceded, "I see your point."

"Good. Then you understand why I have to ask you to surrender your EIS encrypting device, and why I must insist that you not communicate with Forrand again, except on my explicit instructions."

"That would create more problems than it would solve, Chief. The Forrands have a lot of clout on Stragon."

"They have clout? What's that supposed to mean?"

"Ask our new liaison officer." And with that, she got smartly to her feet and walked through the privacy shield and out the door.

One hour later, Vinson Trager was sitting across from Drew, his long legs extended and crossed at the ankles as he said, "Ruby is not mistaken. I'm well versed in the history of my home world, and the name Forrand comes up frequently in our archival records. They've always been a very influential political family on our planet. In fact, there are even a couple of Forrands on the Directorate, and directorships are not easy to come by."

"And it can't possibly be a coincidence that a Forrand on Earth—?"

"—should have ended up in a position to exercise tremendous power? Not at all. Running other people's lives is the Forrand family business, on Stragon as well as on Earth, and they've never shrunk away from using questionable tactics if they felt the end was worthy."

Townsend picked his words carefully. "So, if a Forrand had set up a line of communication and it were suddenly to be silenced...?"

The blue eyes acquired an interested gleam. "If you're implying what I think you are, trust me, there would be unpleasant repercussions at both ends of that line. Like any powerful Stragori family, the Forrands do not take betrayal lightly."

"And it's beyond doubt that Dennis Forrand belongs to that family?"

"Forrand is not a common name on either of our planets. So, it's safe to say that any Forrands born on Earth — and any Terrans with a Forrand ancestor — are almost certainly the fruit of this one family tree."

That made Drew and Olivia's mother part Stragori, which made them hybrids as well. And how many others were running around, unaware of their alien genetic heritage? According to the data O'Malley and his detail had already dug up, there had been thirteen, including Adam Vargas, on the Stragori task force that had come to Earth some 230 years earlier.

Drew swallowed hard. "And how many family trees were there in total, once the Reorganization had been established?"

"In total? There were thousands, Townsend. Vargas's team was just the first wave of migrants. The Directorate's standing order was not to form a separate colony, but rather to merge with the Human population, producing hybrid children if possible."

Drew's world took a sudden leftward tilt. So, the Stragori weren't just annexing Earth—they were annexing Humanity itself. Thousands of Stragori procreating with Humans over multiple generations … and the Doc had detected no immediate differences between Karlov's (now Trager's) DNA and the gene maps in the crew's medical records. According to Steve Bonelli, every crew member had been specially selected by someone back on Earth. Had they been chosen because that someone knew they were hybrids? Or was every Human on the planet now that much closer to being Stragori?

Townsend's thoughts were spinning, blurring his senses and fanning the embers in his stomach. Forcing himself to breathe deeply, he leaned back in his chair and closed his eyes for a moment. When he opened them again, the chair across from him was empty, and Trager was on his way to the tube car.

"Damn!"

———— «◊» ————

The object sitting on the Doc's work table was the same shade of brown as her skin and resembled a half-inflated football. As the four of them stood around it, staring, Trager said with audible dismay, "That's Moe's egg? It can't possibly be viable."

"Kind of flat, isn't it?" Townsend observed.

"Well, what did you expect?" the Doc demanded. "It spent extra time inside his body, being attacked by his immune system and squeezed by his internal organs."

"I'm just glad to be rid of it," declared Moe, his complexion once more a healthy shade of green as he neared full recovery from his surgery. "Now, about my final request...?"

"It can't be your final request anymore," Drew pointed out patiently, "because you're no longer dying. Now it's just asking for a favor."

"Meaning what? You're going to stiff me on a technicality?"

Townsend recognized the syntax. "You've been talking to Hagman, haven't you?"

"Yes. Your Head of Security has been a wellspring of counsel and information."

"Uh-huh. Well, nobody's getting stiffed, Moe. I'm just waiting for my people to locate the notes that our previous liaison officer should have left behind. With luck, they'll contain the comm codes for making direct contact with the First Shield of House Trokerk. In the meanwhile—"

Drew's wristcomm buzzed.

"Chief, they've found something. Lydia is bringing it up to your office," said Ruby's voice.

"I'm on my way," he replied. Addressing the rest of the group, he added, "This may be what I was talking about."

Several minutes later, Townsend stepped off the tube car onto AdComm and found Lydia Garfield pacing back and forth in front of his office door.

"Please, tell me you've found Holchuk's notes!" he entreated without breaking stride.

She gave him a pained look. "We're still searching for those. Sorry! But I remembered saving a bunch of data relating to the Nandrians on our old SPA room server." She held a datawafer out to him. "I was on duty and recording everything when Gavin set up the meeting between Ajda Gray and Trokerk's high speaker, just before our *ssalssit essendi*. Maybe it will help."

Swallowing his disappointment, he took the wafer from her hand. "I certainly hope so. Thanks for this. And keep digging."

———— «◊» ————

Unfortunately, Lydia's notes weren't really relevant, since there had never actually been any direct contact between the *Hak'kors* of Daisy Hub and Trokerk. Townsend's request for a meeting of high speakers had had to travel along an established chain of communication. As Drew recalled, Gavin Holchuk, a warrior of the Fifth Shield, had contacted Chief Officer Nagor, also of the Fifth Shield, who had relayed a message to Chief Officer Agnosk, a member of the Third Shield, who had then petitioned the *Kalufah*, Trokerk's second in command, who had finally passed the request to the *Hak'kor* for consideration.

It was a convoluted process, one demanded by the rigid caste structure of Nandrian society. However, *Hak'kors* were considered to be equals, regardless of the size of their respective Houses. Even though the First Shield didn't leave the home world except on matters of extreme importance, there had to be a way for them to communicate with one another without going through channels. In fact, being represented by a subordinate might send an entirely wrong message. In certain circumstances, it could even be construed as an insult.

Then Townsend remembered: The warmaster belonged to the First Shield, and Trokerk's warmaster had earlier sent Agnosk to beg a favor on his behalf from the *Hak'kor* of House Daisy Hub. That probably meant Third Shield was an acceptable go-between — when favors were involved, at least.

All right, then. Holchuk had assigned each crew member a number to make it easier to deal with the Nandrians when they were aboard, and he'd also drawn up the list of delegates to the Hub's *ssalssit essendi*. Drew had seen that list. He closed his eyes, willing it to reappear in his visual memory, and saw...

Drew, Ruby, and Ajda Gray were First Shield. Rodrigues was Second Shield. Lydia was Third Shield. She was also the station's officer in charge of communications, and Townsend knew that she'd been in possession of the commcodes for Agnosk's ship, the *Nannssi*. Perfect! As he was reaching for the intercomm button to summon her to his office, however, the speaker blurted to life, startling him.

"Chief, we've just been hailed by the *Marco Polo*," said Ruby's cheerful voice. "ETA is in roughly twelve hours. Captain Takamura says he'll be only too happy to let you give him a tour of the station."

This was even more perfect. The *Marco Polo* had gone to Kula'as. Takamura had welcomed aliens aboard, had even taken his ship on a stealth mission for them, deep into alien space. There had to be data he could add to what O'Malley had removed from the ship's logs, information that could help Townsend build his case against the Great Council. It could mean reading Takamura into Daisy Hub's next mission, of course. And if he was considering doing that, then there was someone else who needed to be brought up to speed first.

"Ruby, I want you to find Captain Rodrigues for me. If he's free, tell him we need to talk privately."

"On it, Chief!"

About twenty minutes later, the Ranger captain stepped off the tube car and strolled into Townsend's office. "Have you finally decided to tell me what the hell is going on?" he grumped, dropping onto a guest chair as Drew activated the privacy shield. "And please don't say that I can't report any of it. I'm getting tired of lying to my handler."

"You won't have to for much longer, Paul."

The other man's scowl deepened. "And what is that supposed to mean?"

"You know that I arrived here five standard years ago with a mission from Earth Intelligence. When Novak briefed you, did he tell you what it was?"

"He told me you were assigned to co-opt the station's crew and turn them into an off-world EIS cell with yourself as leader. He advised me to give you plenty of latitude, because your job wouldn't be easy. He also stressed that, contrary to appearances, you and Daisy Hub and all the misfits and boatrockers under your alleged command were vital to the continuing operation of the organization. Therefore, my detachment was to safeguard all of you, with our lives if necessary. And since I haven't received any verifiable countermanding orders, his instruction stands."

"You must have wondered at times about that."

"Of course I wondered about it, for a while. I figured there had to be more to the story, but that it must be above my clearance level. Then everything went crazy and I was too busy even to think about it."

Townsend filled his lungs and said, "What I'm about to tell you is top secret. Only three people know. You'll be the fourth. Unless you'd rather remain at your current clearance level…?"

Rodrigues shot him a look.

"The second part of my assignment was to turn Daisy Hub into a fall-back base of operations, in case the EIS became compromised or could no longer continue functioning on Earth. Apparently, that scenario has come to pass."

"You're telling me that Earth Intelligence is moving to Daisy Hub?"

"Half of it has already arrived. The outgoing Chief of Intelligence stopped by earlier to hand over a couple of memory cores."

"You wouldn't happen to know who the new Chief of Intelligence will be…?" Rodrigues ventured.

"I would," Drew replied, straight-faced. "It's me."

"Not funny, Townsend."

"This isn't a con, Paul. I'm still trying to wrap my own brain around it. Apparently, both the Chief of Intelligence and the Chief of Operations have been compromised and are stepping down, and I was their unanimous choice to take over running the entire organization."

"And if I were to ask Novak to verify this?"

"Going straight to the source? Good luck with that. He'll probably deny everything I just said, because, as you've pointed out, it's way above your clearance level. For now.

"The important thing is this: you were right earlier when you said I had something going on. But you called it a rogue operation. Once the transition and the change of command are completed, I'll have the authority to sanction it as a covert op by Earth Intelligence. I've given you this heads-up because you're already a key operative. Now you have to decide how deeply you want your detachment to be involved in EIS operations, if at all."

"If at all? Do you really think you can manage a black ops organization from this station without any of my men — sorry, any of my *people* finding out about it?"

"No. I'd have to run a con to keep them in the dark. I'd rather not, because that would divert resources from the upcoming mission."

"Which you can't read me into until Novak turns up here, resignation in hand, and makes you the head of Earth Intelligence." Lips pressed together, Rodrigues shook his head. "You're asking me to take a huge leap of faith, Townsend."

"I know. It's a lot to process. However, since you and the original Zulu detachment are already the Second Shield of House Daisy Hub, I'd say you're more than halfway there."

"Past the point of no return. Terrific," growled the Ranger. "I'll have to think about this and get back to you."

Townsend pinned a benign expression on his face and watched him head toward the tube car.

Turn him or terminate him. No matter how hard Drew tried to silence them, the words kept repeating inside his head.

Chapter Eleven

Townsend waited for Lydia to begin her shift on AdComm, then gave her a message to transmit to the Chief Officer of the *Nannssi*: "Please let the *Hak'kor* of Trokerk know that the *Hak'kor* of House Daisy Hub has important information for him and wishes to trade it for a favor."

"State the need, then let the other party decide how to satisfy it. Isn't that how it works with Nandrians?" he added.

Lydia gave him a dubious look. "What if he doesn't think he needs a favor? Or he decides you need a different favor than the one that you want?"

"Have you found Holchuk's notes yet?" he asked. She shook her head in response. "Then send the damn message and let's see what comes back at us."

She uttered a small sigh and obeyed.

Several hours after that, the *Marco Polo* docked at Portal 7, and Captain Hiromasu Takamura came aboard the station. His hair was a little grayer, but Takamura had otherwise not changed since their last encounter. Just as Drew remembered, he was weathered and wiry and emanated authority.

The captain was duly impressed by the new and improved Daisy Hub. He expressed his approval of the expanded dining facilities, the diagnostic gear in Med Services, and the cutting edge technology now installed on AdComm. But his favorite upgrade was the privacy shield that Townsend could now place around his office.

"Earth has repaid you handsomely for your role in winning the Corvou war," Takamura observed. "But I can't help noticing that you're still located at a distance from the Terran spaceways. Aren't you afraid it might be a little too quiet out here?"

"Actually, Captain, we prefer it this way. Besides, now that we're reclassified as a way station, anyone who needs a temporary change of scenery can put in for recreational leave, something we couldn't do before."

Takamura frowned. "I hope you won't be sending anyone to Ginza Hub. Fleet Command has issued a directive placing that station off-limits to all personnel, due to its suspected connections to organized crime."

Suspected? Right. Every investigator in every Security agency knew what was going on out there. They just couldn't prove it. Ginza Hub, ironically the only resort hub to emerge unscathed from the Corvou war, was the undisputed sex and drugs capital of Earth space. Rumor had it that the station was the largest ongoing credit-laundering operation in Human criminal history. Unfortunately, evidence had a habit of getting misplaced, amnesia was rampant among potential witnesses, and rumor didn't carry much weight in the tribunal chambers.

Meanwhile, Riviera Hub, with its family-friendly beaches and bistros, had been completely destroyed. It was old and would have been scuttled soon anyway, meaning it would probably not be replaced. Vegas Hub, the gamblers' paradise, had beaten the odds and survived. However, it had sustained enough serious damage to keep it offline and under repair for the last four Earth years, and most likely for several more. At least, that was the official story.

The upshot of all this was that spacers who didn't want to spend their R and R on a moon or planet were left with just one risky option — the fleshpots and toxcubbies of "Sins-a" Hub.

"If the Space Installation Authority has an official position on this, I'm not aware of it," Townsend pointed out. "However, even if it did, I doubt whether any of my crew would take much notice. That's just a natural consequence of their previous experience with government agencies, I'm afraid." He activated the privacy shield. "Much as I love showing the station off, I had another reason for asking you to stop by, Captain."

"Yes, I thought that might be the case."

"It has to do with an interest we plan to pursue."

"Oh?"

"It's a research project. We're setting up a databank focusing on the Galactic Great Council. That means collecting information about the history of the Council itself, and about its dealings, past and present, with other worlds."

"That sounds like a very ambitious undertaking, Mr. Townsend."

"It's a long term activity. Before the war we couldn't have done it, but we have resources now that we didn't have then."

"Am I correct in assuming that these resources include all the data that your man O'Malley removed from my ship's onboard intranet a few standard years ago?"

"You are."

"Then I'm not sure what more we can do to help you."

"Captain, this privacy shield is proof that not every thought given expression aboard the Hub gets recorded or reported, and I'm sure the same can be said about every ship in Earth's Fleet. You took the *Marco Polo* into alien space and interacted with multiple races. You must have learned things from them that you felt it would be in everyone's best interests to keep off the record. For example, hypothetically speaking, if we were looking for evidence of wrongdoing by the Great Council, where would you recommend we start digging?"

"Ah! I gather the purpose of this initiative is to hold them to account. While I applaud your intent, Mr. Townsend, I'm afraid the richest soil may be beyond your reach. I have no doubt that the Council has committed terrible crimes against numerous races, including our own. The Great Council claims that everything it does is for the purpose of preserving peace in the galaxy. However, almost every alien we've spoken to has warned us that the Council is a puppet organization, serving the interests of a single race: the Reyota. It seems the Reyota always have an agenda, and it always takes precedence, even sometimes at the expense of peace."

This was precisely the kind of information Drew had been hoping to acquire. Keeping his tone conversational, he asked, "And does your own personal experience bear that out?"

"My experience and observations have shown me that anyone dealing with the Reyota needs to remain alert and watch out for traps. About the Council, I cannot say. However, still speaking hypothetically, if you were looking for witnesses to testify against the Council at a Galactic Tribunal, the Thryggians and the Mitrades would probably be the most willing to do it, since they seem to have suffered the most. Unfortunately, the Thryggians are sealed away in a pocket universe, and all the Mitrades have mysteriously disappeared."

"The Thryggians have suffered? But aren't they the ones who developed the Angel of Death virus and released it into the galaxy?"

"Yes, but it now appears that they may have been coerced into doing it by the Reyota. While we were in alien space, we rescued a Thryggian from a crashed ship. He later died in our trauma unit. But his final words were—" He paused. "You should hear them for yourself. Come to my office aboard the *Marco Polo* and I'll play them for you."

"If they were part of your ship's logs, then shouldn't I already have them?"

"This particular record was heavily encrypted and moved to a datawafer, then permanently wiped from the ship's intranet before we set course for Earth space. Once you see it, you'll understand why."

⸺ «◊» ⸺

"*They promised amnesty, but there was no forgiveness,*" croaked the voice of the pathetic, dying creature under the blanket. "*All were punished, and it never ends. Make diseases, they ordered us. Make them sick. Make them die. Keep their numbers small so they won't attack...*"

"*Who gave this order?*" demanded Takamura's voice offscreen. "*Who were they afraid of?*"

"*They are here.*"

"A second later, he was dead," said Takamura, removing the wafer from the port in his desktop.

Townsend leaned back reflectively in his chair. "And there were Reyota in the room at the time?"

"Two. Yorell Enne and her son, Arfan D'Ull. Be doubly careful if you ever encounter him. He's cruel as well as devious — quite a piece of work, that one."

Wordlessly, Drew watched Takamura lift the lid of a small compartment at the rear of a larger one, drop the wafer inside, then close the lid and press his thumb to the lock. As the compartments retracted into his desk, first small, then large, the captain turned his attention back to his visitor.

"Did the Thryggian know they were there?" Drew inquired.

"Yes, but I don't believe their presence deterred him from speaking the truth. He knew he was dying and couldn't be punished for it."

"So, like an arrested hench, he pulled the plug on his bosses. And you figure Humanity was the target of all this biological warfare?"

"It was the most logical conclusion to draw, given Earth's history and what Odysseus also told us about the Reyota. He said that they had turned the Great Council into their servants and the Thryggians into weapons, and that they'd done it *after* the galactic war was over."

"Promising amnesty, but delivering punishment," Townsend murmured.

"Telling people what they wanted to hear, then doing as they always intended," Takamura agreed, "which was evidently to grab power so they could rule over all the other races. You know about the ancient treaty?"

"Yes. Drawn up by the Reyota?"

"So we were told, by more than one alien with no reason to lie."

"I'm sure they would have made its terms harsh, to prevent anyone from gathering enough strength to mount a challenge," Drew said, continuing the chain of logic. "Then, thousands of years later, Humanity popped up on their screens — 'a threat to peace in the galaxy' — and that must have been when the pandemics began. 'Make them sick. Make them die.'"

"You do realize that everything we've just posited is pure conjecture?" Takamura pointed out.

Townsend nodded. "We'll need concrete evidence before we can bring charges. Meanwhile, I would love to get my hands on a copy of that treaty. Any ideas, Captain?"

"It's most probably locked away in the forbidden section of the Central Archives. But Yorell Enne might agree to help, if you can contact her. She's a former Prime Docent and quite knowledgeable about the history of the alien races. And she's apparently wanted on charges of treason by the Great Council. It's claiming that she incited rebellion among the protectorates of the Council's member worlds in the year leading up to the Corvou war."

Townsend gazed a question at him.

"The Reyota wanted us to stand alone against the swarm, but she defied their orders. She quit her post and traveled around, drumming up support for us among the alien races. Consequently, the Great Council is anxious to find and punish her. She won't be easy to locate, Mr. Townsend, but if anyone can tell you the contents of the treaty, I believe it will be her."

——— «» ———

Finding a single alien in alien space — or in Earth space, for that matter — might be beyond Human capabilities, especially in the aftermath of the Corvou war. However, an alternative had already occurred to Townsend. After returning to the station, he took the tube car to AdComm.

"Ruby, do you remember the name of the ship that brought us the Night Cloud fleet, a few intervals before the Corvou war? Yorell Enne was a passenger, and the captain's name was—"

"Trost." She swiveled her chair to face him. "Vother Trost. The ship was called the *Melkarit*. Why?"

"If she's still aboard, I need to speak with Madame Enne. If she isn't, Trost may know how to reach her. Do you have a record of the *Melkarit*'s commcodes?"

She spun back to her console and punched a few keys. "Not here, Chief," she replied over her shoulder, "but they might be backed up on one of the data servers."

"Okay. Send a request to the data team, marked 'immediate attention'. Once you've received the intel, start broadcasting feelers. Bounce them through as many Gates as you can. And let me know as soon as you get a response."

"Will do, Chief."

Drew returned to the tube car and traveled south to Deck C-1, where the data miners had set up their office at the heart of a maze of server panels. The air possessed a different quality here. It practically crackled with electronic impulses, raising gooseflesh along Drew's arms. He couldn't help thinking about the glowing effervescence that had filled the space between Ixbeth and Lania as they combined their mental powers to create Kularian shields around the *Marco Polo* near the end of the Corvou war.

And the Reyota thought Humanity was a dangerous race? They had no idea.

O'Malley sat alone at the work station, his eyes fixed on the text that was rapidly scrolling upward on one of a series of light screens. It was moving too fast for Townsend to read, but the few characters his brain managed to capture were Anglo.

"What can I do for you, boss?" O'Malley muttered.

"I want you to search for something in the files you've downloaded from the Central Archives. It may be written in transliterated Standard, or in the Reyot language, or it may not even be there, but I think it's worth a shot. It's the treaty that you mentioned to me earlier, the one that ended the galactic war."

"If it's anywhere in the sections that I stole, I'll find it for you. Meanwhile, would you like to see what else has turned up on the Stragori database?"

"Show me."

He pressed some buttons on a console and the three screens to Townsend's left flared to life, each showing a different image.

Drew read the first one and cursed under his breath. The translation from Stragori wasn't perfect, but this was clearly an evacuation order issued by the Directorate in advance of the arrival of Terran refugees. They were to be settled on a large island directly south of the mainland, a land mass that already housed a couple million but could comfortably accommodate up to 25 million more. The memo provided a timeline for transferring the residents to another secure location and advised that all the barrier gates be removed, so as not to give a wrong impression. However, the tall fences and covert electronic surveillance were to remain in place in case they were needed later.

Tall fences, barrier gates, and constant monitoring? It was impossible for a former slammer rat like Townsend to read this and not experience a shiver of recognition.

"They're being housed in a detention center," Drew murmured. "A massive one if it can hold that many people."

"Oh, it gets better," O'Malley told him. "Try the next one."

Drew gave him a look, then turned his attention to the second screen and read the first few lines aloud: "In the interests of planetary security in this time of unrest, it is imperative that as many of the Terrans as possible accept cybernetic implantation. We need to convince them that doing so will provide advantages and opportunities not otherwise available...!"

"Planetary security," O'Malley repeated sourly. "It isn't enough that the island is lousy with hidden mics and securecams. They want everyone connected to the intellinet, most probably for tracking purposes."

The refugees weren't only being housed in a detention center — they were being treated like inmates.

"Son of a bitch," Townsend growled.

"Now for the *pièce de résistance*." With a flourish, O'Malley pointed toward the third screen.

This was a memo from someone in the Directorate's office to the Island Supply Unit. Owing to the residual toxicity of the soil from earlier waste dumping, it would be necessary to continue food shipments from the mainland for the duration of the Terrans' stay.

Townsend cursed again, this time more loudly.

"It's been three standard years since the first wave of refugees landed. I've been searching for medical reports related to the Terran settlement," said O'Malley. "There's nothing in the records so far, but we've just begun going through them.

I'm sure we'll find something eventually. It can't be healthy to live in a place like that for any length of time."

Drew thought for a moment, then came to a decision. "We need to leak these documents. There are agents on Stragon, but their handler is on Earth. Do you have a secure way to send files to Ops at EIS headquarters?"

O'Malley looked startled. "Not directly, boss."

"Leave it with me, then. I know someone else who does."

Zulu had moved into what would have been Decks K, L, and M of the old Daisy Hub, and that was how Townsend's crew continued to refer to them. K Deck was the Rangers' version of AdComm. Townsend stepped off the tube car as a meeting in Rodrigues's office was breaking up. The three sergeants acknowledged the station manager in passing as they returned to their desks.

Meanwhile, Rodrigues stood in the doorway, staring expectantly at him.

"We need to talk, Paul. Privately," he added as the captain waved him inside and closed the door.

The Ranger's desk was identical to Drew's own. When they were both seated and the privacy shield was in place, Rodrigues asked quietly, "What's going on, Townsend?"

"We need to get a message to Barry Novak, right away. I know that he's planted agents among the Terran refugees on Stragon. My people have been data mining. They've found documents showing that the Terran colony is actually a detention center on the site of a former toxic waste dump, and that the Directorate has known about it all along. Every one of the 27 million Humans on that island is at risk of sickness or death. Forcing the Directorate to evacuate them to safety has to take priority over any other operation in progress."

Scowling, Rodrigues leaned back in his chair. "Maybe we should just agitate to bring all the Terrans home."

"We can't. Apparently, the Directorate has been pushing for them to be optimized, and you know what that means. Anyone with implants will be connected to the intellinet."

"...and unwittingly spying for the Stragori." Rodrigues made a face. "It's never easy, is it? All right, Townsend, I'll send the message. But before any action is taken, Ops is going to want hard proof, and we can't have any of it traveling through official channels. Have O'Malley prepare copies of those documents for transmission and give them to me as a file on a datawafer. Tell him I'll do the encrypting."

"Thank you, Paul."

"Don't be too quick with your gratitude. If these documents are authentic, they're probably going to trigger an interplanetary incident. And when everything hits the fan, I plan to be standing directly behind you."

Chapter Twelve

On Stragon

On arrival at Stragon, the *Liberty* was assigned a stationary orbit and instructed to hold its position pending an inspection.

Dedrick turned to Ross Posey in the co-pilot's chair and said, "We're going to be boarded. Make sure everything is properly stowed. These Stragori officials are picky about every little detail. One container out of place could hold us up here for days."

"Not to mention what they'll do if they discover that our passenger is traveling with forged documents," Posey remarked. "I sure hope you're right about this Barry Novak. If her creds don't hold up, we'll all three of us be fried."

"They'll hold up," Dedrick told him. "Novak was my Uncle Dennis's fixer for years, and Dennis Forrand only employed the best."

"In that case, no offense, but we've all gotten about thirteen standard years older since Forrand died, so I'll be keeping my fingers crossed that Novak's skills are still as sharp as they used to be. I don't relish the thought of saying, 'I told you so' from the adjoining cell of a Stragori detention center. And now, if you'll excuse me, *Captain*, I have some hatches to batten down before the Directorate's bureaucracy descends upon us." And with an emphatic nod of his head, he got up to leave.

Olivia had been standing just outside the cockpit door, listening to this exchange. She stood aside to let Posey pass, then came forward and took his vacated seat. Dedrick glanced up briefly as she sat down, but his thoughts were obviously elsewhere.

"I understand why he's worried," she began, "and I want to assure you—"

"He's not just worried, he's smacked off at me for accepting this job in the first place," Dedrick said. He swiveled his chair to face her. "When Posey signed on as my first mate, we made a pact. We're Fleet-trained, and we both retired with honor, me from the Fleet and him from Space Installation Security. We agreed that no matter what happened, the *Liberty* would stay firmly on the right side of the law."

"And by helping me, you've broken your promise to him, and now you're both angry. I'm sorry, Gael. I never would have put you in such a difficult situation—"

"You didn't. Novak made the request, realizing that I couldn't turn it down."

"Because you knew who to thank for your acquittal on charges of data tampering six years ago?"

"Partly. I did recognize you on the tribunes' dais at my hearing. Mainly, though, Novak had seen how far I was willing to go to protect my family. My connection to Dennis Forrand is pretty much common knowledge, and so is his protégée Juno Vargas's. But very few are aware that Drew and Olivia Townsend are his grandchildren. Neither one of you would be safe for long if Forrand's enemies ever twigged to that. Novak knew he couldn't trust anyone outside the family with your escape. So, he came to me."

"He told you about Drew and me?"

"He didn't have to. Of course, he didn't realize that at the time."

"But how did you—?"

"Let's just say that Dennis Forrand did not take his secrets with him when he died, and leave it at that. Meanwhile, you're nearly at your destination, Ms. Townsend. Are you ready for this?"

As if on cue, a small ship popped up on the sensor screen.

"Martian vessel *Liberty*, prepare to be boarded for inspection," came a sharp-edged voice over the commlink.

Dedrick pressed the button to reply to the hail. "Stragori shuttle, this is Captain Gael Dedrick. Our Terran passenger is ready to debark. Is it your intention to transport her to the surface for immigration processing, or will you be doing it aboard ship?"

"I don't handle immigration. My instructions are to conduct a full inspection of your craft, its cargo if any, and all passengers and crew. Based on that, I decide what will happen next."

His face darkening, Dedrick inquired, "Is this now standard procedure, sir? Because the last time I was here, it wasn't."

"It's standard for all alien ships in Stragori space, by order of the Directorate." They could practically hear his chin rising as he spoke.

Dedrick's lips compressed, evidently holding back words that could make the situation worse. After a beat, he replied, "Very well, then, we'll await your arrival." He closed the link and turned to meet Olivia's questioning gaze. "It sounds as though they're determined to have their civil war and they don't want any more of us interfering with it."

Her eyes widened momentarily. "You overheard my discussion with Drew?"

"Couldn't help it. These are close quarters. If you're concerned, we still have time to abort your mission. They won't be here for another twenty or so standard minutes."

"No," she decided. "We're Forrands. We stand our ground."

"Then," he said, returning his seat to the piloting position, "I'd better prepare the docking portal. Wouldn't want them to think we're not cooperating."

Once the umbilical walkway was sealed, Dedrick escorted Olivia and her baggage down to the boarding deck. The inspector stepped through the portal to meet them. He was a tall, thin man with watery eyes and very little hair.

"This is your passenger?" he snapped.

"Yes," she replied, "I'm—"

"Speak when you're spoken to, please. It will make things go much faster that way."

Olivia and Dedrick exchanged disbelieving looks.

"Her name?"

Gael replied, "Olivia Townsend."

"Documents?" He was looking at Dedrick, apparently expecting to receive them from the ship's captain. Olivia had to clear her throat to get him to notice that she was the one offering them to him. With a dissatisfied, "Hmph!" he snatched the datawafer from her hand, adding to Dedrick, "She didn't surrender this to you on boarding?"

"No," she told him. "Why should I?"

"I'll ask the questions, if you don't mind," he informed her haughtily, then turned his back on her while he slipped the wafer into a device he'd pulled from his pocket.

"So, Ms. Olivia Townsend of New Chicago, Americas, Earth," he said, reading from the screen. "This says you graduated from Fairhaven University with a degree in the laws of Earth and a sub-degree in urban management. This combination spells politician to me, and we have too many of those on Stragon already."

"I'm a licensed, practicing advocate," she said. "I speak for those who can't speak up for themselves."

"We have too many of those as well, and they're a tremendous pain in the—"

"Well, what sorts of jobs are available to me, then?" she broke in.

With a hint of a smile, he replied, "Terran cuisine is becoming popular on the mainland, so there's a demand for all kinds of food establishment workers — cooks, servers, table cleaners... Also for child care givers, transportation facilitators, and agricultural laborers. And they're crying for maintenance and custodial staff on the island. You don't like any of those? Then tell me, what else can you do?"

This had gone far enough. She drew herself up, gray eyes cold as ice, and skipped to plan B. "I can get you fired if you don't start showing me some respect. I'm a Forrand."

His expression became smug. "Really! I'm just shaking in my shoes. Have you any idea how many people have come here claiming to be part of a powerful Stragori family? Too damn many, as far as I'm concerned. So if you think—" He halted abruptly, apparently receiving a message through one of his cybernetic implants.

As Gael and Olivia watched, his grin evaporated, and his face lost several shades of color.

"Bad news?" Dedrick ventured.

"It — ah — it seems both your identities have been authenticated by the Directorate, and I am ordered to escort

Ms. Townsend down to the reception center on the planetary surface, immediately."

"So, you won't be inspecting my ship?"

"I've been told that's not necessary. If I've said or done anything to offend you, please permit me to offer my deepest apologies."

"You have, and you may," said Dedrick. As Olivia passed him, carrying her suitcase, he put a hand on her arm and murmured, "You don't know what's waiting for you down there."

"I'll be all right, Gael," she replied. "Quite frankly, this is the first time in my life that I've been grateful for the Stragori intellinet."

—— «》 ——

Seen from the air, the spaceport looked like a child's toy — a series of geometric shapes strung together, all with smooth reflective surfaces in pastel colors. Olivia stepped off the shuttle and was met on the tarmac by a matched pair of stern-faced, uniformed officers. For a moment she wondered whether they were about to arrest her. Then they smiled (in unison, with disturbing effect), and one of them said in a chasm-deep voice, "Welcome to Stragon, Ms. Townsend. Your great-grandparents are waiting for you inside. This way, please."

The officers ushered her through two sets of sliding doors, past long curving lines of people waiting with documentation in hand, then through a third door and into an austerely furnished space that reminded her of the High Council meeting chambers on Earth. At least, it would have if the walls had been transparent and the table and chairs made of wood instead of the other way around.

At the head of the table, looking like monarchs on thrones — or like pieces on a chess board — sat a man and a woman with identically styled white hair and smooth features. These were her great-grandparents? Except for the hair, they didn't look a day over fifty. Then again, she reminded herself, they were Stragori. Nestor Quan claimed to be nearly a hundred and eighty years old, but he appeared younger than many of the senior Councilors she'd known on Earth.

The Forrands in front of her were clad in tightly wrapped garments fashioned from a lustrous fabric. The woman's was a delicate violet color and the man's a lightly toasted orange, and their faces wore expressions that were simultaneously benign and expectant.

"Step closer, child," said the woman. "Let us see you more clearly."

Her senses on high alert, Olivia approached them. Their seats had no visible legs. Evidently equipped with antigravity, they rose slowly as she drew near, until both Forrands were looking down on her from nearly a meter in the air. In response, Olivia elevated her chin and stared right back at them.

The woman leaned forward and narrowed her gaze. She sat like this for the space of two breaths, peering at Olivia as though inspecting her for dust, then turned and said to the man, "There. Around the nose and in the shape of the mouth. Do you mark it?"

He nodded slowly. "Definitely a descendant of Gervais Forrand. And if she has that much of him, she may also have inherited his gene for longevity. We'll have to test for it to be certain, of course."

"And if it turns out that I have this gene," Olivia asked, refusing to be left out of the conversation, "does that mean I'll live another two hundred years?"

"That is hard to predict, my dear," the woman told her. "You're a hybrid, after all. But it would certainly extend the productive adult portion of your lifespan. Oh, my!" she exclaimed, catching herself up. "I am so sorry! You've just stepped off a shuttle. We haven't properly introduced ourselves. And now we must whisk you away to meet your — how many times great, Gilles?"

"I haven't been keeping count," he grumbled. "Just call him an ancestor, Linda. She'll get the idea."

"Will my grandfather be joining us?" Olivia asked.

"No," Linda replied. "We aren't sure where he is right now, or how to contact him. He told us to expect you, but Gervais was the one who first realized you'd arrived. He sent us to meet you here."

"But Dennis Forrand is on Stragon?" Olivia persisted.

"Oh, yes. I confess, we were somewhat surprised when Dennis joined us here only twelve years after our own migration, but he assured us that he had left the project in capable hands. And events have demonstrated that he was right."

"He's told us how proud he is of you and your brother," Gilles added. "Proud of what you've accomplished together."

Now Olivia was confused. "Together?"

"Starting the Corvou war like that, and using it to cut the legs out from under the Relocation Authority. It was a stroke of genius," he declared. "And now you're going to help us do the same thing on Stragon."

With blinding clarity, Olivia finally understood. "You're radicals."

Linda's laughter was a descending series of half notes, sung in a soprano voice. "No, child. We're Forrands. We don't fall into someone else's line. We create the path and let others choose to take it."

"Are you saying that you're behind this civil war?" Olivia demanded.

Smiling indulgently, Linda turned to Gilles. "*Esta minona.*"

"*Esta juverna,*" he replied, sounding a little disgruntled. "*Ma elva apprentay.*"

The Stragori language sounded very similar to one of Earth's ancient tongues. French? Español?

"And now, come," said Linda, speaking Standard once more. "We really mustn't keep Gervais waiting any longer."

As though of their own accord, Gilles's and Linda's transparent chairs floated downward, permitting them to dismount. A lot of things floated on this world, Olivia noted, including the cartridge-shaped transportation modules tethered in a row outside the door of the terminal. As Linda scrutinized each one in turn — checking for dust, perhaps? — Olivia turned in place beneath a broad blue sky, letting her gaze sweep the area. She half-expected to see daylight beneath the buildings that had been connected end to end to make up the spaceport, but they all appeared to be securely planted on the ground. In every other direction, the terrain was perfectly flat and green all the way to the horizon, where angular structures jutted upward, glinting in the sun like polished blades stabbing the air from beneath the soil.

Linda had finally found a module she liked. "Come, child! He's waiting for us."

Once they were aboard and moving, Gilles sank into silence. Meanwhile, Olivia's great-grandmother became quite chatty and informative. There was a reason for the streamlined profile and opaque hull of a Stragori transportation module, she explained. The planet was riddled with a complicated network of above- and below-ground express tunnels. They regularly merged and intersected with one another to ensure speedy delivery of goods and passengers to every part of the mainland. Bullet-shaped cars shot along these tunnels at top speed, their routes and timing coordinated by an artificial intelligence housed in a hackproof server somewhere inside the Directorate.

Hackproof? Maybe. Or maybe not. Olivia filed the information away for possible future use.

Only a couple of minutes later, she felt the module begin to slow down. Finally, it came to a halt, and the hatch in its side unsealed with a hiss and slid open.

Gervais Forrand apparently dwelled underground. The three passengers stepped out onto a platform paved with multicolored tiles. It was surrounded by concealed light sources that shone down from every direction, creating an island of brightness amid the surrounding gloom.

As she debarked, Olivia's mind flashed back to her arrival in Veggieville, at the plaza where the MPVs stopped to let off passengers. Now, as then, she squared her shoulders and shook off the feeling of being lost in a strange place. She wasn't that teenaged girl anymore, and she wasn't alone. Whether the Forrands were her friends or her enemies was a question yet to be answered. Until it was, she told herself, she would consider herself to be undercover — observing, and listening, and scooping up every bit of intel that came her way.

As though someone had flipped a switch, it was now Linda's turn to be quiet and Gilles's to be talkative.

"Hard to believe that it's just past noon up top, isn't it?" he remarked abruptly. "But perpetual midnight is the way the Directorate likes it. This way, Olivia." Without a second's hesitation, he set off into the darkness, forcing her to hurry after him.

He strode unerringly to a patch of wall that glowed blue as he approached. He pressed his hand to it and waited. A moment later the wall spoke to him in a soft alto voice.

"Fideto. Entray."

A door materialized in front of them, then slid noiselessly away. Gilles jerked his head toward the opening, signaling that she was to follow him through it. She glanced behind her, expecting to see Linda, but the other woman was nowhere in sight.

Stifling her unease, Olivia stepped through the doorway and found herself in a smallish room, facing a screen that took up one entire wall. This was evidently how they were going to have their meeting: face to face but not in person.

"Now what?" she asked.

"Now we wait," came the response.

"Is Gervais in the Directorate?"

"He's the second Forrand to receive a directorship," Gilles confirmed brusquely.

"And is it unusual to have more than one director in a family?"

"Extremely. Only three families have been so honored. And only one hybrid has ever been granted an audience with a director — you."

That sounded suspiciously like a warning to behave herself. Olivia's hackles rose. She was forty-eight years old and they persisted in treating her like a child. From their perspective, perhaps, it was understandable, but that didn't make it any less annoying.

As she was opening her mouth to make her feelings known, the screen activated. First it glowed green, then it morphed into a storm of pixels, and finally it settled into the image of a man sitting behind a desk. For a moment, words escaped her. This couldn't possibly be Gervais Forrand. Like Gilles and Linda, he didn't look much older than she was.

"Are you sure he's the right person?" she whispered to Gilles.

"Of course, I am!" the man declared. "Are you sure *you* are the right person?"

Olivia drew herself up and gave him Juno's frostiest stare. "That depends. Who am I supposed to be?"

Gervais chuckled. "She's got spirit, Gilles." To Olivia, he replied, "According to your grandfather, you're the best choice to lead the uprising."

"Wait a minute. Are you saying the Directorate *wants* a war?"

"*Neh comprenta,*" said Gilles in that same alien tongue.

"Then let's help her to understand." Addressing her again, Gervais said, "Olivia, is it?" She nodded. "What do you see when you look at me?"

"I see the image of a man."

"Exactly. This is an image of the man I used to be. It's a memory of myself in corporeal form, at a time before my consciousness was uploaded to the Directorate."

Olivia inhaled sharply. "The Directorate is a computer? But we thought—"

He leaned back in his chair, his gaze piercing. "I know what you thought. What are you thinking now?"

"That you've found a way not only to live forever, but also to hold onto your power while doing it," she replied.

He paused, then explained, "We developed this technology hundreds of years ago. After much debate, it was decided not to make it publicly available. Rather, it would be used exclusively for preserving the greatest and wisest leaders among us, so that they could continue to guide our society. Whenever a worthy individual emerged, a directorship was offered. Most candidates leaped at the chance to continue governing the planet indefinitely, keeping the peace and ensuring that the Stragori remained on the best possible path to the future."

"That sounds very noble, and it's perfect in theory," she remarked. "But if you're asking me to foment a revolution for you, then I'm guessing things haven't worked out that well in practice. Sort of like the changes Adam Vargas made to the Relocation Authority on Earth." All at once, something clicked into place in Olivia's mind, and she realized: "And the Reformation! It was a dry run, wasn't it? Testing the feasibility of something you actually wanted to do here."

Gilles and Gervais shared a look. Gilles's expression appeared a bit strained, she thought.

"Dennis was right," Gervais declared. "She's a bright one."

"The larger the Directorate became, the more power it gathered and the more control it exercised over the lives of the Stragori population," said Gilles. "Like the Relocation Authority. Early on, that wasn't a bad thing. But once the number of directors exceeded one hundred, they expanded their influence to include Earth. That was when the problems began."

"Immortality wasn't the blessing everyone had anticipated," Gervais continued. "The directors were doers. It was why they'd been chosen in the first place. But they needed to keep busy in order to stay sane, and things ran in repeating cycles. From generation to generation, the same problems, the same mistakes, the same obsessive behaviors for the same wrong reasons — it was maddening. Most of the oldest among us simply gave up. They firewalled themselves and retreated permanently into their memories.

"The rest of the Directorate worked that much harder to break the cycle. To change the pattern. They took on more responsibility and imposed ever stricter control, until even they were forced to recognize that they might have gone too far. Unfortunately, by then it had also become clear how much danger Earth was in from the Great Council. Drastic action became necessary to preserve Humanity. Almost without exception, these measures were unpopular on Stragon."

"So, helping us to survive has split your people into factions," Olivia summed up. "And now you want us to do what, exactly?"

Locking eyes with her, Gervais leaned forward across his desk. "We can accomplish a great deal from inside this machine. The intellinet keeps us abreast of everything that's happening on-world and allows us to communicate with the flesh-and-blood workers at the various government agencies. We can issue orders and instructions, and we command a loyal military that makes sure they are obeyed.

"However, we have limited control over the mainland servers. We can work within the protected boundaries of our own programming, to modify the virtual world in which we live, for example, but we cannot effect physical change outside of it. And, as some of us have learned from experience, we can't simply delete ourselves. Corporeal hands are required in order to upload specific files and subroutines." He gave her a look that instantly shortened her breath.

"Subroutines. Are you talking about viruses?"

"Whatever it takes to corrupt the server and put the Directorate beyond recovery," said Gervais.

"But you're part of the Directorate," she pointed out. "Can you back yourselves up?"

"Those of us who wish to have already done so, and the backups have been safely stored off-site. You won't be killing anyone who does not want to die."

At the sound of the K-word, Olivia went cold all over. Back on Earth, she had promised herself that Juno Vargas would be the last hit she ever ordered. Her whole purpose for being on Stragon was to support an op designed to prevent bloodshed. And now, "You're asking me to commit mass murder," she protested. "I don't care if they're willing. I won't do it!"

Gervais leaned even closer, projecting an intensity that almost leaped off the screen at her. "We're asking you to help us save our people, just as we helped you save yours from annihilation by the Corvou. We're convinced that ending the Directorate can break down the barrier between the factions and in so doing avert a Stragori civil war. But if the rift is ever to heal, then it's important that neither side be perceived to be responsible for our deaths."

Olivia's chin rose, straightening her spine in the process. "You want Humanity to be the threat from outside that reunites your planet?"

"Not all of Humanity. Just a small group of Terran agents, who will conveniently blow themselves up while trying to escape — or so it will appear. Dennis will help you orchestrate that. It's a deception he perfected while on Earth."

"I gather the revolution you mentioned earlier is meant to provide a cover for that mission?" she said stiffly.

"Yes. Revolution, protest, call it whatever you want. It will be a wholly justified reaction by the Terrans on the island. The groundwork has already been laid, but we'll leave the details to you."

Now her mind was in overdrive, speculating as to what might trigger a Terran revolt on alien soil. "I need to think about this. And I'll need more intel."

"She suspects that we might be drawing her into a radical trap," Gilles translated.

A faint smile slid across Gervais's face. "And she's right to be cautious. We've given her a great deal to consider." To Olivia, he added, "Will three days be enough time for you to verify what I've said and come to a decision?"

"I believe so."

"Then let us talk again once you've made up your mind. Gilles and Linda know how to reach me."

"There's one more thing," she said. "I'll need to speak with Dennis Forrand. Can you locate him from the intel on the servers?"

"I can. But he may not wish to meet with you."

"Tell him that if I don't get answers to my questions, you won't get an answer to yours."

Gervais's eyebrows shot up. "In that case, I'll just have to persuade him, won't I?"

The screen went dark. As she and Gilles retraced their steps back to the transportation module, he leaned closer and whispered, "Dennis taught you well, my dear."

———— «◇» ————

So, the Directorate wasn't a group of flesh-and-blood people, as she'd earlier believed. It was a massive computer, containing the uploaded consciousnesses of more than a hundred Stragori leaders, many of them insane and, apparently, most of them suicidal. It explained a lot, Olivia reflected darkly, as the mode of transportation she'd decided to think of as a "bullet car" carried the three of them through the network of tunnels to the Forrand family home.

Gilles had fallen back into silence, which Linda seemed compelled to fill with amiable chatter. It would be so nice having a guest in the house, she declared. Everyone would want to meet her. They could issue invitations and order up some treats. It would bring all the cousins together. It would be *fun*.

Olivia listened with half an ear. Meanwhile, her thoughts were on things more important than tea parties — and much more dangerous.

If she went along with Gervais's plan, Gilles and Linda would help her, she was certain. Would Dennis? He seemed to be avoiding the rest of his family, making it difficult to determine exactly where he stood. That was one of the questions she would need answered before she could commit to anything. She also wanted to know precisely what Gervais had meant by "the groundwork for a Terran revolt".

Once she had spoken with Dennis Forrand, Olivia's next order of business would be to go to the island and find Angeli, hopefully without exposing her as an EIS agent. Olivia worried about that. As Chief of Intelligence, she'd never actually gone into the field. She'd sat at a safe distance from the action, behind an official title, receiving reports from operatives who were embedded where intel was likely to be collected or exchanged. If a contact's cover was blown, it was always someone else's fault. However, now that she was Olivia Townsend again, things were going to be quite different.

Juno Vargas had negotiated the halls of power on Earth in the ways that Forrand had taught her, playing the political game and pulling strings when necessary to ensure that his master plan came to fruition. But Olivia Townsend had shed Juno's clout along with her baggage. Worse, she was now on an alien world. She had no personal influence here. Olivia would have to rely on her blood connection with the Forrand family to provide protection while she did whatever needed to be done ... once she'd figured out just what that was. It wouldn't be an easy puzzle to solve, regardless of what the various Forrands chose to tell her.

The Reformation was a *fait accompli*, and her responsibility to Dennis Forrand was over. However, another puppeteer might be trying to control her, now that she was, figuratively, within his grasp on Stragon. Gervais Forrand was apparently just as much a scheming, manipulative bastard as her grandfather was.

And if she refused his proposal, what then? Would he simply let her go?

Turn her or terminate her. She smothered that thought the instant it reared its head. Then she reconsidered. What she needed was an ally in the Forrand family. Apparently, Olivia had plenty of relatives on this world. Would there be any among them that she could trust?

Around and around her thoughts revolved, like an ever-darkening carousel. Meanwhile, Linda was still enthusing about the party she planned to host the following evening.

The bullet car let them out below ground, on a platform very similar to the one at the Directorate. Once again, a blue square lit up, a handprint was registered, and a portion of wall slid aside to admit them into a medium-sized, pale green area with no doors or windows. The room was rectangular. Centered at the top of each wall was a small grate, for air circulation, Olivia guessed. And embedded in one of the vertical surfaces was something resembling the light screen at the Directorate.

Gilles led the way to the middle of this space, then announced loudly, "Living room for three!"

As Olivia watched, open-mouthed, the room responded. It shimmered all around them, then settled into shapes. A long black leatherish sofa, an overstuffed dark green easy chair, a sprinkling of low wooden tables with built-in shelves and compartments. Against one wall, the large light screen remained. Against another, an artistic arrangement of framed pictures had appeared. Against a third, a tall, plastiplex display case held a collection of what appeared to be awards and trophies. Against the fourth, she saw an Earth-style door (non-functioning, she suspected) and a fall of drapery, probably meant to suggest a window. It had all materialized in a matter of seconds, leaving her at a loss for words.

Gilles chuckled. "You can sit down if you wish," he assured her. "Everything in this room is solid. We use holographic technology, programming it to create the environment we're most comfortable with. It's costly to run, so not every habitat is equipped with it. But it means we can live in just two rooms instead of ten, repurposing them as necessary. On Stragon, unlike on Earth, the wealthiest among us leave the smallest footprint."

"This was the living room of our first home together on Earth, before we built the mansion in Millbrook Enclave," said Linda.

"But what if you need privacy?" Olivia asked.

"Ah! That's what the second room is for," she replied. "Let me show you."

Linda walked over to the display case. She pressed her hand to the blue square that had appeared beside it, and a moment later, a section of wall dissolved into shimmering air and was gone. Peering through the opening, Olivia saw two Earth-style sliding doors, angled at sixty degrees to each other. Together with the exit from the living room, they created a tiny, triangular vestibule.

"Gilles subdivided and reprogrammed this part of the house before we left to meet you at the spaceport," she explained. "The bedroom on the left is yours. It just needs your voiceprint. Put your hand flat on the door and say your name."

Olivia complied. Nothing happened. She turned puzzled eyes on her great-grandmother.

"Now tell it what you want to do," Linda instructed her. "Say, 'Olivia wants to enter,' or 'Olivia wants to exit,' and it will let you through but no one else. If you wish to entertain company, say, 'Olivia plus one' instead of just your name. Why don't you try that last one out?"

There was a note of urgency in Linda's voice. Her curiosity now aroused, Olivia repeated, "Olivia plus one wants to enter." Again, nothing seemed to happen.

"Now try to touch the door," Linda said.

Warily, Olivia extended a hand and watched her fingers disappear into the door. She wiggled them. When they met no resistance, she realized: this had to be a holographic projection. Olivia stepped through the image without further hesitation and found herself in a bedroom that would have been identical to the one she'd occupied in the Forrand mansion on Earth, except for the light screen that took up most of a wall.

Linda arrived right behind her. "Dennis helped us with some of the details. We wanted you to feel at home here for the duration of your stay. My dear," she said, lowering her voice, "I may play the part, but don't assume that I am in fact a fool. I know what Gervais is planning, and what he wants you to do for him, and why. If you decide to turn him down, don't tell him — tell *me*, and I'll help you however I can."

Now Olivia was confused. "What about Gilles? Is he opposed as well?"

"Yes, but I'm afraid he's given up. On Earth, he was a man of great influence, controlling an entire industry. Here, he feels powerless to stand against the Directorate."

"But you don't."

Linda smiled. "There is more than one way to knock down a bully, child, as I'm told you well know."

Olivia had heard this same message in different words from Isabela Bakshi back in Veggieville. Perhaps there was someone she could trust on Stragon after all.

"Linda, about this party that you want to throw for me tomorrow..."

"It was just talk, *minona*, for the benefit of whoever might be listening in."

"There were mics in the bullet car?"

"Beyond the walls of this dwelling, there are mics everywhere. It's how the Directorate stays informed. You'll need to bear that in mind as you go about your business. And just so you know, if you should decide to remain on Stragon once that business is completed, Gilles and I would be proud to introduce you to the rest of the family."

"What if I decide not to stay?"

"Then we will miss you, and think of you often, and hope that you'll choose to visit us from time to time. You will always be welcome here, dear child."

After her meeting with Drew on Daisy Hub, Olivia had resigned herself to never hearing those words again. Fighting back tears, she replied, "Thank you, Great-grandmother."

Chapter Thirteen

On Earth

Zane 'Man Mountain' DeWitt leaned through the door of Novak's office. "He's in the chair, boss, just as you ordered."

"Good." His messages sent, Novak closed the lid of his concealed desktop keyboard and locked it back into place. "How long until he wakes up?"

"Doc Chin says about an hour. He put a double dose of sedative in Quan's java, just to be sure. That little ninja has some serious fighting skills."

"I want you and Croft in there with me. Chin can monitor the session from next door, but he's not to enter the interrogation room until I ask for him."

The big man's brow furrowed. "Something's changed, hasn't it? You haven't been the same since that day you came back from Med Services. Are you okay, boss?"

"I wanted to see whether my mother had survived the war, so I had my DNA compared to the updated population databank."

"And the results weren't what you were hoping for?"

He paused. "No, but they explained a lot. They showed me who I really am. And today we're going to make Nestor Quan wish he'd never met me. Or Chin, for that matter."

"Sounds messy," DeWitt remarked. "Do you want the surveillance eye turned off?"

"No. Chin's going to want to watch this. Warn Croft not to react to anything he hears. I'll do all the talking. When I give the two of you an order, I want you to follow it without saying a word."

DeWitt gave him a toothy grin. "A blast from the past, boss?"

"Long overdue," Novak muttered grimly.

One hour later, he walked through the door of the interrogation room and found DeWitt and Croft standing stolidly to either side of the EIS's specially designed interrogation chair. Leather cuffs buckled Quan's wrists and ankles firmly to its bent-pipe arms and legs, and a matching leather collar fastened his neck to its head support, permitting no more than a couple of centimeters of movement in any direction. A feature of these restraints was that they grew tighter if the subject struggled against them. Apparently, Quan had forgotten that fact in the seven years since he'd last occupied the chair. The collar looked uncomfortably snug around his throat.

"Finally!" he exclaimed. "Will you please tell your mute henchmen here that they've made a mistake and order them to release me?"

"It's no mistake, Quan."

A chair had been brought in for Novak, but he chose not to sit.

"I beg to differ," spat the prisoner. "When my people find out—"

"How? How are they going to find out? We've kept you incommunicado for seven years. For all you know, the war might already be over, and your side might have lost. And yet, there you are, making threats as though you actually have some power over me." He paused. "Do you remember my telling you earlier that when I run out of patience, you've run out of time? Well, it's happened, Quan. I've heard enough of your lies."

"They weren't lies!"

Novak shrugged. "Maybe. Maybe they were half-truths, spun dizzy to serve your own personal agenda. But that's all they were, and we both know it. In any case, I'm done listening to you. Now you're going to listen to me." Turning to DeWitt, he added, "Gag him."

"No, wait!"

Too late. Croft had already produced a strip of cloth, knotted in the middle, and handed it to DeWitt. For the first time since they'd met, Novak saw concern on Quan's face. Fear would have been preferable, but he'd settle for this, for now.

Quan fussed and protested for several moments after the gag was in place. Then he fell silent, the apprehension in his eyes giving way to a baleful stare that made Novak glad 'the ninja' was securely buckled down.

"I should have realized what you were much earlier," said Novak, leaning in and returning the stare, with interest. "But I finally figured you out. You see, we have something in common, Quan. We make a show of playing by the rules, but deep down, we're both criminals. People like us don't work for other people. We work for ourselves. That's why you don't have any implants. It's hard to skulk around in the shadows if you can be electronically tracked."

Novak glanced at DeWitt and Croft. They were standing like statues. Their expressions were masks of indifference.

"So, I'm certain you've never worked for the Directorate, because all of their agents are optimized. And your claim to be working for the radical faction is probably bogus as well. You might have conned them into thinking you were on their side, I suppose, as long as you saw an opportunity to get something for Nestor Quan. Like the credits for selling Naguchi's patents out from under him, and the reward for retrieving the experiment he'd stolen. And maybe a ready-made spy network that you could use to grab some power for yourself on Stragon. Nod if I'm getting close to the actual truth here."

Quan's fists were clenched, and the visible part of his neck was a taut rope of muscle, giving Novak his answer.

"Now, the trap that you threatened my agents with earlier might actually exist," he continued. "But really, that's irrelevant now, because while you were snoozing, I cut them all loose."

The ninja eyes widened briefly with surprise.

"You heard me correctly, Quan. Earth Intelligence is closing up shop. I've aborted all current missions and discharged my operatives. And all the resources they've been able to call on here on Earth have already begun going away. Will any of my former agents align themselves with the radical faction? They might. I don't know. The important thing is, I won't be ordering them to do it. And neither will you, because you're going away as well.

"You've enjoyed our hospitality long enough. Now it's time to clear your account. You've abused my trust. You destroyed Nayo Naguchi. He was my friend. And street justice dictates that we now destroy *you*." Turning once more to DeWitt and Croft, he said, "Get Dr. Chin in here. Tell him to bring enough sedative to put this little scrag out of our misery for good."

Quan tried once more to speak, but the gag was too effective.

Novak leaned in and told him quietly, "Like I said, I'm a criminal, clearly a more powerful one than you are right now. And in case you were wondering, Barry Novak doesn't exist anymore. There's just me, Rex Regum, king of the Warrior Kings."

"How long do you want him to sleep?" asked Naguchi's voice behind him.

Still staring into Quan's now-fallen face, Novak replied, "Forever. I want him dead. Do it." Then he stalked out of the room.

Thirty minutes later, Naguchi came to the conference room on the sixth floor to find him. Novak was staring darkly into his second cup of java. He glanced up, keeping the frown on his face, as the doctor stepped through the doorway.

"How long did you put him out for?" Novak demanded.

Naguchi threw him a reproachful look. "You knew I couldn't actually kill him."

"Yeah, but *he* didn't. How long, Nayo?"

"I've put him into a chemically-induced coma. It will last until the counteracting drug is administered." Naguchi pulled out the adjacent chair and sat down. "Do you know what you're going to do with him?"

"I know what I'd *like* to do with him, but I don't think you would approve." Novak exhaled gustily. "Where is he now?"

"I've had him moved to the infirmary. He can stay there as long as necessary. And did I hear you say you've aborted all the missions on Stragon?"

"Quan didn't leave me much choice. I've alerted our agents that they may have been compromised. Their instructions now are to suspend activities and await further orders. Which, if I can figure out a way to extract them all without arousing suspicion, will be to report to a rendezvous point."

"So you were lying when you said you'd just 'cut them loose'." Naguchi sounded relieved.

"Of course. I may not be able to bring them all the way back to Earth, but I'm sure as hell not going to leave them within reach of Quan's radical friends."

"Boss?"

They turned and saw DeWitt filling the doorway.

"There's an 'eyes only' transmission sitting on your computer from whoever's been using that unassigned channel."

That would be Paul Rodrigues, now posted back on Daisy Hub. Novak excused himself and headed for the lift.

When Rodrigues specified "eyes only", it was something important. The last such message had been a warning about the start of the Corvou war. As he strode down the eighth-floor corridor toward his office, Novak could feel a stirring in his gut. This was going to be bad news. He could practically smell it.

He dropped onto the chair at his desk, activated the decrypter, opened the file, and read:

These documents speak for themselves. They came from a backup copy of the Stragori archival server. The Terrans on Stragon are at serious risk of illness and/or death. Townsend strongly advises leaking the documents through agents already on Stragon to motivate Terrans to evacuate the refugee settlement.

Intrigued, Novak pulled up each of the documents in turn. By the time he'd finished absorbing their contents, his jaw was so tightly clenched that it ached.

Townsend had recommended an evacuation, but Novak knew from experience what leaked information generally led to. He'd witnessed the violence on Earth in the months just before the Corvou war. When nearly 27 million Terran refugees rose up in outrage, it would take far more than his eleven agents to control the chaos. The EIS would be forced to reach out for help. The moderate and radical factions would see this as an opportunity to swell their respective ranks. They would vie to form alliances, creating division among the Humans as well and placing them, as Olivia had once put it, "smack in the middle of someone else's civil war".

It was a lose-lose situation. Novak could either do nothing and let untold numbers of Terrans slowly sicken and die, or order Angeli to leak the documents and spark a revolt that could quickly cost just as many people their lives. If there was a third possibility, he wasn't in a position to see it.

He filled his lungs and let out a loud and heartfelt curse. Then, feeling only marginally better for it, he made his decision and got busy at his keyboard.

《 》

When the message from R. Bascomb appeared in Novak's InfoComm inbox one week later, the first thing that came to his mind was suspicion. There was no good reason for anyone with that last name to be contacting him.

Warily, he opened and read the text. Richard Bascomb, the general's youngest son, was requesting an in-person meeting the following morning in the most public location in the District. Logic and experience told Novak to refuse this invitation. However, his curiosity had been piqued.

He agreed to the talk.

Arriving early, Novak positioned himself behind a vacant pedestal — the statue that had once occupied it had been an early casualty of the pre-war rioting — and watched as a man emerged from the front doors of the District Administration Building. The man sat down on a bench halfway across the square. He was the only other person in the vicinity, and the way he kept glancing around fairly broadcast the fact that he was waiting for someone. This could only be Richard Bascomb.

Gazing at his half-brother was almost like looking in a mirror. Bascomb had the same build and coloring as his own, wore his hair the same length, even parted it on the same side. His face was a little narrower than Novak's and adorned with a neatly-trimmed blond beard. Still, the resemblance between them was unmistakable.

"He's alone, boss," said DeWitt's voice in Novak's ear. "Unless he's miked. Hard to tell from this distance."

"Copy that, Zane. I'll be careful."

It was time to show himself. Stepping out from cover, Novak strolled toward the bench.

"Richard Bascomb?"

"Call me Rick," the other man replied, getting to his feet to shake hands. "And you're Barry Novak?"

"I am."

They sat down side by side.

"You were probably surprised to hear from me," said Rick. "Supreme Adjudicator Lynette Ellenshaw recommended that I contact you. She told me that you and Madame Vargas had been friends for a long time."

Novak slipped a surreptitious hand into his pocket and activated the jamming device he'd brought with him. "For more than thirty years," he confirmed.

"You must have been devastated when Regional Security found her remains in that firepit in The Flats."

"Yes. It all happened so fast ... quite difficult to accept." In fact, Novak had nearly had a fit when Ridout had mistaken the timing and put them within a hair's breadth of blowing the entire operation.

Rick looked as though he wanted to say more about that. Did he suspect it had been a con? Novak remained tensely silent. He didn't dare disappear two Chief Adjudicators in less than a month, but that didn't stop the EIS mantra from repeating inside his head: *Turn him or terminate him.*

"Lynette also told me that you and Madame Vargas sometimes did favors for each other," he said at last.

"Yes, as friends often do."

"Giving warnings, solving problems, fixing mistakes...?"

"Providing comfort and support in a variety of ways," Novak summed up warily.

"Lynette has mentioned to me that, as the new Chief Adjudicator, I would be well advised to have such a friend."

"That sounds like wise counsel. Are you saying she suggested asking me to be that friend?"

"Would it be an improper request if she had?"

"No, only I can't help wondering why a man with two older brothers would need to ask a stranger to watch his back."

"He would if those two brothers considered him to be a stranger as well."

"Ah. I see."

"You and I have things in common, Barry Novak, starting with a father who wishes we were both dead. Don't worry — he doesn't know about you, and I'm not about to tell him. In fact, the general and I haven't spoken to each other in years. When DNA testing was made publicly available, I asked to be quietly notified about anyone whose analysis revealed a connection to the Bascomb family."

"Why?"

"So I wouldn't have to ask a total stranger to watch my back. And I wanted the information kept confidential so that relatives with a different last name wouldn't have to worry about watching their own. Sadly, even though we just met, you're already more of a brother to me than Hugh and Darren ever were or will be. I'd like to get to know you better. From the way Lynette talked about you, I'm pretty sure you already know a lot about me. I'm hoping we can build a relationship, maybe not as close as what you had with Juno Vargas, but ... something. What do you think? Is it worth pursuing?"

Turn him or terminate him. There were possibilities opening up here. Perhaps it wouldn't matter what Rick Bascomb knew.

"I think we can give it a try," said Novak with deliberate casualness. "Just out of curiosity, who are you concerned might come after you?"

"Any number of my father's enemies. Once upon a time, the Bascomb family business was tailoring. My grandfather made uniforms for all the Security forces. Then my father decided that revenge would be *his* business. I don't know exactly when or why. All I know is, by the time I was born, he was a cold, bitter man, driven by hatred and not even bothering to hide the fact. Growing up in that family was like living in a war zone. I tolerated it for as long as I had to. Then, on my sixteenth birthday, I celebrated my majority by crossing The Flats and becoming a farmer.

"When I returned to New Chicago as the District Councilor for the Agricultural Zone, I discovered how many powerful people my father had managed to smack off during my absence. In some circles, just saying the name 'Bascomb' is enough to raise hackles, and being a Bascomb is enough to raise fists. My father does an excellent job of protecting himself and my brothers. Me? I'm the traitor, not worth his time and effort. That makes me an easy target for anyone with a grievance against the other three, just because we share a last name."

"Have you thought about changing it?"

"It's a little late for that. Besides, the way everything is recorded these days, anyone who wanted to could track me down, no matter what name I was using."

"Have you had any problems so far? Any confrontations?"

"Not really. There have been a lot of snide comments and innuendo. And a couple of veiled threats. Lynette overheard one of them. That's when she gave me your commcode and recommended I get in touch with you. She also said that you would be interested in knowing who had made that threat. It was Supreme Adjudicator Patricia Chen."

If Chen was spewing venom at a Bascomb, it meant Novak's suspicion was correct — the general had something on her and was using it to his own advantage.

"All right, Rick. I might be able to help you with this. And there might be things that you could help me with as well. Let's start with getting Chen on your side and go from there. I'll do some digging and get back to you."

———— «◊» ————

Back at his office in the Zone, Novak composed a carefully worded message to Lynette Ellenshaw, the Supreme Adjudicator for Americas.

She replied promptly: *Let's talk.*

Late that afternoon, as he pulled into the driveway of Juno Vargas's former residence in Millbrook Enclave, he saw an imposing, dark-skinned woman with purple hair standing on the verandah, waving at him. This was Lynette Ellenshaw, exactly as Olivia had described her.

She watched him stop his vehicle and step out of it, then called out cheerfully in a warm alto voice, "I understand you're in the market for a house."

Evidently, she thought the mansion was still under surveillance. He grinned at her and went along with the charade. "I always wondered what it would be like to live in a place like this. Have you had any nibbles?"

"Nothing serious," she replied, pressing her thumb to the front door lock. "These homes are expensive to maintain, and the last couple of years have taken their toll on this one...."

Once they were inside, Novak put a silencing finger to his lips and swept the front of the house for bugs. As he'd anticipated, there weren't any. With Juno Vargas gone and the mansion empty, there was no longer a reason for anyone to be listening in. Still, the Supreme Adjudicator watched him, nervously biting her lip.

"We're clear," he told her.

"Thank goodness! When Juno made me the executor of her will, I didn't realize I'd end up the custodian of so many secrets."

"What made you buy this place?"

"Juno left it to Gael Dedrick, the last legitimate Forrand heir. He told me he had no use for the house or anything in it and instructed me to sell it all off. When I heard a rumor that General Bascomb was preparing to make an offer on the property, I snapped it up myself, just to keep it out of enemy hands. Now I'm thinking of fixing it up and renting it out. But you didn't set up this meeting to discuss real estate, did you?"

"No, I didn't. I need a favor," he told her. "A small one. Can you get me a private audience with Patricia Chen?"

"She'll want to know what it's about."

"Tell her I'm aware of her problem, and that I believe I can help her solve it."

She raised an eyebrow. "In exchange for...?"

"You're complaining about having to keep Juno's secrets. You want to add mine as well?"

"I guess not," she sighed. "No promises, Barry, but I'll relay your request. Then I'll step aside. If she's interested, she'll contact you directly. If she doesn't, you'll have your answer."

It was the best that he could expect. "Thank you, Madame Supreme Adjudicator. I appreciate your assistance. By the way, what would you be charging as rent on a place like this?"

She appraised him up and down before replying, "I doubt that you could afford it."

"Could a junior District Councillor?"

Her lavender eyes twinkled mischievously. "Perhaps."

Novak knew what she was thinking: It would drive the general crazy if his least-favorite son ended up living in a larger and grander home than his own. Truth be told, it would look good on both of them.

——— «◊» ———

The bench in the square outside the District Administration Building was getting a lot of use lately, Novak reflected wryly. This morning, Patricia Chen was sitting in the middle of it, holding a cup of java in one hand and a serviette-wrapped pastry in the other, and not looking genuinely interested in either one of them. Patricia was a good name for her. A dark-haired beauty with classical features, she projected an ageless, aristocratic air.

He activated the jamming device in his pocket, then strolled across the pavement toward her.

"Do you mind if I sit here, Madame Supreme Adjudicator?" he asked.

She'd been deep in thought. His voice startled her into glancing up.

"You're Mr. Novak?" she replied. "You look familiar. Where do I know you from?"

"I own SecuriTech. We hold the installation and maintenance contract for all the surveillance gear in this building. I visit the premises from time to time, so you've probably seen me around."

"Ah." She smiled briefly at him, then frowned and turned away. "According to Lynette, you're the man who knows what everyone else is doing. And you think I have a problem." She gestured to him to have a seat.

"I'm pretty sure you must," he said, easing himself down onto the bench beside her. "If George Bascomb feels safe about pulling your strings, then the odds are he's holding something over you. I'm assuming that's the case, based on your attitude toward the junior District Councilor who shares his last name. Of course, I could be wrong. If so, tell me, and I'll walk away now and never mention this meeting again. But if I'm right, and you tell me what he has on you, I'll make it go away."

She threw him a disbelieving look. "And then *you*'ll have something on me. Or, even worse, what if you fail? Then two people will know my secret instead of just one."

"Normally, that would be a risk. But I won't fail. One way or another, I'll see to it that your secret is ... buried."

She gasped. "Do you realize what you've just suggested doing?"

"Yes. And once I've succeeded, you'll have something on *me*." He turned and locked eyes with her. "There's a small price for this favor, Madame Supreme Adjudicator."

She stiffened in her seat. "What is it?"

"Richard Bascomb is a decent man, new to the ways of power. He also hates his father even more than you do, and the feeling is mutual. All of that puts him in a very vulnerable position. It would be a shame if the job of Chief Adjudicator turned out to be too much for him."

"And the enemy of my enemy is my friend," she said thoughtfully. "All right, Mr. Novak. It isn't a small price, but I'll pay it. We have a deal. I'll tell you what Bascomb knows, but not here." She darted a glance over her shoulder. "Too much surveillance."

"I know a secure place where we can talk. Tell Lynette that you're interested in seeing the house she has for rent. Set up a viewing time, and I'll meet you there."

——— «⟨⟩» ———

Unlike the rooms upstairs, which had been "decluttered" in preparation for showing the house to potential buyers, the clean room in the basement was almost exactly as Juno Vargas had left it. Novak stood in the doorway for a moment, taking in the pair of midnight blue loveseats, the lighter blue padded armchairs, and the large, glass-topped wrought iron coffee table.

There was a slight chill in the air. Also a slight echo. Chen stepped around him, hugging her shoulders. "She's still here," she whispered hoarsely. "I can feel her presence."

No, he thought, Juno was definitely gone. Her silver tea tray that would have completed the picture had been sold at auction.

Out of habit, he pulled the bug detector out of his pocket and scanned for listening devices. "We're clear," he said. "Shall we sit?"

Wordlessly, she settled herself onto one of the chairs. He took Juno's customary place on the adjacent loveseat.

"Tell me what Bascomb knows about you," he said.

She shuddered a little. "Patricia Chen isn't my real name. I was born on Ginza Hub, to an indentured sex worker. As was the practice there, the birth was never registered with Data Management on Earth."

"And...?"

She dragged in a breath, then continued, "When I was fourteen, my mother's owner wanted to sell me to a porn show. My mother objected, and he beat her, badly. That night, I stole into his bedroom with a wrench and hit him in the head with it, more than once. Then I stowed away aboard a supply ship that was leaving port the next morning. The ship-owner found me shortly after departure. As it happened, he'd recently lost his wife and fifteen-year-old daughter in an accident out on one of the colonies. I resembled his daughter physically and was alone in the world, so he offered to help me. When we got to Earth, he took me to a Data Management center, told them the death report from the colony was a clerical error, and had them process me and issue me a fresh biowafer with his daughter's name on it. After that, I was Patricia Chen. And Abe Chen became the loving father I'd never had."

"You never told him about the murder?"

"I've never told anyone, until now."

"Then how did George Bascomb learn about it?"

She dropped her gaze to her lap. "I let my curiosity get the better of me. I wanted to find out whether my birth mother was still alive."

Novak could relate to that.

"And because you were already in his crosshairs, he knew that you'd initiated the search. That gave him a starting point for a search of his own," Novak concluded.

"He came to me with the results," she said bitterly. "Apparently, there's an outstanding arrest warrant on Ginza Hub with my birth name on it. If the truth came out about me, my family on Earth would be ruined, and I would be arrested and extradited to stand trial in a jurisdiction where every rotten thing that owner did was just business as usual." She raised liquid brown eyes to his face. "If you're having second thoughts about helping me, I don't blame you."

"Was your birth mother still alive?"

Frowning now, she replied, "No. I wasn't able to find out her cause of death, but I can guess how it happened. I saw a lot of it when I was a kid."

He didn't press for details. "What about your adoptive father? Still living?"

"He was fatally injured in a flash riot in Vancouverville, just before the war."

"I'm sorry."

She leaned back in her seat with a sigh. "He was eighty-five. I warned him to stay indoors, but he insisted it was his civic duty to protest."

"Is there anything you still haven't told me?" Novak asked. She shook her head. "Did you ever try to verify what Bascomb told *you*?"

"Quite honestly, I was afraid it might give him even more to hold over me."

"In that case, it's clear what you have to do now."

"What *I* have to do?" she repeated uncertainly.

"Don't worry, Madame Supreme Adjudicator. Everything you've told me is strictly confidential. I will take care of your problem. Meanwhile, Lynette is waiting outside to drive you back to your office. You're going to return to your daily routine and pretend we never had this conversation. I'll make sure nothing leads back to you. When it's all over, you'll know."

———— «» ————

Sufficient time had passed. Novak called DeWitt into his office and activated the signal jammer.

"I have a special assignment for you, Man Mountain."

DeWitt perked up. The use of street names generally signaled that violence was about to ensue. "What do you need, boss?"

"I want Quan terminated. He's been cluttering up the infirmary long enough. Make sure Chin isn't around to see it. Unplug 'the ninja' from whatever he's plugged into. Then take him for a ride into The Flats and finish him off. Make sure no one will find his body until long after you and I are dead of natural causes."

"He won't be missed?"

"According to the official records, he died seven years ago. So no, I don't believe his absence will be noticed. Think of it as housecleaning. The Warrior Kings are back, and we don't keep prisoners. Not any more."

Chapter Fourteen

On Daisy Hub

The *Liberty*'s **on** approach, Drew," said Lydia's voice on his wristcomm. "And the *Nannssi* is on her way here as well. ETA is about ten hours for Captain Dedrick, seventeen for the Nandrian vessel."

"Dedrick's coming back?" he said. "Did he mention whether he's carrying passengers?"

"No, but he did request caf and SPA privileges for two. Himself and his first mate, Ross Posey."

So, he'd already dropped Olivia off on Stragon, and he was choosing to remain in the vicinity. Interesting.

"All right, Lydia. Assign him a docking portal and tell him he and Mr. Posey are welcome to enjoy our hospitality. And have someone let me know when they arrive, so I can greet them personally."

"Roger dodger!"

"Have we located the *Melkarit* yet?"

"Still no response. Sorry!"

Well, Takamura had warned him it wouldn't be easy.

Nine hours later, as Townsend was in his quarters getting dressed, his wristcomm buzzed again.

"The *Liberty* will be docking in just over an hour, sir," said Jason Smith's voice. "Lydia warned me to give you time for breakfast before they arrived. She also said to tell you that we received a food shipment from the Hestia colony yesterday, and Chef Jensen is making the eggs Benedict with real eggs this morning. She says they're delicious and he's saving some for you. And there's real cream in the caf to go into your java. Good for your — you-know-what."

Townsend took a moment to gather his patience. His stomach was already doing a bang-up job of keeping him aware of his ulcer. He really didn't need any further reminders from the members of his crew.

"Was there anything else, Mr. Smith?" he said, enunciating carefully.

"Just that the *Liberty* will be docking at station 7, and Captain Dedrick is looking forward to meeting with you."

"Very good. If anything comes up before then, you know where I'll be."

———— 《》 ————

Right on time, the hatch unsealed at docking portal 7, and Gael Dedrick and Ross Posey stepped onto the station. This wasn't the first time Drew had seen them together. Today, however, he was struck by how much they resembled the positive and negative sides of a single image — the two of them equally tall and powerfully built, but one with dark hair and eyes and the pale complexion of a spacer, and the other one dark-skinned and fair-haired.

"Gentlemen, it's good to see you again," Townsend said. "But I can't help wondering what brings you back here."

"He's got a thing for your sister," Posey replied with a grin. "And, if you'll excuse me, I hear some decent cooking calling my name." With that, he walked past Townsend and along the corridor to the nearest tube car stop.

Drew said nothing, just stared at Dedrick in bemusement.

The other man gave a little shrug. "Officially, we wear the titles, but in practice, we're more partners than we are captain and first mate. And he isn't wrong about me. We're staying close by because I'm worried about Olivia."

"Brief me, Captain."

Dedrick complied, concluding with, "I had a bad feeling about sending her on-world, but she was so confident that she would be all right that I let her go. Now I'm wishing I hadn't."

Drew had been having bad feelings as well, but he saw no point in sharing them. "Olivia has always been able to take care of herself. When she was sixteen years old, she convinced Dennis Forrand to become her mentor. By the time she was twenty-five, she was a political force to be reckoned with. She may not have known what she was walking into on Stragon, but, trust me, the ignorance is mutual. They have no idea who they've just let into their house, and what she might be capable of.

"That being said, in the unlikely event that it becomes necessary to mount a rescue operation, I will expect to be included. Daisy Hub is much more than a way station with a caf and a SPA room. We have resources that not even Earth is aware of. So, if she gets herself too deeply into trouble, we can help you get her out of it."

"Good to know."

Just then, Townsend's wristcomm buzzed.

"Urgent message from Captain Rodrigues, sir," said Jason Smith's voice. "He needs to meet privately with you on K Deck."

"Tell him I'm on my way." Returning to his visitor, Drew said, "Until we see how everything shakes out, you're welcome to make yourself at home here, Captain. In the meanwhile, I'd better get back to work."

"Of course," Dedrick replied.

Rodrigues was pacing impatiently inside his office when Townsend stepped off the tube car and strode briskly across the deck to join him. The Ranger captain activated the privacy shield as soon as they were both seated.

"I've heard from Novak," he said. "He was just as alarmed by those documents I sent him as we were. He's promised that action will be taken. He's also assigned you a private channel to EIS Ops, so that he can communicate with you directly from now on instead of going through me."

So, no more handler, just as Olivia had promised.

Wearing a disgruntled expression, Rodrigues dropped a datawafer on the desktop between them. "He sent you a message. It's encrypted. He said to tell you to use the 'victor codes', whatever the hell that means."

Drew scooped up the datawafer. Then he locked eyes with the Ranger and said with calm intensity, "It means I've been straight with you about the changes in the EIS. And it means you can trust me. I said I would do my best to keep you in the loop, Paul, and I will. Let me decrypt this message and get back to you."

"All right, maybe you will," Rodrigues allowed, reluctantly relaxing in his chair. "In any case, I hope you know what you're doing, Townsend, because I damn sure don't."

—— «» ——

If you're reading this, it means you've figured out how to use the EIS confidential command codes to link your DNA-specific encrypter to mine, ensuring that any future communications between us will be direct, secure, and hack-proof.

In case you're wondering, I've been your handler for the past four or five years. I sent Gow on an undercover assignment to Stragon just before the Corvou war and arranged for all his field op contacts to be redirected to my office. So, without realizing it, you've been reporting to the Chief of Ops — or, to be more accurate, you've been touching base to let me know you're still active, without giving anything away.

Yes, I know about that. Don't blame Rodrigues for keeping me informed. He's just been following orders.

Anyway, your reporting days are over. Now that you're taking over the EIS, all the reports will be coming to you, including mine, incomplete though they may need to be in order to give you necessary deniability. As well, until I've wrapped up Ops on Earth, some of our agents will be continuing to report to me. I'll do my best to share this intel with you as an equal at the top of the EIS hierarchy.

Let's begin with what you need to know about the operations on Stragon, and the extraction op that I may need you to mount...

By the time Drew had finished reading the full text of Novak's transmission, his mouth was dry. Gael Dedrick's instincts had been spot on. Twenty-seven million Terran colonists were about to find out that they'd been dying by slow degrees for the past five Earth years, and that the Stragori not only knew about it but were also responsible for it. Meanwhile, a dozen operatives, including Olivia, might need to be extracted on short notice if revealing this information sparked a violent reaction.

In less than seven standard hours, a Nandrian warship would be docking, no doubt to deliver a response to the message Drew had earlier sent to the *Hak'kor* of Trokerk. Between now and then, the new Chief of Earth Intelligence had a hell of a lot of work to do.

So much for letting him step into his new job one foot at a time.

Townsend's intercomm buzzed. "Sir," said Jason Smith's voice, "we've had a response to our earlier queries about the *Melkarit*. She was spotted salvaging debris from a battle site out in Sector Four, about an interval ago."

This was promising. Takamura had mentioned that Yorell Enne was hiding from the Great Council. If Trost was still in Earth space, then she might be as well.

"Very good, Mr. Smith. Keep trying to reach the captain of the *Melkarit*. Let him know that I have an important question for the very important person he brought us earlier and would appreciate meeting with her as soon as she's available."

"Aye, Mr. Townsend."

——— «» ———

The Nandrian ship *Nannssi* arrived an hour ahead of schedule. Chief Officer Agnosk honored the *Hak'kor* of Daisy Hub by remaining aboard her until informed by Ruby that Townsend was ready to receive him. Then he came onto the station, filling the width of the portal almost completely as he stepped through it. His pebbly green snout bore several more scars than Drew remembered, but the huge reptilian warrior was otherwise unchanged.

"Greetings, *Hak'kor*!" he bellowed. "I am honored that you deemed my request to dock worthy of being granted."

Reflexively standing tall and expanding his rib cage, Drew lowered his voice half an octave and replied, "Greetings, Agnosk ban Sitgaram. It is my honor to welcome you to my House. Do you bring me a message?"

"I do, *Hak'kor*. Javar ban Mitoram, the *Hak'kor* of House Trokerk, sends you wishes for long life and victory in battle.

He is intrigued by your offer and very much desires to know how you believe you can benefit him."

"We recently learned of a problem the Stragori were having with the hybrid child they created for their *ssalssit essendi* with House Trokerk. Our Doctor Ktumba was able to solve this problem. If it has arisen as well with the child entrusted to Trokerk fifty-five years ago, then it would be my honor to share the Doc's solution with your *Hak'kor*. In exchange for this information, I would ask that he grant the wish of the hybrid now on the station to meet with the one on Stragon. They are twin brothers, two halves of a whole, and our hybrid greatly desires it. If your *Hak'kor* agrees to this, the meeting can take place at a time and location of Trokerk's choosing."

Agnosk cocked his massive head. "With your indulgence, *Hak'kor*, I would like to meet this hybrid myself, and record an image for my *Hak'kor* to see."

"Of course. He is called Moe. Does your hybrid have a name as well?"

"His name was given to us by the Stragori at the time of *ssalssit essendi* — Ssorryass. We were honored that they had chosen the Nandrian word meaning 'courage' for the symbol of our alliance."

Townsend nearly sprained a vocal cord holding back his laughter. *Homo* and *saurius* had become Moe and— His brain balked at even thinking it. Evidently, the Stragori language and Anglo were quite different from each other, or someone on Stragon would have caught this before the ritual took place. And the Nandrians clearly had no clue what their word for courage would sound like to Humans from Earth. In any case, the *Hak'kor* of House Daisy Hub knew better than to enlighten either alien party.

Loudly clearing his throat, Drew buzzed AdComm.

"Ruby, would you please find Moe and have him brought to Med Services? And you'd better give the Doc a heads-up that Agnosk and I are on our way down there as well."

"On it, Chief!"

As the hulking warrior lumbered along beside him to the tube car stop, Townsend was grateful for the height and breadth of the ring corridor. It spared him from having to decide who would precede and who would follow. Gavin Holchuk was no longer around to advise him, but Drew knew this much: toxed or sober, Nandrians could be tetchy. Even a friendly one could take offense where none was intended and respond with immediate violence. And Agnosk was larger and more powerful than most of his Shield brethren, definitely the last Nandrian in the galaxy that anyone would want to anger.

A couple of minutes later they were standing in the Doc's laboratory, staring at the object she had placed on her metal work table in advance of their arrival.

"It's an egg," she announced unnecessarily.

"What have you done to it?" Agnosk demanded.

Far from being intimidated by his tone, she elevated her chin and snapped back at him, "Other than relieve Moe's pain by removing it from his belly, not a thing."

"Apparently, Moe can make an egg but not lay it. Learning what was causing his problem made me wonder whether his twin might be experiencing it as well," Drew explained.

"I am not aware of any problems with our Ssorryass, *Hak'kor*, but I will be honored to pass this information along in case one arises."

Too late, Drew realized he should have given the Doc a heads-up about that as well. Her eyes were practically starting out of her head, and her lips were writhing as she struggled to contain herself.

"Where is Moe, anyway?" Townsend asked.

As if on cue, the door slid aside, and Moe and Hagman entered the room.

"I found him," Hagman reported. "He was in the caf, drinking lemonade with Racine, Detmar, and Flanagan. Looks like no one's going to win the pool," he added.

Agnosk had been looking Moe up and down with great interest. Now he turned and repeated, "The pool?"

Once more under her control, the Doc's expression contracted with disapproval. "The betting pool. They were trying to get him toxed, to see how long it would take. The closest guess would have been the winner."

Agnosk's head tilted one way, then the other. "Ah! It's an *isshamm*. We have those too. And no prize could be awarded because...?"

"He never got toxed," Hagman replied.

"Of course not!" the Doc informed him. "His biochemistry is part Human. It's able to process citric acid without impairing brain functions."

Agnosk leaned toward Hagman and said in an undertone, "Next time, try whiskey. It always works with Humans."

"Wait a minute," Drew interjected. "Before the war, when we were aboard the *Hak'kor*'s ship for *ssalssit essendi*, there was a betting pool?"

Agnosk emitted the snorting, wheezing sound that passed for Nandrian laughter.

Clearly, it was time to change the subject.

"What now, Agnosk ban Sitgaram? How do we move things forward?"

In response, the Nandrian addressed himself to the hybrid who had been standing silently nearby, taking in every word of their conversation. "You are called Moe?"

"I am."

"And it is your wish to meet in person with Ssorryass?"

Drew tensed, willing Moe not to understand the *double entendre*. Or, if he did, not to react to it.

Moe's eyes widened briefly, but his almost-reptilian features remained otherwise impassive. "If that is what you're calling my twin brother, then yes."

Agnosk returned his attention to Townsend. "I have recorded the image I require. Now, I will transmit your information and Moe's request to my *Hak'kor*. If he gives his consent, I will escort Ssorryass aboard the station."

"And how long do you estimate for the voyage to pick him up from Nandor and bring him back here?" Drew asked.

"There is no need to travel to Nandor, *Hak'kor*. Our hybrid is an officer aboard the *Passpessil*, one of our warships. It can be here in a matter of hours."

On her way to return the egg to storage, the Doc halted and spun, nearly dropping it onto the deck. "A warship? You would send the symbol of an alliance into combat?" she scolded.

As Agnosk slowly swiveled his head to look at her, a deathly stillness fell over the room.

Marion Ktumba was a woman of imposing bulk and stature. She exuded the kind of authority that could make a charging rhino stop and rethink its plan. But this wasn't a rhino she was facing down, it was a Nandrian warrior who stood nearly half a meter taller than she did and carried at least twice her mass. A warrior with the jaws of a T-Rex and a venomous bite, who wouldn't hesitate to kill if he felt he'd been insulted.

Trying to ignore both the cold sweat popping out on his forehead and the heat slowly intensifying in his stomach, Townsend did some rapid mental math. Agnosk was Third Shield, a high caste in the Nandrian social hierarchy. Larger numbers meant lower status and less wiggle room when it came to showing respect. Holchuk had assigned every crew member a ranking, taking into consideration how they might have to interact with the warriors who came aboard the station. Where had he placed the Doc?

This was not a good time to be asking that question aloud. Mouth shut and fingers crossed was a much better way to go. Drew waited, tight as a coiled spring, to see what Agnosk would do.

At last, the Nandrian replied, "Of course, we would let him go into combat if that was his wish and he had been properly trained." Townsend let out a long, relieved breath. "Once an egg exchange is concluded, each egg is turned over to an appropriate-numbered Shield, to be added to their crèche for incubation. After emergence, this offspring is treated no differently than any other young Nandrian. Ssorryass was placed with the emergents from the Fifth Shield of Trokerk. When he reached the age of first testing, he chose and passed a warrior's *tekl'hananni*, and that became the path that he trained to follow."

If this explanation was meant to mollify her, it failed miserably.

"But in order to become an officer, he had to pass a second *tekl'hananni*, didn't he? The kind that would show up on a scoreboard. Did he fight in the war?" she demanded.

Drew winced inwardly, debating with himself whether to step in and shut the Doc down. Agnosk's complexion was growing darker, which probably meant he was losing patience. And blood might still be shed if the Doc took vocal exception to being overruled.

The big alien lowered his snout, putting his eyes level with hers, and said softly, "You believe we should have protected him from what he had spent years preparing for? Ssorryass himself would have rebelled at that. Every Nandrian is taught from his earliest days of life that only the symbol of his House, the *tseritsa*, is immortal. All creatures die. What matters is not *that* one dies but rather *how* one dies, and the best way for a Nandrian to die is with honor."

Her eyes widened. This talk of death had apparently made the Doc aware that she had put herself in danger. Injecting a more deferential note into her voice, she said, "I am not disagreeing with you. However, I would still like to know whether your hybrid's ship was involved in the Corvou war."

"The warmaster felt that it would be foolish to leave Nandor completely unprotected, so two warships were held back. One of them was the *Passpessil*."

As her chin came up, Drew caught the gleam in her eyes and remembered something Ruby had said to him on the day he'd first arrived on Daisy Hub: *"Never argue with the Doc, because she always turns out to be right."*

Chapter Fifteen

On Stragon

Dozing on the sofa, Isabela was startled wide awake by the sound of someone leaning on the buzzer outside her apartment.

Who could possibly be at her door at this relatively late hour? With a glance over her shoulder at Angeli's bedroom, she opened the spyhole Vikram had made in the wall and peered out into the corridor.

A young man was standing there with embossed shoulder patches on his two-tone blue jacket and an expectant expression on his face. His blue and white billed cap bore the logo of the island's delivery service. Even more curious now, Isabela thumbed the latch release and waited while the door slid aside.

"Good evening, ma'am," he said brightly. "I have two transmissions from Earth for this address, one for a Ms. Anna Sturtevant and another for a Mrs. Isabela Bakshi."

Her stomach dropped. Only one person on Earth would be contacting both of them, and it was sure to be something Isabela didn't want to hear.

"From Earth?" she repeated.

"Yes, ma'am. They arrived about a week ago. Sorry about the delay. It was a massive commburst. Had to be two thousand messages, all marked 'expedite'. It's taking time to track everyone down." He pulled a device resembling a compupad from a pouch at his waist. "I'll need to record proof of delivery."

Isabela pressed her thumb to the screen and accepted the datawafer. As she turned away from the door, Angeli came up beside her.

"I'm Anna Sturtevant," she announced. She gave him her thumbprint. Then, slipping the datawafer into her pocket, she smiled the message-bearer on his way.

While Isabela was securing the latch, Angeli went into the living room and switched on the jammer. "Messages from Ops for both of us?" she said, her expression now grim. "This can't be good."

Isabela handed her a commpad. "You're the mission coordinator. You first."

Angeli made a face, then dug out the wafer and inserted it into the port. A second later, the screen came alive with text. On its surface, it was a chatty letter from her fictitious Uncle Henry about Aunt Matilda's problems with her garden. Then Angeli plugged in her EIS decryption device. It activated at her touch. Isabela watched the letters on the screen rearrange themselves into a quite different message, which Angeli read aloud rapidly in a voice devoid of expression.

"To all EIS personnel in the field. Warning. Code orange. All previous intel about Stragon is confirmed unreliable and its source has been neutralized. Some or all operatives on-planet may be compromised. You are ordered to keep cover but discontinue current ops and avoid contact with other agents if possible. Instructions re extraction will follow. Authentication code..." She read this part silently, then turned to Isabela and said with audible disgust, "It's genuine. Basically, it's telling us we're screwed and we're on our own until Ops can figure out a way to get us off-world. Wonderful."

Angeli plucked out the wafer and her decryption device, dropped them both onto the coffee table, and thrust the commpad toward Isabela. "Your turn."

The second wafer contained sincere condolences from Isabela's cousin Selma — another nonexistent relative — and an offer to pay her way back to Earth if remaining on Stragon was too painful. Decrypted, it transformed into the same message as Angeli's. If Isabela was receiving it, that meant support was being pulled back. Without support in place, there could be no future missions to this world. Ops was apparently removing the EIS presence from Stragon, entirely and for good.

That would leave the colonists at the mercy of whatever war broke out here.

Worse still, it would tear Isabela away from the final resting places of her brother and her husband before she could obtain justice for them and peace for herself.

For a long moment, the two women stood staring helplessly into each other's faces. Then Angeli flopped down onto one of the chairs.

"Damn! I sensed from the beginning that someone was surveilling us. This confirms it."

"And now what?" Isabela exclaimed, not bothering to keep her voice steady. "You said you were getting close to finding out who ordered the inquiry into Vikram's death. Are we supposed to just sit on our hands now and do nothing until we're extracted?"

Angeli turned her upper body to face Isabela and said firmly, "No. You're a teacher and I'm a data clerk. We're going to keep our covers, abort the operation mentioned in our orders, and continue working on our other project. I'll go on digging in dangerous places, and you're going to turn this place upside down looking for the copy of Vikram's proposal. If it says anything like what I suspect it will, we may be able to make our farewell to this world one that the Stragori will never forget."

⟨⟩

Three days later, the message carrier was back.

"Special delivery from Earth for Ms. Anna Sturtevant," he announced brightly as Isabela opened the door for him.

When the datawafer was in hand and the door was closed once more, Isabela remarked, "Not extraction coordinates, I hope."

Angeli shook her head. "It's probably too soon for that." She found the commpad and slipped the wafer into the slot. "It's a 'fat' message — files attached," she said, then read aloud from the screen: "Grandma's hands are shaky, so you may have to use your imagination when viewing the attached snaps she took of Cousin Grace's new home. Love, from Uncle Henry."

Angeli inserted her decrypter into the port and reread the covering message. Then she opened the attachment. Her features contracted and hardened as she scanned the text.

"What does it say?" Isabela demanded.

Lips tightly compressed, Angeli handed her the commpad.

By the time she'd reached the bottom of the third document, Isabela was thoroughly confused. "What does Novak expect you to do with this?"

"He says he wants me to spread the word," said Angeli. "Inform the Terran public and stir up protests against the Directorate so they'll be forced to move us all to a safer part of the planet."

"That makes no sense," declared Isabela. "Inform them of what? Everything in these documents is common knowledge on the island, and we are actually safer here than the Stragori are on the mainland. As for the toxins in the soil, the Directorate has not only made us aware of them, it has also gone to great lengths to protect us from them."

"Well, I'm afraid that's not the picture these documents painted for Novak. I can understand why he might have felt alarmed. But he and I were both on Earth during the rioting in the months before the war. We witnessed the mindless destruction that erupts when large groups of people feel trapped and in danger. That's why Novak decided to send agents here, to protect the colony from that kind of violence by finding a way to prevent the Stragori civil war from breaking out. That was our mission.

"And now he's aborted it and is ordering me to foment unrest among the Terran population? Organize protests and marches? Manufacture anger and frustration? That's not right, Bela. It doesn't sound like Novak at all."

"Are you certain the order is authentic?"

"All the verification codes match up."

"Then it appears that you have a decision to make, *chica*. What are you going to do?"

Angeli hesitated, then replied firmly, "Not a damn thing. As far as this loose cannon is concerned, I never got the message."

———— ‹‹›› ————

The man on the screen in Olivia's bedroom had a bland face, a stocky build, and familiar-looking features, but he was definitely not Dennis Forrand.

"You're his advocate," Olivia declared. "I remember you from the reading of his will."

"Indeed," he replied. "And now I represent his interests on Stragon. I am Ira Chase, at your service. Mr. Forrand regrets that he is unable to meet with you in person at this time. However, he has empowered me to answer any urgent questions you may have about his dealings both here and on Earth."

"Really! You can answer all my questions? Are you telling me that you know absolutely everything about him?"

"Almost everything. I watched him grow to adulthood on Earth. I'm his half-brother, making me your great-uncle, I believe. And I must say, it's a pleasure to see you again, even if the feeling is not mutual right now."

Olivia straightened her shoulders. "Were you one of the people he instructed to keep an eye on me after he left for Stragon?" she asked stiffly.

"No. The task of keeping Forrands out of trouble was given to others. My responsibilities on Earth began and ended with the legalities of running the Forrand business empire. And the disposition of the estates of Gilles Forrand and the members of his family, of course. Now, you indicated that you had questions?"

"My questions for him are for his ears only, but I do have two for you," she replied. "Where is Dennis Forrand, and why is he avoiding his family?"

The advocate smiled. "He did warn me that you would be extremely direct."

"Did he instruct you to give me direct and truthful answers? Because I'll accept nothing less," she informed him in Juno's frostiest voice.

"Of course. Dennis began severing his ties to the Forrand family on Stragon in protest when he learned how the

Directorate plans to use the Terran colony on the island. He knows it was Gervais's idea, and that the older generations of Forrands support it. Dennis believes it would be disastrous for the Human population, both here and on Earth. He also was certain that you would agree with his assessment once you had been briefed by Gervais himself."

"Just to be clear, then, you're telling me that Dennis Forrand is against starting a revolution?" Chase nodded. "And where is he now?"

"In seclusion, attempting to plot a course of action that will counter it or, at the very least, mitigate its effects." He paused. "Dennis spent his formative years on Earth. He has great empathy for its inhabitants and harbors no wish to see them come to harm on either of our planets."

"That's what he told you?"

"It's what I personally witnessed. With rare exception, no one is born cold and cynical, Ms. Townsend. The way in which we're treated and the examples that are set for us determine what we'll become as we mature. Gilles may already be having regrets about the way he raised his children, but Linda had a hand in their upbringing as well. She's a very strong, very clever woman, and I see a lot of her influence in the way Dennis turned out."

Olivia bristled as she recalled seeing far too much of Dennis Forrand in the way Juno Vargas had been turning out.

"I knew him as a cruel and ruthless man," she declared.

Unruffled, Chase replied, "He wasn't always. By the time he met you, he'd learned how to be whatever the circumstances demanded. He may have appeared hard-hearted, but everything he did, whether it succeeded or not, was with the greater good in mind."

Forrand wasn't getting off the hook that easily. The greater good? Perhaps, but it hadn't been her good, and it definitely hadn't been Drew's. They were his grandchildren. They should have mattered to him. Clearly, they hadn't.

"Is he tracking me now?"

"Do you wish him to?"

"No." Not that that would stop him, of course. "However, now that I know where he stands on the Terran revolution, I want to be able to contact him if I need his help."

"Are you formulating a plan as well?"

"Beginning to. First, I'll need more intel."

"Set to work, then. When it's safe, he'll get in touch."

As the image on the screen winked out — for a false image was all that it was — she thought, *Thank you, Dennis, for helping me make up my mind.* Then she went to look for Linda.

———— ⟨⟩ ————

The ferry to the island was part boat, part aircraft. It skimmed along the surface of the strait, sped by a wind that churned the dark water into choppy waves all around its hull. Olivia stood at the portside railing, near the bow. She watched in fascination as whitecaps were born and reborn, tumbling and whispering over the deeps, rolling and roaring as they neared the shore. Meanwhile, a constant chilly breeze whipped at her hair and burned her eyes and cheeks.

Being exposed to the elements like this reminded her of the year she had spent touring the Industrial Wilderness with Angeli and Ronny, their driver. Ronny ... what? He had told her his last name, but for that entire year nobody had used it, and now she couldn't recall what it was.

With a pang, she realized that this was the first time she'd even thought about him since that day when he'd delivered them safely back to New Chicago. She'd been seventeen years old. Ronny had been Forrand's tool. After serving his purpose, he'd merged back into the faceless crowd, a non-person once more. And now, far from home and wearing her own identity as a disguise, Olivia was feeling like a non-person too.

On Stragon, her connection with the Forrand family afforded her some borrowed status. That helped. However, it couldn't protect her from being used as Ronny was, to advance someone else's agenda. Only she could do that, and only if she knew what the agenda was.

As the ferry dock came into view, Olivia caught the scent of something so utterly foul that it threatened to turn her stomach inside out.

"A waste disposal vessel must be upwind of us," remarked the male passenger who had come to stand next to her. "Don't worry — you'll get used to it."

She turned to face him, noticing for the first time that they were the only ones braving the weather on deck. Reflexively, she performed a threat assessment. He looked harmless enough. Of course, so did she. Locking eyes with him, she challenged, "Now, why would you say that?"

"Because everything about this place stinks," he replied, giving a little shrug. "You'll be amazed at how quickly your brain will learn to ignore it."

"What I meant was, why assume that I'll be staying long enough for that to happen?"

Still gazing into her face, he lowered his voice. "Because we've been expecting you. Mr. Chase sends his regards, along with this." He pulled something out of a pocket, placed the object in her hand, and closed her fingers over it. "If you feel the need to contact his client, that gives you a direct, secure commlink." Raising his voice again, he added, "I'm going below to get warm. Enjoy your visit to the island, Miss."

Enjoy her visit? He had to be kidding.

Stepping away from the railing, she carefully uncurled her fist. Sitting on her palm was something that resembled a scaled-down EIS decryption device, a small black tube with ridges along half its length and a port connector at one end. If it was real, and if it worked the same way as the full-sized model she and Novak had given their operatives back on Earth, then it was keyed to her DNA, making it useless to anyone else if it were lost.

Then again, it could be a tracking transmitter, cleverly disguised as EIS gear and planted on her by an agent of the Directorate.

Her first impulse was to drop the device into the water. Fortunately, her common sense cut in and stopped her. Whoever had sent this to her knew she was en route to the island. Her best course of action, therefore, was to keep her suspicions to herself until she could determine who it came from and what their intentions were.

Olivia slipped the item into her pocket and joined the other passengers in the enclosed cabin. She looked for the man who had spoken to her on the upper deck. He was nowhere to be seen.

Once the ferry had docked, she adopted a pleasant, tourist-like demeanor and debarked with the others, following a fence-lined walkway to a windowless, flat-roofed hexagonal structure. Walkway, supports, and building were all apparently made of the same dark brown, non-reflective material.

It was a deception. From inside the terminal, the walls were transparent, affording 360 degrees of unhindered view while preventing anyone outside from seeing what was happening within them. Strategically, this could be important. Olivia filed the information away for possible future use.

Meanwhile, she was mentally reviewing her second audience with Gervais. It had gone well enough, she thought. Calling up Juno Vargas's considerable powers of persuasion, she'd assured him that she was finally comfortable with the idea of killing off the Directorate, as long as he promised her a free hand in arranging the details of their demise. He had agreed to this, but only after a hesitation long enough to trigger several mental alarms.

Forced to fake his death and leave Earth before the Reformation could be implemented, Dennis had assigned a team of agents to spy on her, ensuring that she stayed on the course that he had set. If Gervais was monitoring her for the same reason, then it was doubly important that Olivia keep her business on the island a secret from him.

What, then, should she do with Chase's "gift"?

As she gazed around the ferry terminal, Olivia's attention was captured by a sign that said "Security Lockers" in Standard, Anglo, and (she assumed) Stragori. Beneath the sign was a counter, staffed by two uniformed officers.

Perfect.

Ten minutes later, with the suspicious device tucked away safely in a lockbox, Olivia left the building by a side door and found a row of vehicles-for-hire waiting on the pavement outside. They came in different shapes and sizes, everything from a moto with sidecar to a small MPV. She selected one that resembled a PV and fed the address Linda had found for her into the on-board navcom.

Approximately half an hour later, she was standing in front of a barracks-like, stucco-clad building. There were structures just like it aligned close together all up and down every street. Some were a dirty yellow color, but most were terra cotta orange, like this one, with different numbers appearing above their main entrances.

Olivia squared her shoulders and filled her lungs. Then she walked up to the front door and hauled it open.

——— «·» ———

Peering through the spyhole, Isabela almost didn't recognize the woman standing out in the corridor. Then the memory clicked in, and she hastened to switch on the jamming device.

"Angeli, we have company," she called over her shoulder as she opened the door. "Juno Vargas! Please, come inside."

"It's Olivia Townsend now, Mrs. Bakshi."

"Is it? Well, I am glad to see you, whoever you are. And this is not Veggieville, so you can call me Isabela."

Angeli appeared then, her mouth forming an O as she came to a halt two meters away. "Juno? Does Novak know you're here?"

"Yes. In fact, he's the one who sent me. And I'm Olivia Townsend. Juno is dead."

"And why are you on Stragon, exactly?" she asked quietly.

"It's a long story."

Silence.

Something was wrong. These were best friends who hadn't seen each other in five years. They should already have fallen laughing into each other's embrace. Instead, they both had their guards up, and the tension in the room was growing thicker by the second. Finally, Isabela couldn't stand it any longer.

"Who would like some tea?" she broke in.

Olivia looked grateful for the interruption. "I don't suppose you still have any Earth blends on hand?"

"I'm afraid not. But the native varieties are interesting. I will see what I can do."

Isabela purposely made their tea the old-fashioned way. It gave her time to take her guest on a tour of the apartment, leaving Angeli to steep in the living room while their beverage steeped in the kitchen. Unfortunately, only the tea grew more flavorful as a result. Angeli just seemed to get darker and more bitter.

By the time the three women had settled together onto the sofa and chairs, Isabela was primed to break up an argument. She leaned forward to pour the tea, then remained taut and ready at the edge of her seat.

At first, the conversation was carefully polite, so innocuous and superficial that Isabela wondered why she'd even bothered to activate the jammer.

Then Angeli set her cup down deliberately on the coffee table and stared a challenge directly into their visitor's face. "I want to hear this long story of yours," she said. "Why are you here? And why aren't you Juno Vargas anymore? What's happened on Earth that we need to know about?"

Olivia paused for the space of two breaths. "Juno had to die because the High Council was about to arrest her for treason."

"Fallout from the Reformation?" said Angeli, adding in a dubious voice, "After five Earth years?"

"The war threw every level of government into disarray. It's taken that long for the High Council to learn the fates of its missing members and find replacements for them," Olivia explained. "Novak and I decided that I would be safer here, helping with the mission, than if I stayed on Earth."

Isabela and Angeli exchanged freighted looks.

"The mission?" Isabela repeated uncertainly.

"There is no more mission," Angeli cut in. "Novak must have transmitted the abort order while you were en route. We've been instructed to stand down and wait for extraction coordinates."

Olivia's expression hardened, along with her voice. "Show me the abort order."

An unsettling silence filled the room while Angeli found the datawafer, commpad, and decrypter, and brought them back to the sofa to assemble. After pulling up Novak's message to all personnel, she passed the device to Olivia so she could read it for herself.

She stared at the screen for nearly a minute. Then, letting out a small sigh, she returned the commpad to Angeli's hands.

"I guess that's that," said Olivia. "All right, then, since it appears the two of you are at loose ends for a while, I have a special project for you. And by no small coincidence, it happens to be the best possible way to accomplish the mission you originally came here to carry out."

"What's the catch?" Angeli asked her.

"Novak doesn't know anything about it, and it was one of the Directors who gave me the idea."

Angeli narrowed her gaze. "We're not working for the Directorate now, are we?"

"Hardly. Their plan involved an uprising on the island that would have cost more Human lives than I care to imagine. Apparently, they've already laid the foundations for it. At least, that's what Gervais told me, although he never specified how."

"Son of a bitch," murmured Angeli. Isabela could practically see the light going on behind her eyes. "I think I know what he was talking about. You need to see this."

She pulled up Novak's second transmission and opened the attached files for Olivia to read. Olivia's hand was shaking — with anger, Isabela assumed — as she passed the commpad back to her.

"These came into Novak's possession how, exactly?" Olivia asked, enunciating sharply.

"The cover message said they were from a trusted source with access to the Stragori archival backup servers."

"A trusted source?" Olivia echoed. "Trusted by Novak, maybe. This has Gervais's hand all over it. And Forrand always told me that the most effective lie is one that is wrapped inside a truth."

Angeli stiffened. "So, you're taking the lead on this special project?"

"I am," said Olivia. "I have a plan to remove the Directorate and reunite the two factions. It isn't what Gervais will be expecting, and it won't cost Human lives. However, once I've read you into the op, I'll be depending on your absolute discretion. So if you'd rather not—"

"Count me in," Angeli interrupted her. "Idle hands, devil's playground."

"I suspect you will have need of my special skills as well," said Isabela. "And I have a personal favor to ask, involving *your* special skills."

Olivia raised a curious eyebrow. "Go on."

"You remember my brother Carlos, and my husband Vikram, from Veggieville?" Olivia nodded. "They both died on this world — Vikram, at least, under questionable circumstances — and the Directorate's staff has not been forthcoming with answers."

"You want me to help you get closure."

"I want justice," Isabela corrected her. "That will give me closure."

"They weren't only her family," Angeli put in. "They were also EIS agents, and I have reason to believe that something about their deaths was suspicious." She switched the datawafers in her commpad, then passed the device back to Olivia.

After reading the text on the screen, Olivia turned and impaled her with an accusing gray stare. "Where did you get these?"

"I stole a copy of the folder while someone with authorization was downloading it. Don't worry, I didn't leave anything traceable behind."

"That's not the issue, Angeli. I know you're good at what you do. But didn't you find it peculiar that these two documents, completely out of context, had somehow found their way into a single folder that then happened to be downloaded at a time when you were available to co-opt it?"

Angeli's face lost two shades of color. "You think they were bait?"

Olivia gave her a pained look. "I suspect you've been in the trap for a while now and someone is just playing with you. Feeding you disinformation, stringing you along, dropping you a crumb here and there to keep you going in a direction of their choosing. Or simply sending you in circles, to keep you busy. Under the circumstances, I think Novak was right to assume that the team had been compromised, and to call for an extraction."

Isabela straightened in her chair and said, "Nonetheless, I need to know the truth about Carlos and Vikram."

Olivia paused, her lips pressed tightly together. "No promises, Isabela, but I'll do whatever I can."

"If our covers are blown, then time will be short," Angeli cut in. "Tell us about your plan."

"All right, but first, there's something you need to know about the Directorate." With that, Olivia launched into an explanation that left Isabela speechlessly clutching a mug of cooling tea.

"Are they evil? The sane ones are, for sure," Olivia concluded. "Can anything they say be trusted, including what Gervais told me earlier? No. We're on shifting ground here, and I have no idea how Gervais will react when he learns that we're deviating from his instructions. That's why it's essential that everything be kept secret for as long as possible."

"Agreed," said Angeli briskly. "What do you need us to do?"

"Isabela, you're the chemist. How quickly can you produce a supply of aerosolized knockout drug?"

"Assuming that I can find a growth of the right kind of plant, a couple of weeks."

"And Angeli, do you remember how you interfered with Novak's op about six years ago, when he was trying to wipe Lania's identity from Earth's databases? Do you recall how he planned to do it?"

"Ye-es."

"We're going to do something similar to the Directorate's server, only we're going to do it better. If we can hang onto the element of surprise, and if we time everything right, we'll be extracted along with all the other operatives immediately afterward, leaving nowhere for the Stragori to pin the blame. In the meanwhile, we'll stay in contact using our decrypters. If anyone gets curious, we're just three old friends from Earth who finally reconnected and have a lot of catching up to do. Understood?"

Angeli and Isabela exchanged looks and replied in unison, "Understood."

Chapter Sixteen

On Earth

The sixth-floor conference room had been converted into a classroom where Zane DeWitt conducted classes in spycraft each morning and afternoon for ten promising new EIS recruits. Properly groomed and wearing the right-sized clothing, the new generation of Warrior Kings had cleaned up nicely, Novak noted as he replayed that day's session on a monitor screen in his office.

"We know that the old man's got a routine. You can set a clock by it," DeWitt was saying. "It's the younger Bascombs we need to nail down. That's where you'll come in. You're going to be our moles — those are snoops who go inside one organization to spy for another."

"When do we get to use weapons?" demanded one of the recruits, a tall, solidly-built boy about eighteen years old with heavy-lidded eyes. Novak searched his memory and came up with the kid's name: Rufus Jaholovich. He would need a new identity, for sure. His birth name was much too memorable. So was his street name — Sluggo.

On the playback, DeWitt replied evenly, "You get weapons when you need them. But this isn't that kind of mission. Being a mole means staying low. If you fade into the background, people tend to ignore you. After a while, it's as though you don't even exist. Their guard goes down when they think they're alone, and sometimes interesting intel slips out. So, your job for the duration of this assignment is all about keeping your eyes and ears open without attracting any notice, then reporting to us what you've seen and heard."

"But what if we get caught?" challenged another King, a little older and a lot thinner than Rufus.

Loudon Beecher sprang to his feet. "With a gun? Then you're the dumbest ganger on the planet," he said with disgust. "What have I been teaching you for the past ten years?"

"Don't get caught holding," the kid recited shamefacedly.

"The best spies are the ones that no one detects or suspects," DeWitt pointed out, taking back control of the briefing. "So, if you're found somewhere you're not supposed to be, play dumb and pretend to be lost. Smile a lot. Ask for directions, and say 'thank you' when they're given. Then get yourself to where people expect you to be. After that, assume that you've aroused suspicion, and that you'll probably be followed around for a while.

"In any case, never come directly here from work. Stop for a java, or go for a walk in the park. When you're certain you've thrown off anyone who might be hugging your tail, report in. We'll check and decide whether it's safe to send you back into the field. Not safe for *you*, by the way. Safe for the rest of us."

"But what if we can't talk our way out of it?" demanded another student. "What if we're cornered and have to fight?"

"Then you're of no further use to us," DeWitt replied flatly.

The kid's face fell.

"You were chosen for this program because you're street savvy and have shown you know how to deal with Security. You're able to look and act innocent, and you're convincing liars. So, if you can't talk your way out of a situation, it means someone was already looking sideways at you, and you never noticed. That's strike one.

"If they come at you, you'll need to escape. Run away if you can. But if you can't run, then you'll have to fight your way free. If you injure someone in the process, that's strike two and a mess to clean up. But if you kill someone, or get arrested, that's strike three. And that's why we're not issuing any of you weapons for this mission," he concluded sternly.

"We'll provide each of you with a cover that will get you inside. After you've planted the listening devices — which we will be monitoring remotely — it's strictly watch, listen, and report, all the while keeping your cover. And staying the hell out of trouble."

Hearing a sound, Novak halted the playback and glanced toward the doorway, which was currently filled with Zane DeWitt.

"What do you think, boss?" the big man said with a grin. "Are they ready?"

"You've been at this for a month now. You tell me." Novak leaned back in his chair and beckoned DeWitt into the room.

"Okay," he said, dropping onto one of the guest chairs and counting off on his fingers. "I've taught them everything I know about tracking and following. Eastman has given them a crash course on how and where to plant the surveillance devices. Mendez says they're scrappy fighters, with some acrobatic moves that even he's never seen. They all know how to keep a secret, so no problem there. Rufus bothers me a little. He's just so damn big that it's impossible not to notice him, and what he really wants is to have an adventure, not disappear into the woodwork. He'll be the weak link in whatever team we put him on."

"And yet you kept training him."

DeWitt gave a little shrug. "He kind of reminds me of myself, back when we started up the gang. And I think his size and strength could be useful in certain situations."

Novak agreed. In fact, he even had a situation in mind.

"All right, then. Hold Rufus back and divide the other nine into three teams, one to surveille each of Bascomb's sons."

"Not the general?"

"He's already got official eyes and ears on him. We'll have to approach him a different way. The kid wants an adventure, you said?"

DeWitt's eyebrows rose. "Are you sure about this, boss? He's not ready to solo yet."

"He won't be alone. Don't worry, Zane — you'll get him back in one piece."

———— «◊» ————

General Bascomb had managed to avoid arrest for the murder of Juno Vargas, but he was by no means cleared of suspicion. That was the good news. However, there was bad news as well: Regional Security had taken over the murder investigation, and they had put him under tight, even intrusive surveillance, claiming that it was for his own protection until an arrest could be made.

This was going to throw a wrench into Novak's plans. District Security Chief Ridout swore up and down that he'd had nothing to do with it. The order had come from the High Council and had to be obeyed. Everything Bascomb said and did was to be recorded and scrutinized. He was to have no privacy anywhere: not in public, not at work, not at home, and nowhere in between.

The more Novak thought about it, the more convinced he became that Patricia Chen had to be behind the order. Maybe she feared being implicated in a murder if Novak followed through on his earlier promise. Or maybe she simply wanted the satisfaction of boxing Bascomb in and watching him chafe. Either way, she'd made it nearly impossible for anyone to approach him without Security's knowledge.

Nearly was the operative word here. Bascomb occasionally had to visit the hygiene room to relieve himself. Not even Regional Security was foolhardy enough to eavesdrop on a general's bodily functions without damn good cause. So, Earth Intelligence had done it instead.

As far as Novak knew, the device he had installed during his earlier visit to Bascomb's home was one of only two in existence. Specially designed by Naguchi and Nate Eastman, they looked and functioned like everyday objects, but were keyed to a particular individual's DNA. Until touched by the right person, they were undetectable by a standard surveillance sweep. And they contained their own memory, which could be dumped remotely by keying a unique code into another device located within a five-meter radius of the first one.

One of these special objects — installed months earlier during a routine maintenance inspection of the surveillance system at Planetary Security Headquarters — was doing double duty as the "decrypt" button on the general's office computer. His follow-up discussions after receiving classified messages had proven extremely enlightening. The EIS mole on the office cleaning crew was able to collect the intel every night or two and bring it back to Ops HQ for analysis.

The second device, planted in Bascomb's house, had replaced the standard model thumbprint lock on the inside of the hygiene room door. This was where it was assumed he would go to have conversations that were none of anyone else's business, including whoever might be spying on him via his home security system. Lately, to Novak's chagrin, that someone had been Regional Security.

Not content with simply tapping into the system that Novak's company had earlier installed in Bascomb's residence, Security had used their own devices to hijack it completely. At SecuriTech, the dedicated monitoring screen was dark and silent. Meanwhile, sound and images were being fed to a field command center somewhere in Millbrook Enclave. The officers on duty had to be close enough to react immediately if a trespasser or an active signal jammer — or an unauthorized data download — were detected in the vicinity. (The general had opted for the deluxe watchdog package when selecting his system.)

For Novak, having his hands tied was frustrating. However, it had been weeks since the memory cache in Bascomb's hygiene room had been cleared, and that was dangerous. Something needed to be done about it right away.

The SecuriTech receptionist looked up and waved at Novak as he passed her desk and pushed through the double plastiplex doors. He thumbed the lock on the entrance to the monitoring center and paused to let the metal panels slide apart. Then he stepped into a high-ceilinged area with enormous light screens that covered the walls and illuminated the room. In front of each screen sat a SecuriTech employee, keeping an eye on twenty or more "windows" onto spaces currently being surveilled by the company. As Novak scanned the multitude of images, his gaze alighted briefly on interior views of the District Administration Building, the stockrooms and counters of several large retail stores, and the triage area of a Medical Services center.

Clients paid extra for this level of vigilance, and SecuriTech was happy to provide it.

Novak crossed to the long work table that divided the room. District Security had sent them half a dozen malfunctioning InfoComm units to either repair or cannibalize for spare parts. Now the machines were lined up in a row, their screens dark, their cords dangling.

Seated at the far end of the table, with a loupe in one eye and something small balanced on the tip of his index finger, was Nate Eastman, SecuriTech's Head of Research and Development. Without so much as a glance in Novak's direction, he said, "Don't ask. I'm good, but I can't perform miracles."

Novak came to stand beside him. "And what did you think I was going to ask?"

Still not looking up, Eastman replied, "You want to be reconnected with the system in Bascomb's house so we can loop in a decoy feed while one of our agents sneaks close enough to dump the memory of my superbug. That trick may have worked before, but it won't work now. Not with Regional Security's firewall in place. So, unless you've got a plan B…"

"It's more of an idea, actually. What if we had a legitimate reason to send someone inside Bascomb's home with a toolkit?"

Eastman considered for a moment. "Oka-ay. But it couldn't be just that one home, or even just homes that we service. Regional Security would be suspicious of us right away. In fact, to prevent us from tapping back in, they've set up their command base outside our monitoring network altogether. They still need to be close by, though … so I'm guessing their stationary surveillance gear would have to be inside one of the houses either next door to the general's or just across the street. What did you have in mind?"

"Tell me what you think of this: Whichever house they're in will be drawing power from the same source as all the other homes in the vicinity. The nearest energy distribution box is located on a street corner just a block away. If it were physically damaged, say by a vehicle 'accidentally' hitting it at low speed, what would happen?"

"Actually, that wouldn't be a huge deal. The power system has failsafes to isolate faulty components from the rest of the grid, and emergency backups in each affected home would kick in. However, the local power disruption would set off security alarms all up and down the street."

When Eastman paused, Novak continued, "And to remain under warranty, every system would then have to be visually inspected and rebooted by the company that installed it. They would have to let us inside the Bascomb residence to do that."

"Meanwhile, our agent could clear the memory cache, right under Security's noses," Eastman concluded. "That'll work. So, when do you want this 'accident' to occur?"

"How about yesterday?"

———— «» ————

Four days later, the braking system mysteriously failed on a delivery vehicle that had been left idling on a street in Millbrook Enclave, causing it to collide with a power distribution box. That same day, SecuriTech received alarm notifications from five houses, including the one belonging to General Bascomb. The agents on duty followed standard protocol and were able to generate work orders for four of them.

"But not Bascomb's place?" DeWitt said doubtfully. "I thought that was the whole point of this exercise."

"Don't worry, Zane. It'll happen. But first we're going to have some fun."

The big man shook his head in puzzlement. "If you say so, boss."

Feigning ignorance, Novak then contacted District Security, at the Millbrook Enclave Precinct. The officer who took his commcall confirmed that the alarms were false, the result of a minor traffic mishap in the neighborhood. He concluded with, "Is there anything else I can do for you, Mr. Novak?"

"Yes. We've been able to obtain authorization to enter premises from only four of our five affected contractees. We may need a constable to give us access to the fifth residence."

DeWitt's eyes went saucer-wide. He looked about to say something. Novak silenced him with an off-screen hand gesture.

"House number and street name?"

"Seventy-nine Willowbranch Way."

"That's General Bascomb's address." He paused, frowning. "I'm afraid we can't help you, Mr. Novak. Regional Security has instructed us in no uncertain terms—" Another pause. The corners of his mouth were twitching. "Tell me, is the alarm still sounding?"

"Loud and clear. We can't turn it off until we've ascertained that all is well inside the building, and since Regional Security redirected the audio and video feeds, leaving us blind and deaf…"

They heard a deep chuckle from the other end of the transmission.

"Yeah, Regional does seem to enjoy elbowing us lesser beings out of the way. I wish you good luck in your quest for authorization, Mr. Novak. However, since there's already Security on site, perhaps you should just leave this situation to them to take care of."

"Well, thank you anyway, Officer…?"

"Jones."

"Of course." Novak nodded at the screen as it blanked. Turning to DeWitt, he continued, "And now that we've fulfilled the letter of the law, we can sit back and wait for Regional Security to contact us."

"Are you certain they will, boss? Their techs are the ones who diverted the feeds in the first place. What's to stop them from going over there and dealing with the alarm themselves?"

"I'm sure they'll try it, with or without a warrant. However, legalities aside, you and I both know there's no neat and tidy way to silence one of our alarms once it goes off, not even by cutting the power. The general likes to throw his weight around. If he wasn't willing to let Security physically enter his house for the purpose of keeping an eye on him, how do you think he would react if he found out that they'd broken in and ripped his wall apart because of a false alarm?"

"He would probably have a fit, and then he'd have their jobs," DeWitt responded, visibly warming to the idea.

"Yep. Wait for it. They're not stupid. They'll be in touch."

One hour later, SecuriTech's service department received a priority request via Regional Council commconnect. The expression on the face that appeared on the screen looked chiseled out of granite and had a gravelly voice to match.

"Are you Barry Novak?" demanded the face.

Novak counted the bars on his caller's epaulet and replied, "I am. What can I do for you, Captain?"

"Your company installed the security system in General Bascomb's home. Now you can damn well get someone out there to shut it up."

For the next ten seconds, Novak pretended to be calling up the account information. Then he said evenly, "You're referring to 79 Willowbranch Way in Millbrook Enclave?"

"Yes!" The other man's jaw muscles were working hard. It was fascinating to watch.

"First of all, I'm afraid we can't enter that building without authorization from the legally registered homeowner. To do otherwise would be trespassing."

"Even with an alarm going off?"

"Even then. If there were a genuine emergency — which we would determine using the surveillance technology we'd installed — then we would follow the legally mandated protocol by alerting District Security to handle the situation," Novak explained patiently. "Once they'd arrived on the scene — again, ascertained by means of our surveillance technology — then we would silence the alarm. Unfortunately, by depriving us of both the audio and the video feeds, you've made it impossible for us to do that."

The captain looked as though steam would be coming out of his ears any moment. Off screen meanwhile, DeWitt was convulsing with silent laughter, and the shoulders of every employee in the room were shaking as well.

"You already know that it's a false alarm, Novak," grated the captain. "What do you want?"

Novak squared his shoulders. "With respect, Captain, until your people let me see what they're seeing inside the house right now, I'm afraid I know nothing of the kind."

The officer exhaled gustily. "Fine. Keep this channel open. I'll have them show you their screens. And then will you turn off the goddamned alarm?"

"Of course. There's just one more thing."

Wearing a martyred expression, the other man said, "And what is that?"

"Just one of those legal details that can trip us up so easily," Novak replied with a shrug. "In the absence of an emergency, I'll need the general's permission before my technicians can enter his home to perform the safety inspection and reboot that are required by the terms of his warranty with us."

"And if you don't get it?"

Another shrug. "Then his warranty is invalidated, and we are under no further obligation to provide service free of charge. I don't think he would appreciate that," he added unnecessarily.

"Can he authorize this through a third party?"

Novak arranged his features into a portrait of regret. "I'm afraid not. It's a legal matter and requires the transmission of a living thumbprint."

"All right," snarled the captain. "You'll have it within the hour."

As instructed, Novak kept the channel open. But he muted the sound so that no one at the other end would hear the laughter that erupted when he stood up and spread his arms in a silent *ta-dah!*

It was like old times, except that no laws had been broken. And it felt good. Novak had missed this.

"Where are Croft and Rufus?" he asked DeWitt.

"Already on site, briefed and waiting for our signal. I told them to stretch things out, take long lunch breaks, stuff like that, in case there was a hitch. And may I say, boss, it was an education watching you work."

"Thank you. And now I would like the privilege of watching *you* work."

"Yes, *sir*," said the big man, displaying a toothy grin as he spun on his heel and strode out of the room.

⟨ ⟩

Early the next morning, a van emblazoned with the logo of SecuriTech Security Solutions made the turn onto Willowbranch Way and parked at the curb in front of number 79. There was supposed to be no one home. The general lived alone. According to the surveillance reports, he arrived at his office every morning at six o'clock sharp, without fail. And yet, in the driveway sat an unmarked vehicle with darkened windows, so obviously from a Security transportation pool that it might as well have borne an insignia.

"This could be trouble," Croft murmured.

Sitting in the passenger seat beside him and clad in a service uniform identical to his own, Rufus frowned in confusion. "He's still at home?"

"Dunno. If he is, he's picked a bad day to deviate from his schedule. And if he's not, we may have picked a bad day to deviate from ours. I guess we'll find out which one it is pretty soon. I've got the work order," he added, patting his shirt pocket. "You remember all the signals we practiced?"

Rufus swallowed audibly. "Yes, sir."

Croft spotted a tic in the kid's left eyelid and sighed inwardly. "Listen," he said, "there's no need for you to be nervous, not today. Today you've got one job to do, and that's to be an apprentice technician. I'm the one working the con. You're the one following the work order. You know how to do this. I watched you all day yesterday, and you've got the aptitude to be a very good technician. There's nothing in your toolkit that shouldn't be there, nothing to arouse suspicion. So just relax and do what you did yesterday in those other houses, and don't react to anything I do or say. If you find something different or puzzling about any of the securecams or mics, call me over to have a look. Understood?"

"What if someone asks me a question?"

"If it's strictly about the work that you're doing, answer it if you can. If it involves the work that I'm doing, or if you're not sure what's safe to tell them, then refer the question to me. Remember, you're an apprentice. You're not expected to have all the answers."

"Got it."

"Okay, then! Grab your kit and let's go inside."

They were halfway up the driveway when the front door swung inward. A tall man wearing a dark blue business suit and a forbidding facial expression emerged from the house. He stood on the porch, watching them approach.

Selecting his strategy, Croft was the first to challenge. "Are you the homeowner?" he called.

"I'm his son, Hugh Bascomb. And who are—?"

"Good! I was hoping someone would be home today," Croft declared briskly. If Bascomb wanted to call them something, he could use the names embroidered on the front of their uniforms. Meanwhile, it was important that Croft take control of the conversation.

"Oh? Why?"

"Because there's nothing routine about this routine inspection, not with a gang of cops camped out next door. They could have mucked things up any number of ways. And I may need a witness besides my apprentice here to testify that I had nothing to do with it. How's that for a reason?" he bristled.

Bascomb took a step backward and raised his hands in a gesture of appeasement. "It's a good one," he conceded. "But before we go inside, I'll need to see your copy of the work order."

Wordlessly, Croft pulled up the document on his compupad and handed him the device.

"Your boss gave Captain Worth a hard time yesterday," Bascomb remarked, his gaze fixed on the screen.

"He gives everyone a hard time. Novak's a stickler for the rules and doesn't much care whose feathers he ruffles. Especially when they've ruffled his first."

"A stickler? Funny. That's not what I've heard," he muttered under his breath, then continued in a normal voice, "I understand his position. Really, I do. And you can tell him that the general's not too happy about this 'protective detail' arrangement either." Bascomb handed the compupad back. "Shall we enter the premises?"

Casting a glance at his apprentice, Croft saw a new level of respect in the youngster's eyes. And not a trace of apprehension.

"Lead the way, Mr. Bascomb."

———— 《 》 ————

"What sort of intel are we gleaning from our moles?" Novak asked.

DeWitt closed the office door and came to stand in front of his desk. "At first, not much, but things are getting interesting." Gestured to sit down, he settled onto a guest chair and continued, "Beecher's cell reports that the new Chief Adjudicator is pleasant and accessible and genuinely cares about the people in the District. In fact, it sounds as though he may be the only honest politician in Americas. Perhaps even the world."

"I sense a 'but' coming."

"He has enemies, mainly in his own family. They don't contact him at the office, only at his home, on a private channel. Eastman has been monitoring the feed from our audio surveillance there and has already recorded a couple of openly threatening conversations." The big man narrowed his gaze. "You already knew about that, though, from talking to him."

"I knew what he told me. Now that it's been confirmed, I know it's the truth."

"Uh-huh. So, are you thinking of changing careers once the EIS closes up shop, boss? Getting involved in politics, maybe?"

Novak pretended to consider the idea. "I wouldn't want to be a public figure, but it would be a shame to waste all the skills and resources we've managed to gather over the years. Perhaps we could work behind the scenes, helping to make things happen. Or preventing things from happening. What do you think, Zane? Is that something our crew might be interested in besides keeping SecuriTech going?"

"I can't speak for anyone else, but it's something *I* would be interested in. Certainly worth keeping in mind for later, after the dust settles."

"If it settles. What about the other two brothers?"

"There's plenty of blackmail fodder there, but to be honest, I can't see us turning either one of them, boss. Darren's ex-husband, Saul Stuebing, is an event promoter, with controlling interest in several live sports and entertainment venues. Darren's joining the Space Installation Authority was apparently Stuebing's idea, to make it easier for him to expand his business off-world. And the general most likely saw an advantage in it for himself and twisted an arm or two to make it happen. After the war, Stuebing invested heavily in Vegas Hub. He must have figured that it would be up and running fairly quickly. But it's still under reconstruction, and the delays have already cost him a fortune."

"Delays that were the direct result of Daisy Hub getting priority treatment from the High Council?"

"Yep."

Novak grimaced. "So, now there are two powerful people with grudges against the station: Stuebing and George Bascomb."

"And Darren's been taking a lot of pressure from both of them. In fact, getting the Hub reclassified was his attempt at appeasement."

"Did it work?"

"Not according to the audio from the mics we planted."

"And you're certain we can't turn him?"

"Boss, he makes regular trips to Ginza Hub, where he likes drugging and raping little boys. This man is blackmail bait for so damn many people that we'd never be able to trust him. In my opinion, it would be foolish to bring him anywhere near the organization."

"Does Stuebing know about his ex's off-world activities?"

"He does. In fact, I checked out Saul Stuebing, thinking he might be useful."

"And?"

DeWitt made a face. "That son of a bitch has some unsavory habits of his own, involving the grooming of young athletes and entertainers. And don't even start me on how he and Darren met. Like I said, there's lots of blackmail fodder."

"Just not for us," Novak concluded. "All right, then. What about Hugh Bascomb?"

"Hugh's the oldest son. He used his inheritance from his grandfather to start up a deal brokerage firm. Basically, he plays with companies. Buying, selling, building, dismantling … and everything he does is for profit."

"Including destroying Forrand Pharmaceuticals?"

"We're still looking into that. It's not like him to waste the assets of a perfectly good corporate enterprise. One of the moles reported overhearing the end of a commcall that suggests to me Hugh might have plans to either parcel it out to other pharma labs or build it back up under a different name."

"Thus pleasing his father and turning a profit at the same time?"

DeWitt shrugged. "It is what he does. When he's not threatening to have his youngest brother murdered, that is."

Novak perked up. "Sounds like you saved the best for last."

The big man grinned. "We have the audio from Hugh's end of the conversation as well. It was very specific. There's apparently a piece of legislation relating to corporate taxation on the table at District Council, and Hugh wants it killed. If it passes in any form, he's promised that Richard will end up just like Juno Vargas did. His words."

Novak leaned back thoughtfully in his chair. "Now, *that* I can work with."

"It gets better. Our team has returned from the mission to Willowbranch Way. You should have a look at the report Croft uploaded after he and Rufus left the general's residence."

"They pulled off the memory dump?"

"Yes, while having a very interesting conversation with Hugh Bascomb. I won't spoil it for you, but I think you'll love where it ends up."

With that, DeWitt got to his feet and left the room.

Curious now, Novak pulled up the relevant file on his screen. The more he read, the higher his eyebrows rose. And the more he thought about it, the broader his smile became.

Hugh Bascomb had evidently gone digging for dirt on both Dennis Forrand and Juno Vargas and now thought he had something on their "fixer", Barry Novak. That was why he'd met Croft at the house — to send a message to SecuriTech's owner.

All the veiled references to rumor and hearsay that Bascomb had slipped into his remarks to Croft were almost certainly the preamble to a blackmail or extortion demand. Novak had a pretty good idea what it might be: Rick Bascomb was an obstacle to his brother's plans and therefore needed to be removed. Who better to take him out than Forrand's private hit man?

After all, companies weren't the only thing that could be parceled out or repurposed.

A soft bell tone announced the arrival of a message in one of Novak's EIS inboxes. The transmission was from Angeli, meaning it concerned something important. Novak pulled it up onto his screen, saw the three word confirmation — "Dear Uncle Henry" — and activated his decrypter. As he read the decoded text, a sick feeling invaded the back of his throat. He cleared it with a colorful expletive. Then he got busy on his keyboard.

The three documents from the Directorate's backup server were disinformation.

Townsend needed to be warned not to trust their source.

Chapter Seventeen

On Daisy Hub

The Nandrian warship *Passpessil* announced its approach to Daisy Hub exactly one interval after Agnosk's visit. Evidently, the *Hak'kor* of Trokerk had agreed to grant Moe's request for a favor.

Before the warship docked, Townsend made a point of warning his senior staff about the names that had been given to the two hybrids.

"Sorry ass? And it means 'courage' in Nandrian? That's unfortunate," Walt remarked.

"Which part?" said Ruby.

"All of it," he declared. "How could those scientists not have realized—?"

"Don't blame the scientists for using standard nomenclature," the Doc cut in. "*Homo saurius* describes a hybrid creature that is part evolved anthropoid and part reptilian. The language of science is derived from Old Latin. Perhaps there were some ancient Romans in that control group long ago. In any case, 'sorry ass' is Anglo, which is only spoken on Earth. It means 'courage' in Nandrian. It may mean nothing at all in Stragori."

"And that is why we're going to be gracious hosts and not react when our guest's name is spoken aloud," Townsend told them, "especially if there are Nandrians around. Making fun of their word for 'courage' can only be construed as an insult. And we all know what will happen if a Nandrian takes offence."

Heads bobbed and meaningful looks crisscrossed the room.

"Spread the word to every department and detail. No chortling, chuckling, or any other indication of amusement, for as long as we have Nandrians aboard the station," said Townsend.

"You've got it, Chief," Ruby caroled. "Straight faces all around."

One hour later, Drew was standing in the docking ring, watching two warriors step through portal number 3. The one who towered over him was Agnosk. The other was much shorter but almost as broad in the body, and both were clad in full battle armor.

They halted side by side and struck identical military poses.

As dictated by protocol, Townsend was the first to speak. Earlier, Holchuk would have written him a script for this occasion, but by now Drew didn't need one.

"Greetings, honored visitors, and welcome to House Daisy Hub. Daisy Hub has a long and glorious history, dating back to—"

"Apologies, *Hak'kor*," Agnosk interrupted. "Ssorryass is needed aboard his ship and can only spend a short time on the station. With your indulgence, may we proceed to the introductions, and then to your Med Services to meet his twin?"

"Of course. It would be my honor to introduce myself. I am Drew, son of David, First Shield of House Daisy Hub."

"I am Ssorryass, son of Stragon, Fifth Shield of House Trokerk," said the hybrid in a clear, reedy voice. Apparently, despite the Nandrian musculature on his frame, he was still preadolescent by Stragori age reckoning. This kid had no idea what was about to happen to his insides.

"And I am Agnosk, son of Sitgar, Third Shield of House Trokerk. We bring you greetings from our *Hak'kor*."

Drew gave the formulaic response: "Please return my best wishes to him," then added, "and follow me to Med Services," as he wheeled and led the way to the nearest tube car door.

Moe and the Doc emerged from her office — a real room this time, no longer just an alcove off the Trauma unit — when the three of them entered the triage area. Moe halted in the middle of that space. As Ssorryass stepped forward and walked a circle around him, his head tilted curiously, Moe drew himself up and expanded his chest in a vain attempt to match the dimensions of his twin.

Meanwhile, Drew was getting a very bad feeling about this situation.

"I am Ssorryass, son of Stragon, Fifth Shield of House Trokerk, Warrior Officer aboard the Nandrian heavy cruiser *Passpessil*," the hybrid announced to the air beside Moe's head. Then, finally turning to face him, he added in a voice loaded with puerile disdain, "And what are you?"

"I am your twin brother," Moe replied bravely. "I have waited a long time to meet you."

"In battle?" Ssorryass looked him up and down again. "Then where is your armor? Was it taken from you in a fight?" A pause, then, "You look small and weak to me. Have you ever worn armor? Miserable creature, do you even know how to defend yourself?"

Moe opened his mouth, looked about to reply, then closed it and dropped his gaze. As his shoulders drooped, his whole body seemed to sag and deflate.

Meanwhile, the embers in Townsend's stomach were stirring back to life. This had been a mistake. It was not going to end well. Thinking wishfully about the bottle of antacid tablets in his desk drawer, he cast a sidelong glance at Agnosk. The Nandrian stood as though carved out of stone, his eyes directed stolidly frontward.

He knew. They all must have known, yet they decided to let it happen. Why?

"We cannot be twins," Ssorryass declared to the room. "We are nothing alike."

"You're right," Moe told him, raising his eyes once more. Drew saw the sadness that filled them and felt his heart twist. "We may have come from the same egg, but we were raised on different worlds. Viewed through different lenses. You have many brothers, and no need for any more. I— am glad that you have found your place, and that you're happy there. Now please go. Live your life. I won't bother you again."

With that, Moe turned his back on everyone in the room.

Drew and the Doc exchanged a worried look before she mimed sweeping him toward the door.

Townsend escorted Agnosk and Ssorryass back to the docking ring, where they went through an abridged version of the Nandrian leave-taking ceremony. At the end of it, the youngster pivoted without another word and disappeared through portal 3. Agnosk hung back, apparently sensing that not everything had been said.

"With respect, *Hak'kor*, do you have a question?"

"I do. What exactly happened back there?"

The massive head tilted to one side. "The twins were reunited, as your hybrid requested."

"But you'd met Moe, and you must have realized he would be rejected. Why go ahead with it?"

"Our *Hak'kor* deemed it wise, based on the information you provided him. Ssorryass believes himself to be the same as any full-blooded Nandrian. He will soon discover that he is not. When that happens, he will feel alone. His Shield brothers will see him differently, perhaps treat him differently as well. He will remember that there is one other who shares that same loneliness, and who reached out to him in the past. Tell Moe to be patient. He will see his twin again."

Townsend waited for the portal to seal behind Agnosk, then hurried back to Med Services to pass the Nandrian's message along.

As he stepped into her lab, the Doc glanced up, stern-faced, from the display on her screen. "You just missed him," she said curtly.

"Did he tell you where he was going?"

She pursed and unpursed her lips. "No, but I think we can guess. He said he was going to find someone who could teach him to fight."

Wonderful.

Drew buzzed AdComm. "Ruby?"

"Right here, Chief. What can I do for you?"

"Moe may be headed for K Deck. Rodrigues needs to be warned. Tell him I'm on my way there as well."

"I'm on it."

Townsend had guessed correctly. As he stepped off the tube car on K Deck, he could see the Ranger captain and the hybrid in Rodrigues's office, their complexions darkening and their arms energetically sculpting the air. Paul saw him coming and unsealed the door.

"Apologies for being late," Drew told them, his arrival hitting pause on what had clearly been a heated discussion.

"Do you know what this is about, Townsend?" the Ranger demanded. "Because there's no way I can recommend him for SIS training."

"I do know, and I have a solution that may solve more than one problem here."

"Go on," said Rodrigues, in a voice that brought to mind raised eyebrows and a toe tapping impatiently on the deck.

"Moe wants to learn some self-defense skills, and that's always a good thing. Wouldn't you agree?" Grudgingly, the other man nodded confirmation. "But he doesn't need to enlist in Security for that. He just needs a teacher who can spare him some time. I suggest you give Madeline Holchuk the assignment."

"Turn over a trainee to a rookie constable?" Rodrigues protested.

"A rookie constable with years of prior experience at the Regional Security level. She's more than qualified, Paul, and she and Moe have a great deal in common. I think they'd be good for each other, in more ways than one."

The Ranger leaned back thoughtfully in his chair. "All right," he said at last. "We can give it a try. I'll have her sergeant modify the duty schedule, putting her in the exercise room for a half hour every second day, beginning tomorrow. The whole detachment doesn't have to know about this. Show up and you'll have a lesson," he added, addressing Moe. "Pass and she'll have a workout. Deal?"

Somehow managing to form a grin with his lipless mouth, the hybrid replied, "Deal."

——— ‹›› ———

Things were quiet on C Deck. Townsend was at his desk, drafting his usual noncommittal report to the Space Installation Authority and wondering when the other shoe would drop. It had been a while since the recommissioning of the station. Six or seven intervals, at least. Rodrigues had warned him to expect surprise inspections. So far, none had materialized. Perhaps there would be one today.

Better now than later, he thought, while secrets were still safe and there were only two aliens in residence. The Stragori craft on the landing deck could be easily explained. Vin Trager was a practiced liar. And Moe would certainly be complicit in concealing his own presence aboard the Hub.

Then Lydia made a whooping sound that brought Townsend to his feet and out of his office to investigate.

"I didn't think we'd be seeing *this* type of craft again," she declared, pointing at the ship profile depicted on the screen over the main console. "It's ten hours out and headed our way."

He recognized it from its silhouette. Instantly, the day became much more interesting. "We have an Eggenali Night Cloud on approach? Hail it. If the pilot is Gorse Pirrit, welcome him back and clear him to tie down on our landing deck."

"What if it's not him?"

The Night Cloud was uncloaked at the moment, but this class of alien ship was a stealth fighter, and it was currently in Earth space. Townsend didn't *think* the Eggenali had a bone to pick with Terrans — they'd fought fiercely on the side of Humanity in the recent war. Nonetheless, it was probably better to be safe than sorry.

He amended his instructions. "Find out what he's doing way the hell out here and ask whether he needs our assistance. And put it on speaker."

She opened the commlink. "This is Daisy Hub Control to the approaching Eggenali vessel. Please identify yourself and your purpose in Earth space."

After a pause, they heard a familiar voice. "This is Night Cloud One, and we're carrying a passenger we understand your station manager wishes to confer with."

Yorell Enne. Finally!

"Mr. Pirrit, we've reserved your parking spot and will meet you on the landing deck when you arrive," Townsend told him.

Now, with luck, they might get some answers.

Townsend was halfway back to his office when Lydia called out, "A message just arrived, Drew. It's from Earth, addressed to you and marked 'eyes only'."

Townsend frowned. A transmission from Novak? This had to be important. "Put it on a datawafer for me. I'll read it once I've sent off my report."

Half an hour later, with an antacid tablet still dissolving in his mouth, Drew stormed onto the data mining deck and found Walt Garfield studying the contents of a text file.

"What can I do for you, Mr. Townsend?" he inquired evenly, never taking his eyes off the screen.

"You can tell me that every precaution was taken to keep the data from the Stragori memory blocs on the outside of our firewall."

The urgency in his voice made Walt glance up.

"Yes, and nearly all of it still is. We've been uploading one memory bloc at a time, to a dedicated server, and we're using rogue technology to sift the contents. When we come across a relevant file, we make sure it's clean before moving it over. That's why it's taking us so long to process this stuff. We knew we'd have it for a while and figured you'd appreciate the increased security."

As Walt watched, Drew snagged the nearest chair and collapsed onto it with relief.

"Is there a problem, Mr. Townsend?"

"Other than the fact that I'm kicking myself for not following my first instincts? I suspected a con the second Trager offered to give us the decryption key. But, just like any mark, I was greedy. I convinced myself the potential reward was worth the risk."

"You're certain we're being played? How?"

Townsend said grimly, "Best case scenario, they've seeded every memory bloc with disinformation. Worst case scenario, I'm not sure I even want to imagine. Their technology is far superior to ours."

"All right, then. How do you want us to proceed?"

"I want you to sanitize the entire station. Blow out the dedicated server. Reinitialize the rogue technology. Run diagnostics on every part of our InfoComm network. Do whatever you need to do, but remove every trace of the Stragori data from our systems. Then you're going to pack up those memory blocs, seal them inside their cases, and put them into storage. If the Directorate survive what's coming, they may want their stuff back."

"And if they don't survive?"

"I'll make that decision when the time comes." Townsend buzzed AdComm. "Lydia, I need you and O'Malley to report to Deck C-1 as soon as you're individually available. The three of you have a priority job to take care of. Walt will explain when you get here." Closing the channel, he added, "Keep me apprised of your progress. And expect the unexpected."

Walt shrugged philosophically. "We always do."

—— «» ——

Yorell Enne was still a force of nature. The former Prime Docent was a Reyot female of advanced years and imposing stature, a powerful figure topped with a striking mane of pure white hair. The Reyota and Kularians were felid races, bipedal but with legs better constructed for running than for walking. Wherever the environment permitted it, they ran. That was what they were doing now, all three of them, bearing down on Townsend from the other side of the landing deck. He repressed a sudden urge to jump out of their way.

As they came to a halt a respectful distance from him, he let out the breath he'd been holding. Then, bowing from his shoulders, he greeted them. "Madame Prime Docent, thank you for making the time to come see me. And Mr. Pirrit and Dr. Minegar, thank you for transporting her here."

Yorell gestured dismissively with one long-fingered hand. "Thank *you*, Mr. Townsend, for requesting my presence. We've been helping out, working salvage aboard the *Melkarit*, and this gives us a welcome break."

"And, I must confess," added Pirrit, "we've been curious to see your new station. I trust this one contains no troublesome alien technology?"

Drew replied truthfully, "The Nandrian field generators on both Daisy Hub and Zulu were damaged in the final battle. Earth has not requested replacements for them, and the Nandrians haven't offered any. And as you can imagine, we're all quite happy about that."

Pirrit laughed.

"Mr. Townsend, your transmission mentioned an important question for me," said Yorell.

"Yes. It concerns a rather puzzling visual record that Captain Takamura recently showed me, and the terms of a certain treaty...?"

Everything about her stiffened. "Perhaps we should take this discussion somewhere private." She threw a significant look at Pirrit.

Responding to the cue as though he'd been anticipating it, he said, "Ixbeth and I are feeling a little hungry. Perhaps Mr. Townsend can direct us to the caf? If you're still calling it that."

"Of course," Drew replied. "We'll find you there when our meeting is over, and I'll take all three of you on a tour of the station."

After dropping Pirrit and Dr. Minegar off on D Deck, Drew escorted Yorell to his office and invited her to sit. Gesturing for silence, he activated the privacy shield, then told her, "One of the privileges of being the station manager is that not everything I do or say gets recorded. We're inside a jamming zone, Madame Prime Docent. Shall we talk?"

She inclined her head in assent, then gazed inquiringly at him.

"Captain Takamura suggested that your position as Prime Docent might have given you access to information not readily available to others."

"It did. However, as you must know by now, I no longer occupy that post. In fact, I don't even dare to show my face on Reyi'it again, since the Great Council has branded me as a criminal. Any information I give you will be from memory only, and therefore should not be considered authoritative."

"Understood. Nonetheless, you know more than any of us about the history of the alien worlds, and I do have questions. It would make our work much easier if you could share whatever you remember learning regarding the origins of the Great Council and the terms of the treaty."

"You are looking for factual historical data?"

"As much as possible, yes."

A smile was tugging at the corners of her mouth. "Now I am the curious one, Mr. Townsend. Precisely what sort of work are you and your crew engaged in?"

He paused, weighing how best to answer, then finally said, "It's an archiving project. For now, at least. There isn't a lot to do out here, and my people need to stay busy. It keeps our minds off our own unpleasant memories of the war."

"So, you have decided to collect information about ancient alien history?"

"And anything relating to alien interactions with Humans in the distant past."

"You are not telling me the whole truth, Mr. Townsend," she reproved him gently. "But I will help you as much as I can. As an exile forced to remain in Earth space, I too need to keep busy, and metal salvaging is an occupation better suited to the young. Can you accommodate me with temporary living quarters while 'picking my brain', as I've heard Humans put it?"

"Of course. What about Pirrit and Dr. Minegar? Will they need quarters as well?"

"On the *Melkarit*, they prefer to live inside their Night Cloud. I cannot say what they will choose to do aboard your station. However, I am reasonably certain that Captain Trost will not miss them if they decide to stay here with me. I trust that will not present any problems for you?"

"Not at all, Prime Docent."

"Well, then, since there is no longer any urgency, shall we go have a bite of something in the caf?"

It was phrased as a suggestion, but something in the tone of her voice and the way she held her head reminded Townsend of the first time he'd met Doctor Ktumba. He'd been after information then, too, interviewing her as a possible witness to the suspicious death of the previous station manager. Like Enne's, her manner had been condescending to the point of being insulting. Eventually, Townsend and the Doc had reached an understanding about who was in charge of what. This time around, Drew opted for a short cut.

"Actually, I was hoping to ask you a couple of questions now," he replied, locking eyes with her across his desk.

She had leaned forward in anticipation of getting to her feet. Eyebrows elevated, she stopped and sank back into her chair. "Very well, Mr. Townsend, if you insist."

"I have a theory that you may be able to confirm or disprove. One of our alien allies has told me that it's common knowledge in alien space that Humans and Stragori both came from Earth. That we are actually the same race. Is that true?"

"That it is common knowledge? Yes. And there are documents in the Central Archives that corroborate your common origin."

"Did the Stragori ever sign the treaty?"

"I think you know they didn't."

"Because they refused? Or because they were never invited to?"

"When that treaty came into effect, your race was millennia away from achieving any kind of space travel. Earth was observed and occasionally visited, but never asked to join the Great Council."

"And Stragon? They've had interstellar capabilities for centuries. Never invited?"

Reluctantly, she repeated, "Never invited."

"Why? Was it because the Humans of Earth were so backward?" he persisted. When she failed to reply, he told her, "Madame Enne, we already know that the Stragori were the control group of an experiment being conducted on Humanity."

"I should have guessed that would be the case," she said with a sigh. "You're right, Mr. Townsend. A unified race with space flight technology might have been asked to join the Council. But Humanity was neither. And you're still a broken race, no matter how advanced your technology may be."

Throwing caution out an airlock, Drew asked her, "Would we still be considered a broken race if all the Humans of Earth had been annihilated by the Corvou, leaving only the Stragori?"

She gazed reproachfully at him for a moment. "You're searching for reasons. I'm afraid I cannot help you. Is the experiment still ongoing? I do not know. Would the Council feel safer if your kind were extinct? I do not know, nor does it give me pleasure to speculate about such things. I am only glad that Humanity survives, on both your worlds and out in space. Now, if we are done here…?"

"We are, Madame Enne. Thank you for your patience. I'll instruct my staff to prepare your suite while I'm giving you that tour I promised."

——— «» ———

Townsend saw Ruby crossing the deck toward his office. She looked worried. He waited until she was standing in the doorway to assure her, her, "Madame Enne is comfortably settled in her quarters. She appears to be quite satisfied with the arrangements you made. Pirrit and Dr. Minegar are choosing to sleep inside their ship, but will be joining us for meals and meetings."

"That's nice, Chief, but it's not why I came over. O'Malley says there's something on his screen that you need to look at. He sounds scared."

"Scared?" he echoed. "O'Malley is never scared, even when he ought to be."

"Exactly."

"Tell him I'm on my way."

Townsend stepped off the tube car onto Deck C-1 and saw all three members of the data mining detail huddled around one of the monitors as though trying to warm themselves in its glow. He shuffled his feet to make some noise as he approached. O'Malley was the only one who glanced up to greet him.

"Boss, I'm not sure what you'll want to do about this," he said.

Drew caught the slight tremor in the ratkeeper's voice and frowned. Coming around the table for a view of the screen, he saw two words: PLEASE DON'T.

"Please don't what?" he demanded.

"I was about to reinitialize the dedicated offline server, as you ordered," Walt Garfield explained. "I keyed in the instruction, but before I could hit 'execute', the screen refreshed and these words appeared. It's not a joke, Townsend. None of us did this."

"You're telling me the server is talking to us?"

"We can't think of anything else it could be," said Lydia.

"All right, then, let's ask it." Drew sat down and typed: *Who or what are you?*

MY NAME IS GERVAIS FORRAND.

I AM A SENIOR DIRECTOR OF THE STRAGORI GOVERNMENT AND THE *HAK'KOR* OF HOUSE STRAGON.

"Damn!" muttered Walt behind him.

A sudden icy sweat tattooing his forehead, Townsend typed: *Where are you?*

I AM NOT SURE.

I WAS DOWNLOADED ON STRAGON INTO MEMORY BLOC 2472.

I SUSPECT I AM NOW SOMEWHERE ELSE.

SOMEWHERE I AM NOT SUPPOSED TO BE.

CAN YOU TELL ME WHERE I AM?

"2472? That was the bloc we were processing when you gave us the priority assignment, boss," O'Malley said softly. "Third out of a total of about thirty."

"A downloaded consciousness?" said Lydia. "That sounds familiar. Remember back before the war, when Rob was trying to con Karlov into thinking his mind had been moved onto a computer?"

"Yeah," said Townsend, recalling. O'Malley had given it his best shot, but Karlov hadn't believed him for a second. The Stragori knew that Humanity's technology, unlike their own, wasn't advanced enough to digitize and transfer a living consciousness.

He continued typing.

We believe that you've somehow copied yourself onto our server.

ARE YOU SURE I AM A COPY? IS THE ORIGINAL STILL ON THE BLOC?

We can't know that without reinserting the memory bloc to check, and we're not about to do that. If we're able to locate an empty bloc, can you download yourself again?

NO. NOT AT THIS LEVEL OF TECHNOLOGY.

"Boss, I've got a really bad feeling about this," O'Malley murmured. "If we're being played—!"

If? Townsend gave him a look. For certain they were. And he wasn't about to fall for the same con twice.

So, you're an uploaded consciousness, and you're trapped inside our server?

YES.

Are there any others like you embedded in the Stragori memory blocs?

NO. THE REST OF THE BLOCS CONTAIN DATA ONLY.

Can you see and hear us?

NO.

Uh-huh. Deliberately turning his back to the screen, Drew signaled to Walt to keep an eye on it, then said, "We can't take the chance. Reinitialize the server."

Walt's eyes widened briefly. When Townsend swiveled his chair, there was a single word on the screen: WAIT!

"Oh, jeez," O'Malley moaned.

"Cheer up, Rob," Lydia advised him. "It could have been worse. He could have been on the first bloc we searched instead of the last one."

"I'm not convinced that he wasn't," said Walt, lowering his voice. "We don't know how long he's been in there, only what it took to flush him out."

Addressing the entity in the server, Drew said, "So you *can* hear us speaking. Why did you lie about it?"

I DID NOT INTEND TO SPY BUT I FEARED YOU WOULD NOT BELIEVE ME.

"And your fear was justified. Someone in the Directorate planted bogus documents in these memory blocs. Why should we believe anything you say, including that you are Gervais Forrand?"

THERE ARE NO FALSE DOCUMENTS IN THE BACKUP FILES. BUT SOME OF THEM HAVE BEEN PURPOSELY TAKEN OUT OF CONTEXT TO PROVOKE AN EMOTIONAL RESPONSE IN TERRANS.

"Well, they've certainly succeeded in getting a rise out of *me*. Assuming that what you're telling me now is the truth, what Terran emotional response were you hoping for?"

ULTIMATELY, THE DESTRUCTION OF THE DIRECTORATE. BUT NOT OF HOUSE STRAGON. THE NANDRIANS WOULD NEVER PERMIT THAT.

"And you claim to be the *Hak'kor* of that House."

I AM THE *HAK'KOR.* BY PROTECTING MY BACKUP SELF YOU WILL ENSURE THE SURVIVAL OF OUR HOUSE, REGARDLESS OF WHAT HAPPENS ON STRAGON.

"What about your *Kalufah*? And your high speaker? Where is the rest of your First Shield?"

THEY ARE CORPOREAL AND REMAIN ON STRAGON. OUR FIRST SHIELD IS MANY IN NUMBER. SOME WILL SURVIVE TO LEAD.

For a moment, Townsend froze. According to Vixor ban Jorisam, the First Shield were all members of the same family, its leaders related by blood. If Gervais Forrand really was the *Hak'kor* of House Stragon, that meant Dennis Forrand and all his descendants — including Olivia — were heirs to power on an alien world. Perhaps Stragon was where she belonged after all.

"It's your call, Drew," said Lydia, breaking into his thoughts. "What do you want us to do?"

"The one thing we cannot do, unfortunately, which is to reinitialize the server. He may just be a backup copy, but he's been entrusted to a fellow *Hak'kor* for safekeeping, and the honor of our House hinges on not betraying that trust. All right," Townsend decided. "Keep this server isolated and disable the audio and video functions on the rogue monitor attached to it. We'll communicate with Gervais Forrand using the keyboard only. And he's going to earn his keep by providing reliable intel to aid our activities on Stragon." He turned steely eyes on the monitor screen. "Aren't you, Gervais?"

There was a pause of several seconds.

IF THAT IS THE ONLY WAY I WILL GET TO TALK TO ANYONE, THEN I HAVE NO CHOICE BUT TO AGREE.

Chapter Eighteen

On Stragon

Olivia returned to the ferry terminal alone, reasoning that the less she was seen in the company of the other two women, the safer all three of them would be. Not that it would make a difference if Angeli and Isabela were already under surveillance by the Directorate. Pushing that unsettling thought to the back of her mind, she paused long enough to retrieve the mini-decrypter from its Security locker, then joined the stream of travelers being funneled onto the walkway to the boarding dock.

Olivia remained below decks for the return trip to the mainland, finding the sour smell of bodies crowded together preferable to the sinus-scouring pungency wafting from the barges anchored farther along the shore. As a bonus, those bodies also generated heat, and the temperature outside was perceptibly falling.

When she disembarked on the other side of the strait, she found Linda Forrand waiting for her, one hand resting on the curved roof of a bullet car.

Hurrying toward her, Olivia called out, "Your timing is perfect. But how did you know which ferry I would be on?"

"Let's get inside," Linda urged. "We'll talk on the way home."

As the car jerked into motion, a gentle warmth began drifting through the cabin.

"There, that's better," said Linda. "Oh, and I have a gift for you." Reaching into her pocket, she brought out a small, familiar-looking object and depressed a button located on its side. Immediately, the air filled with beautiful orchestral music. "For those times when you need to have a private conversation," Linda explained. "The symphony has a jamming signal embedded in it that turns specific voices into static. For now, it's programmed for yours and mine. Later, I'll show you how to add more."

"This is brilliant."

"Thank you. It's my own invention. Completely illegal, of course, but forgivable when it's used by a Forrand. Now, to answer your question, the Directorate is able to track the whereabouts of every one of us. Members of certain families may have access to that information."

Olivia frowned. "Optimized or not, we're being tracked?"

"Yes. Not every technology our scientists develop is shared with the general population. In order to stay in power, the Directorate needs to maintain an advantage. This is how they do it."

"So, the families in question...?"

"...are those of the Directors."

"I see. And what happens to the secret technologies if I do what Gervais wants?"

"I don't know. Losing them may be the price of reuniting the two factions."

Olivia gazed into her great-grandmother's eyes, noticing once more that they were gray, like her own. "I need you to tell me the truth, Linda, about everything."

"I know, *minona*, and I'll do my best to give it to you."

"You used that word when I first arrived. What does it mean?"

Linda's features softened. "It's a term of endearment. On Earth, I would be speaking Anglo and calling you 'sweetness' or 'darling'. Here on Stragon, it's *minona* for a girl, *minian* for a boy."

"Gilles didn't look happy when you called me that."

"He knew that you were about to be given a very important mission. He felt the need to point out, correctly, that you're still a child, with a child's naive idealism, and that you will soon learn how cruel the world can be when it is governed by the Directorate."

Olivia had heard something quite similar from Dennis Forrand, back when she really was a naive, idealistic child. It stung to hear it again, even coming from someone three times her age.

"Whatever happened to 'Forrands don't fall into line behind others'?"

"We don't. However, we do defer to our oldest living members. The first Forrand to join the Directorate was Louis. His consciousness survives, but no one has heard from him in decades. Gervais now controls the family, and has effectively taken control of the Directorate as well. Once it falls, his political power will be gone, and the rest of us will be free to create a new and better order."

To Olivia, that smacked of the same sort of naive idealism that Gilles had been so quick to disparage. The temptation to comment was strong, but her curiosity was stronger. So, she asked, "Now that I've seen the island, I can't help wondering. It was originally meant to hold prisoners, wasn't it?"

"Yes. But not criminals, not in the usual sense. They're a disruptive element. We call them objectors."

This was sounding awfully familiar as well. Olivia stared a question at her. Linda replied to it.

"Stragori society — the one the Directorate created — is highly structured, with levels of privilege and responsibility, and well defined boundaries. For most of the population, this was a tolerable arrangement, even comforting for some. They always knew where they fitted in and what their limits were."

"And this was the system that Adam Vargas brought to Earth?"

"A version of it, yes. It was the fastest way to bring order out of the chaos on your planet. But not everyone on a world will be satisfied to live under the same set of rules. So, the island was designated as a place reserved for those who objected to the Directorate's vision. It allowed them to establish their own, different kind of society."

The Stragori social order wasn't the only thing Vargas had brought to Earth, Olivia mused darkly. Daisy Hub had been classified as an experiment in self-contained deep space living, but it too had been intended as a gulag for dissidents.

A sickening suspicion hatching in her mind, she demanded, "Where are the objectors now?"

Linda lifted sad eyes to meet her gaze. "The surviving population was removed to another part of the planet. That's all we were told. The Directorate picked the location, but the coordinates are being kept secret."

"The surviving population?" Olivia echoed. "What did they survive?"

"The island. After five years, people began dying. It turned out they'd been poisoned by the chemicals in the soil. By the time our scientists had figured that out and come up with an effective broad-spectrum antitoxin, ninety percent of the objector population was beyond help.

"According to the official records, none of them were supposed to have been there that long. After a year, two at most, they should have been relocated to one of the new colony worlds. But there was a terrible accident, and the Directorate had to cancel our colonization program."

"According to the official records," Olivia repeated. As a former politician, she'd used that phrase often enough to know how empty it was, and at the same time how opaque. From the look on her face, Linda knew as well. "And no one thought to evacuate these people as soon as they began falling ill?"

"The island was under quarantine until it could be determined whether or not the sickness was contagious," Linda replied. "At least, that's what people were told at the time."

"According to the official records," Olivia said again, a little more harshly. "The Terrans have been on the island for about five years. Are they going to begin to die too?"

Linda gasped. She looked genuinely shocked. "Of course not, *minona*. Every Terran refugee received an injection of the antitoxin at the spaceport on arrival. Administered before exposure to the chemicals, it's one hundred percent effective."

"Really? Or just according to the official records?"

Linda sank into wounded silence and remained there for the rest of the journey home.

Meanwhile, Olivia was processing what she had learned. In her experience, nothing was completely effective. There was always a margin of error. Carlos Calvera had died of an inoculation within a year of settling on the island. If his blood test results were being suppressed, then perhaps he hadn't been the only one to die this way. In any case, Olivia doubted whether quoting statistics to Isabela would quench a grieving sister's thirst for justice.

When the bullet car stopped at the Forrand residence, Olivia went directly to her bedroom and plugged the mini-decrypter into the light screen on the wall.

This time, the face that appeared was Dennis Forrand's. It, too, was just an image and could easily be counterfeited, but she was too angry to care.

"Well?" grumped the face. "You called *me*, Juno. In trouble already?"

"I've learned some more about the Directorate. Now I'm thinking that death may be too good for them."

He chuckled. "I agree. So does every other Stragori who was born and grew up on Earth. It's ugly behind that curtain. Unfortunately, there is no longer any way to cause the Directors physical suffering. The best we can hope for is to delete them permanently from the servers."

"What about backups? Gervais told me that the Directors who wished to live had stored copies of themselves off-site. Can you find out where that is?"

"I can try. Contact me again in a couple of days for an update." A second later, the image pixelated and dissolved into darkness.

Olivia's plan was still nascent, but little by little, it was firming up in her mind. Take out the backups first, wherever they might be. Then destroy the Directorate's dedicated, supposedly hack-proof server and get the hell off-world. Their escape route would have to be carefully mapped — with the traffic-controlling AI disabled, the transit grid on the mainland would be out of commission as well.

She hoped there was a contingency plan in case of a computer failure. Bullet cars shot through those tunnels, crossing paths with split-second accuracy. If the cars couldn't all be stopped at once, people would die in a rapid-fire sequence of high-speed collisions.

That would be unfortunate. After all, the whole point of her plan — of her even being on Stragon — was to avoid bloodshed.

———— 《》 ————

Two days later, Olivia returned to the island. Now that she knew the mini-decrypter functioned as she'd been told — and that the Directorate had other ways to track her — there was no longer any point in leaving it with Security at the ferry terminal. However, as she passed the counter staffed by two uniformed officers, one of them yawning with boredom, she couldn't help wondering: Why would a dozen lockers need to be watched by personnel on site when the area was already bristling with surveillance technology?

Olivia added this to the growing list of questions at the back of her mind. She waved pleasantly to the guards in case she needed to chat them up later. Then she hired a different vehicle than before and let it carry her to Angeli and Isabela's apartment building.

Isabela served her something that looked and smelled like java. In answer to Olivia's inquiring glance, she explained, "Angeli found this on the mainland. Apparently, some of the Terrans who have moved there are maintaining gardens for bartering purposes, using seeds they brought from Earth. One of them is growing java plants."

Olivia frowned. She certainly appreciated the hospitality. However, "Which of your most precious belongings did you have to part with in exchange for this treat?"

A pause, then, "A paper-and-ink edition of *Frankenstein*, by Mary Shelley. It wasn't a great sacrifice. The book carried sad memories for me."

"Speaking of sad memories," said Angeli, "we finally found Vikram's report yesterday, and it raised a lot of questions." She handed her playback device with the datawafer in it across the table to Olivia. "As you can see, he measured the depth of the soil at various locations on the island..."

"'...and struck a hard, flat surface that was too smooth to be natural rock,'" Olivia said a moment later, reading from the screen. "'It could not be drilled or dissolved by anything at my disposal and consequently could not be further analyzed. But by extending my sampling area, I was able to establish its dimensions.'" She read silently for a few seconds more, then glanced up, her eyes wide with sudden comprehension. "It sounds as though he's describing a roof. And if there's a roof, there has to be—"

Of course! What better place to store an untouchable server array than inside a bunker on a gulag surrounded by water, buried under half a meter of toxic waste?

That explained what she'd noticed about the ferry terminal as well, Olivia realized. The two-way walls, the Security officers on duty — it all made sense now.

"If there is a building beneath that roof, then there must be another entrance on a lower level," she declared. "A service door, maybe, for receiving supplies."

"If it were up to me, I'd put it in the Wilderness Zone," said Angeli, visibly warming to the idea.

"There are caves along the foot of the bluff on the south shore," Isabela put in. "I do not know how deep they are, but it's possible that one of them could be concealing an entrance."

Everyone paused for a breath.

"I suggest we surveille the area to see whether anything is delivered," Angeli said. "Then, if we're right, we'll also know which cave to explore."

"I can do that," Isabela told them. "Before Vikram died, I used to come and go all the time in the Wilderness Zone, sometimes after dark."

Angeli put a hand on her arm. "Bela, are you going to be all right there on your own?"

"I'll be fine, *chica*. It is you that have to be careful."

———— «» ————

"Your contact is correct. There is a bunker under the island," said Dennis Forrand's image on the screen in Olivia's bedroom. "According to the archives, it's been there for thousands of years. The bunker, not the island. The island came much later, built up around the bunker to conceal it, at a time before Stragon had 'clean' industry. Hence, the toxic chemicals in the soil."

"Is that where the Directorate is? Inside the bunker?"

The image let out a sigh. "None of my sources are willing to commit themselves by answering that question, so all I can tell you is this: if I were Gervais, that is where *I* would be. Considering by how much the bunker predates the existence of the Directorate, I would also wager that there's much more down there than just a collection of servers in a clean room. Unfortunately, there's only one way to find out anything for sure, and it's not going to be easy."

"We're already working on that problem. What about the offsite backups that I asked about earlier?"

"I've located multi-level server installations on all three of the major land masses. Unfortunately, none of them are as thoroughly firewalled as they'd need to be in order to protect the Directorate's uploaded consciousnesses."

"So Gervais was lying to me?"

"Maybe. Or maybe there are installations that only a handful of people with above top secret clearance are aware of. Or perhaps, in this case, 'offsite' is code for off-world. This may or may not be relevant, but a friend of mine on the Directorate's staff was able to learn that a diplomatic shuttle departed a while ago under cover of darkness after taking on some sort of mysterious cargo. Only the pilot was aboard."

"Did your friend give you any specifics about this flight?"

"The flight plan was classified above my friend's security level. But he noted that another member of the Directorate's staff was transferred off-world without warning that same night and hasn't been heard from since. A fellow named Vinson Trager. And before you ask, he's a qualified shuttle pilot with diplomatic envoy status. It's only a guess on my part, but he could easily have transported a server backup through the defense grid unchallenged."

So, it was entirely possible that Olivia's plan had already been foiled. Wonderful.

"Thank you, Dennis," she said tightly. "I think we can take things from here."

"So do I. Good luck, my dear."

⸺ ‹‹›› ⸺

One week later, Olivia was back on the island.

Isabela had completed her part of the mission prep. She had concocted and aerosolized the knock-out drug as requested, creating three spray containers, one for each of them. She had also identified an inlet on the southern shore of the island, where a small craft had offloaded three large packing containers two nights earlier.

Meanwhile, Angeli had enlisted the assistance of one of the other EIS cells to assemble several small devices for her: two EMP generators and four heat bombs. A frankenstein of Terran and Stragori technologies, each one was half the size of a commpad and, as she explained to the other two women, could be set to detonate on a time delay.

"Are you sure these will work?" Olivia asked, picking one up and turning it over in her hand.

Angeli took it from her and put all six devices into her own bag. "They'll do what they were designed to do," she replied briskly. "Whether they'll accomplish what you want is another issue." Under Olivia's questioning gaze, she placed the bag with the other two beside the door, then continued, "We have no idea what we're going to find inside that bunker, but I'm assuming it's current Stragori technology.

"The best way to corrupt a database, Terran or Stragori, is with a strong electromagnetic pulse. If the bunker is EMP-shielded, the servers might not be. But just in case they are, we can plant the heat bombs to take out the power supply and control consoles as well. The data will remain intact but unreachable, and the chaos and confusion should last for a while, giving us a chance to escape. Look, I know it's not perfect," she bristled, "but it's the best I could do with the intel I had."

"I know," Olivia assured her. "That's all anyone can ask."

Isabela had been looking out the window. She turned and told them, "It will be dusk soon. When the sun touches the horizon, we leave."

At Isabela's insistence, Olivia was wearing a mismatched combination of garments, half of them belonging to Angeli. It was a good thing they would be traveling in near-darkness, she reflected. Every item she was wearing would look gray or black. Even the color of her skin would be disguised by the hood attached to her jacket and the long sleeves and trousers that swathed every possible bit of her body. "Ouf! I'm drowning in fabric," she complained.

"Better that than what the plant life out there will do to you," Isabela told her. "On Earth, in The Flats, there are certain flora with the word 'poison' in their names. Poison ivy, poison oak, poison sumac. In the Wilderness Zone, every growing thing is poisonous, potentially lethal. So, you must not touch anything with your bare hands. Always wear gloves, and make sure you tuck your sleeves into them, to protect your wrists."

"It's time," Angeli cut in. "Bela and I have devices that should jam up the securecams between here and the gates. Let's go."

Moving stealthily from shadow to shadow, the three women negotiated the five-block route to the edge of the district. Then they walked double-time to the first gate, hugging the post as they sidled through it. Isabela led the way to the second gate and past it into the Wilderness Zone, where they stopped for a "bare skin check". Seeing by the light of hand-held glow-rods, they then proceeded into the woods. Half an hour later, they had reached the bluffs above the coastline.

Isabela hunkered down and pulled something cylindrical out of her pack. She put one end of it up to her eye, then turned and peered through it, down the shore to their left.

To see what, exactly? The area below them was pitch dark and the glow-rods had limited range. Olivia heard the sibilant mutter of waves breaking below them and couldn't help wondering how Isabela planned to get the three of them safely down there from this ridge.

"Have a look," Isabela urged, placing the cylinder in Olivia's hand.

She complied and saw clearly the stretch of beach, the water seeming to breathe beside it, and the gnarled and pitted rock surface that rose at its back, all appearing bathed in an eerie orange light.

"The Stragori call it 'night sight'," Isabela explained. "It's actually a coating applied over a regular glass surface. Angeli came across the formula in one of her restricted files."

Which probably meant the Directorate knew what they were up to, and what they would need in order to accomplish it. Wonderful, Olivia thought glumly.

Well, that answered one of her questions. There was still the matter of getting themselves down and back up again.

As though reading her mind, Isabela said, "Point the glass to the right, along the top of the bluff, and tell me what you see."

Again, Olivia did as she was told. In the middle of the grassy fringe at the edge of the drop sat a brown lump with a disturbing resemblance to the feces of a very large animal.

"It's ... a pile of something," she said.

"It's a climbing ladder. Vikram made it for Moe," said Isabela, "and we are going to use it to access the beach."

"Will it hold our weight?" Angeli asked.

"It should," came the response. "It is securely anchored at the top. Just to be safe, however, we'll need to climb it one at a time."

Despite its off-putting appearance when lying on the ground, the ladder had been cleverly engineered. A single length of reinforced rope with sturdy loops pulled from it to act as hand- and footholds, it wasn't the easiest thing to negotiate. Nevertheless, it got all three of them to the foot of the bluff, and as it hung over the edge, it was dark enough to blend into the background when seen from the water.

"They carried the supplies into the fourth cave from this end of the beach," Isabela told them in a whisper. "But it might not be the only way in."

"We'll have to be careful," Olivia agreed.

Keeping their backs to the rock face, they moved along in single file, testing their footing with each step and holding their breath as they scurried past the first three cave openings. At last they arrived at number four.

"Knockout spray," hissed Olivia. Isabela dropped her pack in order to distribute the canisters, then shouldered it again.

Cautiously, they entered the cave mouth, senses on high alert, spray cans at the ready. But alarms were already going off at the back of Olivia's brain. There was something in the air, something familiar that she couldn't quite identify, like a name that she was struggling to put to a face she recognized.

All at once, she recalled where she'd experienced the sensation before.

"Stop!" Olivia commanded them, bringing everything to a halt. "Have either of you touched the walls yet?"

"Not yet," said Angeli.

"Nor I," Isabela replied. "What are you thinking, *chica*?"

"The Stragori have advanced holographic technology," she said tautly, "and it feels just like this. These rock surfaces could be an illusion. Someone could be watching us right now. And if so..." With sudden decisiveness, she shrugged out of her pack, took a long stride deeper into the cave, and declaimed loudly to the air, "Listen up, people! We know you're here, and we know why you're here, so you may as well drop the disguise and talk to us."

Behind her, Angeli and Isabela froze in place. For the next few seconds, they were immersed in a silence so thick and heavy that they could practically feel it pressing against their skin. Then, with a sound like static, the cave pixelated and dissolved, leaving behind a large room made of metal, with a glowing domed ceiling. The entire innermost wall consisted of a pair of featureless sliding doors. Hissing ominously, they slowly parted, releasing a shaft of bright light into what was clearly an antechamber of some sort.

Olivia's legs were shaking. They wanted to turn and run back to the beach. But she'd issued a challenge, and now she had to see it through.

I'm a Forrand. I stand my ground, she reminded herself sternly.

As the women stood staring at the opening, three beings emerged from the inner room. They were short and stocky, with gray skin, beaklike mouths, and large hairless heads. All three were clad in shiny, one-piece garments. Olivia had only ever seen such creatures in news feed images, but she recognized the race immediately.

So did Isabela. "*Madre!*" she breathed. "Those are Thryggians."

The aliens took a step forward.

"You appear surprised. But you said you knew we were here?" one of them chirped.

"We knew *someone* was here," Olivia replied, savagely bringing her voice under control. "We just weren't expecting it to be you."

"You say you know why we are here," piped up a second alien. "But we do not know why *you* are here."

Olivia paused, selecting a safe response. Meanwhile, the third Thryggian produced a wand of some sort and pointed it at each of the women in turn. Then he (it?) turned to the other aliens and chittered at them for a moment.

"You are from Earth. Who else have you told about this place?" demanded the first alien.

Olivia's thoughts were racing. Which would be more dangerous? Saying that no one else knew? Or saying that everyone else knew?

Before she could speak, Isabela declared, "We are not sure how many others know about you. But my mate was murdered because he stumbled onto your secret. That is why *I* am here, to see for myself what someone decided my husband's life was worth sacrificing to protect."

Unexpectedly, the aliens' arms burst into spastic, fluttery motion. "They are killing? No, no," chattered the first Thryggian, and the second chimed in, "That is wrong. It cannot be."

"Well, it's happened," Angeli broke in angrily. "And it will probably happen again. If we could figure things out, so can others. How many have to die just to keep your presence on this world a secret?"

"This is terrible. What can we do?" chirped the second alien.

It wasn't addressing the women, but Olivia felt compelled to answer anyway. "You can help us mend the rift in Stragori society by showing us where the Directorate is stored."

"Then you can leave Stragon," Angeli added.

Forming a huddle, the aliens chirped and chattered excitedly at one another for several long moments. When they turned back to face the intruders, it was clear which Thryggian was the leader.

"We cannot leave. We are the observers. The experiment must continue. It is all that protects the Humans on this world now, from the Great Council," it explained, the skin of its head visibly pulsing.

"Experiment?" murmured Isabela. "Do you know what this alien is talking about, *chica*?"

Unfortunately, Olivia did. "I've seen a lab report written in Thryggian. It dates back thousands of years. In that language, Stragori means 'control group'."

"A control group exists to show what would have happened if the experimental group had not been treated," Isabela said.

"Or, in our case, interfered with," Olivia added grimly.

"So, the Stragori are us if we'd just been left alone?" said Angeli. "And the Humans of Earth were experimented on? All of us? For thousands of years?" A storm was brewing on her face and in her voice. Her hands were curling into fists at her sides.

"Why do you need to see the Directorate's server?" asked one of the aliens.

Olivia looked it straight in the eyes and replied, "To destroy it. The Directors have chosen death as the only way to heal Stragori society. Since they cannot delete themselves, I have been tasked with corrupting their programs in order to avert a civil war."

"You were told this?" said the Thryggian leader. "It is a lie."

"How do you know that?" Angeli demanded.

"We observe all Stragori, including those in the Directorate. Any Director wishing to die can move into a designated compartment of the server. We monitor and clear it every eight days."

"Well, you can't be observing very closely," said Olivia, "because it was a Director who gave me this assignment, and everything he said was backed up by a senior member of his family."

Isabela laid a cautioning hand on her arm. *"Chica,"* she said softly, "are you quite certain the person you were speaking with was a Director?"

In that moment, every suspicion Olivia had had since landing at the spaceport slammed into her stomach at once, driving a sour taste up into her throat. "No. No, I'm not," she admitted. "I've been played so many ways since arriving on this world that I'm not sure what to believe anymore."

There was another huddle, and another spate of chatter by the Thryggians.

When they'd finished, the leader turned to face Olivia and chirped, "We will show you to the Directorate to find the truth. This way, please."

Exchanging wary glances, the three women followed the aliens into the bowels of the bunker. At the end of a circuitous, featureless hallway sat a metal slab of sliding door. One of the aliens pressed its hand to the wall and chittered a password, and the door moved ponderously out of the way.

Olivia stepped into a room that was more like an aquarium display. Three of the walls were transparent panes holding back some sort of aqueous material, and suspended in it she saw numerous small … jellyfish?

"Where is the server?" she asked.

"This room is the server," a Thryggian replied. "Each node contains the consciousness of a single Director."

"Are these— Are they inside living creatures?"

"Living, yes, but not sentient. Just as your brain is physically transported by your body, each Director now moves through the hyperconductive fluid of the server by means of an organic node."

"This is old technology on Thrygg, but it is compatible with what the Stragori have developed," said another of the aliens. "Until they perfect their programming, it will need to be supported herewise."

"Which Director gave you your task?" asked the Thryggian leader.

"Gervais Forrand," Olivia replied.

"A recent addition," supplied another of the Thryggians.

As Olivia watched, the third alien opened a panel in the wall beside the door and thrust a hand inside. A moment later, a round pedestal rose from the floor in the middle of the room, stopping when it was about a meter in height.

"Contact him," the leader instructed the second alien, who then busied itself with a strange-looking array that had appeared in one corner of the room.

A moment later, all eyes were drawn to the top of the pedestal, where a three-dimensional figure had materialized. It looked solid enough to be real, but this fearful child — ten years old at most — couldn't possibly be Gervais Forrand.

"What is that?" Olivia demanded.

"It is a memory. This Director is still adjusting to his current state," said the leader. "For the first hundred years, it is difficult to focus on the present. But if you speak to him, he will answer."

"Can he see me?"

"Only if we project your image into the hyperconductive fluid, or if it is already in his memory. This will be a test of his memory."

"So, if it was really Gervais that I spoke to earlier…?"

"…then his consciousness will have a visual record of you. Elsewise, he will hear you but be blind."

Summoning her courage, Olivia called out, "Gervais Forrand!"

At the sound of her voice, the image shifted. Now it showed them a man near the end of his life. Pale, deeply wrinkled skin hung at his jowls. Wisps of white hair barely covered his mottled scalp. "Who is calling me?" he demanded, his image appearing to gaze around the room.

"Olivia Townsend. I'm Gilles and Linda Forrand's great-granddaughter."

"Gilles and Linda," he repeated. The image shifted again, becoming more recognizably the man she had seen on the light screen. "Gilles and Linda are on Earth. What is your name again?"

"Olivia Townsend. Linda says I look just like you," she declared. "Do you see the resemblance?"

His eyes glazed over. "No. It's too dark here." His features went slack. "If she says so," he sighed. A second later the man was gone, replaced by a boy who looked to be in his early teens. He was staring directly ahead with an expression of gleeful anticipation on his face. "This is going to be fun!" he exclaimed.

The Thryggian leader gestured to the alien at the array, and with an electronic sizzle, the image dissolved.

"The Gervais Forrand that I spoke to was completely focused on the present, very logical and persuasive," said Olivia. "And he was on a light screen, interacting with Gilles and me." She turned apologetically toward Angeli and Isabela. "It was a con. I should have known better."

"Then you will not be destroying the server?" chirped one of the Thryggians.

Angeli's gaze hardened. "That depends. Are you going to let us leave?"

The Thryggian wrung its hands. "We are scientists. We observe. We monitor. We do not interfere. And we do not imprison," it maintained. "We ask only one thing."

"Don't worry," Olivia assured it. "We're used to keeping secrets. Yours will be safe."

The alien leader turned to Isabela. "We regret the loss of your mate. If we were suddenly reduced to two, we would be stricken with grief. In a paired society, the sadness must be much more. We will carry yours with us for the rest of our days."

Tears shining in her eyes, she replied, "Thank you."

———— «◊» ————

They still had a problem.

The journey back to Angeli and Isabela's apartment had gone relatively smoothly. They'd scrambled up the climbing rope with only a couple of near-mishaps, and, to Olivia's surprise, had managed to find their way back out of the Wilderness Zone without incident. Isabela had then led them quickly along the paved streets of the district, picking the shortest route to the quadplex.

After removing their protective garments, the three women had stared mutely at one another for several heartbeats. Normally, an operation would have been followed by a debriefing. Tonight that had been unnecessary. It was fortunate, because Olivia doubted whether she would have believed what had happened if she hadn't been there herself.

There was no way any of them would be able to sleep that night.

At last, Isabela had broken the silence. "I think I would like some tea," she'd said, and had gone to the kitchen to make a pot of it.

Now they sat in the living room, sipping from cups of dark, strong brew. Angeli and Isabela were chatting quietly at one end of the sofa. Meanwhile, Olivia slouched in an armchair, mired in thought.

She had been betrayed. Again.

Whatever had possessed her to come to this world? What arrogance or half-baked idealism had convinced her that she, of all people, could make a difference here? Did Olivia even dare to go back to Gilles and Linda's house, knowing what she now knew about the Directorate, and about the impostor who'd passed himself off to her as Gervais Forrand? How could she look either of her great-grandparents in the face again without wondering whether they'd helped him to trick her? And whether they'd do it again?

Gilles had called her a child, and he'd been right — the political power games she'd learned to play on Earth had done little to prepare her for the cold war being waged on Stragon.

"They said it was an experiment and they never interfered," Isabela was pointing out. "But if they have linked their server to the ones the Stragori are using in order to compensate for flawed Stragori programming, is that not interfering?"

It was blindingly obvious now to Olivia that the Forrands were undeclared radicals, conspiring with person or persons unknown to murder the entire Directorate. But who was using whom? Dennis Forrand had been opportunistic as hell back on Earth. Linda had seemed anxious to build a new world order and hadn't hesitated to go behind her husband's back. That the Forrands hadn't become powerful on this world by "falling into line" was a gross understatement. Scheming and backstabbing were apparently written right into the family's DNA.

And Olivia shared part of it. Once she'd shown her mettle by carrying out an act of mass murder, Linda and Gilles had promised to introduce her to her cousins.

Angeli's raised voice dragged Olivia back to the moment. "So, the Stragori have had this consciousness-uploading technology for centuries. By now they must think it works perfectly, when in fact, the Thryggians have been secretly plugging the holes in the Stragori's programming. They've been using Thryggian technology to safeguard the Directors, while fooling the Stragori into thinking they're more advanced than they actually are. That's not just interference, Bela. That's cheating."

"No," Olivia cut in, "it's protection. You heard what the Thryggian said. They have to ensure that the experiment continues because as long as the Stragori are a monitored 'control group', no one is allowed to interfere with them, including the Great Council."

"But they did not say they were protecting the Stragori," Isabela reminded them. "They said 'the Humans on this world'. To me, that means the Terrans as well."

"Including us?" Angeli returned. "Are *we* allowed to interfere? Because if the objective of this op is to destroy the Directorate, it seems to me the only way to accomplish it is to take out the bunker."

"And betray the Thryggians," Olivia added bleakly. "And end the experiment, and with it any protection Stragon has enjoyed from the Great Council. I'm aborting the operation. We can't do it."

Angeli cursed under her breath. "So basically, we're right back where we started, but with more intel and a lot more questions."

"And a half-dozen or so devices that we'll have to either use or destroy," Olivia added.

"Hmm." Angeli deliberately wrapped both her hands around her teacup. "If Vikram was killed by Stragori to keep the existence of the bunker a secret, then it's a safe bet that whoever is impersonating Gervais also knows about it. That's probably why he wants violence to break out on the island. It makes it a lot easier to blame the Terrans when the server containing the entire Directorate gets destroyed. Meanwhile, the ones who have backed themselves up can step in and take control, with Gervais as their leader."

"But we are not going to destroy the bunker," Isabela reminded her.

"Which will smack Gervais off something fierce," said Angeli. "Well, if we're going to ruin his plan, let's do it right. Let's scramble or blow up a couple of servers on the mainland that *might* contain a Director or two, then get ourselves off-world before the dust clears. We'll need to coordinate our timing with Novak's, though, since he's arranging the extraction."

"He can't," said Olivia.

Isabela nearly choked on a mouthful of tea. "What? What are you talking about?"

"The timing will be too tight. We're here, he's there, and it takes too damn long to communicate with Earth."

"So you're saying we're screwed?" Angeli said flatly.

"No. There's an alternative. Daisy Hub is less than three days away, with access to both intel and transportation."

"How sure are you that your brother can help us?" Angeli asked.

Olivia debated with herself for a second, then swallowed a sigh. She was no longer the Chief of Intelligence. Drew's new role in the organization was not for her to reveal. "He's one of us. He has an EIS decrypter, so we should be able to communicate directly with the Hub. Angeli, you're the coordinator of the original mission. Would you set that up, please?"

The other woman gave her a startled look, then replied, "Of course."

"We still have to locate the servers on the mainland, *chica*."

"Leave that to me. Once I've identified our targets, we'll split up and attack them simultaneously."

"I have a better idea," said Angeli. "Neither one of you knows your way around the mainland the way I do. Let me plant the devices, setting them all to go off at the same time. Then I'll rendezvous with you at the extraction coordinates."

Olivia was too tired to argue. "All right. Just promise me you'll be careful."

"Always."

Chapter Nineteen

On Earth

The man who strolled through the storefront door of Securi-Tech Security Solutions was tall and thin, with graying hair that lay in fashionable curls along the back of his neck. His dark brown suit was impeccably tailored, and he was looking around smugly, as though he'd just won the company in a game of chance and was already planning how he could profit from it.

This was going to be interesting.

The receptionist cleared her throat loudly to get his attention. "Can I help you, sir?" she asked.

His smile broadened at the sight of her. Hers became more forced.

"I'm looking for a Mr. Barry Novak," he said. "Tell him Hugh Bascomb is here to parlay."

Watching this on Eastman's monitor in the surveillance room, Novak caught the reference to pirates negotiating under a flag of truce and couldn't help smiling as well. Clearly, this mark believed they were equals, or at least both operating under the same set of rules. He had no idea what he had just walked into.

The receptionist said coolly, "Do you have an appointment, Mr. Bascomb?"

"No, but I'm certain he'll want to talk to me."

"Cocky son of a bitch, isn't he?" remarked DeWitt over Novak's shoulder.

"Pam knows what to do. She can handle him," Novak assured him.

"I'm afraid he's not in the building at the moment." She swiveled her monitor to show the visitor a screen titled "Appointments: B. Novak". It was filled with both real and fictitious meetings, the last one beginning at 7:00 p.m.

"Let me see that," Bascomb growled, grabbing the monitor before she could turn it back. "Lunch *and* dinner meetings? He's a busy man."

"A very busy man," she confirmed. "Perhaps it would be best if his assistant contacted you to arrange a mutually convenient time to 'parlay'."

He paused and stared at her, apparently reacting to the note of irony in her voice. To her credit, Pam met and held his gaze with an expectant one of her own. "Perhaps," he said at last. "But I don't deal with executive assistants. Tell Mr. Novak that I'll expect his personal commcall sometime this evening. And he'd better not disappoint me. What we need to discuss is time sensitive."

And with that, Hugh Bascomb wheeled and departed the way he'd entered.

"You gonna call him, boss?" DeWitt asked.

"Eventually. First, there's someone else I need to talk to. By the way, how is that data search coming along?"

"Ginza Hub's an interesting place. Space Installation Security had a detachment housed on the station for a while, but now they're based elsewhere. Away from temptation, I guess. Anyway, we found seventeen outstanding arrest warrants for crimes committed on Ginza Hub, mostly for trafficking in *pilenti*. That's the alien drug that supercharges whatever else you happen to be on, including prescription meds and even vitamin pills. Nasty stuff," the big man remarked with a shake of his head. "Apparently, the cops out there have their hands full just keeping the *pilenti* contained to the Hub. Imagine what would happen if any of it reached Earth."

"Did any fifty-year-old murder warrants pop up?" Novak reminded him.

"No, but there was a murder investigation of sorts about fifty years ago. A pimp was bludgeoned to death in his sleep. The killer turned herself in as soon as SIS began asking questions."

"Was there a tribunal?"

"No. She died of an overdose while in custody, and the case was officially closed. That's it. That's all we could find."

Unbidden, the memory of Patricia Chen's voice surfaced in Novak's mind: *"I can guess how it happened. I saw a lot of it when I was a kid."*

"Are you going to tell me why you wanted us to look into this, boss?"

Novak let out an audible breath. "Trust me, Zane, it's better if you don't know."

And probably better if she doesn't as well.

The message Novak transmitted to Patricia Chen later that day was succinct, and meaningful only to her: "He lied. No warrant. Kick some ass."

Her reply was equally cryptic: "Thank you. Expect fireworks."

———— «◊» ————

There was an art to setting a trap. The best ones were laid with finesse and subtlety. This one would have neither, but that was all right. As Hugh Bascomb himself had pointed out, they were fighting the clock. Patricia Chen had agreed to postpone the arrest of General Bascomb for the murder of Juno Vargas, but only by 36 hours.

After conferring with Chen and District Security Chief Melville Ridout, Novak had made an evening commcall to Hugh Bascomb's home. The conversation had been brief, conducted in short, sharp syllables. A time and place had been agreed upon for a meeting the following afternoon.

The next day, Novak was in his office at SecuriTech, performing a final check of his cams and mics before heading out to the rendezvous, when Naguchi burst into the room.

"Good! I've caught you," he said with obvious relief. "I have a question for you."

"Then make it a yes or no and ask it quickly. I've got no time for a drawn-out discussion right now."

"Knowing what you know about this man, did you really agree to meet him one on one in a public place?"

"I did. And knowing what he thinks he knows about me, I've taken precautions. Neither one of us is actually going to be alone. But only one of us is going to be recording."

"Don't underestimate him, Barry," Naguchi warned. "I've heard some things about him that should be deeply concerning."

"I've got this covered, Nayo. Trust me." Novak emphasized the last two words with a look.

And, wearing an expression that clearly said, *I hope you know what the hell you're doing*, Naguchi stepped aside to let him pass.

Forty-five minutes later, Novak's PV pulled into a parking spot in the gridded lot beneath the sports complex. He rode the lift to the main floor and stepped into a sleek, shiny space lined with light screens displaying looped images of male and female athletes in low-grav flight. Without exception, their uniforms were abbreviated to show off bulging muscles, and their expressions were strained to the point of contortion. The depictions were unnatural, their proportions even a little disturbing. But the only thought running through Novak's mind was, *I wonder how many of them were 'groomed' by Saul Stuebing?*

Glowing arrows embedded in the floor snagged his attention. His eyes followed them first, toward the refreshment lobby, where a blank light screen seemed to hang in the air. As he drew nearer, Novak realized that the screen was actually suspended from the ceiling on a slender metal rod. It was equipped with proximity detectors as well, for it flared to life as he approached, showing him that day's game schedule for each arena in turn.

Bascomb had specified Arena B. When it came up, Novak read: *Closed for technical inspection.* Ah. It appeared they would have privacy after all. Sort of.

The floor-arrow was flashing insistently at him now, urging him onward.

Not yet.

"Audio check?" he murmured

"We're reading you five by five," came the voice in his ear. "Ready when you are."

Novak arranged his face into an impassive mask and strode into the spectators' circle of Arena B.

Low-grav sports were played in tall cylindrical spaces enclosed by reinforced transparent plastiplex and surrounded by two types of seating: stationary rows that began at ground level and rose higher the farther away they were from the barrier; and groups of chairs enclosed in gondolas that moved vertically while swinging around on a track to follow the action. Before the Reformation, being able to book a gondola seat had been one of the many perks of being designated Eligible. Now, it was just an expensive way to watch a match.

It was also a private space in the middle of a public place, the ideal venue for a clandestine meeting. That was why the last thing Novak expected was to find Bascomb ensconced in the middle of the highest row of "cheap seats", with one foot propped against the seat-back in front of him. Casually dressed, he was reaching into a container of snacks and popping them one by one into his mouth.

Novak climbed up to the top row and lowered himself onto a seat one space away from him.

"They used to call this the nose-bleed section," Bascomb remarked conversationally. "Personally, I don't see it." Remaining comfortably slouched, he held his cup of potato crisps across the empty seat, offering to share.

"You're full of surprises, Mr. Bascomb," Novak said, waving it away. "Do you come here often to watch a technical inspection?"

The other man chuckled. "Sometimes. I own a piece of this place. Figure I ought to know how it works."

"You said you had something time sensitive you wished to discuss with me?" Novak reminded him.

Bascomb straightened in his seat. "Yes. I want to acquire your business."

Novak thought he had prepared himself to hear just about anything. Evidently, he hadn't. "Really! You want SecuriTech? Why?"

"I think you know why." When Novak failed to respond, he continued, "I've done some research. You started up with funding from Dennis Forrand."

"A loan that I have long since repaid. And you started your business with an inheritance from your grandfather. So what?"

"Don't pretend you're not aware of the feud between Forrand and my father."

"I knew there was bad blood, but I wouldn't call it a feud. That implies enmity on both sides. Dennis and Gilles are both dead, so I think the correct term for what your father has going on here is 'vendetta'. And, for your information, SecuriTech was never Forrand's company. It's mine. It's a sole proprietorship, without a board of directors that you can trick your way onto, and it's not for sale."

"I never said I wanted to *buy* it."

Now they were getting closer to what Novak wanted to hear. With effort, he kept his expression neutral and asked, "Then what? Did you think I would simply hand it over to you?"

"Not at all. But I'm going to make you an offer. And I think that once you've heard what I have to say, you'll not only accept it, you'll thank me for it."

"And I think you're delusional. But we're both entitled to our opinions, aren't we?"

A familiar reptilian smile crept across Bascomb's face. "I've been hearing rather dark things about you, Novak."

"And you believe everything you hear?"

"Oh, I'm much more thorough than that."

Bascomb pulled something resembling a miniature metal briefcase out of his pocket and turned it so that the other man could see the flashing green light on one end.

"That's an interesting looking gadget," Novak remarked coolly. "Are you saying that you've been recording this meeting?"

"No. But on the assumption that you came here wearing some cleverly designed surveillance gear, I've been jamming it. You see, for information to have power, it needs to be secret, and the information I've obtained about you is quite potent."

Now they would see whether Eastman's invention worked.

Mentally crossing his fingers, Novak leaned back in his seat. "Really! And what sort of information is that?"

"You didn't just get start-up funding from Dennis Forrand. You worked with him on other projects."

Novak shrugged. "Of course. Part of the loan was repaid with trade."

"And becoming Juno Vargas's fixer after Forrand died — was that part of repaying the loan as well? Don't deny it. You two were very close."

"It's no secret that she and I were friends. As for being her 'fixer', as you put it... Is there a point to this interrogation, Bascomb?"

The other man leaned in and lowered his voice. "What if I told you it was an interview?"

"Now you're saying you want to hire me?"

"No. I want you to take me on as a controlling partner in SecuriTech. Fifty-one percent of the business. While conducting my due diligence I couldn't help noticing what a perfect cover you've got for espionage activities."

Novak's heart leaped. Assuming a shocked expression, he exclaimed, "Espionage? Is that what this is about?"

"Why not? You've already insinuated yourself into people's homes and offices. That gear of yours works both ways. You can spy on them at will. Why not do it for profit?"

"Besides the fact that it's illegal, it would be a serious violation of our clients' trust. SecuriTech keeps them and their property safe. We only look in when an alarm goes off so we'll know who is needed on site."

"I'm sure that's what you've led them to believe, along with everyone who works in the various public buildings where you've installed your surveillance technology. How long do you think SecuriTech would survive if word got out that you'd been using illegally-acquired information to further your own agenda?"

"Long enough for me to prove that you're a damn liar."

"Mmm ... I wouldn't take that bet, Mr. Novak. I've got clout and very deep pockets. And everything I've done is within the letter of the law. Can you say the same? No need to answer that. Fortunately for you, I don't care about your past. However, others will, so it's in your best interests to accept my offer. Give me what I've asked for and your reputation will remain intact. And before we part company, I just want you to know that several weeks ago I placed a document with my advocate to be unsealed in the event that any harm comes to me. Do I need to tell you what it contains?"

Novak had to consciously unclench his jaw. "No. The wording is probably very similar to what's in *my* insurance policy. Just in case you decide to expedite matters."

As they both got to their feet, Bascomb advised him, "Think carefully about this. And remember that even though they couldn't hear our words, there were witnesses to this discussion. You know how to reach me with your answer. Don't wait too long."

It took every gram of his self-control, but Novak said nothing, just stared balefully at him for a moment and walked away.

Once back on the lift, he took a full breath, let it out slowly, and said to the air in the empty car, "Please tell me you heard all that."

"Every word, Mr. Novak," chirped the voice in his ear. "Chief Ridout says we've got enough to justify opening an investigation into all of Bascomb's business dealings. Good work! Oh, and we'll need you to return the electronic gear to HQ, including our prototype of the differentiating signal disperser."

So that was what Ridout had decided to call it. In order to keep everything aboveboard, the Chief had classified this operation as an authorized District Security sting and staffed it with his own officers. On the official record, all the surveillance technology Novak had worn had come from Ridout's department, including Eastman's jammer-jamming device. "Consider it a cost of staying in business," Ridout had told him when Novak had opened his mouth to object.

Nate hadn't been happy about it, but the Chief's offer was one Novak couldn't refuse.

So… District Security could have this prototype. Eastman would design another. It was all good.

——— «» ———

Turn him or terminate him. It was standard procedure whenever someone got in the way of an EIS operation. Except there *was* no EIS on Earth, not any more. That had left private citizen Novak with only one alternative: give

Hugh Bascomb enough rope to incriminate himself, make sure District Security was in on the operation, then trust Ridout to make it all turn out legal.

Just one problem. It wasn't enough.

Bascomb knew too much. The fact that he had been expecting an attempt on his life and had taken precautions to prevent it was a clear sign of that. And he'd been right — trust was an important part of SecuriTech's business. Even a manufactured scandal could send that part of Novak's life straight down the sewer, leaving him and the Warrior Kings right back where they'd started. No, he corrected himself, they'd be left where Forrand had warned him they'd end up if they turned down his offer.

Bascomb was too dangerous to let live. He needed to be silenced.

Unfortunately, if Novak and the Kings were to have a future after the EIS, they had to at least appear to be operating within the law. That meant murder was no longer in their toolkits, and ordering a hit was no longer in Barry Novak's purview. However, as he was driving back to SecuriTech after dropping off his cam and mics at District Security, he could feel Tomasz Novotny stirring and stretching inside him.

Tommy had never felt constrained by legalities. Maybe he could figure out a way to get this done.

Arriving at the office, Novak found DeWitt and Naguchi waiting for him in the clean room.

"It looked pretty tense for a while there, boss," DeWitt remarked. "Pretty tense where I was sitting too, with a couple of Bascomb's men staring at me the whole time."

"Yep. Hugh Bascomb is quite a piece of work. He's just as canny and manipulative as Dennis Forrand ever was, and that's saying something. I'm glad Security was backing us up."

"Speaking of which, I really wish you'd told me the rest of your plan, Barry," Naguchi scolded. "It would have saved me a lot of worry."

"There wasn't time. I did tell you to trust me," Novak reminded him.

"And everything turned out well?" said Naguchi.

Novak paused. "I don't know. Security is going to launch an investigation into Bascomb's business dealings. Based on our conversation alone, they can probably bring him up on a number of charges. What they can't do is keep him in solitary detention between now and his tribunal. He's got too much clout, as well as a whole battery of high-powered advocates working on his behalf. And someone like Bascomb can do us a lot of damage if he remains at large."

"So, I gather we're terminating him?" asked DeWitt.

"Can't. He's set up an insurance policy," Novak replied.

"Gentlemen, if I may make an observation?" said Naguchi. As all eyes turned toward him, the scientist continued, "The Bascomb family presents us with four targets. The general is about to be arrested by the High Council on charges of murder and treason. That's one down. Hugh Bascomb will shortly be arrested as well. Two down. Since he will not immediately be suspecting Barry of having betrayed him, it seems to me we have an opportunity here to cut him off and at the same time eliminate a third target by simply pointing Hugh in the direction of one of his brothers."

"Richard already has a motive," DeWitt pointed out. "His whole family hates him, and Hugh threatened to kill him."

"No," said Novak. "He may fit perfectly into a frame, but Richard's the only decent man in the bunch. The one we should be serving up to Hugh on a platter is Darren. Blackmail bait, remember?"

DeWitt uttered a throaty chuckle. "Three down and we keep our hands clean. I like it, boss. Never thought I'd hear it from a fine upstanding citizen like Dr. Chin here, but I like it a lot."

Naguchi gave him a disapproving look. "Clearly, I've fallen in with bad company."

"Maybe, but it's a good plan if we can make it work," said Novak. "Now all we need to do is convince Hugh Bascomb that Darren was the one who pulled the plug on him to Security."

"I'll get right on it," DeWitt promised him. "Oh, and by the way, a commcall came in for you earlier, on an open channel, from someone claiming to be the Chair of the

High Council. Pam told her you'd get back to her at the first opportunity."

Three days later, the InfoComm network was buzzing with news of a pair of high-profile arrests, and Novak was striding across the square in front of the District Administration Building. Patricia Chen was waiting for him on the bench where they'd first met. This morning she was holding two cups of java, one in each hand. She lifted one in invitation as he drew nearer, and gave it to him once he was seated beside her.

"Mr. Novak," she said, "thank you for agreeing to meet with me."

He took a sip and tasted just the right amount of creamer and sweetening. This boded well, he thought. Relaxing against the back of the bench, he told her, "You know I'm always available if you need me, Madame Supreme Adjudicator."

She paused. "Are you carrying one of those...?"

He pulled the device out of his pocket and let her watch him activate it. Then he placed it on the bench between them. "Now we can talk."

"Good! Because I have a business proposition for you."

"Oh?"

"Space Installation Security has a Covert Operations branch that works behind the scenes to troubleshoot dangerous situations on our colonies and hubs. Recent events have demonstrated to the High Council that we need a similar organization working confidentially for us here on Earth. It would consist of a group of operatives who are independent of the various Security forces, and who will be loyal to — and report only to — the members of Earth's highest level of government. You and your team have acquitted yourselves extremely well of late. And you're no stranger to this kind of work, as some of us are already aware. Therefore, I am authorized by the Council to make you an offer."

"You want me to head up a sort of Earth intelligence network?"

"That would be a good name for it."

"And we would be expected to do what, exactly?"

"Whatever the High Council needs you to do on-world in order to maintain the effectiveness and integrity of the government. The sort of thing you've done in the past for individuals such as Dennis Forrand and Juno Vargas ... and myself. Only you'll be doing it with our knowledge and our permission."

"And would we be paid for this service, Madame Supreme Adjudicator?"

"Operational expenses would be covered, of course. When not needed, you would continue to run SecuriTech as a profit-making enterprise and pay your employees' salaries out of company revenues."

"I have a relatively small staff right now. What you're describing would require me to hire a network of agents around the world. How am I supposed to afford that?"

"You can't, on what you're currently charging us for security surveillance. That's why we've decided to budget for a fifteen percent increase in SecuriTech's fees. We're also prepared to offer a further incentive: amnesty for any misdeeds committed in the past, and a conditional pardon for any that your operatives may be required to commit in the line of duty in the future."

Novak smiled inwardly. To Tommy Novotny, this was all sounding very familiar. "A clean slate, in other words. A fresh beginning."

"Yes, but only for those who sign on. And not all future crimes will be forgiven, just the ones we sanction," she warned. "Do we have a deal, Mr. Novak?"

"I'll have to confirm that all of my team are on board with this before giving you my final answer, but I believe we do, Madame Supreme Adjudicator."

———— «» ————

Back in the clean room, Novak downloaded his discussion with Patricia Chen onto a datawafer and played it for his second in command.

DeWitt's jaw dropped.

"Are you sure she meant you'd be pardoned for this too, boss?"

"Do you want to hear it again?" Novak asked.

"But you recorded a High Councilor without her—! Never mind," the big man said with a sigh.

"I was taking precautions, Zane, just in case it was a con. If it's not, there's no harm done."

"And if she finds out, she can claim we frankensteined it from a bunch of other recordings, just like Eastman did with the audio feeds from Darren Bascomb's place."

On that project, Nate had outdone himself, as far as Novak was concerned. By the time Eastman had finished intercutting words and syllables and adjusting the tones and cadences, Darren's voice had sounded completely natural. Anyone listening to the file would swear that the middle Bascomb brother was speaking to someone at District Security, offering to testify in front of a tribunal about Hugh's illegal business practices.

The original had ended up on Chief Ridout's InfoComm unit as an incoming commcall. A copy had been downloaded to a datawafer and delivered by a mole armed with a spot-jammer to Hugh Bascomb's office desk during the night. And because the file had been created on rogue technology, there was no way for anyone to trace it back to a source.

Interesting events were about to ensue. What form they would take was yet to be revealed. Ideally, it would be an attempt on Darren's life that would land Hugh in even deeper trouble than he was already in. But Novak would settle for keeping Hugh Bascomb too busy to interfere with SecuriTech until he was so thoroughly discredited that no one would believe a word he said.

"It will be all right, Zane. Trust me."

———— «◊» ————

The tribunals had been short and, as far as Novak was concerned, very sweet.

Chen wasn't the only high official Bascomb had been extorting. When it appeared the refiled murder charge wasn't going to stick after all, a number of his other victims came forward, determined not to let him slither free a second time. New charges were laid, with first-person witness testimony. The scandal sent all the news feeds into overdrive. The tabs practically burst into flames. General Bascomb got a thoroughly dishonorable discharge and a twenty-year sentence in detention.

Meanwhile, Hugh had taken the bait and hired someone to arrange an "accident" for his brother Darren. Attempted murder carried a penalty of only fifteen years in detention, but Novak was confident that Darren and Saul would find a way to keep him locked up for good, either aboveground or below it.

The sentencing hearings had been broadcast live. As he blanked the screen of his InfoComm unit and leaned back in his chair, Novak was smiling. He hadn't felt this relaxed in a long time.

Not that long ago, he wouldn't have given odds on him and his crew having much of a future. Now, thanks to his new friends on the Earth High Council, it was looking very promising indeed.

Chapter Twenty

On Daisy Hub

"I understand this was your idea?"

Townsend gazed from the Doc's stern face to the two bruised and battered beings sitting side by side in the triage area of Med Services. They'd definitely been in a fight … with each other.

Madeline had a broken nose and two black eyes. She was cradling what appeared to be a broken arm, and there was a line of nasty-looking puncture wounds on her other hand.

"Doc, is that—?"

"A Nandrian bite mark? Yes. Fortunately, I began synthesizing antivenin as soon as Moe came aboard. I administered it in time to save her hand. She'll have some residual numbness in her fingers, nothing more. But that was the least of her injuries. Between them, these patients have two broken arms, several broken ribs, and more scrapes, bruises, and shallow lacerations than I can count. I wanted you to see their condition before I began treatment so I could ask you: What the *hell* were you thinking, Mr. Townsend?"

"They both had issues to work out," he replied, realizing as the words left his mouth how lame they sounded.

Moe's reaction to hearing them was either a grin or a grimace. With that face it was hard to tell.

"So you thought it would be a good idea to put an angry Nandrian hybrid and an angry Human together and let them take their feelings out on each other?" the Doc scolded.

Wearily, Townsend asked, "Have you notified Rodrigues?"

"Not yet."

"Please don't," Madeline piped up. "I'll report it, and I'll take responsibility for it."

Townsend and the Doc turned together and stared at her.

"I was teaching him self-defense, and he kept holding back," Madeline explained. "So I ordered him to show me what he had. It was more than I expected. This was my fault."

"No, it was mine," Moe declared. "I was angrier than I realized, and before I knew it, I had lost control."

"You went *hartoon*," Townsend told him. "It was a very Nandrian thing to do."

With difficulty, Moe straightened in his chair. "I assaulted Constable Holchuk with deadly force, and I must take full responsibility for her injuries."

Madeline had to turn her whole body to look at him, wincing as she did so. "I wasn't exactly helpless, Moe. I got my licks in, so don't try to paint me as a victim," she warned him. "Next time it'll be *me* mopping the deck with *you*."

The Doc made a disgusted face. To Townsend she said, "Next they'll be claiming they both tripped over a loose wire. All right, Constable," she continued, addressing her patient, "I'll let you break the news to your commanding officer. Tell him whatever story you like. But not before I've put that arm into a regen unit."

As he left Med Services, Townsend was quietly congratulating himself. Moe and Madeline had bonded, just as he'd hoped. That was one problem taken care of. Now, to deal with the rest.

«»

"Is it my imagination, or have we begun collecting aliens?" said Ruby from the door of Townsend's office.

He blanked his screen, activated the privacy shield, and settled back in his chair. "You're not imagining it. By the time we're ready to move against the Great Council, there may even be a few more. Do you think it's going to be an issue?"

Pursing her lips, she eased herself onto one of the guest seats in front of his desk. "I don't know, Chief," she finally said. "So much has changed since the war. I'm not just talking about Daisy Hub. Earth's government isn't courting the approval of the alien races the way it was before. And it's going to be a lot harder for us to keep secrets from now on. Sooner or later, Earth's government is going to find out who's taken up residence on the station. Having Trager and Moe here makes it look as though we're choosing sides in the Stragori conflict. And Yorell Enne is a wanted fugitive. So you tell me: How many risks are you prepared to take for the sake of your new mission?"

"Is this you I hear worrying, Ruby? Or is it Dennis Forrand, speaking through you?" he countered.

Elevating her chin, she replied stiffly, "It's me. I sent Forrand my final report an interval ago." Reaching into a pocket, she placed her EIS decryption device on the desktop between them. "As you stipulated. You were right. You can't have your hands tied by the presence of a mole aboard the station, even if you know who it is. I told him that, and I also assured him that the future of the EIS was safe as long as you remained in command here. Now I'm wondering whether that assessment might have been a little premature."

He placed the device in his desk drawer. "I guess we'll both find out soon enough. I have a meeting with Yorell in half an hour. If she's the information source I'm hoping she'll be, keeping her on the Hub will be a risk worth taking."

Through the plastiplex wall of his office, Townsend saw Jason Smith step off the tube car and begin his shift at the main console. Now officially off-duty, Ruby got to her feet.

"I told you I'd always back your play, Chief, and I meant it. This is your call. But if things go wrong, we could all be fried before we've even had a chance to begin, so I really hope you know what you're doing."

I do too, Ruby.

About thirty-two minutes later, the Reyot force of nature arrived on AdComm. Yorell was clad in a dark blue robe that billowed behind her like a wind-blown sail as she swept from the tube car door to the entrance of Townsend's office. The word that sprang to his mind at the sight of her was "regal". This alien not only had the bearing of a queen, she also radiated the attitude of one.

"I'm ready to answer your questions, Mr. Townsend," she declared, taking possession of his guest chair as though it were a throne. "What part of the forbidden files would you like me to remember for you today?"

"What interests me at the moment is the treaty that we were discussing earlier. Were there other races besides mine that were excluded from it?"

"Just one in this arm of the galaxy," she told him, frowning. "The Praxt. The treaty was meant to end a war and ensure that there could never be another. The Praxt had remained neutral bystanders to the conflict. They objected to some of the terms of the treaty and demanded to negotiate an exception clause."

"Because the terms were so harsh?"

"And because the treaty lumped them together with those who had taken sides and participated in the battles. Apparently, that especially rankled them."

"I see. And how did the Great Council respond to their demand?"

"The Council stood fast. Since there could be no further negotiation, Praxim rejected the terms of the treaty outright and refused to sign it."

"But the other races did sign on."

"Yes, and as soon as the treaty had been ratified on all their home worlds, the Council issued a strongly-worded recommendation that member worlds trade only among themselves. One by one over the years, those worlds complied, until Praxim was cut off completely."

"That's it? The only punishment the Council meted out was a slow-motion trade embargo?"

"I've seen the records. Officially, there were no sanctions passed in Council against the Praxt. Unofficially, however, I have absolutely no doubt that punitive actions were taken." A pause, then, "The Praxt are no more, Mr. Townsend. Most of the race perished when an asteroid collided with their home world. A distant colony of them survived, but that world was later settled by members of another race. When the two cultures merged, the Praxt lost their individual identity."

That last sentence launched a shiver of recognition across Townsend's shoulders.

"You're saying that there are no Praxt left alive? That's a shame. I would have liked to hear their side of the story."

"No pure-blooded Praxt remain alive. They're all hybrids now. In fact, one of them accompanied me to your station," Yorell told him.

"Gorse Pirrit? He's Eggenali."

"The colony world was Eggenar," she confirmed, "and the Eggenali are a hybrid race, combining the Praxtan and Kularian genomes. The Eggenali place a high value on remembering the past. I believe you would find it quite instructive to sit down for a chat with Mr. Pirrit sometime."

"Thank you, Madame Enne. I think I will. Now, would you happen to recall what some of those harsh terms of the treaty involved?"

She paused, apparently to gather her thoughts. "Permanent disarmament, primarily. The treaty's stated purpose was to preserve the peace, so any weapons deployed during the war were completely and forever banned, and the technologies that had produced and powered them were outlawed. As a result, many societies were summarily stripped of all but the most rudimentary machines. This was especially hard for a race like the Kularians, who had been using psi energy for millennia and now had to discover alternative ways to generate power."

"And yet they all agreed to abide by these terms. Why?"

She gave a little shrug. "The war had stretched on for a long time. Their resources were depleted. Their people were exhausted. I cannot produce any proof of this, Mr. Townsend, but my personal suspicion is that they simply did not have the strength to resist the dictates of a neutral power determined to impose peace at any cost."

"Wait a minute. The Reyota were neutral, like the Praxt?"

"To all outward appearances, yes. But not like the Praxt. My ancestors were dedicated to profit, in its many forms. And war can be extremely profitable for those who don't take sides."

There was no need for her to elaborate that statement — Townsend was a former cop.

"One last thing for now, Madame Enne: Are the Reyota as influential on the Council now as they were back then?"

"I'm sure there are those who believe the Reyota *are* the Council. Every planetary government has an agenda, Mr. Townsend, and Reyi'it is no exception. Since I have not been home in several standard years, I'm afraid I cannot comment regarding the current political situation on my world. However, I can say this much with certainty: Fourteen independent member worlds have voting rights on the Council. Only one of those worlds is Reyi'it. Theoretically, the Council has the ability to defeat any motion the Reyota may bring before it, but in all my years as Prime Docent, I cannot recall a single instance when that has happened."

"So, unless there have been some drastic changes since the Corvou war, it's probably safe to say that the Reyota are still exercising control over the Great Council, only they're doing it quietly and behind closed doors," he summed up.

The Prime Docent let out a sigh. "And that will make them extremely difficult to expose. I hope you have a plan, Mr. Townsend, because I would dearly love to go home again."

"I will have, Madame Enne, never fear."

—— «» ——

The message from Stragon was brief, direct, and encrypted, and Townsend's jaw nearly struck his keyboard after the VICTOR code had transformed the text on his screen.

TWELVE TO BE EXTRACTED. PLEASE ARRANGE AND TRANSMIT PICKUP DETAILS.

If they were communicating with him directly, the situation had to be serious. He couldn't delay any longer.

The intercomm buzzed. "Mr. Trager is requesting your presence in the caf, Chief."

"Tell him I'll be there as soon as I can."

On arrival, Townsend saw Gorse Pirrit and Vin Trager sitting together at a table in the middle of the room, mugs of java cooling at their elbows. He took the chair across from them and said, "I understand you were looking for me."

Trager leaned forward and said in a lowered voice, "Yes. We believe we have found a solution for your problem."

Intrigued to know which of his many problems they were talking about, Townsend leaned in as well. "Keep talking."

"Word has reached me through diplomatic channels that you need to move about a dozen Terrans covertly from Stragon to Daisy Hub. That will require a ship that can slip through the Stragori defensive perimeter unnoticed," said Trager. "The Night Cloud is just such a ship."

"Word travels fast through your diplomatic channels," Drew observed, narrowing his gaze. "I just found out about it myself."

Trager said nothing, only gave him a faint smile and a helpless shrug.

"Mr. Pirrit, have you agreed to this? If not, please say so."

"I still have to discuss it with my mate, Mr. Townsend, but if she approves the mission, then you'll have your ship."

"Is there any reason to think she might not?" asked Drew.

"Just one: It will mean leaving Earth space. Like Yorell, we are fugitives, considered to be dangerous criminals by the Great Council."

Now Townsend's curiosity was truly piqued. "And what crime, exactly, are you supposed to have committed?"

"I modified this particular Night Cloud to use psi-driven technology. It's forbidden by the treaty. Eggenar never signed it, so on that world, psi energy is just another power source. However, I made the modifications while we were living on Kula'as."

"What treaty is this?" Trager wanted to know.

"It ended the last galactic war," Pirrit explained. "It's been in effect for several thousand years now."

"And it has remained unchanged over time?" said Trager.

"Unfortunately, yes, and it's being enforced just as rigidly now as it was back then," Pirrit replied bitterly. "Every one of its terms contains the phrase 'in perpetuity'. Every new generation is punished as if it had personally taken part in the war. And if one individual or a small group of beings breaks the treaty, their entire race is penalized. That was why Ixbeth and I had to leave Kula'as before the Great Council could discover what I'd done to the ship. Otherwise, half a million people would have paid a heavy price for it."

"Mr. Pirrit, if you'd rather not take this risk—"

"It's a small act of rebellion, Mr. Townsend. I ran away once, and it hasn't sat well with me. In full stealth mode, the Night Cloud is undetectable. Once Ixbeth agrees to go, we and it will be at your disposal."

⟨⟩

All right. Townsend had the transportation required for the extraction. Now he just needed to figure out where to send it. A map of the colony would be a good place to start.

His first stop was Deck C-1, where Gervais sat trapped inside his dedicated server. As O'Malley watched, shaking his head in disbelief, Townsend sat down at the attached computer and keyed in the beginning of a conversation.

Hello, Gervais. This is Drew Townsend.

MR. TOWNSEND. IT'S A PLEASURE TO HEAR FROM YOU. HOW MAY I BE OF SERVICE?

I need to extract a group of Terrans from Stragon.

THIS WILL BE A COVERT MISSION, I GATHER?

Yes.

ARE ANY OF THEM OPTIMIZED?

No.

THAT SIMPLIFIES THINGS CONSIDERABLY. IS IT IMPORTANT THAT THEY ALL DEPART TOGETHER?

Yes.

THE TERRAN COLONY IS ON AN ISLAND.

I know. Is there anywhere on it large enough for a shuttle to land?

THE BEACH, ON THE SOUTH SHORE, AT LOW TIDE. ONCE THE WATER HAS COMPLETELY EBBED, THERE IS A WINDOW OF TWO HOURS BEFORE IT RISES AGAIN. A VERTICAL-DESCENT CRAFT COULD TOUCH DOWN AND TAKE ON PASSENGERS, PROVIDED THE LANDING WAS CAREFULLY TIMED.

PROBLEM: HOW DO YOU INTEND TO AVOID DETECTION BY THE DEFENSE GRID? NAVIGATION SATELLITES ARE CONSTANTLY MONITORING THAT AREA.

Not sure yet. I'm working on it. Thank you for the intel.

O'Malley had paused his own work to follow these exchanges. He watched Townsend shut down the computer, then commented, "You're just going to take his word for it, boss?"

"Of course not. But I did tell him he would have to earn his keep by providing reliable information. Now I'm going to talk with our new Stragori liaison officer, to see whether Gervais is living up to his part of the bargain. In any case, for this op to succeed, we're going to need map coordinates and tide data, and we'll have to synchronize our chronometers and calendars as well."

The ratkeeper perked up. "You're not just testing him, then? It's a real op?"

"Yes. It's our first official extraction."

"You know, since the Nandrians won't be throwing victory parties on the station anymore, maybe we should celebrate something else instead. Like, every time there's a successfully completed operation we throw a party. What do you think?"

Townsend tossed him a grin. "Tell Nora my favorite cake is devil's food with vanilla frosting."

Chapter Twenty-One

On Stragon

Olivia was on the first ferry returning to the mainland the morning after their mission. As before, Linda was waiting to escort her back to the Forrand home.

"How was your visit with your friends, *minona*?" she asked.

"We had a lot to talk about. None of us got a wink of sleep," Olivia replied, pointedly stifling a yawn. "I think I'll be spending some time in bed today."

That was as much as she was willing to share. They rode the bullet car in uncomfortable silence. Although visibly disappointed, Linda did not pry, and for that Olivia was grateful.

Back in her bedroom, she plugged the mini-decrypter into the light screen to summon the image of Dennis Forrand.

He looked rumpled today, as though he'd been torn from sleep by the sound of his comm.

"What now?" he grumped. "I thought you were going to handle everything."

"I still am, but I need a bit more intel from your sources."

"Such as?"

"The servers on the mainland. How many, and where are they? And specifically, I want to know which one houses the AI in charge of traffic control."

His eyebrows rose. "This is your idea of 'a bit'?"

"Can you get the information for me or not?"

A pause, then, "Stay where you are, and contact me in a couple of hours."

The screen pixelated out.

Two hours was just enough time for a refreshing nap. When she plugged her device back in, what came up on the screen was not Dennis Forrand's image. It was a map with three locations marked. One of them sprouted an arrow pointing to an Anglo notation printed in block letters: MAIN SERVER–AI HERE

She captured it on her EIS commpad and transmitted the image to Angeli.

Angeli's response was immediate: I WORK DIRECTLY ABOVE MAIN TARGET. WILL INVESTIGATE.

It took all of Olivia's self-control to maintain comm silence after that. Unaccustomed to being a team player, she had to keep reminding herself that she had done everything she was supposed to. The problem was, she didn't know whether she had done everything she could.

The Terrans on the island weren't going to sicken and die. Not only had they all been inoculated against the toxins in the soil, but every square centimeter of ground in the residential districts had been either paved over or covered with fabricated turf. According to Isabela, the Terrans were self-sufficient in all respects but one — they could not grow food on the island. However, as long as the Stragori kept sending them edible supplies, the colony could survive there for many years to come.

As long as the Stragori kept feeding them.

All at once, pieces were falling into place in her mind, forming a picture so clear and sharp that just looking at it gave her a headache. The radical faction didn't only want the Directorate gone, they wanted the Terrans gone as well. And, just like Earth For Terrans back home before the war — like Juno Vargas, in fact, before the Reformation — they were prepared to go to any lengths in order to accomplish that. Including tricking Terran agents into committing an act of terrorism that would start a bloody war.

Olivia went cold all over. Pouncing on her commpad, she tapped out an urgent message to Angeli: ABORT MISSION! EXPLANATION LATER.

Then she called Dennis Forrand up on her light screen. He did not look happy.

"Olivia, I've given you all the information I have—"

She cut him off. "Tell me about the fringe radical groups. Which one would you say is the most likely to want to blow things up?"

The image's eyes widened briefly. "That would be Stragon First. It was started on Galandra — that's our largest land mass — by someone named Nestor Quan. About six years ago, he went to Earth space and got himself arrested. Word is, he died in custody, before a tribunal could be held."

She let out an impatient syllable. "You know damn well that's not true. Quan was alive and well at EIS Ops when I left to come here." Not waiting for his response, she went on, "Is there a chapter of Stragon First on the mainland?"

"As far as I know, they're trying to establish themselves here, but haven't had much luck. Security's tightened up considerably since the Terran refugees arrived."

"Dennis, I think they are established. In fact, I think they may have found a way to impersonate the Directors. I don't know how to prove it, but maybe you can mobilize your resources and do something about it."

Her commpad chose that moment to buzz. She picked it up and decrypted a message from Angeli: D.H. SAYS EXTRACTION FROM MOE'S BEACH IN TWO DAYS AT SECOND LOW TIDE. I'LL INSTRUCT EVERYONE.

They were on the clock. A ship was already on its way from Daisy Hub.

"I have to go, Dennis. Do whatever you can."

"Good luck, Granddaughter."

For just a second, she saw sadness in his eyes, as though he knew they would never speak to each other again. Then the screen went dark.

———— 《 》 ————

The following day, in the late afternoon, an explosion rocked the mainland. It shook the foundations of buildings and rippled the water of the strait. It cracked or collapsed the walls of a section of transportation tunnels, triggering an automatic shutdown of the entire system.

Olivia felt the floor shift under her feet. "Olivia wants to exit!" she cried, and raced through the door into the living room.

Linda was sitting on the sofa, staring at the light screen. Her face was the color of chalk. "What have you done, *minona*?" she whispered through bloodless lips.

"I haven't done anything!" Olivia wheeled and saw a scene of disaster on the screen, with a death toll crawling across the bottom of the image — 25, then 27, then 31. Blood-smeared bodies were being pulled from a pit of rubble, their skin coated with gray dust. Some of them appeared to be missing limbs. Olivia tried not to look at the faces of the victims.

"Which building was this?" she murmured faintly, her own voice sounding distant in her ears.

"The Directorate's office. The explosion happened on the tunnel level, where the main servers were located," said Linda. "Without a foundation, the whole building collapsed."

At the bottom of the screen, the numbers were still climbing.

Olivia's gorge was rising with them. "Olivia wants to enter!" She ran back to her bedroom and snatched up her commpad. She tried to reach Angeli. There was no answer.

"Olivia wants— wants to— exit." The words came out in a series of gasps. She had to repeat them before the door dematerialized to let her through.

"Linda, my friend works in that building. I have to get there. I have to find out—"

"—that she is dead? There is nothing there anymore," Linda told her woodenly. "I was afraid of this. Gervais must have realized you weren't going to follow his plan, so he went ahead without you."

The illogic of what she was saying stopped Olivia in her tracks. "Went ahead how? An uploaded consciousness couldn't have planted a bomb by itself. Someone — some flesh and blood person — must have done it, believing they were following the instructions of a Director."

"Of course, that's what I meant. But, child, Gervais *is* a Director."

"Yes, but that's not who we've been talking to. Trust me, Great-grandmother, I've met the real Gervais Forrand, and he is not capable of something like this."

Linda got to her feet, determination sharpening her voice. "It wasn't Gervais? Then who was it, *minona*? Who is responsible for this carnage?"

"I don't know, but I have suspicions. And yesterday, Dennis told me about a radical group called Stragon First."

"Yes, Dennis would know about radical groups," she said bitterly. "We will have to get to the bottom of this. And I am truly sorry about your friend, *minona*. But right now, the important thing is to get you somewhere safe."

Olivia's mental alarm went off. "Why?" she demanded. "Am I in danger?"

"Whether or not you actually caused the death of the Directorate, it was always Gervais's intention to blame a group of Terran agents—"

"—who would conveniently blow themselves up while trying to escape," Olivia recited from memory. "But it was going to be a decep … tion." Struggling for her next breath, she said, "He's not going to let us leave, is he?"

Linda's gray eyes turned as flat and hard as granite. "He'll try to prevent you. We'll just have to make sure he fails. Whoever this criminal is, he has picked the wrong family to toy with."

That evening, encrypted messages flew back and forth. Second low tide would be reached at the end of the twentieth hour, which at that time of year was shortly after dusk. The bullet car system was still unsafe to travel, but the ferry was running. Terrans who lived on the island but worked on the mainland were making their way to the docks in twos and threes, using whatever ground-level transportation they could find. Slipped in among them were the nine EIS operatives Angeli had been handling. Four of them lived on the mainland. With luck, they would all be on their way to Daisy Hub before fake-Gervais realized they were gone.

Anna Sturtevant was still among the missing. The explosion had occurred at the end of her shift, making Olivia hopeful that Angeli hadn't been in the building at the time. Of course, she might have been nearby. If she'd been knocked down by the shock wave and lost her commpad, that would explain why no one was able to contact her.

Still, she knew where and when the extraction was taking place. She would turn up to be taken to Daisy Hub. Olivia was certain of it.

The following day after lunch, Olivia emerged from her bedroom, carrying her packed bag. "I have to leave," she said. "I'm sorry. It will take time to get there, and I can't miss the rendezvous."

"And I'm sorry you won't be able to stay longer," Linda said with a sigh. "You're right. You must go. But not on foot. At least let me transport you safely to the mainland ferry terminal."

"You have a personal vehicle?"

"You keep forgetting, child. We're Forrands. We have everything we need, when we need it." Linda picked up a device and spoke into it. "Linda plus one wishes to enter the rooftop. Ready copter."

The air in the room shimmered for a few seconds as a stairway materialized in the middle of it, ending at a trap door in the ceiling.

"Come, *minona*. Your chariot awaits," said Linda, leading the way up the steps.

They emerged in daylight, at the edge of a pad. In front of them sat a more streamlined version of the Earth-designed aircraft used for flights between urban districts. Unlike those planes, the "copter" shone as though newly-made.

"It isn't as fast as a tunnel car," Linda explained once they were both seated inside it. "That's why we don't use it very often. And this model's programming isn't voice-responsive." She proceeded to press a series of keys in rapid succession. "But it will get us where we need to be, and that's all anyone can ask."

The copter rose straight up, turned in place, then found its bearings and flew. About twenty minutes later, it landed vertically on a pad surrounded by trees, a short distance from the ferry docks.

"You're here," Linda announced. She leaned over and gave Olivia a hug. "We're going to miss you, my dear."

"You've been very good to me, Great-grandmother. I'll never forget it."

"When it's safe once more, perhaps we'll see you again. You have family here. Who knows? You might even choose to make Stragon your home some day."

It wasn't likely. However, since nowhere really felt like home right now, anything was possible.

«◇»

Once more securely wrapped in protective clothing (her own this time), Olivia strolled with Isabela to the food kiosk that had been designated as the staging area. This was where all the EIS agents would meet up before heading to the beach as a group. Since the extraction was supposed to be secret and the Directorate had a way to track all their movements, it made sense to use a location where people naturally tended to gather. Normally, they would have traveled separately to the extraction coordinates. However, Isabela was the only one who knew her way around the Wilderness Zone well enough to guide them there.

None of the agents knew who Isabela was, but they all recognized Juno Vargas on sight. One by one, they spotted her in the crowd and made eye contact with her. Olivia kept a head count. Including herself and Isabela, eleven men and women were present. Angeli was not.

"We can't delay any longer, *chica*," Isabela whispered.

Olivia shook her head. "She's coming. I know it."

One of the men wandered over and asked quietly, "What's the hold-up?"

"Waiting for Anna Sturtevant," Isabela murmured in reply.

"She won't be coming," said the man. "There was a late news report. Three bodies were pulled out of a collapsed section of tunnel. One of them was identified as Anna Sturtevant."

NO!

Olivia felt as though she'd been kicked in the stomach. All at once the air was driven out of her lungs, leaving her gasping for breath. Then her legs dissolved beneath her. She would have fallen if Isabela and the male operative hadn't taken her by the arms and helped her to a bench.

He was confused. "I'm sorry. Was she—?"

"They were friends," Isabela explained. "This is a shock."

"One more reason not to form attachments in this line of work," muttered a woman's voice nearby.

At the back of her mind, Olivia heard Dennis Forrand's remembered voice, warning her about the price one paid to wield power. She'd heard his warning and taken the risk anyway. Thought she could handle anything. And she was right. She could. She just hadn't realized how much pain would be involved. Or that it would strike her at the worst possible moment.

She had no time for this. Channeling Juno Vargas, Olivia sat up straight and wiped away her tears with the back of her hand. Grieving could come later. Right now, there was a job to do. She had to be strong. Lives depended on it.

"Are you going to be all right, *chica*?" Isabela whispered.

"I'm fine," she grated. "Let's get going."

As before, Isabela led them in the waning daylight, through the gates and the woods, to the bluff overlooking the beach. She showed them how to use the rope ladder, then dropped it over the edge.

"It's awfully dark down there," said one of the women. "Are we sure this is the right place?"

Then a voice floated up to them, speaking in accented Standard: "Do you want a lift home or not?"

Someone laughed. The sound pierced Olivia's heart like a knife.

There was a ship on the beach. One by one, they clambered down the rope and headed for the light spilling from the hatch in its side. When it was Olivia's turn, Isabela gave her a long hug and said, "I'm staying here, *chica*. Carlos and Vikram are buried on Stragon, and my students are important to me. This is home now. Besides, someone needs to pull the rope back up and conceal it. You go now. I will miss you more than you know. But you have work to do elsewhere. Never forget where your power lies."

Reluctantly, Olivia left her and began the climb downward. The man who had broken the news of Angeli's death waited at the bottom to help her aboard the ship. She was grateful for the assistance.

The hold of this vessel was roomy enough. It had been outfitted with benches and blankets, and someone had stocked it with bins of food packets. Someone had also been counting passengers.

"That's just ten. There are supposed to be twelve of you."

Olivia glanced up and found herself face to face with an alien. Meeting aliens on Stragon didn't surprise her anymore. This one was male, she guessed, dark-skinned, with features that were almost cat-like.

"One didn't make it," she told him. "And one decided to stay behind."

"And where is Olivia?" he demanded.

"That's me," she said, startled.

"Good. I was instructed to bring you back whether you wanted to come or not." He sealed the outer hatch, then leaned over and pounded on the forward bulkhead a couple of times. Straightening back up, he turned and addressed the entire group. "The tide will be coming back in at any minute, so I'll be brief. My name is Gorse Pirrit. My mate and co-pilot is Ixbeth Minegar. This is a stealth craft, and she has just activated the cloak that will allow us to pass through the Stragori defense grid undetected. I understand that the Directorate has ways of tracking your movements. Well, you can relax, because no technology in the known galaxy is capable of penetrating an Eggenali dispersal shield. From this point onward, we and the ship are all invisible. Food is over there," he said, pointing. "Eat when you're hungry. Blankets and deck space are for sharing. Sleep when you're tired. For hygiene, go past the food and find the door on your left. If there's something else you need, or a problem you can't solve among yourselves, let me know. And in case you're in no mood for this three days from now, you're very welcome."

With that, he went forward to the cockpit.

Olivia closed her eyes and leaned back against the bulkhead, arms crossed, hugging her shoulders. Three days without privacy. It was going to be a torment. She was drowning in misery, this moment, these people, all pressing down on her like a leaden weight. Crushing her into place.

Robbing her of the will to breathe. How could she possibly be safe? How *dare* she be?

By the second day of the voyage, an emptiness had taken root inside her, darker and deeper than the vastness of space, and with it a fury she had no wish to control. She wanted to scream and break things. She wanted to tear a hole in the universe and watch it bleed. If a woman's power was fueled by rage, then Olivia Townsend was the most powerful being alive.

By the third day, her energy was depleted. All she wanted to do was curl up in a corner and disappear inside her mind. Shrink to a pinpoint and wink out of existence. Because there was no point anymore, in anything. She didn't belong here, not on Earth, not on Stragon, and not on Daisy Hub.

And then she remembered Gorse Pirrit's words: *"I was instructed to bring you back whether you wanted to come or not."*

Of course. First there had to be a debriefing. Then she could die.

Chapter Twenty-Two

On Daisy Hub

"The Night Cloud just emerged from the Gate, Drew," said Lydia's voice over the intercomm. "Captain Pirrit says there are ten passengers aboard. ETA is about fifteen hours."

With a gnawing sense of dread, Townsend asked her, "Only ten? Is Olivia with him?"

She relayed the question, then turned and told him, "He says yes, she's safe and sound."

Townsend drew his first unfettered breath since transmitting the extraction data some five standard days earlier. The rescue had been successful. Now there was one more thing to attend to.

"I want a general meeting in the caf at shift end," he said. "All of our crew, our current alien guests, and Captain Rodrigues. They should all be there. I have an important announcement to make."

"You want Moe as well?"

"Absolutely. It appears he's going to be with us for a while, and he'll need something to do when he's not fighting with Madeline Holchuk. So, I'm going to put him to work."

"He's the symbol of an alliance. Can we really do that?"

"If Trokerk can send Ssorryass into battle, I can give Moe a job," he replied firmly. "Send the notices. I'll clarify everything at the meeting."

Five hours later, Townsend was standing in the caf, with Jensen's serving counter behind him and a roomful of curious people in front of him. He scanned the crowd to ensure that everyone he needed to address was in attendance. Then he began:

"When we first came out here to our new and improved Daisy Hub, I spoke with each crew member privately, and I made several of you promises. Today I'm going to keep one of them. It's important — especially to those in a situation like ours — to have a day-to-day purpose. A reason to get out of bed in the morning. That's what Nayo Naguchi was doing when he set up the duty rotations forcing each of you to work on multiple details. Your task was to learn about the technology aboard the station and acquire the necessary skills to keep it running smoothly. That was really all there was to do on Daisy Hub as long as it was classified as an experiment in self-sufficient deep space living. Well, we've been reclassified, and that has opened up some interesting new pathways for us.

"Technically, we're supposed to be a deep space way station. If we were located on a spaceway, we would all have jobs to keep us busy. But we're not. So, I've come up with something that I think will fill the gap. Before the war, you were all champing at the bit to get involved with the resistance on Earth. Now that the Relocation Authority has lost most of its power, the resistance on Earth has more or less fallen apart. However, with what we know about recent events, it's clear to me that a resistance is still necessary. Therefore, I'm proposing that Daisy Hub become the headquarters for a new and improved Earth resistance. We can do everything that the old resistance did. We can secretly recruit and train agents. We can mount covert operations anywhere in Earth space and perhaps even beyond its borders. And we can gather intelligence, analyze it, and share the truth with those who have the means and the will to act on it.

"That last part has given me the idea for a cover that we could use. The Great Council has established a massive collection of data, called the Central Archives. A lot of information has come into our possession recently, from a variety of sources. And Earth's government very kindly provided us with enormous data storage capabilities when they rebuilt this station. Why not set up our own Central Archives right here on Daisy Hub?"

O'Malley was grinning from ear to ear. "We can't call it a Central Archives, boss," he shouted out. "That name is taken. And we're not on Earth, so it can't be the Earth Intelligence Service either."

"If you don't mind, I'd rather leave the word 'intelligence' out of it altogether," said Ruby. "Just call it a library."

"But we're going to be far more than a library," protested Walt Garfield. "We're going to be a resource center. A wealth of information. A repository of knowledge."

"That's it!" Lydia exclaimed, raising both hands in the air. "We can call it The Repository, capital T, capital R." Her cheeks dimpling, she glanced around as though waiting for applause.

"I like that," Drew said. "The Repository. It has a ring to it. And of course, we're going to need an experienced curator to be in charge of it, at least until she's able to go home again. Madame Enne, would you be interested in becoming our Head Librarian?"

Yorell got slowly to her feet. "Mr. Townsend," she replied solemnly, "it would be my honor to fill this post for however long you require my services."

"Thank you," said Drew. "Now, you'll need to assemble and train a staff. May I suggest that you include Moe in that group? I understand that he is fluent in several languages and could be quite an asset."

"Of course." She looked around the room, found Moe sitting off to the side, and gave him a nod of acceptance.

Meanwhile, Townsend couldn't help noticing, Vin Trager was standing with his arms crossed over his chest and a concerned expression on his face. It matched the one Rodrigues was wearing. The Ranger captain had taken a seat near the caf door. He'd been leaning forward all during Townsend's announcement. Now he sat back, slowly shaking his head.

Okay. Drew hadn't really expected an effortless transition. There were still a few wrinkles to iron out. But at least the residents of Daisy Hub no longer had to keep secrets from one another. He would take that as a win.

——— «‹›» ———

"That was quite a show you put on, Townsend." Trager stood on the other side of Drew's desk, gazing sternly down at him. "Am I to understand that it's your intention to make the contents of the Stragori memory blocs publicly available?"

"No. I ordered all the Stragori data to be removed from our systems. The memory blocs have been sealed back inside their cases and placed in storage. Except for the contents of bloc 2472, which appears to be a download of your *Hak'kor*'s consciousness. At least, that's what it's claiming. It also says it cannot put itself back where it was because our technology is not advanced enough to permit that operation. Personally, I think it's lying about that."

Slack-jawed, Trager sank onto one of the guest chairs. "A consciousness? And where is it now?"

"Trapped inside a dedicated server, physically isolated from the rest of the network. Fortunately, my people take precautions. It will remain there until you are able to confirm that your *Hak'kor*, Gervais Forrand, is alive and well on Stragon. At that time, we'll reinitialize the server."

"*Gervais* Forrand? He is not the *Hak'kor*. Louis Forrand is. Gervais wasn't even offered a Directorship until after the *ssalssit essendi* with Trokerk. I don't know who or what you have on that server, Townsend, but it's not what you think it is, and it's not what I was told I would be bringing here."

Trager looked genuinely upset.

"Could it be an artificial intelligence?" Townsend inquired.

The Stragori considered for a moment. "Programmed with a false narrative? It could be. And if it's lying about who it is, nothing it says can be trusted. Honestly, I think your safest course of action would be to delete it, permanently and immediately."

Drew got to his feet. "I agree. And ... welcome to The Repository, Mr. Trager."

Rodrigues arrived as Trager was leaving. The Ranger captain stepped through the privacy shield, a gathering storm in his eyes.

"You're putting a Reyot in charge of sensitive information. Are you out of your mind, Townsend?" he demanded. "What she's going to know about us when she goes back to alien space—"

"—will be nothing compared to the intel she is prepared to give us about the alien races, and the Great Council, and the Central Archives. But you needn't worry, Paul. She won't be going back to Reyi'it until the arrest warrant against her has been rescinded, and that won't happen until we've taken down the Great Council and put something else in its place. That's the operation I couldn't read you into earlier."

His mouth an O of shocked comprehension, Rodrigues sank slowly onto a chair. "That's the operation?" he repeated when he could find his voice. "You're going to—? How?"

"Bloodlessly, I hope. Only time will tell. But I think we're off to a good start. Don't you?"

Townsend watched with interest as a parade of expressions crossed the Ranger captain's face. Finally, Rodrigues said, "We're certainly off to something. And since you included me in that meeting, you must have a role for me to play. What is it?"

"To begin with, we're going to need a proper Security arm to protect the secrecy of the organization as it develops."

"You want Zulu to continue being a Second Shield for House Daisy Hub, in other words. My men would go for that. The women weren't with us before the Corvou war, so I can't be sure about them. Of course, they did demonstrate a flagrant lack of respect for the SIS chain of command when they pressured the commandant to assign them here. Do I still have discretion over when to brief my detachment about this?"

"Absolutely. We can talk about possibly involving some of your people more deeply in Repository operations later. And eventually we're all going to need training in the use of the Hub's defensive weapons."

"You know, you really are a dangerous man when you're thinking, Townsend," growled the Ranger.

Drew leaned forward and crossed his arms on the desktop. "Daisy Hub and Zulu are a team, and we're going to need everyone read in and pulling together if our new mission is to succeed. Fortunately, it's a long term project.

That gives you time to get all your people onside so that I can bring them up to speed and integrate them into the operation."

"Even if we all agree to this, Zulu still needs to patrol the sector, and I still need to file regular reports with Space Installation Security," Rodrigues pointed out. "It's not just a cover for us. It's our job."

"Understood. Like I said, it's probably going to take years just to set this con up. A lot can change between now and then. I meant it when I told you earlier that you're a key operative, Paul. I wouldn't have confided in you otherwise, and I wouldn't be trusting you now. So let's begin by establishing the Second Shield, and see where we go from there."

Rodrigues considered for a moment, a smile playing at the corners of his mouth. Finally he said, "All right, *Hak'kor*, deal me in."

———— «» ————

Drew and Ruby met the Night Cloud on the landing deck. Quarters had been prepared for the extracted operatives, and Ruby had warned Chef Jensen to expect a larger than usual dinner crowd. Debriefing and orientation could wait until after everyone was fed and settled, Drew had decided.

According to Pirrit, it had been an uneventful voyage. Now, four women and five men came through the hatch, one at a time. Each one carried a go-bag. It was obvious just from looking at them (and sniffing the air around them) that they'd been stuck together in close quarters for several days. Fed and settled and *showered*, Drew added to his earlier thought.

Jerald Gow, his former handler on Earth, was among the extractees. The two men made eye contact as Gow passed.

Olivia was the last passenger to debark. Something twisted in Drew's chest at the sight of her. Safe and sound? He didn't think so. She moved as though things were broken inside her. Her expression was dazed. Pirrit had to help her down from the ship, placing her bag beside her feet once she was on the deck.

Drew kept his gaze fixed on her face. "Show the others to their quarters, Ruby. I need a minute with my sister."

"Not a problem, Chief."

As she led the group into a waiting tube car, Pirrit and Ixbeth climbed back inside the ship and closed the hatch, leaving Drew and Olivia standing alone, separated by two meters of silence.

When she finally raised her eyes to meet his, he could see that she had been crying. There were tears in her voice when she spoke.

"Drew, I'm sorry. I know you don't want me here, but I have nowhere else to go."

What was there to say?

He covered the distance between them and opened his arms, and she toppled into them and hung on tight, burying her face against his chest. "Angeli's dead," she said, choking out each word. "I didn't find out until just before we were extracted. She was my best friend, and she died on Stragon, and I had to leave her behind."

Holding her while heaving sobs wracked her body, he filled his lungs and let his breath out slowly. He knew exactly how much she was hurting inside. He'd wept this same way over Bruni Patel.

Tightening his embrace, he finally found the necessary words. Drew lowered his head and whispered, "I'm sorry, Olivia, for everything. Welcome home."

——— «·» ———

Five days later, all the agents from Stragon had been debriefed, and Olivia had calmed down enough to discuss her experiences there as well. Townsend was wishing he'd been able to extract Anna Sturtevant. As operation coordinator, she could have provided the perspective that tied everything together.

The mission objective outlined to him earlier by Novak had been threefold: first, to monitor and assess the status of the colony; second, to gauge the volatility of the situation on Stragon; and third, to suss out potential ways to defuse or head off developments that could result in an outbreak of civil war. According to the debriefing reports, the colony on the island was doing just fine, thanks; the situation on the mainland was becoming increasingly unstable as the radical faction grew bolder; and the EIS agents had constantly felt as though they were being blocked from gathering any useful intel. One of them had described her time on-world as "walking a tightrope over a quicksand bog for the enjoyment of an invisible audience".

The consensus among the agents was that a civil war was inevitable. The colony was safe for now, but bound eventually to be dragged into the conflict. And the political situation on Stragon was such a quagmire of plots and counterplots, lies and deception, that there was very little to be gained by adding any Terran operatives to the mix.

Townsend had interviewed Olivia last. Her insights regarding the Forrand family and Stragon First had been most interesting, but what she'd had to tell him about the Directorate and the bunker under the island had been especially eye-opening.

Boxing up and storing the Stragori memory blocs and deleting the Gervais entity from the server had clearly been the right call. In her debriefing, Olivia had theorized that Dennis Forrand might have been behind this particular con. After all, making sure he had eyes and ears on every one of his projects at all times had always been his style. He'd left agents behind on Earth to monitor the Reformation. Why not put an avatar of himself inside the station's computer system to let him oversee Daisy Hub's activities?

Drew had thought immediately of Ruby, of her EIS encrypter sitting in his desk drawer, and made up his mind. Whether or not the Gervais on the server had been a version of Dennis Forrand, Townsend was done with him.

Drew and Olivia had spent most of their lives playing Forrand's game by Forrand's rules. Now the game was over. Daisy Hub was Townsend's House, and he was its *Hak'kor*. The Repository belonged to him as well. Once he'd explained the situation to them, each of the nine agents he'd extracted had signed on to join his crew without a moment's hesitation. Olivia was his sister, now under his protection for as long as she needed it. Grieving was a process, and she wouldn't be going through it alone. The coming years would give them a chance to rebuild their relationship.

Drew Townsend had his turf, and Daisy Hub had its mission. He'd already contacted Olivia's information sources on Earth and made O'Malley their handler. There remained just one last thing to do. Townsend sat down at his desk. Surrounded by the privacy shield, he plugged in his decrypter, keyed in the applicable VICTOR codes, and composed a message to Barry Novak:

Ten agents were successfully extracted. One was deceased. One remained voluntarily and is deactivated. There is now no official or covert EIS presence on Stragon or on Earth.

The new organization on Daisy Hub is fully staffed and ready for business. You have friends in Sector Three. Let us know if we can be of assistance.

D. Townsend, Station Manager, CEO of The Repository

If you enjoyed this read

Please leave a review on Amazon, Facebook, Good Reads or Instagram.

It takes less than five minutes and it really does make a difference.

If you're not sure how to leave a review on Amazon:

1. *Go to amazon.com.*

2. *Type in The Identity Shift by Arlene F. Marks and when you see it, click on it.*

3. *Scroll down to Customer Reviews. Nearby you'll see a box labeled Write a Review. Click it.*

4. *Now, if you've never written a review before on Amazon, they might ask you to create a name for yourself.*

5. *Reviews can be as simple as, "Loved the book! Can't wait for the Next!" (Please don't give the story away.)*

And that's it!

Brian Hades, publisher

About the Author

Born and raised in Toronto, Arlene F. Marks began writing stories at the age of 6 and can't seem to stop. Although she's been published in multiple genres, her first love has always been speculative fiction. Her work has appeared in *H. P. Lovecraft's Magazine of Horror*, *Onder Magazine*, and *Daily Science Fiction*. Her science fantasy novel, *The Accidental God*, was nominated for the 2015 Stephen Leacock Medal for Humour. Arlene lives with her husband on Nottawasaga Bay but spends an inordinate amount of time in the Sic Transit Terra universe.

Have you read these other novels in the Sic Transit Terra series?

The Genius Asylum
(Book 1 in the Sic Transit Terra Series)

by Arlene F. Marks

The truth is out there...

Earth Intelligence and Space Installation Security each think Drew Townsend is working for them. They're wrong.

Sent undercover to set up a covert intelligence operation on Earth's remotest space station, Drew Townsend finds himself managing a crew of brilliant mavericks, making friends with the most feared warriors in the galaxy, and feeling more at home in the controlled insanity of Daisy Hub than he ever did on Earth. Then he learns the truth about his mission there, and it's time to choose. In the coming interplanetary conflict, which side will Daisy Hub be on?

"Facinating story. It has you hooked with intrigue right from the beginning and each chapter reveals more and more about the characters and the plot. I found myself not wanting to take a break after each chapter, as I couldn't wait to find out more about what happens next."

— *Cheryl L Warringtonon*

The Otherness Factor
(Sic Transit Terra Book 2)

by Arlene F. Marks

"I know where the Angel of Death plague originated, and so does every other 'patient' who left Thrygg that day..."

Fourteen years ago, Thryggian scientists permitted a mass escape of test subjects from their laboratory on Thrygg, including Abner Dedrick, the youngest member of the powerful ForrandDedrick family on Earth. These patients all thought they'd been receiving an unapproved longevity treatment. In fact, they'd been infected with a bio-engineered virus and their escape was the first step in a horrific experiment.

The plague unleashed by the Thryggians has finally been brought under control and they're on trial for this and other scientific crimes. The viral strain Abner was carrying has wiped out an entire Human colony. Only his young daughter Lania and his voice log have survived. Aboard the Earth ship that rescues Lania is Ixbeth Minegar, a lone alien who becomes convinced that Lania is part of a prophecy that could spell life or death for Ixbeth's entire race.

The Relativity Bomb
(Sic Transit Terra Book 3)

by Arlene F. Marks

Earth's Ancient Past is Coming Home to Roost...

Earth's ancient past is coming home to roost, and it's making Barry Novak, the Chief of Operations of the Earth Intelligence Service, very nervous.

A document written in an alien language surfaces at an archaeological site on Earth.

But earth isn't yet ready to learn these truths. Making them public would cause worldwide xenophobia. So, Novak does the only thing he can think of. He sends them as far away as he can—to Daisy Hub.

Picking up where The Genius Asylum left off, long buried secrets arrive aboard the space station, carried by a mysterious one-eyed man who calls himself Max Karlov and claims to have been assigned there. But there are things happening on Daisy Hub that need to be kept "in the family", and too many unanswered questions about this new crew member. Determined to unravel Karlov's story, Townsend and his crew of maverick geniuses start digging for the truth. What they discover will shake them to their core.

The Genome Rally
(Sic Transit Terra Book 4)

by Arlene F. Marks

The most dangerous race in the galaxy is the race against time.

And the second most dangerous race? The Galactic Great Council believes it's the Humans. However, as the captain and officers of the Earth ship Marco Polo are about to find out, Humanity has plenty of competition for that title.

While visiting Kula'as, Captain Takamura and his crew are recruited by aliens for a covert mission. The Thryggians may be close to breaking out of their pocket universe using a psi-powered heavy ship left over from an ancient war. If they succeed in activating the ship, they'll be unstoppable. Can a bickering bunch of Humans and aliens work together to find and steal the vessel before it is too late?

Picking up where the The Relativity Bomb left off, The Genome Rally introduces more mystery, more secrets and more hidden agendas. And where no one and nothing can be taken at face value.

The Cockroach Crusade
(Sic Transit Terra Book 5)

by Arlene F. Marks

The Corvou are swarming, and they're headed for Earth.

When a botched first contact at Daisy Hub results in a declaration of war against Humanity by an alien race, battle lines are drawn. Not that they're likely to be respected by an enemy determined to wipe out every Human they can find.

As the Terran government scrambles to prepare for an attack they fear no one will survive, Drew Townsend and his crew of maverick geniuses set to work, trying to find a way to prevent it.

Fortunately, the fiercest warriors in the galaxy will be fighting on their side. But will that be enough to save the Human race from annihilation?

**For more EDGE titles and information
about upcoming speculative fiction
please visit us at:**

www.edgewebsite.com

Don't forget to sign-up for our Special Offers

www.ingramcontent.com/pod-product-compliance
Lightning Source LLC
Chambersburg PA
CBHW021135110726
47900CB00002B/360